AND HE SHALL APPEAR

AND HE SHALL APPEAR

KATE VAN DER BORGH

4th ESTATE • London

4th Estate
An imprint of HarperCollins*Publishers*
1 London Bridge Street
London SE1 9GF

www.4thestate.co.uk

HarperCollins*Publishers*
Macken House, 39/40 Mayor Street Upper
Dublin 1, D01 C9W8, Ireland

First published in Great Britain in 2025 by 4th Estate

1

A catalogue record for this book is
available from the British Library

ISBN 978-0-00-863654-8 (hardback)
ISBN 978-0-00-863655-5 (trade paperback)

This novel is entirely a work of fiction. The names, characters
and incidents portrayed in it are the work of the author's imagination.
Any resemblance to actual persons, living or dead, events or
localities is entirely coincidental.

Set in Adobe Garamond Pro
Printed and bound in the UK using 100%
renewable electricity at CPI Group (UK) Ltd

MIX
Paper | Supporting
responsible forestry
FSC™ C007454

For Leo: a believer.

All good music, whatever its date, is ageless – as alive and significant today as it was when it was written.

Peter Warlock, composer

For myself I could but pity him ... he was not one of those fortunate who has the gift to possess his love and not be possessed by it.

Robert Nichols, friend of Peter Warlock

PROLOGUE

Nobody is afraid of the past. What we're afraid of is the past coming loose. We're afraid that it might free itself from where we left it and, like a lengthening shadow on an empty street, slip silently after us until we feel it brushing at our heel.

I can't prove what happened between him and me all those years ago, behind those exalting college walls. Nor can I prove what's happening now. But plenty of truths defy physical evidence. Yes, we can make claims, but could you prove to someone that they were the best friend you ever had? Could you verify your regret at how terribly you let them down? What about your fear, your implacable, immeasurable fear that they will never forgive you for it – never forgive, and never forget?

Before I met him, I'd only had one experience I couldn't explain. Something that happened when I was a child. It surprised me, because it wasn't like the stories we told as we sat cross-legged behind the dilapidated science block, hidden from the dinner ladies who circled the asphalt like blue-rinsed sharks. In our Ghost Club tales – about the spirit that crept between the row of sari shops and the big Tesco, about the creature that stalked the wasteland where, long ago, the cotton mills stood – the fear was clear and sharp, like sherbet on the tongue. But what happened to me was hazy, as if it existed at the very edge of understanding, of reality. I remember it like this:

I was sitting up in bed, wrapped in my ThunderCats duvet, peering at the shapes made unfamiliar by the dark. In the corner, my music stand leaned like the mast of a sinking ship, next to my battered clarinet case and a neglected football. On my chest of drawers my action figurines stood, all – I knew without being able to discern their faces – with their gazes turned towards me. The silence felt a long way from morning. Something had woken me, I realised. Not a sound. A feeling, maybe.

There was someone in the house.

I had never been a brave boy, and there's no denying that I felt deeply frightened then. But I also felt a low, irresistible pull. While I was terrified to discover whatever was moving in the night, I was somehow more afraid of *not* seeing it. Which is why I rustled softly out of bed and stepped soundlessly out of my room.

When my eyes finally adjusted to the darkness, I looked towards the bedroom at the end of the landing. Through the door, open just a crack, was my mum's sleeping body, reflected in the mirrored wardrobe, made sickly by the light of her clock radio. There was no spectral figure floating beside her, no maniac raising a flashing blade. No movement but for the rise and fall of her chest with each unconscious breath.

I moved on to the bathroom. The streaks of moonlight on the tiles, the faint smell of bleach – all this made the space feel strangely antiseptic. My tongue became sticky at the thought that I might discover a figure stretched out in the bath, its clawed hands ready to curl around the candy-striped shower curtain. But when I edged forward and peered into the tub, there was only the dripping showerhead dangling like a hanged man, gazing sightlessly into the blackness of the plughole. Bare toes plucking at the cold vinyl, I reversed out of the room and back onto the landing.

Clutching the banister, I descended the stairs (stretching myself over the final step, which, for reasons I couldn't articulate, I never liked to touch) and made my way into the living room, where the battered recliner hunched in the corner and the rug reached tasselled fingers across the floor. Fearful of what I might see, or perhaps of what might see me, I left the lights off as I padded across the carpet, peeking behind the sofa and beneath the coffee table as I went. The house, unremarkable during the day, was peculiar in the gloom. It crouched and whispered behind my back. When I looked towards the curtains, drawn tightly across the bay window, I had the vertiginous sensation that what was behind them was not normal, and that if I opened them and looked out into the night I might see something other than the usual pebble-dashed terraces, the ordinary, overgrown gardens. Approaching the window sidelong, I took the edge of one curtain between my fingertips. Peeled it delicately from the glass. From the darkness beyond emerged a face, so close I could see the shadows under its eyes, and I would have cried out had my breath not seized in my chest – but the face was only my own, reflected ghastly, and beyond it the street, empty and still.

Nerves thrumming, I carried on, past the dining table piled high with laundry ready for ironing, past the sagging spider plant and its crisping fronds. Finally, into the kitchen, lit only by the faltering street lamp outside. On my left was the sink, where metallic drips landed on sauce-crusted pans, overseen by the stained kettle and crumb-dusted toaster. Opposite these was the cooker, flanked by cupboards of plates and bowls, chipped mugs and old jugs and empty jam jars. As ever, there was the smell of damp cloths and cooled cooking fat. But beneath this, something else – something organic, like freshly turned soil. There, straight ahead of me, the door leading into the little pantry, with its panel of frosted glass.

And someone behind it.

I froze. Stared. The silhouette was blurred but for small, dark rounds where its fingertips pressed on the glass. Its head swayed from side to side, a serpentine movement that made me shudder. I wondered whether it – whatever it was – could see me in the darkness. Whether it could hear me, or smell me.

The important thing was to avoid alerting it to my presence, to stay perfectly still while I worked out what to do. How did it get there? The door behind which it stood was the only way into the pantry, the only way out. Perhaps, I thought with a shiver, the thing had always been inside and we'd simply never known.

As I stood, it rapped hard at the door.

I skittered backwards, terror thrilling through my body, my legs charged with the impulse to run. I wanted to call my mum. But still I felt that grim, reckless need – urgent now – to stay, to see it for myself. Taking a moment to slow my breath, I forced my feet towards the door, my body hunched as if braced for impact. Inhaled, exhaled.

I clasped the door handle, turned. Pulled.

Waiting behind the door was my father. But he wasn't the right age, not the age he was when I last saw him, the age at which he died. He was a boy like me, maybe ten or eleven. Instead of being florid and riddled with spider veins, his cheeks were now fair and dappled with freckles, while his strawberry blonde hair was styled neatly in a short-back-and-sides. He looked like a character from an Enid Blyton book, like he did in the black and white photos I'd once found in a disintegrating carrier bag. Alongside my terror, there came a confusion of feelings: anger for everything that had happened, relief that the person I'd thought was gone was, in fact, not. Here was a chance to speak to him again. But it seemed strange to call another child Dad, and I found myself fumbling over how to say hello. I felt babyish then, standing mute in my too-short pyjamas, and I thought perhaps I might cry. He didn't notice. He looked past me, into the darkness that hung deeper in the house.

Then, somehow, my mum's hands were on my shoulders, her voice soaring over my head. *Can I help you?* she asked him, her tone blandly tolerant, as if she were speaking to a very old person or a salesman.

They stared at one other. Then my dad opened his mouth, so wide that it looked as if he might dislocate his jaw, as if he were letting my mum inspect his teeth. Then he reached out, would have touched me had Mum not drawn me sharply backwards. I realised that she didn't recognise the person in front of us.

I wriggled, straining to see her face, but she only held me tighter. I called out: *Don't you see who it is? Look at the eyes.*

But with a swipe, Mum slammed the door and dragged me out of the kitchen. My feet skidding on the linoleum, I started to scream. There was the shadow, still shifting, restless, behind the door, with nothing to do but keep waiting to be let in.

When I told them, the members of Ghost Club were unimpressed. 'So it was a dream?' one said.

'Well,' I said. 'Sort of, but—'

'So it's not true, then. Not a proper ghost story.'

I wondered how to explain that this dream world had contained a jagged tear of reality. 'But it really was my dad. Coming back.'

'How'd you know?'

'I know.'

'But how?'

'I just do!'

'What did he want, then?'

I shrugged. I hadn't understood my dad even when he was alive.

'So your dad,' whispered one slow learner, the knowledge arriving in her head like a long-delayed train, 'is *dead*?'

That afternoon I noticed children whispering and pointing. Some gave me extra room as they passed, as if I were carrying a population of head lice or a virulent strain of flu. Later, I found I'd been nicknamed – in that on-the-nose way of primary schoolers – Spooky, and I resolved not to talk to the others about my dad again.

Some time later, puzzling over my dream, I asked my mum: If a person was born with no legs, would their ghost have no legs too? Rummaging in the fridge, she said she supposed so. But what if, I went on, someone was born with legs but lost them in an accident? If *they* came back as a ghost would they have legs or not? I remember staring down at my boiled egg, at my toast soldiers queuing for a dip, trying not to look at the pantry door. My mum handed me a glass of orange squash and told me I was being a very morbid boy.

But I couldn't stop thinking about it. Why wouldn't an old man revisit his loved ones as his younger, stronger self? Why did we assume he'd spend eternity with arthritis in his fingers and a bend in his back? And if I died (because at that age I was still convinced that death would happen to everyone but me), would I get to choose my own eternal form? Or would it be chosen by God, by the Devil, or by something else?

I thought of the silly little boy I'd been only a few years ago: the one too scared to cross the road by himself, who couldn't sleep without his ladybird nightlight. I couldn't stand to be like that for ever. Even worse, what if my mum spent eternity as a child too? How, in the afterlife, would she make my favourite sandwiches, crisp-and-ketchup, with the crusts cut off? She wouldn't be allowed to use a knife.

I also worried that the dream might come back. It hadn't been scary as such – not a proper nightmare, scrabbling at the walls of a well or shambling down a twilit hospital corridor. But it had sunk beneath my skin, left a memory like a bruise. On the edge of sleep I sometimes jolted myself awake, thinking I'd heard that knock again. Perhaps he'd be a teenager this time, or a baby wailing in a Moses basket. Perhaps he'd be a pensioner with eyes dull as an old fish, his mouth puckered, older than he ever became in real life. And, whoever he was, perhaps my mum would still slam the door shut.

I'd almost forgotten about the dream when it returned, in my final year of university. But, this time, when I stood in that spectral kitchen gripping the door handle, I knew that the person behind the door wasn't my dad. It was someone else, someone more recently lost to me. Thankfully, in the moments before the door shushed open, I forced myself awake.

As I lay sweating in the aftermath of the dream, I wondered: Which version of him had been waiting for me behind the rippled glass? Would he have appeared as my best friend? Or my worst enemy?

While I'd never known the meaning of the original dream, I understood this new one all too well. It was a warning that he wasn't gone for good. Maybe one day, terribly awake, I'd catch an uncertain glimpse of him shifting through a crowd at a train station, or I'd pass him at a pedestrian crossing in the driving rain. Perhaps I'd find him waiting in the stairwell outside the flat. Who would he be, then? Would he return to me as the tortured soul or the scene-stealing showman, the conqueror or the conquered?

I didn't know. But I was sure of two things. He would definitely come back. And when he did, he wouldn't bother to knock.

ONE

I

The letter landed heavily on the doormat, its creamy envelope conspicuous in a sea of estate agent leaflets. I opened it while waiting for my toast to pop up, and the name on the elegant letterhead gave me a feeling like a cold hand on the back of the neck. Frances Cavendish was announcing the Cavendish Scholarship: a new bursary for disadvantaged students, to help them pursue their musical studies at Cambridge. The moment Frances had decided to set up the scholarship, she'd wanted to involve me. Not just, I imagine, as director of Voices from Before (which she acknowledged as Manchester's finest ensemble for early twentieth-century vocal works, a phrase that mirrored our website exactly) but as a friend of the Cavendish family.

Frances very much hoped I'd join the judging panel at the auditions later in the year to select the recipients of the inaugural award. After the judging, there'd be a celebratory dinner in college, for the organisers, the judges and their guests, which would of course be an emotional but rewarding experience. Frances ended the letter saying something about 'fond memories'. Not what I'd call them.

My instinct was of course to reply with a firm 'thanks, but no'. Life had settled, the years steady as a metronome, and I'd relished it: the parents, assuring me of their children's genius, the children themselves rolling from one grade to the next at a resolutely average pace. Outside teaching, I clung to the predictable calendar of concerts through which my ensemble performed for undiscerning local crowds. That the vast majority of my university connections were broken was no accident.

And yet. This was a tantalising professional opportunity, the kind of thing usually reserved for my more successful peers. I often came across former classmates conducting at the Proms or talking on Radio 3, and it had started to feel like I'd only imagined sitting behind them in the lecture hall. Like it was another person who had walked beside them down those hallowed corridors. I smelled burning and swore as I retrieved my blackened breakfast from the toaster. No. Of course I couldn't go back.

The letter lay on the kitchen counter for a couple of weeks, and my eyes danced over it each time I heaped coffee into the pot. As I drove to rehearsals, Frances's words rolled around my head like a screw come loose, and when I stood at my music stand, baton in hand, the crotchets and quavers in my score seemed occasionally to collapse into her elegant type. Now and again I set the wrong tempo, forgot to cue a soloist, and the singers shifted gradually from amusement to exasperation. Once, when I turned up late for a pre-concert rehearsal, I blamed it on a death in the family, which I almost convinced myself was true. All the while I had a sensation like a toothache, low and dragging.

I suppose most people would have told their partner what was bothering them. But I didn't say a word, not to anyone. I moved through the quotidian moments, the dinner and the cleaning up and the hour in front of the TV, an actor playing the part of a man who was fine. At night I'd lie in bed, mine the only eyes open and staring into the dark, feeling that the world around me had been invisibly altered. Our moonlit possessions – my slippers sitting lumpish by the door, her hairbands knotted on the bedside table, the mirror hanging slightly askew – seemed to have been swapped when I wasn't looking, little domestic changelings, and everything was imbued with a kind of menace that I couldn't prove and couldn't explain. All of it, I knew, was powered by my fear that, if I went back to college, he'd be there too.

In the end, my reply was inevitable. After going out of my way to buy some fussy note paper from an overpriced museum shop, I wrote Frances a prim reply declaring that I'd be honoured to accept the invitation. But, months later, as I headed back to the place where it all began, I wondered whether I was looking not for honour but for vindication.

~

It all started in the first years of the new millennium, beneath a frail, late-September sun. My stepdad paced around the car, pink-faced, panicking that he was going to get a ticket. Meanwhile, my mum and I dumped cardboard boxes (all of which seemed to have coat hangers poking oafishly out of them) onto the pavement. One box had split at the side and was spilling my two-for-one bottles of antibacterial facewash onto the kerb. I stood back to let a family wheel their matching luggage noiselessly past.

'Bloody hell,' my mum breathed. 'Amazing, isn't it?'

I looked up and inwardly thrilled at the towering building that had stood golden for more than six hundred years. Through the enormous wooden gates was a square courtyard, where sandstone walls looked down on a pristine lawn striped in shades of sage and pear. On the far side of the courtyard was a chapel, its leaded windows jewelled with brightly coloured medieval glass. This, the prospectus had said, was New Court. Somewhere beyond was another courtyard, fourteenth century, the oldest not just in this college but the whole university, imaginatively named Old Court. The whole thing felt a long way from my sixth form, which could have passed for an abandoned Soviet gymnasium.

'It's alright,' I mumbled, turning to watch the bicycles, some of which really did have wicker baskets on the front, sailing up and down Trumpington Street.

I'd already visited the porters' lodge and had been directed towards H staircase: one of several lettered staircases in New Court, each of them an ascending spiral of student rooms. Having liberated my possessions from the car, we started shuttling them to H2, a ground-floor room containing a piano that sounded surprisingly terrible. With every box I delivered, I told myself: this space was mine, and I would belong here. I was a book, slipping neatly onto a new shelf.

I was collecting the last of my boxes when I noticed a girl on the college steps guarding a gigantic suitcase. A pretty girl, peering at a bunch of papers, her brow creasing slightly as her gaze passed from one page to the next. Her hair was arranged in two buns, and she wore that style of flared jeans – low at the hips, pockets studded with diamanté – popular with the MTV stars of the time. Behind me, Mum asked loudly whether I'd remembered my hay fever tablets.

Perhaps I would never have introduced myself anyway. Certainly not in front of my mum and stepdad, whose unnecessarily smart outfits and palpable confusion set them apart from the other parents moving about the place. In any case I didn't get the chance because, somehow, out of nowhere, he was there. He had a broad, open face that you might have described as timeless, the kind that could just as well belong to a Premier League striker as a World War Two fighter pilot. Billowing around him was a dark, wool coat with a grey scarf, an affront to the mildness of the day – neither fashionable nor unfashionable, clothes that couldn't be pinned to a particular era. Dark hair crept from beneath his collar, which to me (someone who could count his chest hairs on two hands) seemed almost indecent. It also contrasted strangely with his long, slender fingers. Most striking was his poise. I was used to my peers holding typical adolescent shapes: slouches to signal disinterest, furtive hunches to disguise cans or cigarettes. But he had an ease, a gravity that I recognised in teachers or police officers or politicians. While I drifted, an untethered balloon, he was a monument that had stood for centuries.

I paused where I stood, as if taking stock of my CD collection, and I saw him say something to the girl. The expression on her face made it clear they were strangers to one another. He moved close to whisper in her ear, his smile revealing small, straight teeth.

Then, something odd: the girl stepped back, chin tucked, her mouth a stern line. She seemed alarmed, or offended, and I wondered if she might walk away from this guy. Maybe even slap him. I remember that he reached for her narrow wrist – cautiously, as if handling a bird – and turned her hand palm upwards. I wasn't sure, but it looked as if something moved in the pale bowl of her hand.

Then the girl threw back her head and gave the most astonishing laugh, like the jangling of bells. When she turned her face to him again, chattering wildly, her fingers landed gently on his forearm. They were conspirators now.

My stepdad called out to my mum, anxious for them to get back on the road. It was a four-hour drive, remember? Arms straining beneath the last battered box, mortified at the smallness of my possessions beneath the illustrious Cambridge sky, I turned and passed through the enormous gate and across the courtyard to my room, past that strange and spellbinding theatre, feeling like I'd missed my cue.

Typical, that I start the story at the point he entered it.

I know where my mum would start. She'd say that she'd known since I was a baby, when I'd clap along to her Culture Club cassettes perfectly in time, that I was going to be a musician. She'd tell you about the piano lessons that began when I was five, the ones she worked overtime to pay for, and the book tokens I brought home from junior school talent shows. She'd describe the scales and arpeggios that thundered through our tiny house, the evenings when 'You Can Play Simon and Garfunkel: Book One' drowned out her favourite soaps. Later, the Bach suites whose leaping left-hand parts required hours of repetition, the Poulenc pieces whose liquid harmonies still sounded wrong even when I'd checked the score five or six times. With no small pride, she'd tell you how, after some adventures with the clarinet and saxophone, I took up the bassoon (so exotic, she'd say), which led to the youth orchestras, the town hall concerts, the teacher who was the first to say that I really should think about Oxbridge. And, even though she wasn't present for any of it, Mum would describe yet again my bizarre Cambridge interview, during which I played an impassioned Brahms piece on the piano while an interviewer in a dressing gown fiddled noisily with his kettle. Who cares what he wore, she'd say. He offered you a place, didn't he? She'd paint you a picture, filled with music and applause, my arrival at Cambridge the triumphant finale to my teenage years.

But my mum's version is half a story, a Disney version of a tale that was Grimm. Because, in *my* version, music was my joy and my curse. At the poorly performing small-town school I attended, being academically successful – and making an effort to be so – was considered unforgivable. Classical music was for the snooty and the precocious. And the bassoon? A provocation, a gift for piss-takers. The only people in school who liked me were the teachers, and I'm sure even some of them thought I was a bit much.

Things didn't get any better for me once we'd skulked up to sixth form, when it became customary for my peers to spend their weekends Down Town in pubs choked with cigarette smoke, in bars offering free sambuca to girls in boob tubes. I went 'out' perhaps a handful of times, but I didn't like it. Too many people there would recognise me from high school and deliver some wise-crack:

'Oi! Thought you'd be home, playing with your horn.'

'A bassoon isn't a horn. It's a woodwind instrument.'

'I wasn't talking about your bassoon.'

During those A Level years, I socialised almost exclusively in the sixth form canteen with Gaz and Ben and Reedy, guys I'd known since junior school and who enjoyed nothing about classical music except for the fact that the German word for bassoon is *Fagott*.

But at Cambridge, coolness surely wasn't going to be a pre-requisite for social success. On my interview day, I'd noticed how other male applicants had shunned the gels and pomades used by my school colleagues and instead wore their hair in the bouffant style of minor royals. They wouldn't have lasted five minutes in The Rose and Crown. I told myself, surely even *I* couldn't be weird in a place where teenage boys and girls wore gowns to dinner. In any case, by the time I found myself juggling those boxes in front of college, I knew that university was an opportunity for reinven-tion. Your near-total lack of experience with the opposite sex? Erased from the record. That time you farted thunderously during the minute's silence and made Becky Baxter gag? Like it never happened. My high school days were over before Facebook had conquered the world, and I was free to rewrite my history.

So, in those first weeks of Michaelmas term, I started turning up at room parties as if I were the kind of person to do that kind of thing. On hearing the distant thump of a bass speaker I'd head towards the sound, a sailor drawn to the siren of sociability – and on discovering a gathering I'd slip inside, into a room of hulking boat crew or moody thesps dressed in beanie hats and band T-shirts (The Strokes, Gorillaz, Sigur Rós. I knew none of them). Although I didn't drink, and never had, I'd take six-packs of cheap lager and set them ostentatiously on whatever desk or table was serving as the bar, like a dinner party guest presenting a fine claret to the host. Then I'd nod at people as if casting a reel, hoping to catch hold of a conversation, fiddling with my clunky, bottom-of-the-range Nokia if I found myself alone so as not to look too unhinged.

Which is how I met Tim, a neatly dressed medic living on G staircase, who introduced himself at one room party after he over-heard me apologising for standing on some girl's foot.

'Northerners unite,' he said, giving my hand a vigorous shake. 'Give me some more of those flat vowels, they're like music.'

'Where are you from, then?' I asked.

'Derby.'

'That's Midlands at best.'

He laughed as if I were a great wit. 'In Cambridge, everything past Leamington Spa is a savage wilderness. Believe me, we're on the same team now.'

I learned that Tim came from a small, unremarkable village, the kind of place you either left at eighteen or lived in your whole life.

His mum and dad both did something artsy for their local council, and they were surprised but happy when their son chose sciences. When he got his place at Cambridge, Tim's fond classmates clubbed together and bought him the watch he now wore every day, about which I noticed two things: it was acutely ugly, and Tim treasured it. He asked about my own family with genuine interest, and, while I could tell he was the kind of person who would handle the whole truth gently, I gave him the easy, edited version: mum pretty cool, stepdad a bit of a wet lettuce but fundamentally decent. When I was conspicuously silent about my dad, Tim didn't push it.

After that night, I saw him often. We'd regularly study together in the college library, bolstering one another when our spirits failed: *Come on, just another twenty minutes.* Sometimes, we took our books to a glossy American coffee chain that had recently arrived in the city, rewarding ourselves with creamy, syrupy creations whenever we managed a solid stint of focused work. Whenever I found myself frustrated by an essay, Tim would attempt an impression of the music I was writing about – his cor anglais was particularly poor – and if he flagged over the Functional Architecture of the Body, I'd make him laugh by asking for his advice on fictional medical conditions such as Lancashire Gut and Symphonic Toe.

Tim also introduced me to other friends he'd made: a couple of guys from his staircase, one Scottish and one Welsh; a shy girl Tim had nicknamed 'Casio' because of her near-supernatural abilities in calculation, who wore her Cambridge scarf and hoodie with unironic pride. Yes, we went to the odd room party after Freshers' Week. But, alongside our geographical accord and our silly sense of humour, our relationship seemed shaped by a shared commitment to make the most of this Cambridge opportunity. To do the work, and to do ourselves justice. In other words, Tim was exactly the kind of friend my parents hoped I'd make.

But it's worth noting that *Tim* – with his open smile and straightforward manner – was the one who had made and shared friends with *me*. And I didn't make other friends so easily. As the only first year musician in college, I had no ready-made clique. And when I asked others what subject they were reading, their barely concealed eye-rolls revealed that this was a boring conversation starter, something of a faux pas. The same went for my 'fun fact' about The Eagle down the road, it being the pub where those scientists discovered DNA. Half the time, it seemed people could hardly understand my northern accent anyway.

For a while, I tried to broaden my appeal. I pretended to enjoy the indie bands that were popular at the time, like Arcade Fire (whose universally loved debut album just sounded a bit chaotic to me). I watched shows like *Little Britain* and *The Mighty Boosh*, laughing along with everyone else without understanding the jokes. I bought a pair of chinos, for fuck's sake. I ran through all the repertoire I could think of, desperate to find something that would connect with a wider audience. But Cambridge insisted that I know my place and, outside my catch-ups with Tim, my life was like a tune played to an empty hall.

If I ever felt lost, I lay in bed and listened to my favourite composers. Mostly English twentieth-century figures like Britten, Delius, Quilter. Music that feels nostalgic for another time, somehow. My favourite was Peter Warlock: a beer enthusiast who wore a devilish goatee and enjoyed naked motorbike rides, delighted to horrify his respectable neighbours. In his work, memorable melodies dance above darkly surprising harmonies. Elizabethan and folk sensibilities mix with modern influences, giving the music a liminal, timeless quality – like something once loved, now lost, half-remembered. Like how ghosts would sound. In fact, one of his first compositions was a set of three songs titled *Saudades*, a Portuguese word that describes regret for days gone by.

Apparently, Warlock was also good at falling out with people, and he often found himself on the wrong side of composers, conductors, music publishers. Funny to think of our heroes having friends, losing them. Hard to imagine them buying birthday cards and dressing up for weddings, arguing with the neighbours over the encroaching wisteria. Maybe that's another reason I liked Warlock: we both knew what it was like to be on the outside of a circle.

It was during this time that I saw my first Cambridge ghosts. Some were genuinely horrifying, with waxen faces and cavernous black eyes. Others were less polished, formed of rumpled bedsheets. Many were the 'sexy' variety: brides with torn veils and clinging dresses, schoolgirls with blood on their cropped shirts. All were at my first Cambridge formal.

Formals were smart, silver-service dinners that took place in college every Wednesday and Sunday. I hadn't been to any, partly because I hadn't been invited to join any of the drinking societies (those alarming groups made famous by frothing articles in the *Daily Mail*) that made up a large part of the dining crowd. But Tim had asked me to join him for the Halloween formal, insisting it wasn't to be missed. And, that night, I could see why.

Even in its normal state, our dining hall was spectacular. It was a huge, rectangular space, with room for at least two hundred diners, panelled with treacle-dark wood and papered with opulent

Gothic designs. The two long walls were sentried by stained-glass saints in their leaded landscapes and, between them, old, oiled masters in gilt frames who looked disapprovingly down at the tables that stretched across the room in their white linen shrouds. Rafters arced high above us, as if we stood in a great cathedral, while colossal chandeliers blazed coldly in the yawning dark. That evening, the hall was particularly dramatic: the candelabra were gauzed with fake spiderwebs, the bright tablecloths blotted with something that was supposed to be blood.

Not realising how much effort people would make with their costumes, I'd worn my standard college gown with some fangs, face paint and a chocolate medallion on a red ribbon. As for Tim, he assured me that the brown bathmat around his shoulders made him a werewolf.

'Not sure we're in line for the fancy dress prize,' I said to him as we joined the long line of monsters filing into the hall.

'That depends,' Tim replied. 'What if I'm not just a guy in a bad costume? What if I'm a guy dressed as a guy in a bad costume?'

'I think, if you get anywhere near the prize, Margaret Thatcher will rugby tackle you to the ground. You got any idea how long it took him to set his hair like that?'

'Ha, true. I hope his mate isn't planning on a career in politics, because photographs of *that* costume are not going to age well.'

We'd just found ourselves a spot when two girls – one dressed as a cat, the other as a zombie – appeared. Tim gave them a broad smile. 'Hey! No, no, have a seat.' Then, turning to me: 'Have you met?' I shook my head as they took their places beside us.

The cat was called Berenice. Petite, with dark, bright eyes and a slightly unflattering bob. The zombie was Alexa, model-tall and boyish, with a knot of long, dark hair that exposed an inexpertly applied rubber wound. The two of them had a chilly kind of distinction, but when I went to shake their hands I immediately felt overly formal. They offered neat smiles that didn't quite reach their eyes.

Under the pressure of Tim's gaze, I asked Berenice and Alexa lame questions that went nowhere. Yes, the two of them were settling in well enough, yes, they'd been to The Eagle.

'You know it's where they discovered DNA?' I asked, cringing immediately.

'Yes,' replied Berenice. 'And where they apparently forgot about Rosalind Franklin's contribution to the work.'

Not knowing what she was on about, I made for safer ground. 'What subjects are you doing?'

'I'm a medic,' Berenice said, distracted by a bread basket offered by a waiter. 'That's how I know Tim.'

'Philosophy for me,' replied Alexa, vaguely.

'Hang on,' I said, 'Didn't you do that quiz in the bar ...?'

'*Play Your Descartes Right*. Don't remind me. The Philosophy Society made me do it.'

'Oh. I thought it was good.'

She looked at me as if I were an insect she'd never encountered before.

'What about you?' Berenice asked me, relentlessly polite. 'What's your subject?'

'Music.'

'What do you play?'

'Piano.' Then, apologetically: 'And bassoon.'

Alexa jumped in. 'You're in the university orchestra, right? I knew I'd seen you somewhere. I play violin.'

'No way! We can walk to rehearsals together sometime if you want.'

She gave a tight smile. I realised that it sounded like I was flirting, which I definitely was not. Flustered, I busied myself with the wine that I didn't actually want but had brought because, apparently, it was customary. While I was planning to share my bottle with Tim, I'd heard that some people would drink a whole one to themselves before dessert, a fact I found astonishing. I was hardly planning to rush mine, whose bouquet was best described as 'petrol station forecourt'.

The fellows had assembled at high table and were poised to say Grace when a group of students bowled messily into the hall. Even if the volume of their voices hadn't got my attention, their outfits would have. One was dressed like Louis XIV, complete with powdered wig and heels, while another clanked about in what appeared to be a real suit of armour. There was also a flapper in a vintage gown, a riot of tassels and feathers. Behind them, five or six others, decked out in the most detailed and decadent costumes, all shimmering in the candlelight like characters slipped from a cinema screen.

But most noticeable was the one leading them, dressed from head to toe in red – his jacket, shirt and trousers all the vivid colour of a Valentine's rose or a poisonous insect – and carrying a bottle of champagne in each hand. Even in the low light I recognised the impish smile, the steady stride. It was the guy I'd seen on my first day, the one on the college steps. He was the one who led this strange and glittering crew as they clattered between the long tables, the one they jostled to sit beside as they claimed the vacant spaces immediately to my right.

The gong rang. Everyone rustled to their feet, and I peered at the latecomers as they intoned ironically along with the fellow who led us in Grace. At the 'Amen', the guy in red mimed bursting into flames, and the characters around him laughed. Ah, I realised. He's the Devil.

At the second gong we sat, and the waiting staff, preternaturally tolerant, began to file into the room, bearing some thematically acceptable starter (probably pumpkin tart). I hardly noticed, though, too distracted by the figures beside me. On the group's periphery, Louis XIV talked loudly at the armour, whose raised visor revealed a face cold and perfectly handsome as a Greek marble. The flapper – an animated, Sloaney kind of girl – threw bits of her seeded roll at them, scattering crumbs across the linen. But the one who called their attention was the Devil, the true conductor of this impromptu Danse Macabre. When he poured champagne into his friends' glasses he moved with a casual stage-craft, and when he called for a toast it was with the gravity of an operatic hero. Even that suit, which should have looked ridiculous, only accentuated his pale skin and his commanding frame. He seemed part of college's elaborate furniture – not, like me, a visitor passing through.

A conscientious host, Tim brought Alexa and Berenice into the conversation, found topics we could all get on board with. The girls talked about the formals they'd already attended in other colleges (Queen's terrible, John's outstanding), about their membership of various college sports. But, while I nodded along – no, Berenice, I did not know that about mixed netball – my brain was occupied by the fact that although, as instructed by my mum, I'd waited for the people around me to receive their starters before tackling mine, the group on my right followed no such etiquette. In fact, the Devil was directing them in some kind of race, where each person was attempting to finish their own food before their companions' had touched the table. These people had a wildness about them. But it appeared to be an acceptable kind of wildness, one that the staff were willing to suffer rather than challenge.

The mains followed. Several times, poor Tim had to repeat his questions because I was so absorbed by the group beside me. At one point they laughed loudly about their school days, using slang I'd never heard like 'beak' and 'pig', and I realised that many of them had studied at the same place. It astounded me that a group of mates could end up not just at Cambridge but at the same college. Nobody else from my whole year ended up at Oxbridge.

But wherever the conversation went, focus always came back to the Devil. Faces turned towards him. Eyes searched, unthinkingly, for his. When he touched those close to him, just a gentle brush of his fingertips at their shoulder, their faces lit up as if the contact were electric. Some of the group became kittenish when he spoke to them, touching their faces and fussing with their outfits, while others seemed, consciously or otherwise, to copy his gestures, mirroring him as he stretched and reclined. I leaned close myself, drawing the attention of the flapper, who – with no malice whatsoever – told me it was lovely that I'd managed to look spooky even though I didn't have 'a proper costume'. More than once I tried to catch the Devil's eye, smiled stupidly whenever he said something that sounded like a punchline. When I overheard him asking for the salt, I grabbed the nearest shaker and practically threw it down the table.

But the only one who noticed me was Louis XIV, who jogged my elbow. 'Crikey,' he said, pointing at the wine I'd brought. 'Never seen one that colour.'

I leaned towards him, delighted to be of help. 'It's a rosé,' I explained.

A look of glee spread slowly across his painted face. Then, folding his lips into exaggerated, obscene shapes, he parroted back my northern vowels: 'It's a *roh-sey*.'

Unsure how to react, I looked silently across the table at Tim, who only shook his head at Louis like a teacher assessing a particularly foolish pupil.

'I'm aware of that,' Louis went on, arching a precision-drawn eyebrow. 'I'm just not sure I've ever come across one that looks quite so ... noxious.'

I glanced at my bottle, wondering what colour a rosé was supposed to be. 'The guy in the shop said it would be nice with dinner,' I said, apologetically.

'I'm sure it is, if your dinner is mushy peas and gravy.'

The armour smirked. The flapper looked exasperated and threw a napkin at Louis, who shrugged at her: *But it's true.* She told him he was a pig, and he looked back at me with a boozy smile as if to say: *That's true, too.*

A small, proud part of me wanted to challenge this guy, tell him to get some manners. But if I had – which in itself would have violated all social codes by souring the atmosphere – he would surely have said it was just a joke, right? Banter. After all, I couldn't prove the edge in his voice, the derision in his eyes. Maybe, he would say, I was imagining it.

Which is why I laughed along.

Unfortunately, this only served to highlight the contrasting reaction from Tim, who had observed our exchange in disdainful silence. Louis fixed his eyes on Tim, thoughtful – as if Tim were a shopkeeper who owed him some small change. Then, to my alarm, he reached suddenly across the table. But he didn't, as I feared, grab Tim by his bathmat or slap him across the face. Instead, he lunged at Tim's glass, made a movement that produced a small chink. I looked closer. There, sunk at the bottom of the lurid rosé sea, was a penny.

Flapper, armour and Louis leaned in, made exaggerated *oohs* and *aahs*. This was one of the Cambridge traditions I'd heard about but hadn't yet seen in practice.

'You know what to do,' said the armour, his voice sonorous inside his helmet.

They all began to beat their hands rhythmically on the table: *Down it, down it*. But Tim shook his head, continued calmly with his meal. The beat became faster, louder, rattling the cutlery and stuttering the candles, and I stared meaningfully at Tim, sure that the fellows would object at any moment. But neither they nor Tim batted an eyelid. Even as the beat became frenzied, Tim worked at his plate like a parent ignoring a wheedling toddler. Down the table, the Devil looked on.

Eventually, the thumping died away. Louis gave a soft, sustained boo.

In that moment, I remembered how I'd adapted my behaviour to survive at school. I'd learned to minimise the daily calls of 'swot' and 'nerd' by keeping my hand down in class, arriving at school early so that nobody would see me grappling with my stupid bassoon case. But there were new rules here, and I'd found myself transgressing yet again. Now I cringed at Tim's clothes: the supermarket shirt, too short at the wrists, the cheap watch chosen by his classmates. His accent, like mine, a big, sore thumb.

At something of a loss, I snatched Tim's glass and drank.

As I gulped, pink streaking down my chin and onto my shirt, I heard the hammering of fists, invigorating, the jangle of glassware. When the wine was gone, I discarded the penny and upturned the glass above my head with a flourish, pretending not to notice the drops that landed coldly in my hair. Even Louis cheered. I still haven't forgotten the slow smile that slid across the Devil's face.

This was the moment when things turned, like when one of those magic eye pictures suddenly comes into focus. I'd always been careful with alcohol, had avoided the willy-waving of competitive boozing. But that only meant I didn't know what it felt like. What if I was really the party guy, the mad one, and had just never realised it? It hadn't been so hard, draining that glass. And everyone had loved it. I didn't know whether it was the drink or the applause, but I had a pleasant, floating feeling. Maybe I was one of the people who could handle it. Maybe, I thought, as I gave myself a generous top-up, I could stop worrying about what might happen and just let go.

I woke with my face pressed against linoleum. There was an acrid, bitter stink. Heaving myself onto all fours, I saw that the communal bath was smeared with a vivid pink puke, as if it were my actual guts blocking the plughole.

I must not have bothered to close the door after coming through it, as I had vague, flipbook memories of clasping the toilet as figures whispered along the corridor, some giggling, some muttering in disgust. Feeling a chill at my knees, I looked with dismay at my new trousers, torn. A plastic clock on the wall showed it wasn't even midnight. Jesus. My stomach spasmed, and something burned up my throat and out of my mouth.

Once the heaving had passed, I paused to rest my reeling head on the cool rim of the bath. Then I switched on the tap and tried to rinse the mess away. Only partially successful, and disturbed by the colours swirling, psychedelic, around the plughole, I slumped against the wall and tried to work out where the fuck I was. Beyond the bathroom door were stairs leading both up and down, and a pair of doors labelled S5 and S6, which meant I must be in Old Court, on the second floor. What I was doing here, I had no idea.

Directly opposite was a window, its leaded panels dimmed by the night. It took me a moment to realise what was wrong. Although the window was closed, locked, and two floors up, there was a figure on the ledge outside.

Against the lightless sky, the shape was vague and leached of colour. The overall impression was of something crouching. I'd seen no ladders, no bits of scaffolding around college that might have been stolen, scaled. But the thing didn't look like one of the college's gargoyles, as it seemed very gently to stretch and sway. Surely not. I wanted to call out, just to be sure. But, if there really was someone out there, I might startle them and send them toppling to the ground. Through the diamond shapes of leaded glass, I couldn't tell whether the shape was facing away into the courtyard or towards me.

For a moment – I know this sounds strange – I felt like *I* was the one in danger. But I didn't have time to think about it before the thing that might or might not have been a head turned slowly, like an optical illusion that seems to move both left and right at the same time, before my senses became slow, before the room tipped and dropped again into darkness.

The next time I creaked open my eyelids, I saw only a dreamy gloom. And within it, a figure reared and swayed.

Too confused to be afraid, I found myself entranced by the languorous movement of arms and legs. Around me was a low humming, a murmuring of words I couldn't quite make out, and also the slightest scent of smoke, sickening. The figure before me twisted, shifted (was I still unconscious? I didn't think so, although

I did seem to be lying down) and the murmuring grew in intensity, became more of a feeling than a sound. Then the shape raised its arms—

—and its hands exploded into two livid balls of flame.

Consciousness crashed down around me – *Christ, what the fuck* – and I tried to stand, but something pulled at my hands and feet. Panicked, I began to thrash, heard myself whimpering like a child.

But it was only the tangle of soft blankets, on someone else's bed. Eyes wide and sweeping the dimly lit room, I now saw people chattering casually, holding bottles and plastic cups, shifting to the steady pulse of a large speaker on the floor. Everyone was spattered with blood. I almost cried out again, but I stopped myself. Costumes.

Across the room was the figure that had erupted with fire: the Devil in his blazing red. He was standing on a desk, above an Anglepoise lamp that threw dark shapes across his face and sent shadows crawling up the walls. The flames were gone from his hands now and he was busy performing a deep bow, soaking up claps and whoops. Some kind of trick, then? I sat up, swung my legs onto the floor – gingerly, as if my bones were made of glass – and, in a movement that took supernatural levels of effort, heaved myself to standing.

Thanks to the standard-issue furniture and washes of magnolia, college rooms usually had a budget-hotel-chain look about them, an air of incompleteness, like a paint-by-numbers waiting for an artist. But this was a cross between a gentlemen's club and a children's party. On one wall, a large neon sign cast a feverish glow over several gilt-framed charcoal drawings (hung, in clear violation of college rules, on nails). In one corner were shelves full of massive, sprawling plants, some alive, beside a collection of badly painted masks. Beneath these, staggering piles of books, their spines creased to softness, very unlike the handful of pristine textbooks standing rigid on my own bookcase.

As I stepped through the crowd, my heartbeat slowing to match the easy thump of the music, I passed an ornately beautiful chest of drawers, a telescope, the occasional balloon, a disassembled bicycle. A table bearing wine, champagne and a vat of bright pink jelly. Also, on the floor, a boxy thing made of wire mesh, covered in grubby cloths. Beneath the smell of smoke and beer there was a hint of something foul, like rot or sulphur. Almost animal.

On a set of shelves, coils of rope. Piles of coins, a ceramic hand. And on the wall ahead of us, a round mirror, timeworn and slightly convex, about the size of a dinner plate. The glass itself seemed black, but so highly polished that it reflected the whole room. Beautiful and extremely strange. The place was baffling: a room to be accessed with a password or through a wardrobe.

A loud thud made me spin on my heels. The Devil was on the floor now, his audience closing around him like truffling pigs. There, up front, was the suit of armour, helmet removed and pale eyes sharp. Beside him the flapper, looking bleary, the feather in her headband drooping queasily. The two of them put their bodies between the Devil and the crowd, as if shielding an exam paper from cheating eyes.

This wasn't how I wanted to meet him, face-painted and only superficially conscious. But I didn't dare miss my chance. When he lifted an empty wine glass, I grabbed a bottle of red from the mantlepiece and strode through the crowd, forcing my way with firm elbows and feigned apologies until I was in front of him.

Before I could speak, he turned, very slowly. And I swear I *felt* his gaze, in my body, like the chime of a struck bell. There was something playful in his expression, as if to say: *It took you long enough.*

What he actually said was: 'Feeling better, Count?'

'Oh … fine,' I replied, my voice like a broken bagpipe. I offered the bottle, but he shook his head.

'You've been sleeping the sleep of the dead,' he said. 'Well, thankfully not quite, since someone sensible put you in the recovery position.'

The flapper gave a braying laugh before pouting at me as if I were a stray animal. 'Aw, babe,' she said, 'there's a bit of sick on your chin.' She handed me something to wipe my face, and I realised it was one of her silk gloves. 'Don't worry,' she said, 'they aren't mine.' All the while the armour stared, assessing, as if he might set me a trial or ask me a riddle.

There was something about the Devil's presence that caught me off guard. Not his face, striking though it was. Rather his voice. Not loud, but full and grounded, as if it came not from his throat but from the earth. 'We found you in the bathroom a bit worse for wear,' he said. 'You didn't seem sure where your own room was, so we brought you here.'

'Oh … Is this your room?'

'Certainly is. Excuse the smell, that fire trick demands a fair amount of butane.'

Fearful of my own stink, likely of puke, I tugged my cape tighter around me and hoped my make-up hid my reddening cheeks. But he laughed again, turning his body to separate us from the others. When he clasped my hand in introduction – Bryn, Bryn Cavendish – I seemed to feel the flames still beating in his palm.

I smiled, ruefully. 'I really am sorry …'

'Don't be. You've been a much more civilised guest than some. Sajid is particularly messy tonight.' Bryn arched an eyebrow at a glazed-looking chap sitting on the floor, legs outstretched like a rag doll (ah, I realised with satisfaction – this was Louis, minus his wig). 'His father is our family lawyer, so I have to play nice. You won't be surprised to hear he's a Wykehamist.'

I wasn't surprised, but only because I had no idea what this meant. Even so, this introduction was different to the ones I'd had with other students, those polite, stilted interactions about where we'd come from and what we were studying. This was like being reunited with an old friend.

Just then a girl, swathed in cobwebs, shook Bryn by the shoulder. She had a dreamy look, as if she were half asleep or heavily medicated. 'Hey,' she said, ignoring me. 'You promised.'

Bryn rubbed his chin, theatrically pensive. 'What are you offering?'

'One of my famous traybakes. Either that or my eternal soul.'

'Traybake sounds ideal.'

Before I could ask, Bryn took a deck of cards from his pocket and fanned it, face up, allowing us to see all the suits in all their randomness. Then he turned the deck over, shuffled it, and settled it in one hand. The back of the uppermost card glinted with an intricate design that looked like the mechanism of a clock.

'You need to be careful with this deck,' he whispered, as if sharing a great secret. 'Because it's haunted.' He fanned the cards again, face down this time, and held them towards us. 'Pick a card,' he said, 'and point to it.'

Eagerly, I made for a card, but the girl did too. I withdrew casually, as if I'd only ever intended to smooth my artificial widow's peak.

Wary of being led, the girl moved her hand up and down before touching a card around the middle of the spread. Carefully, Bryn lifted the uppermost cards, so we could see the chosen one at the bottom. The two of hearts.

'Don't tell me what it is. But remember it.'

Bringing the cards together, he fluttered the deck, cutting, slicing. His hands moved like those of a virtuoso, with the fluidity and grace that comes from years of practice. After a final cut he allowed the deck to sit, neat and still, in his palm.

'Now,' he continued, 'the only one who can find your card is the spirit that haunts the deck.'

The girl sighed ostentatiously. 'Is the spirit's name Bryn, by any chance?'

'If you like. Maybe you should summon the spirit, like they do in stories, by speaking its name three times.'

They grinned at one another, mischief sparking between them. Then the girl leaned forward, bringing her face close to his, and whispered: 'Bryn. Bryn.'

She came closer still.

'*Bryn.*'

I felt envy, tightening like a screw. But not of Bryn. Of the girl who, in that moment, had his unqualified attention.

We all looked down at the deck, sitting on his open palm. Nothing happened. Behind us someone roared, the loser in some drinking game.

But then – and I'd swear this is how it happened – while Bryn's hands stayed completely still, the top portion of the deck began to move, all by itself, millimetre by inexplicable millimetre. The girl and I gasped. That top portion continued to shift, so far that it eventually teetered on the bottom portion as if it might topple off altogether. But it didn't. In fact, after a pause, it inched back into place, slowly and strangely, so that the cards were all aligned again. Only now, there was a single card left poking from the otherwise tidy deck.

Bryn eased it out, held it up for us to see. The two of hearts.

'You're ridiculous,' the girl murmured, unable to stop one corner of her mouth curling upwards. 'How did you do it?'

'Yeah,' I said, softly. 'How?'

A seriousness passed over his face. 'You don't want to know,' he said, the drama gone from his voice. 'Not really.'

The girl punched him on the arm, allowing the contact to last a little longer than necessary. Then, summoned away by her friends, she disappeared reluctantly into the crowd.

'Make sure the traybake has cherries in it,' he called, bright again. 'I like cherries.'

I stared, bewitched.

Before he could move away, I fired questions at Bryn, as if blowing on kindling to sustain a tiny flame. It turned out he was reading Maths – this was in spite of his parents encouraging him to read Music, a fact that gave us our first piece of common ground and couldn't have delighted me more. Bryn had grown up in London, an only child, had hated the private school to which he was sent to board. 'So how did you get into magic?' I asked.

'My dad's a magician,' he said, with a discernible glow of pride. 'He was on TV for a time, when I was a kid. And he's achieved a kind of … notoriety in certain circles.'

This made so much sense. 'Wow. And he taught you?'

He nodded. 'When I was five or six, he put on a performance for my birthday. He started with stuff I thought was shit, like pulling coins out of ears, you know. But then he wheeled out this set of old-fashioned weighing scales, like the Statue of Liberty carries.'

He held out his hands, palms up, moved them up and down in contrary motion.

'He balanced little metal weights on one side, to show how that side would go down and the other would go up. Then he put a weight on each side so that they were balanced. All the while he's giving us some spiel about how these things are Ancient Egyptian, or maybe from an Arabian sorcerer ...'

'More like Made in China?'

'Ha, exactly! He gave us some chat about ancient, mystical knowledge, about how we measure the worth of things. Then he gave me a rock and a feather, told me to put them on either side of the scales. So I did. And both sides stayed completely level.'

I was slightly underwhelmed. 'I guess there was some kind of mechanism?'

'That's what I said. So he let me take the thing apart, to prove me wrong. Showed me the bar connecting both sides, stiff and straight. Honestly, I couldn't work it out.'

'It's a pretty odd trick.'

'I know. When I got older, I searched every magic shop I knew of, trying to find it. It sounds weird, but it was the first thing that made me think that impossible things really could happen. More than Santa and tooth fairies and all that shit.' Then, shrugging: 'But since I never found it, maybe I made the thing up.'

'So,' I said, 'were you disappointed when you realised that magic isn't real?'

He looked at me, a brightness behind his eyes. Then he laughed loudly, clapped me on the back. 'You're funny.'

It seemed that while I had spent my formative years watching *Masters of the Universe* and eating Frosties straight from the box, Bryn had spent his questioning the nature of reality.

This childhood memory made me think of my own father: of the day he left home, of the flat he'd moved into. Of what that flat looked like at the end, its carpets matted with hair, its corners laced with cobwebs. I brushed the memory away, focused on holding Bryn's interest. 'God, I wish I'd learned magic as a kid,' I said, weakly. 'Although, to be fair, pretty much anything would have been cooler than wind band. But,' I added quickly, not meaning to confess my lack of street cred just yet, 'the past is the past.'

Bryn looked into his glass, and for a moment I worried I'd made things awkward. Then he asked: 'Do you believe in fate?'

'Fate? No.'

'So you believe that, from here, there are millions of potential futures ahead of you, and it's up to you to choose your path?'

'I guess.'

'I think I agree. But what about potential pasts? How many million versions of the past might there be – or have been – to bring you to this exact moment?'

'What?'

He refilled his glass with a wine different to the one I'd offered. 'We see time running in one direction. Morning to night, young to old, right? But time and space, they're not reality. They're tools we use to *understand* reality, to help us make sense of things our minds can't manage.'

'Okay ...'

'So, if we're all moving forward in time, why can't we see the future? Most laws of physics work as well backwards as they do forwards.'

I frowned. 'Bryn, I'm a musician. I'm out of my depth here.'

He took a long drink, continued as if I hadn't spoken. 'I mean, what can we be absolutely sure about other than the moment we're living in? We have no trouble imagining a million different futures stretching out ahead of us. So why not a million different pasts?'

I paused. Blinked. 'Run that by me again.'

Before he could reply there came the sound of raised voices – the crowd surged, as if the room itself drew a breath, and bodies jostled one another. Then, an abrupt quieting, like a TV being turned to mute. I realised: the music had gone off.

There in the corner, a space cleared around him as if he were infectious, was the guy I'd met as Louis, who I now knew to be Sajid. At his feet, scenes of minor carnage: a glass receptacle, broken cleanly at the neck, lying on a sodden, crimsoned carpet.

A shout from the armour. 'Sajid, not the decanter!'

And from the flapper: 'That was from his dad, you fucking idiot.'

Teetering on his aristocratic heels, Sajid looked blearily at his hands as if expecting something to be clasped there. 'Balls,' he mumbled. Then, grinning messily at Bryn: 'Heirlooms are hand-me-downs by another name, right?'

Bryn stepped into the space the others had cleared. He didn't rush to reassure Sajid, like I would have: *It's fine, I never liked that thing anyway.* Nor did he show irritation. His expression remained blank and unreadable, as if he were hearing distant voices over radio waves. The only sounds in the room were the whispers of tipsy concern, of costumes rustling.

Sajid arranged his face in a cartoonish frown. 'Master Cavendish. My sincere apologies.'

I looked anxiously around, wondering whether this party was over.

Then Bryn smiled. But it was a commiserative, almost pitying smile. 'Don't apologise to me,' he said, his eyes bright. 'Since this was a "hand-me-down", you'll have to apologise to the people it came from. My dead relatives.'

Sniggers from the crowd suggested this was understood to be some kind of game.

Bryn took something from a drawer, something I couldn't see. Then he beckoned Sajid into the centre of the room, allowing the rest of us to gather around the two of them. With Sajid in position, Bryn asked certain people to take up some of the candles that flickered on tables and shelves, and as we settled into a circle we made ghostly *oohs* and evil cackles. The tension had become something else now, an anticipation that travelled through us like electricity in a circuit.

Bryn called to a ghost pirate. 'Could you turn off the light, please?'

At a soft click, the room became very dark, very quiet. We were able to discern one another only vaguely in the low light of the candles, the seething glow of the red neon sign. Collectively, we leaned in, Scouts around a campfire.

'I'll call my relatives now, so that you can apologise,' Bryn said. Then, placing his hands on Sajid's shoulders: 'Just do as I say. Because if we don't do it right … We might summon something else. And whatever we summon, it might not leave us. Understand?'

'This is a very silly game,' Sajid slurred.

Now I saw what Bryn had taken from his drawer: a pile of photographs. He riffled through them until he found one of Sajid. 'Here,' he said, holding it out. 'Make an offering of yourself.' Then he took a penknife from his pocket. 'Stab the picture.'

Sajid looked appalled. 'That's horrid!'

Bryn feigned puzzlement. 'But it's just a silly game.'

Sajid glared. But he took the knife. Bryn held the photograph by its edges, pulling it taut. Then, Sajid attacked the image of himself, jabbing and tearing at it with the blade until the photograph came apart between Bryn's hands. The crowd simultaneously laughed and winced.

Approaching one of the candle bearers, Bryn touched the ravaged pieces of the photograph to the flame and dropped them, glowing, into a nearby mug. Then he made for the broken decanter, which still contained a little liquid. Lifting it carefully, he poured the liquid into the mug, creating a red mulch. Back in the circle, he offered this to Sajid.

'Drink.'

In the guttering candlelight, the crowd made delighted noises: *eww, gross*. Sajid would surely apologise properly, and we'd turn the lights back on and leave it at that. Right? But Sajid – unreadable now, suddenly steadier on his feet – only stared at Bryn for ten, twenty seconds. Bryn, congenial, stared back. To a collective cringe, Sajid took the cup.

Then, throwing his head back, he poured the liquid all over his closed mouth, allowing it to run down his neck and over his white, brocade blouse. Wiping his lips with a ruffled sleeve, he twinkled at Bryn, triumphant: 'Mmmm. Delicious.'

The room held its breath at this grimy act of defiance.

But Bryn only shrugged: *It's your funeral.*

As we watched, Bryn suddenly made a strange collapsing movement – like a marionette would if its strings were cut – so that he stood hunched, head bowed, hands covering his face. The rest of us stood rigid, deathly silent. Though it wasn't possible, it seemed the room had got even darker – around me, mere suggestions of cheekbones and eye sockets, brush strokes of seething red. Bryn seemed to be speaking softly through his fingers, but I couldn't make out any words. Then he twitched violently, and out of the dark:

Bang.

The crowd shrieked, grasping at one another, dissolving into horrified laughter: *What the fuck was that?* For a few seconds we strained to see in the shadows, perhaps imagining a shape moving among us. Within the hubbub, whispers: *I don't like it, I'm frightened.* Then, a cry, and a finger, pointing.

Following the finger, we saw it. The door of Bryn's closet had clattered open.

There was general glee and confusion as we confirmed to one another that, no, none of us had gone near the closet. And we'd all seen that Bryn hadn't either. The whole spectacle had a daft, ghost-train-delirium about it – but, one by one, we stopped giggling when we spotted Bryn: seemingly oblivious to our hilarity, turning slowly within our circle like the second hand of a clock, as if his eyes tracked something the rest of us couldn't see.

Having turned a full three hundred and sixty degrees, Bryn stopped moving, focusing somewhere over Sajid's shoulder. Then he raised a hand at nothing, a solemn gesture of welcome. The person beside me shivered. I wanted to shout at the crowd: Do any of you realise how much skill it takes to manipulate an audience like this?

In the silence, Bryn kept his eyes in the space beyond Sajid, occasionally nodding. Then he took a step towards Sajid.

'He's sent you a message,' Bryn said.

His hand moving quickly, like the biting jaw of a snake, Bryn reached into the neck of Sajid's shirt and took from it something rectangular. Then, encouraging us to use our candles as tiny spotlights, he held the thing out for the group to see. It was a card, a little bigger than a playing card. And on it was a picture of a robed man, one arm pointing up, the other pointing down. Around his waist, a snake biting its own tail. Below him was written: The Magician.

We laughed at the cheesiness of it, as if he'd produced a string of hankies or plastic flowers. Sneering, Sajid let the card fall to the ground.

Unbothered by either reaction, Bryn turned and, saying nothing, pointed at Sajid's remarkably skimpy breeches. Despite raising a contemptuous eyebrow, Sajid turned out his pockets. Nothing. It was only when he put his hand right inside his costume, inside the shorts he wore underneath, that he discovered another card. Bryn snatched it from Sajid and held it aloft.

This card also showed a man, but this man was strolling, looking up at the sky, unaware that his next step would take him off the edge of a cliff. Beneath him was written: The Fool.

We laughed again. Me loudest of all.

Looking slightly rattled (and who wouldn't be?), Sajid made to leave the circle. But the ring of bodies tensed and flexed to block his exit. Bryn looked on, smiling. Then, very slowly, he pointed at the mug abandoned on the carpet, its lip still blackened with the now-coagulated liquid Sajid had refused to drink. Keeping his eyes on Bryn, Sajid bent at the knees and picked up the mug. There was something inside it now, something that looked dirty, or even – inexplicably – singed. Another card.

When Sajid had peered apprehensively at the card for long enough, Bryn took it from him and held it up for us to see. On it was a golden, winged thing blowing a trumpet, and below, bodies crawling from graves. The word beneath: Judgement. In the shadows, the closet door gaped as if horrified.

Sajid tossed the mug at Bryn. 'Being scared of dead things is for juvenile intellects,' he said, waspish.

Boos and hisses from the crowd, as if to say: *Bad form*. But Bryn only smiled. 'Careful,' he said. 'Remember what I told you. Just because they're dead doesn't mean they're gone.'

Bereft of clever comebacks, Sajid forced his way out of the circle, grabbing the wig he'd dumped on the table. As he went, the audience broke into a patronising applause. God, this was the best fucking thing that had happened to me since I'd arrived at Cambridge. The room was just refilling with low, delighted chatter when there came out of the darkness an awful, despairing cry.

We turned, craning necks, searching, until Bryn himself flicked on the light.

Sajid stood at the door, his horrified face dripping with a viscous pink ooze. The stunned crowd gave a collective gasp, which gradually turned to shrieks of laughter as people passed the punchline around: someone had filled Sajid's wig with vodka jelly.

Holy shit, it was the greatest trick you've ever seen. The crowd roared, unsympathetic, as Sajid thundered out of the room and slammed the door. I laughed so hard I thought I might be sick again. Finally, the room rearranged itself, with Bryn at the centre, the armour at his side. The flapper also resumed her guard, but not before stealing a freshly lit cigarette from a skeleton's mouth.

Actually, I really did feel sick. The smell of wine, the cigarette smog that began to fill the room – it all set off a sinking feeling in my stomach, a feeling of the floor falling away. I looked around helplessly, as if relief might be somewhere in the books, the bottles, the strange black mirror.

There must have been something peculiar about the mirror's surface, because the reflected bodies seemed to bend and lurch in unnatural ways, out of sync with the laughter and music that swelled about the room. Each echoed figure was odd, misshapen. Even Bryn looked grotesque. Fearful of what my body might be about to do, I stumbled out, searching for the bathroom I'd vacated earlier, unsure as to whether I wanted Bryn to regret my departure or not notice it at all.

Afterwards, I thought about Bryn's father, what he'd passed on to his son. Magic, a language few could speak. A power to manipulate reality as others saw it. Remembering the familial pride that had brightened Bryn's face, I imagined him with Cavendish Senior, hunched over playing cards, dice, delighting in a successful piece of misdirection; the two of them sharing a stage, making grand, simultaneous bows. It must be nice to have a family history that you could be proud of, the kind to be kept in a velvet-lined box and shown off to guests.

I also thought about what my own dad had passed on to me. Things that definitely weren't magic. Some charity shop cutlery. A stained toiletry bag with a blunt razor inside. Mementoes I didn't need, since I was happy to forget.

I suppose my dad gave me music, since Mum says I didn't get it from her. She used to remind me about his incessant whistling – *Do you remember, love, how he'd come down the path, tweeting away?* – and how he, peculiarly, was the one who introduced me to classical music. He used to play it in the car, Mum said, and his friends from the bookies used to laugh and call him maestro. With him, as with me, a blessing and a curse.

After the party, I was keen to cross paths with Bryn again. The problem was, I only ever saw him in snatches, imperfect glimpses at odd times. Once, during my short and ill-judged rowing career, I was cycling to the river at 5.30 a.m. and saw him across the road, strolling in the direction of college. But he didn't look drunk or shabby, as if he might be getting back from an all-nighter. He looked fresh, his coat unbuttoned in spite of the gusting rain. (I raised my hand to wave, but the manoeuvre sent me wobbling towards a lamp post and I aborted it halfway through.) Another time, when I woke in the night and looked idly through my curtains, I saw him crossing New Court by himself, looking up at the stars. He was gone before I could find an excuse to dash outside. Even when I spotted him moving up and down our halls, it was always at a distance. He was a suggestion, disappearing around a corner, or a figure leaving a room just as I entered it.

On the rare occasions I found him settled in college, he was surrounded by people, impossible to reach, with two figures in particular stationed always beside him like diligent sentinels. First was the suit of armour, in reality a Law student named Jamie. I'd learned Jamie was one of those people known to everyone, a 'face' at the Pitt Club, student union, all the rest of it. His dad was Something Very High Up in the Civil Service, which is why Jamie had grown up in Asia and America as well as the UK. He had a wary demeanour and sharp, inquisitive features that seemed to suggest he was storing up every word you said, and I imagined he was the kind of person whose influence depended less on charm and more on duress.

Bryn's second sentinel was the flapper, a Politics student called Sarah whose brother had been at the same school as Bryn. Glossy and gregarious, she'd set up a new college society for women in politics but abandoned it after she forgot to turn up to its inaugural meeting. She'd also been fined in our first week for running naked laps of Old Court – not realising, she claimed, that the provost was visiting the master at the time – but clearly thought the fine a reasonable price to pay for the adventure.

However, these figures featured little in my Cambridge days, which were governed by the rhythms of the music faculty (harmony and counterpoint on Mondays, German Romanticism on Wednesdays, the carelessly defined 'world music' on Fridays). In the mornings, I'd be scribbling furiously on the front row of the lecture hall, or be sat at my piano analysing obscure baroque sonatas. Later, if I didn't have a supervision – a small group session during which I marvelled at other students' knowledge and struggled to showcase my own – I spent long hours with Tim and his friends in the library. Some weekends, the girl Tim called Casio would cook for us, and I'd do jobs like peeling potatoes and washing dishes as she made sausage and mash or cottage pie, hearty, unassuming dishes that reminded us of home.

Sometimes, when the autumn air was particularly crisp, our little group would head to Magdalene Bridge and hire a punt. Tim would take his place at the stern, bouncing us from one bank to the other while the rest of us encouraged him to *give it some welly*. And we'd inevitably fall silent as we moved along the exemplary green expanse of The Backs, past the pale, imperious face of King's Chapel, all of us conscious that these days were opportunities we'd only be given once. On one of these punting trips, someone asked about 'the guy who showed up at Halloween dressed like a Butlin's redcoat', and Casio butted in, keen to show that she knew Bryn's name (even hearing it gave me a superstitious thrill, as if our speaking it might conjure him up right then and there). But Tim upstaged her by revealing two things: first, that 'this Bryn bloke' had chosen to study at our college because his father had studied there too, back in the day. Second, that this knowledge had come from Berenice, who was in fact Bryn's cousin. Astonishing, I thought. The family resemblance wasn't strong.

Hanging out with Tim and his friends – it was nice. But when I joined them for another study session, I had a strange sense that I was looking for answers in the wrong place. A feeling that I was late for something, that there was somewhere else I was supposed to be. Michaelmas term ticked reliably on, and somehow, for all its undoubted gifts, each Cambridge day began to feel like a birthday party where the guests hadn't turned up.

* * *

After that punting trip, I decided: I was being too passive. If I wanted to be a part of Bryn's story, I was going to have to write myself in there. One evening I saw him heading up to hall as I was on my way out. And, I reasoned, if he was eating in college, he might well swing by the bar afterwards. So, taking a stool at the bar with a decent view of the place, I set myself up like a cop-show rookie on his first stakeout. I felt too awkward to ask for the pint of orange squash I actually wanted – so I half-heartedly ordered an ale and settled in with my well-thumbed biography of Peter Warlock.

As I skimmed favourite paragraphs (about Warlock decrying Christianity, about him half-joking about selling his soul), faces came and went. Computer scientists, choral scholars, rugby 'lads'. None of them Bryn. Tim texted – *Me and Casio are watching* Memento, *want to join?* – and I told him I was busy. Time crept by. Feeling obliged, I bought another pint and drank it unenthusiastically, even though my head was unexpectedly beginning to swim.

I'd just decided to head to the toilets when two students arrived at the bar. Had they not caught my eye, I might have kept my nose in my book. Berenice, neat and preppy now that she was out of her Halloween garb. And Alexa, intimidatingly cool in fishnets and fingerless gloves.

Caught, I gave them a meek wave. 'Alright?'

Berenice eyed me as if I were a particularly cryptic crossword clue. 'Fine, thanks. Did you have fun at Halloween?'

Alexa smirked. Christ, I had no idea what they'd seen of me after the main course. But it can't have been good. 'Still getting used to these Cambridge customs,' I said, the ale making me unusually frank. 'Seriously, sorry if I got carried away.'

Berenice's posture softened. 'You're hardly the first.'

Then, seeing an opportunity: 'It was good to catch up with your cousin, though. At his afterparty.'

She folded her arms. 'You know Bryn?'

'A bit,' I replied, irritated by her surprise. Then, flashing my knowledge like fake ID at a bouncer: 'He's very talented, isn't he? With the magic?'

'True,' she said. Then, somewhat confidentially, 'I just wish he didn't make it so creepy. All bones and fake blood, it's foul.'

Curious, the softening of the girls' manner when they assumed I was known to Bryn. I wondered whether those painful, early conversations would have gone better if I'd been able to drop his name.

Alexa jumped in, eyes shining. 'But the creepy stuff is part of the show! And it's family tradition.'

Berenice made a face. 'Not our side of the family.'

Alexa lifted an eyebrow at me, keen to show her own credentials: 'You know Bryn's dad was notorious for being into the occult?'

What the fuck? 'Oh, yeah,' I replied, hoping they wouldn't probe. Then, using my titbit from Tim: 'His dad was at this college, right?'

Competitive now, Alexa leaned in. 'Well, did you know that he also stole a chalice from some religious society, to use in a black mass?'

I made a surprised face, conceding the point, wondering why everyone else's families were so much more interesting than mine. 'Well,' I said, 'it's nice to have a hobby.'

Alexa laughed, a warm, open sound.

Berenice smiled ruefully. 'Sure,' she said. 'But Bryn's hobby might have the accommodation officer asking why his room is covered in burn marks.'

'Shit,' I said. 'You think he'll get in trouble?'

'Always does,' Berenice replied, 'and always gets out of it again.'

'You know, I haven't seen him around much lately,' I said, as if surprised.

'We left him smoking in Old Court just now. He was hiding from an old school friend who wanted him to go to some club—'

I forced the rest of my pint down, stifled a burp. 'Ha,' I said, 'sounds like Bryn.' Then, sliding off my stool, edging towards the exit, I waved again. 'I should let you get on. Good to see you.'

As I stumbled out, Alexa called: 'See you at orchestra.'

Even Berenice offered a quiet smile. I gave them a goofy thumbs-up, immediately regretted it, and dashed out of the bar, ignoring the fact that I was now beyond desperate for a piss.

Old Court was silent and wine-dark. There was nobody circling the smooth cassock of lawn, no other soul inside that dim, sepulchral space. Dammit. We must have come so close to crossing paths.

But then, a slight movement, an adjustment in my perspective, and there he was: standing, stone-still in the darkness, between dull haloes cast by the Dickensian lamps. How had I not seen him? In my delight, I almost called out – but his posture made me pause. His head was tilted back, and he was staring up at the wall, a strange, satisfied smile on his lips. Like an indulgent parent, or an artist admiring their own work.

Scampering noisily around the lawn, I tried to draw attention to myself. But even as I neared him, Bryn didn't move. He just kept staring, his focus somewhere around the second floor. It was only when, almost at his shoulder, I coughed – twice – that he finally turned his face to mine.

Offering a smile and a wave, I was about to ask him how the rest of the party had gone (perhaps even be a little forward and ask him when the next one would be). But the sentence faltered before it could begin. Bryn's expression was faintly blank, as if he were puzzling over a mathematical equation or hearing voices other than mine. Was he annoyed with me?

No. It was worse than that. He didn't recognise me.

I clenched my fists, forcing my nails into my palms, infinitely less painful than the disappointment and the shame. Without stopping, I made my way past him and around the courtyard, as if that had always been my intention.

Wait, I told myself. It was understandable. When we met, I was in costume. And it was dark. *And* we were drunk. Maybe I should have said: You did the trick for me, the one with the haunted cards, remember? But that would have meant reminding him how I'd passed out, post-puke, in his bed, and perhaps it was no bad thing to wipe that episode from the collective memory.

Having made a full, senseless circle of the lawn, I began to trudge in the direction of the bar. But no. Here, uninhibited by hangers-on like Sajid, I had a chance to make an impression on Bryn. It might even be a funny way to start a conversation – me, asking him to work out who the hell I was.

Steeling myself, I turned back, my smile ready. But the courtyard really was empty now. Was the door to Bryn's staircase swinging slightly, as if it had just fallen shut? I kicked at a pebble, swore through my teeth.

And then, that quiet again. This time it was gaping, vast. As if the music and chatter of the bar were coming from a great distance. Or even getting further away. I became aware of the pull of my breath, the clicking of my tongue behind my teeth. The total absence of sound gave me a strange notion, then: that not only was the courtyard vacant but the student rooms too, and that if I went into them at random – not just here, but all across college – I'd find laptop screens staring coldly at nothing, radios talking to themselves. Half-written essays, mugs of cold tea, never to be finished.

There was something else now, too, a horrible smell, maybe some kind of fertiliser applied to the flower beds. It was the stink of hooves, pattering, spattering mud, of ragged things exhumed by foxes. It made me queasy.

Unsettled, I looked up at the place Bryn had been staring at. There, between the second-storey bedroom windows, was a shadowy thing, just about visible against the night-washed stone. Something long, flattened. It was easily the size of a man, but it made me think of a spider, or a beetle, spindly limbs inching imperceptibly in the dark. The sight of it gave me a jolt. A spread of ivy, or something?

Without knowing why, I called: 'Hello?'

My voice was small, a penny landing in a prodigious well. No reply. But, as I stared, part of the thing seemed almost to shudder, the movement like a muscle shivering beneath skin.

Then, a scream like broken glass, so piercing that I felt it in my bones, so all-encompassing that I couldn't tell which direction it came from. I spun, frantic, body desperate to move and brain at a loss as to where to go.

But it was just a student, behind me, in a dishevelled evening dress, being chaotically piggybacked out of the bar by a bloke in a rugby shirt. Jesus Christ. I watched, chill with adrenaline, as the pair stumbled through the door, letting it clatter closed behind them before tottering away. Silence settled again.

I glanced back up at the wall; there was nothing but darkened stone. Just a trick of the light, then. I moved away carefully, as if holding my trembling self together.

But when I was within touching distance of the archway, I burst into a blundering sprint, crashing into New Court and towards H staircase. Because as I hurtled for the safety of my room, past the people who jumped, puzzled, out of my way, I realised that – thanks to that awful scream – a warmth had begun to spread unstoppably around my crotch.

II

The packing slowed me down. I stood for too long at the wardrobe, wondering who exactly I ought to be when I returned as an adult to Cambridge: pinstriped professional? Tweedy artiste? Not that I had much choice in the matter, since my best shirt had been nibbled by moths and my next best wasn't clean. After a period of panic, I picked a slightly corporate-looking button-down, plus my special-occasion socks (lucky charms: I was wearing them on the night of our first kiss), and stuffed them into my case alongside my trusty concert brogues. But my hesitation meant it was well into the afternoon by the time I pulled out of the driveway. Clouds gathered as I snaked through the suburban streets, eyes fixed on the GPS even though I could have found my way back to college without it, a man drawn by a dowsing rod.

Once I was on the motorway, I turned on the radio and was pleased to hear the sounds of Shostakovich's Chamber Symphony. As a kid, I'd been transfixed by the grim, sinuous opening, the frantic second movement, the grotesque waltz and desolate finale. Later, at Cambridge, I'd learned that the piece is filled with fragments of Shostakovich's other works – bits from his symphonies, and from the opera that made him dangerously unpopular with Stalin's regime. Also, his name. Using the notes of the musical scale, Shostakovich wrote his initials into the piece, and this little musical signature repeats throughout every movement. So the composer is not just the storyteller but the story itself, and the music is a reflection on his life. An elegy, for himself.

Raindrops shivered down the windscreen and the wipers' bloodless thunk jarred against the fluid tempo of the music. I must have been halfway down the M6 when I heard something else. A soft scratching.

Shit. If there was a problem with the car, I wouldn't have the first idea how to fix it. But it had only just had its MOT.

I turned the radio off and tried to separate the sound from the hiss of rain. Rather than coming from the engine, it seemed to come from inside the car, alongside or behind my seat. Low and rough. Almost like someone gently dragging a fingernail on leather. Using the rear-view mirror I glanced at the back seats. Nothing. I twisted briefly as if I didn't believe the reflection, scanned the space behind me. Still nothing.

Rattled, I pulled into the nearest service station and got out of the car. Then I opened the rear door and rummaged around the seats, looking between the cushions and in the footwells as rain lashed against my arse. It was hard to work out what was going on amidst the not-quite-legally photocopied pages of sheet music, half-written reports and bony music stands.

Then I spotted it, in the pocket of the car door behind the driver's seat: a little rock, about the width of a pound coin. I nudged it with my finger, and it moved along the pocket with that distinctive scratch. Relief rushed over me, visceral as the rain. The rock must have been rolling up and down as I revved and slowed. I picked it up, felt it cool and smooth in my palm. Maybe I'd accidentally kicked it into the car when I was loading things into the back.

Rock in hand, I collected some of the rubbish from the back seat and took everything to the nearest bin. Then, settling back into the driver's seat, I chastised myself. Silly, to be spooked like that.

No, only silly to be spooked *so soon*. The things I was afraid of, they would surely happen in Cambridge. Our old haunt. Ha.

When I started the car again, the final movement of the symphony was beginning. They say Shostakovich had a suitcase packed, so that when the regime came for him in the night he'd be ready to go. Pragmatic. But the strange thing is, although those in power denounced his music, though they declared him an enemy of the people, they let him live. Other artists disappeared. But for Shostakovich, nobody came to knock.

He couldn't know he'd be spared, though. So he lived in fear for decades. People say he made nocturnal patrols of his apartment block, thinking, smoking. He probably shuddered at every slamming door, every creaking floorboard, wondering whether, this time, those footsteps were hurrying for him.

Nobody knows why they didn't kill him. Perhaps Shostakovich, admired in the West, was too visible to be erased from history. Or perhaps the state enjoyed toying with the man who had dared to displease them. Because all that silence, all that waiting? Take it from me, that kind of punishment is as diabolical as any.

~

Over the following weeks, I got to know Alexa better as we walked frosty streets to and from orchestra rehearsals. I carried her violin case back to college, juggling it alongside my bassoon, when she was burdened with library books. We had a drink in the bar now and again, usually joined by Berenice.

It's funny that I got on so well with Alexa, since we were as different as it's possible for two people to be. She was privately educated, I was not. Her combat trousers and velvet chokers gave her a cool-girl edge, whereas I was entirely without edge (possibly just a bit rough). Initially, our bond was formed over a shared enthusiasm for certain TV shows – *Buffy*, *Friends*, *X-Files* – but I think it endured because of something else. I saw the way Alexa moved like a foal, gangly, as if unsure how to handle her natural elegance. I saw how, whenever she posed for photos, she would pull a stupid face as if embarrassed by her own bright smile. I spotted the chipped nail varnish and baggy jumpers, an attempt to disguise her prep school roots, and I realised: the expressions I'd taken as aloof were often merely uncertain, and the confidence I'd found so imposing was as fragile as my own. Maybe one of the biggest reasons we were comfortable with one another was because there was zero sexual tension – no expectation, no self-consciousness about what people thought when they saw us together. And so, thus protected, we were free to build something like friendship.

One night towards the end of term, Alexa and Berenice suggested that I tag along to a curry night. Wary of anything spicier than Coronation chicken, I almost declined – until Berenice happened to mention that Bryn would be there. So, at the allotted time, I met the girls outside the notorious Curry Prince, a venue clearly geared more towards mass catering than fine dining.

'Ready for this?' Alexa asked. 'I hear Bryn's imposing a "madras minimum".'

'What does that mean?'

'It means you'd better fill up on naan.'

I looked more closely at the girls. Berenice was carrying a teddy bear, Alexa cradling a bust of Aristotle. 'Forgot to say,' Berenice said, seeing my confusion. 'We're supposed to bring a prop that begins with the first letter of our name. Another of my cousin's ideas, obviously. It's no big deal.'

I felt suddenly petulant, my fingers moving subtly around something that wasn't there. Always the one left out of the joke. Pretending not to mind, I followed Alexa and Berenice inside.

A waiter with saintlike patience showed us to an upstairs room, where at least thirty students already sat at a long table. I recognised a few. There was Jamie, dressed not in the cashmere and silk I'd seen him wearing around college, but in his prop: a tightly fitting rugby jersey, apparently from his school, causing much amusement. Beside him was Sarah, who had persuaded someone else to carry her improbable and ambitious prop (a stepladder). I also spied tray-bake girl – whose pencil case could be read as a P or a C – as well as several notable faces from our college's dining societies. All glanced occasionally around as if waiting for a ceremony to begin.

I was busy pondering where Bryn might sit when Alexa forcibly directed me and Berenice to a couple of places at the quieter end of the table. Then she took her own place elsewhere, shrugging regretfully and mouthing 'see you after dinner', as if this were the only possible seating arrangement. I was confused. And frustrated – not just because I was sure to be miles from Bryn, but because Berenice wasn't as fun as Alexa. She was nice, but in the way a digestive is nice: sweet, but a bit dry. She gave me a broad smile, her lips glossier than usual, and I slumped into an unstable chair, pitying the couples about to share their date nights with a room full of rowdy students.

As we settled in, there came a commotion from the staircase. Heads turned, necks craned and people began to nudge and point.

It was Bryn. Just the back of him at first, reversing through the doorway and grappling with something enormous. As he emerged into the room, so did a grey statue – Bryn carried the head, someone else the feet. It was the size of a man, but with the head of a goat, and wings. And breasts. The incredulous crowd laughed and cheered.

Nodding at the chaos, I asked Berenice: 'Who's that?'

'It's Baphomet,' she replied with a sigh. 'Bryn's brought a statue of Baphomet.'

'No, I mean the guy helping him. Is he another old schoolfriend of Bryn's?'

'Oh. No, that's Kenny. Second year from Selwyn. I think his mum was the Cavendish family's PA or something. More importantly, his theatre group has a minivan that is large enough to transport that … thing.'

I eyed this Kenny guy: the oversized glasses, the furry, faux-charity-shop jumper, painfully try-hard. An insufferable Cambridge thesp, then.

Calling reassurances to our agitated waiter, Bryn and Kenny set the statue down at the other end of the table. Then, to the sound of our cheers, they dropped exhausted into the seats beside Jamie and Sarah. And – I remember this very clearly – Bryn put his hand on the back of Kenny's neck and shook him, a gesture somewhere between a mother cupping her baby's head and a tiger worrying its prey. As the excitement at their arrival subsided, the two of them fell into an animated discussion, heads lowered to almost-touching. Wishing for the first and only time that I owned a van, I shovelled some onion onto a poppadom and stuffed the lot joylessly into my mouth.

Before long, waiters delivered plates and people reached for them absently, not remembering whether they'd ordered dopiaza or jalfrezi, not caring. Someone doled out some warm, vinegary wine, and I left mine untouched. While Berenice talked about her studies in an unnecessary amount of detail, my eye was drawn to the head of the table, where Sarah was loudly pressuring Kenny to eat a mound of luminous-looking pickle – and where, stately as the statue itself, Bryn reclined in his chair. Even when we were in the same room, he felt very far away.

'So, what do you think?'

Startled, I looked at Berenice, who was peering over her glasses at me like a teacher. 'Sorry, what?'

'I was asking where we should go after dinner.'

'Go?'

'For dancing! I say Fez.'

'Won't most people want to go to Cindy's?'

She tucked some mousy hair behind her ear. 'So? We could always go on our own.'

Perhaps the realisation came slowly because, as a teetotal member of the wind band, I had never been much of a Romeo. But I finally got it. The make-up she never usually wore, her readiness to sit apart from Alexa? Holy hell, Berenice was flirting with me. If there was any spark between us, it was less like the fizz of fireworks, more like the tickle of licking a battery.

I was subtly inching my chair away when a pair of hands landed heavily on her shoulders.

'Bee!'

Finally, it was Bryn: ruddied by booze, beaming, glorious. I churned with delight.

'Having a good time?' he said.

'The meal was absolutely average, thank you.' She pointed dismissively at Baphomet. 'I thought Sajid was helping you with that thing.'

'I haven't seen him.'

'Is he upset?'

Bryn gasped, feigning offence. Then he looked at me. For several seconds he said nothing at all. Then: 'Did you forget your own name?'

I stared, thrown. Then – oh. He was talking about my absent prop.

'Sorry, I didn't know …' I hurriedly explained which props I *would* have chosen, had I known, being sure to pronounce my name clearly and emphatically. Then, careful in front of Berenice not to make this look like an introduction, I switched subjects: 'What happened to Sajid?'

Bryn leaned so close that I felt his breath on my ear. 'The other night, he saw something in his bedroom, crouching in the corner. Something … not natural. And he says it's my doing.'

I didn't understand. 'He thinks he saw … a ghost?'

Bryn shrugged. 'Ghost, demon. Whatever.'

Berenice sighed, exasperated. 'I don't suppose Sajid was extremely drunk?'

I thought of the Tarot cards at Halloween, the invisible visitor. The humiliating jelly. Something about it reminded me of a story a counsellor told me, after my dad's death. 'I heard about some woman,' I said. 'She had a panic attack every time she got home from work, because she was convinced that there was a killer clown waiting for her just inside the front door. Really, she was lonely. And terrified of going back to an empty house.'

'So,' Bryn said, 'she invented something to fear, because reality was even worse.'

I nodded.

'Then again, what's more likely,' Bryn said, 'that a plonker like Sajid has the sense to be scared of anything at all? Or that he's been successfully cursed?'

I frowned. At the end of the table Baphomet looked on, its long, caprine face impassive, its blind eyes flat and empty. Another image dropped into my head, then: of the thing I thought I'd seen beyond the bathroom window, the thing that seemed to have scaled the walls where Bryn lived. There was an idea in there, somewhere, but it didn't quite land.

Then Bryn laughed raucously, and I joined in, thinking: Okay, I get it. Like Alexa said, this is all part of the show.

'Anyway,' said Berenice, 'we're going dancing.' She placed a hand on my shoulder, and I almost moved subtly to dislodge it. But Bryn smiled at his cousin's proprietorial stance, and I let her hand rest. 'Surely you can't take your statue into town.'

'Nope,' Bryn replied. 'We're heading back to my room to worship him for a bit. According to the scriptures, he likes Bolly, so we'll open a bottle or three.'

Wait, was this a fucking joke? Bryn was going back to his room to party with *Kenny*, some simpering am-dram prat dressed like a children's TV presenter, and I was going to some sweaty club with Berenice? The whole point of coming out tonight had been to hang out with Bryn. There was so much I had to say to him – about how my own hero Peter Warlock was fascinated by the occult, how he once had an astrology reading that suggested 'a Satanic influence'. But, already, students were massing and flapping, cawing drunkenly about who was going with who. Jamie was helping Kenny with the statue, having only just persuaded Sarah out of its lap.

Berenice waved at Alexa, who approached, swinging Aristotle by the neck, and I looked helplessly at Bryn. I was about to lose him again. But at the last moment he turned, pointed at me and Berenice, drew a circle in the air around us. 'Cute,' he said, with a wink. Then he melted into the crowd like an apparition disappearing through a wall.

Berenice lowered her eyes, flushed a little. I pretended not to notice. But I wondered. It was good of Bryn to be so attentive to his cousin, nice of him to spend time with her. And, Berenice and me? Maybe we did look kind of cute together.

Our first date was a mixed bag. On Tim's advice, I'd booked a romantic but relaxed restaurant in town offering something called 'tapas'. On looking at the menu and being pleasantly surprised by the prices, I announced that I'd have the chorizo, but when Berenice suggested that I might need some other dishes to go with it, I realised I was out of my depth. When I chose some other dishes, the waiter's expression revealed that my pronunciation was unconventional at best. Just when I thought nothing else could go wrong, I left my menu too close to a tea light and burned the starters off.

Berenice handled it impeccably. 'You know,' she said, 'I was once on a date and, being flirty, I tried to feed this guy a spoonful of ice cream. Dropped it right into his lap.'

I winced. 'That'll put a dampener on it.'

'It really did,' she said. 'Now, make me feel better and tell me some dating disasters of your own.'

I gave a panicked smile. I hardly wanted to admit that my love life had been limited to an infatuation with a cellist called Tina that, in truth, had little basis but for some text messages about a borrowed Mahler score. 'Oh,' I said, 'I don't … kiss and tell.' The old-fashioned phrase sat on me, preposterous, like a bow tie on a child.

'Or tell me about your family. Brothers, sisters?'

'No. Probably best, my mum had enough on her hands.'

Berenice frowned. 'In what way?'

Fuck. I'd only said that last part because I was awkward, babbling. 'It's just – my dad wasn't around.'

'Oh?'

Somewhere, a woman laughed, a horrible, cutting sound. 'Yeah,' I continued, not liking the way Berenice's face was folding into concern, 'he and my mum split up when I was eight. He died a couple of years later.' The words felt small amidst the rattle of cutlery. Talking about my dad felt wrong, like breaking a confidence or twisting someone's words.

'Oh,' she said, reaching to touch my hand. 'I'm so sorry.'

I waved the sympathy and her hand away, nearly toppling the fizzy water that Berenice had ordered instead of wine. 'Don't be. We weren't close.' Picking some burnt-looking bread from a basket, I tried not to think about my younger self curled in the corner with the house phone, dialling his number over and over.

'Even so,' Berenice said, 'that must be a lot to deal with.'

I tore the bread into bite-sized pieces, left them on my plate. 'Honestly, I don't think I even cried.' For a moment my body recalled the sensation: sinking to my scuffed knees, my jaw hanging open like that of a corpse waiting to be bound, unable to feel my mum's arms around me (All the while bargaining with the universe: I'll tidy my room, I'll eat all my vegetables, I'll do whatever you want if you'll just bring him back. The old him, though, not the new him, be careful about that.)

In the pause that followed, some small, scalding dishes arrived. Berenice explained that we were supposed to share, which was disappointing since she'd ordered weird things like squid and sardines, things I didn't like, and we ate in silence for a while. Everything was too spicy, too oily. All the while I glanced at Berenice's rounded cheeks, her downturned mouth, searching for a family resemblance with Bryn. But her eyes were the eyes of someone who went to sleep at a sensible time, not someone whose bed was largely ornamental. Her hands were hands shaped for folders and notebooks, not for palming pennies or casting spells.

'Your family is more interesting than mine anyway,' I said, with forced brightness. 'What's it like being at university with your cousin?'

'It's funny,' she said, 'I've met a few people at the same college as a family member—'

'I meant Bryn specifically. He's practically a celebrity.'

'Oh. Right.' She pouted, as if she hadn't thought about this before. 'Frankly, my family was always a bit mortified by the Cavendish lot. I mean, Bryn's dad is famous for being a TV magician whose nasty, Hammer Horror tricks were designed for teenagers and weirdos. The best thing about his show is that it hasn't aired for fifteen years.'

A hint of jealousy, perhaps? 'Bryn told me he got the magic thing from his dad. Are they close?'

Berenice tugged at some shellfish with her fingers, exposing the soft, pale flesh. She seemed to find the subject distasteful. 'Louis Cavendish is a complicated man. And one of the few people who doesn't act as if Bryn is the centre of the universe.'

Christ, this whole family was bizarre. 'And you honestly don't like Bryn's magic?'

Berenice set down her knife and fork. A waiter refilled her glass, making me feel inattentive. Eventually, she began. 'When we were kids,' she said, 'Bryn came to visit, and he wanted to show me a trick. I said, okay. So he put his hand in his pocket and took out a mouse. A real, live one, its whiskers were so sweet. Anyway, he put the mouse in a bag – about the size of your hand – and put the bag on the floor. Then he stamped on it.'

I flinched.

'I screamed and screamed,' Berenice went on. 'Bryn stood, grinning. Then he put his hand in his pocket, and what was inside but a mouse.'

It sounded like a very cool trick to me. 'That must have been freaky, for a kid,' I said.

She shook her head. 'It wasn't that. Afterwards, I kept saying, tell me how you did it. Eventually he said: Berenice, it was magic. Deadly serious. Like he was almost angry that I thought otherwise. I found it really ... unsettling. I don't like pretence.' Then, looking me straight in the eye, she added: 'That's why I like you.'

I stuffed a piece of bread into my mouth.

Berenice maintained her gaze, open and unblinking. 'Guys here, they swagger around like the universe exists to give them an audience. Like, they don't actually have anything interesting to say. But they put on this ... *performance*, as if they do. It's infuriating. But,' she said, softer now, 'you're not like other guys in college.'

I didn't respond. This wasn't the compliment she assumed it to be.

'What I mean is,' she added, quickly, 'you don't pretend to be something you're not.'

'So,' I said, switching subjects as if shy, 'reading between the lines, you're not planning on spending much time with your cousin.'

She shook her head. 'The curry was fine, but more than enough for one term.'

I set my cutlery down in the way my mum had patiently taught me (she was determined that people wouldn't judge me for silly things, that they would appreciate me for who I am). The restaurant was so fucking loud. We were interrupted by our waiter, who made a fuss of the food I'd left and, to my dismay, left us with a pair of dessert menus.

Perhaps thinking she'd come across as disloyal, Berenice changed her tune. 'Don't get me wrong,' she said. 'Bryn is great. He's protective of his family, that's one thing. And he's obviously scarily talented. I remember him singing at school—'

'Bryn's a singer?' Of course. That voice.

An idea flared like a struck match. In the run-up to Christmas, I was due to play for the college fellows at some swanky dinner. I'd been preparing some solo piano pieces, but the fellows wouldn't know or care if I updated the programme. 'That's funny,' I said, 'because I've been looking for a singer to perform with.'

'Hmmm. Good luck holding Bryn's attention.'

I thought about my bank balance, gritted my teeth. 'It's a paid gig. A hundred quid.'

'Really? Still, he's not exactly strapped for cash.'

'You know,' I said, being as real as I'd ever been, 'I'm kind of desperate, Berenice. You said he was good to his family. Would he sing with me if you asked him, as a favour?'

She shrugged. 'Maybe.'

'So will you ask?'

'Of course, if you want me to.'

I beamed. She beamed back, and it made her look pretty.

I ordered the most expensive desserts on the menu, my treat, and when they arrived I joked that Berenice should keep her spoon to herself. 'You know,' I said, 'whatever you think of Bryn's magic, it can't be easy to palm a mouse, slip it into your pocket.'

From behind Berenice's smile came a flash of something like disappointment. 'No,' she said, 'it would be easier to use two mice, one of which is disposable.'

* * *

A couple of mornings later, I found a note under my door.

Berenice explained your predicament. Practice tomorrow at 4? B.

Quite chummy, really. A mark of our burgeoning connection, the shift from *vous* to *tu*. I know a guy called Bryn; I've got a friend called Bryn. That 'B'. Bewitched, bothered and bewildered. I folded the note neatly, tucked it into my pocket, and hummed the half-remembered melody as I made my way to breakfast.

One other thing I did that day: I spent hours listening to Warlock, to see what Bryn and I might perform together. I even listened to those songs from *Saudades* with a new fondness for their naivety, wondering at the distance we must travel to find our voices. Perhaps there was a point to everything that had gone before. Maybe it all had to happen to bring me to this exact place and time.

As the clock crept towards the hour, I kicked balled-up pants under my bed and hid some embarrassing CDs (*Smooth Classical II*, *Morning Piano Moods*) in a drawer. I removed a book about Beethoven from my desk and replaced it with one about *The Beauty of Maths and Music*. Some snacks and clean mugs, 'casually' arranged around my kettle, and I was ready.

Bryn arrived just after half past, and I clapped him daringly on the back as he stepped over the threshold. 'A hundred quid for a few songs?' he asked, making for my piano and flicking through my pile of sheet music. 'Sounds weirdly generous.'

Straight to business, then. 'Er, yeah. It's a special thing, for the fellows. They're ... not really advertising the payment.'

'A hundred *each*?'

'Yeah, yeah. Do you want a brew?'

He looked confused. I gestured at my instant coffee and he shook his head. 'So. What are we playing?' he said.

I'd hoped we'd sit, talk, have some of the overpriced biscuits I'd bought. But this was turning out more like a supervision than a social. Okay, fine. It was good that he was keen, wasn't it? Good that I was about to play through my favourite songs with my new favourite singer? I gathered myself, took a seat at the piano. 'Peter Warlock,' I said. 'Early twentieth-century English composer, wrote beautifully for baritone. Listen …' I played a few favourite passages, handling each perfectly constructed bar as if it were a freshly laid egg.

But within moments, Bryn was riffling through my music again. 'Hmmm. Not sure. But I like the idea of something English, saves me learning lyrics in another language.'

Trying not to show my disappointment, I suggested other pieces. Finzi, Howells, Bax. But each time Bryn seemed underwhelmed. Eventually he held up a sheaf of stapled pages. 'What's this?'

I took the music from his hands. '*A Shropshire Lad*, six songs by George Butterworth. Same era, stuff about young men lost in the war.' I picked out fragments of the songs, tried with my reedy voice to conjure the blossoming cherry tree and the bustling country fair. Bryn listened, frowning.

Then, the final song of the set. 'This one's fun,' I said, 'because you play two different characters. One verse is sung by a ghost. Then the next verse, by his friend who's still alive. And they alternate from there. So here, the ghost asks: Do you still play football together, now I'm gone? And his friend says, yes, we're still playing. How's your sight-singing?'

Bryn tipped his hand from side to side, 'So-so'. But, above my accompaniment, he put every note in its place, moving from the eerie question to its full-voiced reply:

Is my girl happy,
That I thought hard to leave,
And has she tired of weeping
As she lies down at eve?

Ay, she lies down lightly,
She lies not down to weep:
Your girl is well contented.
Be still, my lad, and sleep.

My body resonated with excitement like a string cleanly plucked. Jesus, the ease and richness of his voice was unearthly. My musicianship was the one thing I was known for, the quality shoring up my self-worth. But with Bryn, it was merely another thing to be pulled from his bottomless bag of talents. I was both delighted and chilled. 'Shall we work on this one?' I said, grinning.

'Fine,' he replied, without enthusiasm. 'Let's do our best, given the state of this piano.'

At that moment, I saw my room as if through Bryn's eyes, adding up each uninspiring element: the unloved instrument, with its dodgy tuning and twangy strings. The dog-eared music and the plastic metronome, my stupid biscuits and cheap coffee. No wonder he was listless. This was supposed to be an adventure, but it was a disaster—

Or maybe not. 'I've got an idea,' I said.

Unlike New Court, which glowed like a winter sunrise, Old Court was small and closeted and somehow mean. I didn't go there often, except to walk occasionally, hopefully, below Bryn's window. The walls, blackened by age, did a surprisingly good job of dulling the rumbling traffic of the city beyond, leaving the courtyard in solemn stillness.

Bryn followed as I passed through a small door in the far corner, up a twisted staircase and along a gloomy, uneven corridor. At the end was an unassuming door without a number. I'd read there was a piano here, gifted by a particularly generous alumna, and that the room was available for visiting musicians and occasional recitals. Hoping this was all true, I took from my pocket the key I'd just stolen from the porters' lodge (surreptitiously swiped from the board while Bryn distracted the porter, a job he'd performed as faultlessly as expected) and slipped it into the lock. Glancing back, I caught a look of intrigue on Bryn's face. He couldn't know that, up to this point, my greatest crime had been sneaking an extra book out of the library when I was at my borrowing limit. If Tim had seen me here, he would have had a fit.

A click, and the door swung open.

Inside, light bled between two huge cherry-coloured curtains, seeping into the rich hardwood panelling and gleaming across the polished floorboards. Books, harmonious in shades of wine and grain, covered the far wall. In the middle of the room, a wonder: a baby grand, its lid reaching like a great black sail.

'Well,' said Bryn, the trademark grin back on his face. 'This is more like it.'

We stepped around the room, lighting enormous, fringed lamps as we went. It clearly pleased Bryn, to think of this hidden place so close to his own room, to think I'd revealed its secret. This was better, I thought. This might just work.

Stopping at a glass cabinet, Bryn announced: 'Here we go.' Reaching inside, he retrieved two glasses and an ancient-looking bottle. Then he took a corkscrew from his pocket.

I tried to remain nonchalant. 'That's not ... expensive, is it?'

'Nah. They've got cellars full of this stuff.'

'Are you sure?'

'Totally.' The cork was already out, the glasses full.

Bryn motioned at the piano, and I sat. Then, leaning on the gleaming spruce, he handed me a glass. I looked at the syrupy stuff inside, then back at Bryn's irrefutable smile. 'It's fine,' he said. 'Trust me. Here's to us.'

'To us,' I replied, taking a large swig. The liquid was rich and sweet, intensely dark, with a hint of something burnt. Unable to wait a moment longer, I put my music on the stand and touched my fingers to the keys.

Musically, we were tentative at first, like people on a date who accidentally speak over one another and apologise unnecessarily. We each anticipated the other, blamed ourselves for little misunderstandings. But eventually we began to stretch the tempo here and there, intuitively giving space to special harmonic moments or melodic turns.

Bryn drank the majority of the wine – not wanting to make a twat of myself, again, I was determined to take it easy – but soon we both became silly and excitable. We giggled at small things. My fingers occasionally stumbled over themselves. Bryn mixed up his words, and when he mangled the lyrics 'heart and soul' into 'shart and hole' I sank my head onto the keys, weeping with laughter.

Yes, this was fine now. Better than fine.

At some point, Bryn decided we should have a break. He retrieved a second bottle from the cabinet, refilled our glasses, and we each relaxed into a doughy armchair. 'So,' he said, 'you're clearly finding your way around college.'

I didn't feel the need to lie. 'Not really,' I replied. 'It's still a mystery to me.'

'How do you mean?'

I thought for a while. 'The dining hall? Before I came here, I'd never even *seen* a room like that. And now I'm meant to have my Bran Flakes there, as if that's normal.'

Bryn considered this. 'I guess. Our hall at school looked exactly the same.'

'And then there's the gowns and the *Benedic, Domine* business.'

'Ah. We always said Grace, too. Although we had our own slightly ruder version.'

I smiled, sadly. 'You know, in our first week, I got chatting to a girl in a lecture, and it turned out her family had owned coalfields in Northumberland. I told her, my grandad had worked in one of them. The girl made a joke about how she'd keep a position for me at the pit, in case the bassoon fell through. I know she was kidding, but. People must look at me—'

I stopped. The idea that people had any kind of opinion about me was pure narcissism. But someone like Bryn *must* consider how they were observed, assessed.

I changed tack. 'If you could find out what other people secretly thought of you, would you?'

He snorted. 'Fuck, no.'

'Why not?'

'Why would I? Would it make you happier, knowing what other people think?'

'It's not about being happy, it's about knowing the truth.'

He shook his head. 'Nobody wants the truth. We're not built for it. Anyway, whose truth? You think other people know you better than you know yourself? Their version of you is just that: a version.' He stretched, drained the liquid from his glass, and stood. I picked at a loose thread on my T-shirt, feeling like a child getting lost in grown-ups' conversation.

For a moment he ambled silently up and down the bookshelves, stopping to pull a cloth-bound title from its row. 'Here's a truth for you,' he said. 'When I was younger, I took an overdose.'

My mouth fell open but no words came out.

He shrugged, *no big deal*, put the book back in the wrong place. 'I was a bit out of control, taking … It doesn't matter. Anyway, one night, I was out with friends and really, really wasted, and I felt disconnected. Not part of the world, somehow. And I became obsessed with the idea of knowing' – he searched for the right phrase – 'what was on the other side.'

'What?'

'I know it sounds weird,' he went on, without hearing, 'but I felt certain that if I took all the pills in my pocket, if I fucking died, I wouldn't—'

He paused.

'—I wouldn't *stay dead*.'

From beyond the window, the chapel bell moaned. I rubbed my arms. 'What happened?'

'I woke up in hospital.'

'Jesus, Bryn,' I said, my stomach dipping as if I stood at the edge of a cliff. 'That's weird.'

'I can't even remember what I took. Frances was there when I woke up, by my bed. That part was bad.'

'Frances?'

'My mother.' He spread his hands. 'But what would other people make of that? That I'm unhappy, unbalanced? Because that's not what it was. That's the truth you're talking about, other people's truth. Anyway,' he said, 'the main thing is, I can handle illicit substances a *lot* better these days.'

I managed an anxious smile, pretending to understand.

'And you know what?' he continued in a gleeful stage whisper. 'The year after, when we were getting towards A Levels, I'd done no fucking work whatsoever. So I told my headteacher I was feeling depressed, and she was so worried about me doing something stupid that she kept me off school until exams were over. It took her a couple of calls, but Cambridge made my offer unconditional.'

'Bryn, that's terrible!'

'I know!'

We laughed raucously, and the mood shifted, eased. 'So did you find out?' I asked.

'Find out what?'

'What was on the other side?'

And then: a creak from beyond the door. We froze. Another creak, like someone stepping softly up the stairs.

Bryn's expression was a mixture of alarm and hilarity. 'If that's a porter …'

'Could we get sent down?' I whispered.

He shrugged. A cold flush of fear came over me, and I began to murmur feverishly: 'Shit, shit, shit …'

Seeing my rising anxiety, Bryn made a show of tiptoeing to the door. There he listened intently, a finger on his lips. All the while he looked at me, and his sober expression gave me an inexplicable comfort: nothing bad can happen while he's here. I held that thought right up to the point he sprang at the piano and began to pound the keys like a hooligan, howling with laughter above his shapeless, cacophonous chords.

'Bryn!' I said, my voice little more than a hiss. 'What the fuck?'

His words were laced with laughter and his eyes had a delighted gleam. But I was pure panic. He kept swiping at the keys even as I tried to drag him from the piano stool.

The footsteps were louder now, regular. Coming our way.

Jesus. I pictured myself being instructed to pack my belongings, being driven away from college by my mortified parents, watching the burnished battlements through the rear window until they had disappeared irretrievably from view. My breath came sharp and shallow, and I think my eyes burned with furious tears. Finally seeing my petrified face, Bryn stopped his hammering and – still smiling – sprinted to the window, pushed it open. 'This way.'

'Are you joking?'

'We don't have any choice!' Then he sat on the windowsill and swung his feet up onto it. I merely stood, a deer with feet splayed in headlights, gazing around as if the ancient furniture might tell me what to do.

The footsteps sounded closer still.

Bryn threw open the window and peered at the courtyard below. He'd do it, I knew that much, he'd step out into the biting air. Dropping my sheet music, I dashed into a corner and squeezed myself uselessly between a desk and a bookcase, knowing that my arse would be clearly visible to anyone coming through the door. Crouching on the sill, Bryn turned to look at me.

And then, a moment when we were frozen in time, spellbound: one stuck with horror and the other with glee, our fates tied together in mad camaraderie by wine and music and a magical sort of danger.

Silence, from the corridor.

Silence, followed by the sounds of footsteps moving away, further and further away, then a distant door opening, closing.

I exhaled. Bryn leapt from the windowsill and slumped melodramatically to the floor, cackling at the ceiling. I crumpled to my knees and wiped sweat from my forehead. With relief flooding my body, making me feel almost drunk, my face relaxed into a smile. Actually, that was pretty fucking brilliant.

'I think,' Bryn said, 'this might be a good time to leave.'

By the time we emerged into Old Court, I felt fiercely alive. I watched students moving beneath the starred sky, drawn to the soft lights of the dining hall and the hubbub of the college bar, and I felt a kind of synchronicity in my surroundings – as if I were a melody dancing lightly, the ostinato bass line of college firm and reliable beneath me. Bryn clapped my arm, heartily. 'Well played. I think we've got something good, there.'

I smiled, sensing the touch of his hand even after it was back in his pocket. I was about to ask whether we might go to the bar together, but a voice drew my attention. Tim, waving enthusiastically, a small figure beside him. 'Hey! Me and Casio are going up to hall, if you fancy?'

And by the time I looked back, Bryn was sauntering away, illuminated beneath the lamplight as if credits might begin to roll, as if he were taking the evening with him.

We came together a few nights later, fellows looking on, the saints gazing down from sunless glass. I have no memory of whether we were triumphant or merely tolerable.

Because, with Bryn, memory is slippery. Like, what colour was his hair, exactly? I know it shone darkly, like new leather shoes. But while in some of my memories it has a reddish cast, in others it appears completely black. And what about his eyes? Not blue or green. Certainly not brown. In my mind, they're the colour of shadows moving across an icy field, darkening and lightening with the rise and fall of the ground.

And this isn't down to the distance between then and now. My memory faltered even at the time. When Bryn disappeared for days, I had the feeling you get when someone dies: terror, that you'll forget them. In his absence, I forced myself to recall his features, his voice, as if repeating a tricky passage of music. As if he were a skill I might lose without constant and devoted practice.

In those final days of Michaelmas term, I spent a lot of time with Berenice, who was now officially my girlfriend.

Nobody knew better than me that I was punching above my weight. After all, Berenice was charming. Her eyes landed gently on the people around her, encouraging and warm. Her skin was clear, like the women you see in adverts for whitening toothpaste or washing powder, and, in her neatly pressed dresses, she carried herself with a quiet elegance.

She was also much cleverer than me. Don't get me wrong, I was good at my subject. But mine was a simple intelligence, an accumulation of other people's ideas. Where I assumed that lecturers and authors must surely know better than me, Berenice didn't take their words at face value. She turned them over, like a chef might check apples for bruises. She rolled them, squeezed them, and when she finally accepted them you could be sure they were just right. I was struck that a person could have such mastery over their own thoughts.

This did mean that, in our conversations, I was wary of screwing up. Sometimes I'd go quiet, pretending to be pensive, when really I had nothing to add. Or, desperate to show some spark, I'd come out with a grandly stupid idea that Berenice would slice neatly into its individually stupid constituent pieces. When we showed up as a couple in the common room or at Christmas parties, I was nervy, deferential. Perhaps observers thought it was because of the scale of my love for her. Or maybe they decided that, in the balance between us, I merely saw that my side of the scale needed more weight.

In the end, I was almost glad when the Christmas holidays rolled around and I could run away home – to go back to wasting my time on shit reality TV, to making ill-thought-through arguments about news stories without having my logic justifiably challenged. To being the half-arsed person that, for the whole term, I had exhausted myself trying not to be.

During those holidays, my mum interrogated me about my new Cambridge life. As we lay on the sofa, half-watching festive films and stuffing ourselves with Quality Street, she asked hungrily about the modules I was taking, the friends I'd made. I didn't mention Berenice, as it seemed too soon. But I talked about Bryn and our performance, about the pieces I was studying. All the while she glowed with pride like a string of fairy lights. Once, she remembered the teasing of my high school days, and shook her head – sorry for my former self, satisfied that the good guys win out in the end.

I also caught up with my old sixth-form friends. Gaz was doing History at Leeds, Ben was at Loughborough studying Computer Sciences. Reedy was working in his dad's chippy while he waited to re-sit the A Levels he'd flunked, which is where we usually met to talk over battered sausages and pickled onions. It might have been fun had the three of them not spent the whole time taking the piss out of my accent. *Listen to you, you've gone all posh. Go on, say 'beer'. Say 'over there'.* Why then did people in Cambridge still casually imitate my dropped Ts, my loose-jawed northern vowels?

The teasing was a reminder that I was stuck inbetween – sailing from one world, unsure when or if I'd ever reach another.

At one of our meetings, I performed a trick I'd just learned (from *Beginner's Magic: Easy Tricks to Amaze your Friends*, on loan from the municipal library). I started by holding a pen lightly between my fingers. Keeping everything else still, I covered the pen with one hand. Then, when I moved that hand away again, the pen was gone. *Shazam.* Unfortunately, Reedy spotted the piece of elastic, running inside my wrist and up my sleeve, that had whipped the pen away as soon as I let go of it (I must have stood in the wrong place: I was yet to learn that perspective is everything). The lads seemed bored by the solution, and disappointed that, despite my time at Cambridge, I had not been imbued with special powers and had instead remained an ordinary bloke.

One other thing I remember. As Christmas Day neared, Mum asked me to get some table decorations from the loft. And when I clambered up among the cobwebbed suitcases and musty camping equipment, I came across my dad's record player, a record still sitting on the turntable. The sight of it stopped my breath. For a beat, I was back on his knee, his hand gently covering mine as he explained why I mustn't trace my chubby fingertip across the vinyl. I almost heard him telling me patiently that no, these grooves on the record's surface were not a multitude of concentric circles as I'd assumed, but a single path running from the edge inwards. Crouching in the darkness, I remembered the sound that had emerged when he lowered the needle – that unearthly crackle, so unlike the sound from the TV or the radio, so obviously from a distant time, a distant place.

When I climbed down and handed over the box of tinsel and other Christmas tat, I didn't mention the record player. I wanted to forget it. I'd been more comfortable thinking that, after dad's death, it had been – like the pen in the trick – magicked away. There was something deeply unsettling about the idea that it had been up there, with us all along.

Before the holidays were over, I gave up on learning magic myself. I was afraid of people seeing me copy Bryn so blatantly. In any case, I knew I had none of the showmanship on which a performance like his depended: making that contract with the audience, building their trust, concealing the deception until the very end.

III

It was after eight by the time I arrived at my B&B. As the landlady said something about keys, I looked around and realised: it hardly felt like I was in Cambridge. The out-of-date celebrity magazines fanned primly in the lounge, the painfully twee countryside prints that lined the walls – all reminders that life in the city had existed beyond the tastes and experiences of us students. It hadn't crossed my mind at the time. Once I'd dumped my case upstairs and devoured the complimentary Viennese whirls, I headed out into the dusk.

I'd planned to meet Tim at a pub out past John's. While his role as a paediatric surgeon meant his diary was rather fuller than mine, it was mainly thanks to him that we'd caught up once or twice a year since leaving college. Whenever he visited extended family in Salford we made the effort to meet, and I took him to hipster bars and gastropubs as if they, and not the cheaper sports pubs, were my locals. But, unbelievably (for him, at least), this was the first time since we were students that we'd met in Cambridge. We'd agreed to have a quick drink tonight, and then Tim would be my guest for the following evening at the Cavendish Scholarship dinner. He knew nothing about singing except that he was very bad at it, but he was enthusiastic at the idea of a free four-course meal in our old digs.

Walking the once-familiar roads, I found them empty but for the occasional bicycle lamp that sliced through the dark. At one point, my feet took me automatically in the direction of an old supervisor's house, and I spun around just as the first raindrops tapped me on the nose.

Eventually, there it was. The Apple Tree, an image of Isaac Newton on its swinging sign. I was reminded of something Bryn had told me: that Newton wrote more books on alchemy than on any other subject, all unpublished since the work was considered heretical. There can be few schoolchildren in the country who don't know this iconic Cambridge figure, but fewer still who do know about his secret societies or his apocalyptic predictions or his pursuit of the Philosopher's Stone. History has gently edited Newton's achievements such that what we remember is the falling fruit, the bumped head, the discovery of a force that pulls us towards the earth.

As this flew through my mind, it was followed by a picture of something terrible, the thing I'd dreamed (nightmared?) many times – and I thought I felt gravity itself, tugging at me so hard that it might pull me onto the pavement. A passing student looked at me with alarm, likely thinking I was drunk. I hurried, panicked, into the pub, brushing rain from my coat, buoyed by the warmth of an open fire and the tang of vinegar on freshly fried fish.

There at the bar was Tim, his face a shade slacker and his body a little softer, his grin as broad as ever. We hugged and, after he insisted on getting the first round, we did the usual updates (his wife and daughter both well).

'What's the plan for tomorrow?' he asked, touching his lips to the foamy top of his pint.

'Auditions at ten,' I replied. 'Right through until afternoon, with a bit of deliberating between the judges. So I'll probably be back at college, to get changed and everything, by six-ish.'

'Aren't you changing at your B&B?'

'I'm only at the B&B tonight. For tomorrow – you're going to love this – I've booked a room in college.'

Tim raised his eyebrows. 'What's a young professional like you doing in a scummy old college room? And after I said you could stay at ours!'

'I thought it would be fun. Memory lane. I can see what the youth have done to the old place.'

Tim gave his head a baffled shake. 'Have you forgotten what the beds are like? Best get your chiropractor on standby.'

Only then did I realise how odd my plans sounded. But the pull I'd felt since reading Frances's letter wasn't just about the city. It was about college itself, the space we'd inhabited when it all unravelled. I had the feeling that I'd been rehearsing, polishing my memories like scales and arpeggios, fixing them in the mind and body. But why? To carry them back to the place we'd shared? To show, by my service to his family, that I had never wanted things to end the way they did?

Seeing his puzzled expression, it made me sad to think of the deceptions I'd dealt poor Tim. Not just the normal sleight of hand between friends, like when I invited him to my most prestigious concerts but failed to tell him about the ones in poorly ventilated village halls or cabbage-scented care homes. The concealment of the fear and guilt that hung always at my shoulder. At least I'd never needed to exaggerate my love life. I'd done just fine there.

I searched for an easier subject. 'Do you remember Bryn getting kicked out of here?'

'No. When?'

'First year. A charity pub crawl, I think. The blokes were dressed in women's underwear.'

'God, I can't remember that. Was I there?'

'You must have been, everyone was. Weren't you in a red nightie or something?'

'Red always was my colour.'

'They were by the fireplace,' I said, pointing. 'With that American mathmo who left after a term. Ruben? They had a bottle of whisky, like they were in a Western or something. Then Bryn tried to climb up the chimney and they made him leave.'

Tim shook his head. 'Well. Probably best that kind of thing is in the dim and distant past.'

I nodded, stared into my glass. But Tim was wrong. Bryn wasn't distant at all. In fact, I could feel it strongly: he was very close. And getting closer.

~

In those brisk January days of Lent term, my college world expanded like a spotlight growing on a stage. Having established myself as his musical partner, I actually spent time with Bryn's group, at more intimate parties in his room or in pubs by the river.

It wasn't always easy. While Sarah was superficially friendly, she barely remembered our conversations from one meeting to the next. On learning (again) that I was a musician, she'd promise to put me in touch with family friends who worked for Glyndebourne or the Royal Opera House and never follow through. Jamie, on the other hand, didn't even pretend to like me. He kept his distance, regarding me with a steely suspicion, as if I might pick his pocket or try and sell him a timeshare. That Kenny bloke was worst of all – he made a game of my existence, mimicking my accent and asking questions of me as if I were a newly discovered life form ('*You've honestly never heard of the* London Review of Books?'). His most annoying habit was hanging around Bryn's neck, constantly muttering in his ear in a way that left everybody else out.

Those gatherings were easier when I invited Alexa along. She was chatty, she was funny. Crucially, she was familiar with the public school manners I found so perplexing, and – dialling certain parts of her personality up or down – fitted seamlessly into the crowd. It must have been her heightened sense of empathy, a chameleonic social awareness. Laughing easily at people's jokes, whether juvenile or barbed, she was the perfect party guest, the most amenable audience member.

Berenice, though, rarely joined our parties. When she'd said she didn't intend to spend much time on her cousin, she'd meant it.

And so I clung to my place in Bryn's group. I learned to keep up with everyone else – to power through a bottle of wine before dinner without passing out during pudding, to chug alcopops that were sickly enough to make your teeth squeak. All this without ending up in any more Old Court bathrooms. I became intrigued by the oddness of inebriation: the losing of time, the blunting of senses, the muddy memories that differed from person to person.

This meant I had less time to spend with Tim. I began to cut short our study sessions, then miss them altogether, persuaded by Bryn that while our books could wait, this sunset, this film screening, this paddle of vodka shots – well, it wouldn't. Now and again, on my way to another adventure, I'd spy Tim in our old spot in the library, frowning over his books, and I'd wonder whether to ask him along.

But Tim, who didn't crackle with electricity so much as glow with a hot-water-bottle warmth, wouldn't have liked Bryn's gatherings anyway. There were people climbing out of windows and into locked buildings, people breaking into the closed-up parts of other colleges (I'm pretty sure Jamie once stole the TV from Pembroke's common room). Dark feats of endurance, like when some guy poked a needle through the skin of his forearm just because Bryn told him to. Or when a girl tattooed Bryn's initials onto her thigh with a biro and a candle-scorched safety pin. Strange tests of allegiance, offerings that Bryn would receive like an obliging regent. Often, when the porters were distracted and he was feeling particularly reckless, Bryn would lead people out of a New Court window and up onto the college roof, but this was the one jape in which I refused to take part – instead, I offered to act as lookout, staring out across the courtyard while my new friends moved above me.

There was no Truth or Dare, like in other student gatherings, no faux-ironic Spin the Bottle, games designed to help us safely unveil ourselves to one another. And yet Bryn's parties were much more revealing. Unprompted, people told outrageous stories about their sex lives, about committing real, serious crimes. Keen to make an impression, I wondered about telling tales from Peter Warlock's life as if they were my own, but I decided that these tales of Paris jails and naked motorcycle rides were obviously too colourful to belong to me. I felt very strongly the need for stories that would secure my place within the circle.

Perhaps the thing that made Bryn's coterie so different from Tim and his friends: they didn't see Cambridge the same way. They looked upon the city and its traditions with an indifference that bordered on disdain. The age-old structures, the traditions that impressed the rest of us so much, Bryn and his friends would as soon have pulled them all down. They were completely unafraid to break rules, to ignore instructions. That's not to say that they weren't interested in learning – only that, if they were given a reading list, they'd read a wholly different set of books. If they were given an essay to write, they'd write an essay on why the question itself was inherently flawed. Perhaps it's only natural to want to break out of structures when you already sit so neatly within them, when your life is held so securely.

It's funny that I always think of this as 'Bryn's group'. Because, a lot of the time, he wasn't even there. We simply moved around his absence as we did his presence, planets orbiting a great sun.

This was also the time Mona started following us around. As his fellow mathmo, Mona had supervisions with Bryn. She also lived directly below him on the first floor of Old Court's S staircase. These facts seemed to be her entire claim to the group.

I'd thought Mona was okay when we'd met in Michaelmas term. But, the more I knew of her, the more aggressively ordinary she seemed. She didn't drink. Although her tutors described her as a bright star, conversationally she was a thumping great black hole. To paint a picture, she carried a soft toy cat everywhere she went – a reminder of a long-deceased Balinese bought by her parents as a companion that wouldn't aggravate her allergies. It seemed always to be poking out of her bag and annoyed me to an irrational degree.

You might wonder why, as we moved around the common room or the bar, she crept so determinedly after us. But I knew that, like so many, she was in love with Bryn. I saw her lingering outside the porters' lodge early in the mornings, waiting to see whether he'd appear in time for them to walk to lectures together (despite the fact that he hardly ever went to lectures). I was also confident that Bryn's courtesy towards her was directly related to her willingness to share completed coursework. Mona was the Cambridge we were trying not to be: our nerdy pasts made manifest. Rejecting her was our way of protecting the new identities we were so carefully constructing. And look, the fact is – she was really fucking annoying.

So, when Mona trotted into the common room and plonked herself beside Bryn, I'd look meaningfully at Alexa. As she followed us up the stone staircase to hall for breakfast, we'd find a spot where there wasn't quite enough space for her to join us, and when she artlessly copied our gestures and phrases, we made up new, ridiculous ones to see if she'd copy those too. I'm not proud of it. But I'm supposed to be telling the truth now.

One cold February day, perhaps two or three weeks into term, I found Bryn, Sarah and Jamie having lunch in hall. At first I was puzzled as to why, when I gave them a cheery hello, they offered me only sullen mumbles – but when I sat and joined their muted conversation, I learned that Bryn was in a foul mood, having just been bollocked by college. (I didn't dare ask why, but I got the impression that the porters had found something prohibited in his room. And while Bryn didn't care about the ensuing fine, he wasn't too happy about the master having a word with Frances.) Just when I thought the atmosphere couldn't get any worse, Mona came trudging gracelessly towards us, tray in hand.

Jamie, not helping the situation, elbowed Bryn. 'Mate. Your girlfriend's here.'

Bryn looked up, unsmiling. Mona approached the space we'd carelessly left free, her face benign and uninspiring as a cow looking over a gate. She stared at Jamie as he ploughed valiantly through a leathery pork chop. 'Anyone sitting here?' she asked, brightly.

Jamie kept his eyes on his plate. 'Before I answer,' he replied, 'are you expecting a statement of fact or an invitation?'

Sarah guffawed instinctively before checking herself. 'Stop,' she said, gesturing around the table, 'we're being charitable today.' Then, using the generic address she favoured for people she barely remembered, to Mona: 'Have a seat, babe.'

Slightly dubious, Mona turned to Bryn. Then, using what was presumably her most seductive conversation starter: 'Did you finish the paper for Jennings?'

Bryn grimaced. 'Barely started it. I'm fucked.'

Mona looked at him with deep concern. 'If you want to talk through it, come round. Any time.'

I winced at this patronising offer, wondering whether Bryn would feel intellectually undermined in front of his friends. Even so, a curious smile spread across Bryn's face. 'Really?' he said. 'Any time?'

'Of course.'

'Thanks Mona. I might take you up on that.'

And then he reached slowly towards her – it honestly looked as if he was going to grab her by the tit – before putting his hand to the frizzy hair at the back of her head. The action was weirdly, deeply sensual, and we held ourselves in stunned stillness. Mona visibly shivered.

Then, Bryn's hand was in front of her face bearing a shiny red apple.

She squealed and blushed. We feigned indifference.

'Very biblical.'

'Attention seeker.'

'Yeah, but can you do it with a pineapple?'

Perhaps I was the only one who noticed because, rather than focusing on the trick itself, I'd been distracted by the dynamic of this unlikely double act. But when Bryn took the apple from Mona's hair with one hand, I saw that his other hand drifted down to her waist. And though I couldn't swear to it, I thought his fingers dipped subtly into the pocket of her sensible coat. Almost like he was depositing something.

I remembered hearing somewhere that magicians are most worried about those audience members on the fringe of a performance. The ones who aren't in the front rows, who aren't touched by the magician's gaze – they're the ones who might just spot the five-pound note being tucked under the watch strap. And here, on the sidelines, I'd seen something. I just had no idea what the trick might be.

Alexa was particularly irritated by Mona's fawning over Bryn. We laughed about it one evening as we trudged to orchestra rehearsal in the middle of an insistent snowfall.

'Maybe she'll send Bryn a Valentine,' I said, enjoying the sound of my voice as it reverberated around the frigid streets.

'Written in binary. Then she'll invite him round for a study session, to decode it.'

'Ask him to look over her vital statistics.'

'*Eurgh.* No. If Mona ever removed that horrible cardigan, there'd be one underneath it exactly the same.'

'Ha! She's totally cardigan squared.'

'Cardigan recurring.'

'You never know,' I said, 'maybe there's another side to her personality. She might be a bondage queen.'

'She doesn't have a personality to begin with, let alone one with different sides.'

As we cut through King's College, a carpet of white stretched right out back to the river, dappled with lamplight. Christmas-card trees wore a festive dusting of frost, as if they'd lost track of time.

'Speaking of Valentine's Day,' Alexa asked, 'do you and Berenice have plans?'

'Actually, she's got to be in London for the weekend,' I said. 'Family thing. So I'll probably stay in with a takeaway and a box of tissues.'

'Too much information.'

'Tissues for my tears! Get your mind out of the gutter. What about you?'

'Well, as a single person, I'll likely have a chow mein and a wank.'

I cackled. That was *not* the kind of joke I could have had with Berenice. 'Well, I suppose self-love is valid on Valentine's Day.'

'It's for the best, given my track record. Either a guy is obsessed with me and I can't bear him, or I'm the one who's obsessed.'

'Hmmm. My mum used to talk about every relationship having "The Lover and The Loved". One who does all the loving, and one who soaks it all up.'

She slowed momentarily on the icy path. 'Do you think a person can ever really be happy, being The Lover?'

I shrugged. 'I presume most Lovers don't realise that's what they are. And maybe it's worse to be The Loved, knowing that you don't feel that intense passion that you're supposed to feel. Yeah, The Loved get all the adoration, but they get the guilt too.'

'I guess both The Lover and The Loved can be happy so long as they can persuade themselves there's no such thing.'

We made our way out of King's, past The Backs.

'Would you rather,' said Alexa, 'be forced to do bad deeds but have everyone believe you're a good person, or never do anything bad but have people think you're a dick?'

I laughed. 'Is this coursework or something?'

'Just answer the question.'

'How bad are the deeds?'

'Slapping old women. Forcing your loved ones to sit through Hawley's talk about the college's medieval manuscripts.'

I winced. 'Honestly? I'd probably do the bad stuff and have people think I was good.'

'Knowing you're living a lie?'

'It's a lie either way. So, I'm thinking, which lie allows me to live a happier life.'

'So it comes back to self-love. Because it depends whether you value your own opinion of yourself above other people's. You, like many of us, value other people's opinions above your own.'

'Is that such a bad thing? I'm going to need people's good opinion if I'm going to make friends, get a job ...'

She shook her head. 'Do you honestly think people only offer friendship – and jobs, whatever – to people they think are *good*? Do you think being a good person is really what gets you ahead?'

'Maybe not. I hadn't considered the difference between being thought good and being liked. Anyhow, don't change the subject. We were talking about your plans for Valentine's Day. Isn't there anyone who might tempt you away from that chow mein?'

She shrugged, *Maybe.*

I made an educated guess. 'Is it Bryn?'

For a while, she said nothing, and our footsteps landed wetly on the salted pavement. Then she said, quietly: 'What do you think he'd say?'

Honestly, I had no clue how Bryn felt about Alexa. But I thought there was a good chance he'd be interested. Sure, he had his pick of beautiful girls, but Alexa was attractive in an interesting way. Her teeth, slightly gapped, her strong, aquiline nose – hers was a charming, boutique beauty, not the mass-market kind you saw in magazines.

Also, the fact that Alexa asked, that she thought I might know Bryn's secrets – I was flattered. 'I know he's hard to read,' I said, 'but I wouldn't be surprised if he feels the same way. He's very attentive.'

'He's attentive to everybody,' she said, adjusting her woollen hat, now speckled with snowflakes. 'You know, there's part of me that would rather never know. Do you know what I mean? Like, living with the *potential* that something could happen is better than knowing for sure that it never will.'

'Come on. Do you want me to say something to him?'

'Fuck, no! Well. I don't know.' She paused. 'Let me think about it.'

'Fine,' I replied. 'But for now, keep going as you are. The right people will end up together, you'll see.'

'Thanks, Mister Hallmark Cards.'

Throughout that night's rehearsal, I pondered. It could be a very cool thing if she and Bryn were to get together. To people in college, she and Berenice came as a pair. So if Alexa and Bryn got together, our two couplings would make a happy foursome. Alexa and Bryn, me and Berenice. Alexa and Berenice. Me and Bryn.

Wondering about my own dynamic with Berenice, I realised that I couldn't identify either of us as The Lover or The Loved. Of course, I saw her as my better in many – most – ways. She was smarter. She was kind.

Did I like her, or did I think she was good?

In the end, I bought her a card and some chocolates, ready for when she got back from London. And on Valentine's Day itself, I had a takeaway and a wank.

At weekends, locals filled the Cambridge nightclubs. And with no student deals on double spirits, no free entry for those dressed as superheroes, Friday and Saturday evenings revolved around takeaway noodles in the common room with reality TV blaring in the background. So I was delighted when, one afternoon around the middle of term, Bryn caught me in the post room and asked whether I wanted to join him and a few friends for the weekend at his family's home somewhere near Chipping Norton. This invitation was all the more thrilling given there'd be a select group in attendance. There was Jamie, who was willing to forgo a Pitt Club dinner for the trip. Sarah too, especially since she'd recently been reprimanded for her behaviour at a Wine Soc event and was finding college life 'so fucking parochial'. Also that dickhead, Kenny. The twist was that we'd have to leave college in just a few hours, but the spontaneity seemed part of the fun and absolutely typical of Bryn.

At Bryn's request, I called Berenice to invite her along too. But she declined, making some excuse about having an essay due on the Monday. I also had an essay due – two, in fact, neither of them even halfway finished – but I wasn't going to argue. Berenice and I had been bickering lately. She'd accused me of being unpleasant on nights out, told me I turned into someone else when I had too much to drink. Like 'a man possessed'. She was bound to say that, because she had that middle-aged, one-glass-of-wine-with-my-meal approach to booze. I regretted telling her anything about my dad's problems with alcohol, since she was happy to use it against me. I told her, exasperated: We're British, binge-drinking is what we do.

When I told Bryn that Berenice couldn't join us, he didn't seem bothered. He only remarked casually that Sarah might think the whole thing was turning into a 'bit of a sausage fest'. Which gave me an idea. I asked: Why not invite Alexa? Bryn had shrugged, *Sure*, and the whole thing had become an opportunity. What would make me happier than for my two friends to get together? And what would bind me more irrevocably to both of them?

* * *

Alexa and I met the others outside college, at the van Kenny had once again 'borrowed' from his theatre group. Giddy with excitement, we stuffed the van with overnight bags, plus some hurriedly-bought deli foods as mandated by our host (my remit was limited to crisps, which I chose to read as sensitivity towards my bank balance rather than distrust in my taste). Despite me trying to manoeuvre Bryn and Alexa into adjacent seats, he ended up beside Jamie, she beside Sarah. Which left me in the front with Kenny. The whole journey, Kenny bellowed over his shoulder, anxious to be part of the group chat, occasionally dropping his water bottle onto my lap as if I were a side table. But, with two nights at Bryn's on the horizon, I was too excited to care.

The sun sank slowly through the sky, and motorway turned to A roads, to B roads, to rambling country lanes. One by one we fell silent, like an audience when the house lights are dimmed. When we finally passed through a large iron gate, Bryn told Kenny to pull over – we should walk from here, he said – and we set off down a long gravel drive, so thickly canopied by trees that we could hardly see one another in the shadows beneath. As we crunched along in the dark, Kenny crept up and grabbed me suddenly by the shoulders, producing a scream from me and hysterical laughter from everybody else. Just as I was getting ready to trip him, the trees opened up and we finally saw where we were headed.

Naturally, I'd tried to imagine what the house might be like. But nothing prepared me for what awaited us that February evening. Up a path bisecting an immaculate lawn was an enormous farmhouse, its timbered walls thickly cloaked in ivy. Darkened windows reflected the silvery light, while purple flowers spilled from the sills in spite of the cold. A lilac front door beckoned, cheeky as a wink.

The whole house was enclosed by dense woods, like a castle in a fairy tale.

While the others stared in wonder, they missed something strange. They didn't notice that, as Bryn looked at the house, his expression turned to puzzlement. As if, somehow, he'd been tricked. But the look was fleeting, and – like a juggler disguising a fumble – he rearranged his features quickly so that, when everyone turned to him, he was ready with a modest smile.

We followed him up the path to the front door, Kenny trying to look unruffled, Jamie, Sarah and Alexa literally racing one another to arrive first. Again, everyone was too busy shouting and giggling to notice the way Bryn rattled the handle before unlocking the door (why do that, unless you think someone is waiting?). In the entrance hall, we dumped our bags below a row of exquisite family portraits that hung crookedly, a blank space in the middle where something had been removed. One portrait showed a middle-aged woman you might describe as handsome, with high cheekbones and dark hair in an elegant twist. Surely this was Bryn's mother, Frances Cavendish.

Alexa whispered in my ear. 'What a dump, hey.'

I nodded, unsmiling. 'Imagine having your portraits in pastel rather than oils.'

Bryn stalked up and down, throwing on lights and poking his head through doorways, peering up into the darkness at the top of the wood-panelled staircase. I looked myself, up into the glowering shadows, but saw nothing.

He led us hurriedly in and out of the games room, the library, the sitting room, where lamps of all sizes and styles gave the place a cinematic soft-focus. Each space had a signature scent, as if curated by a perfumier – here, firewood and leather, there, old newspapers and chamomile. Waving distractedly up the stairs,

Bryn mentioned a roof terrace overlooking the swimming pool, a relatively new addition that had horrified the locals. I imagined inviting people to my own house, having them squeeze into our spare bedroom between my stepdad's old telescope and my mum's abandoned exercise bike. Finally, when Bryn outlined the available bedrooms – explaining that he'd take his father's – I pleaded for what was usually his room, claiming that I'd prefer one within easy reach of the bathroom.

We followed him into a huge open space with wooden beams overhead and stone underfoot. At one end was a kitchen, featuring the first Aga I'd ever seen in real life, where work surfaces were strewn with ornamental jugs, dried flowers, bowls and bottles, all in an artful mess. At the other end of the space was the dining area, containing a large farmhouse table covered in newspapers, outdated theatre programmes, miscellaneous correspondence. In the corner by the table was a pretty upright piano, encumbered with piles of music books, a violin and cello leaning casually beside it. Everything was so charming that I thought we might conclude this tour with a burst of applause. We all turned to Bryn, expectant: time to start the party?

But no, he was backing out of the room, jabbing at his mobile. 'Crack on with the champagne,' he said. Then, waving half-heartedly at a large wine rack, 'or help yourselves to whatever. I've got to – nip out for a sec.'

We looked at him, perplexed.

His voice faded as he disappeared around the door frame. 'Oh, and if you could make a start on dinner—'

The front door slammed.

In the silence that followed, those of us left behind looked cautiously at one another, puppies abandoned at a roadside. But nobody commented on the frown on Bryn's face, the sudden darkness in his tone. None of us wanted to suggest the unthinkable: that we might not understand our friend Bryn very well at all.

Kenny began organising us as if this were his directorial debut at the National. Jamie, who had studied French cookery on his gap year, was put to work at a chopping board, assisted by Alexa. Sarah – a member of Wine Soc, disgraced or no – was tasked with decanting the wine and preparing the pre-dinner cocktail. At one point I spotted Jamie and Sarah smirking behind Kenny's back, but they worked away like indulgent parents.

I set the table, filling bowls with the snacks I'd brought. Jamie complained that few wines paired easily with Frazzles, while Sarah squealed with delight and said that the last time she even saw those things was at her junior school tuck shop. I was thankful for Alexa, who gamely ate a handful. For much of the time, Sarah monopolised Alexa's attention with chatter about their shared connections, so I retreated to the piano and made familiar shapes with my hands, pressing the keys so softly that they didn't make a sound.

In the time it took for Jamie to prep the meal, including a horrifying starter that appeared to be made of raw meat, our host did not return. But night closed in around the house. With the lights atmospherically dimmed, the edges of the kitchen disappeared into shadow, candlelight bouncing off the wall-mounted blades and copper-bottomed pans. Jamie set out another place at the table, and I, feeling criticised, challenged his counting. But he, as clueless as me, revealed that Bryn had said we'd be cooking for seven. Seven?

We stood around the table, at a slight distance, like police officers arriving at a crime scene. Jamie, who had donned a velvet jacket, looked meaningfully at me. 'Aren't we dressing for dinner?'

Sarah snorted. 'Stop showing off, James, you look like a game show host.'

He scowled at her, poured himself a red wine. Then addressed the room. 'We should start. You know what Bryn's like.'

I bristled. 'I don't know ... That seems rude.'

Jamie sputtered. 'Alright, Mister Debrett's. Tell me, what else would be rude? Licking my plate? Scratching my balls with the salad tongs?'

Kenny guffawed as if this were a much better joke. Turning to me, he asked, giddy: 'What's wrong? Aren't you excited about your tartare?'

It looked gross. 'Course I am.'

'Only I presumed you weren't much of a foodie,' Kenny said, holding out his own glass for Jamie to fill, 'since you've given us soup spoons for the dessert.'

Confused, I looked at the spoons I'd set out. Actually, they did look a funny shape.

Sarah jumped in, waggling her finger between me and Alexa: 'Remind me. How do you two know one another?'

'We're both in orchestra,' I replied, puzzled at the question.

Kenny jumped in again. 'I wondered too,' he said. 'I knew it couldn't be through school.'

I glanced at Alexa, but she busied herself cleaning the chopping board, a nation state attempting to remain politically neutral.

But I wasn't letting Kenny get away with that one. 'Course it wasn't school,' I said to him, sarcastic. 'Because naturally I went to a shitty school with no money, where we foraged our own pencils and shared one gym kit between three pupils.'

Sarah looked stunned. 'God, did you really?'

'And yet,' said Kenny, 'money isn't what separates private and state schools.'

I knew it was bait. Still, I couldn't resist. 'So what does, then?'

Kenny moved around the table making imperceptible adjustments to the cutlery. 'State school students – present company potentially excepted, I don't know you well enough to say – are taught to see the world in a way I'd call *ordinary*. They've been told: Get a nice, safe job, be a doctor or a lawyer if you want to aim high. Get married, pay your bills, blah blah.'

Jamie rolled his eyes as if this were a hobby horse he'd trotted out before. I stared at Kenny as if observing someone with mild cognitive decline.

'Whereas,' he went on, 'private schools say: Go, start your own company. Go and be the Chancellor of the Exchequer. And that confidence, that *belief,* is a skill in itself.'

Jamie spoke into his glass, murmured words that seemed meant for Sarah and maybe Alexa. 'A skill that even the minor public schools can develop, apparently.'

I couldn't get the words out fast enough. 'So, people from poor families and run-down towns would have the same life chances as everyone else, if only they had the right attitude?'

Kenny stared at me as if the answer were obvious. 'You're doing okay, aren't you?'

Jamie squealed with glee: *Ooh, such a bitch.* Sarah tutted and turned sympathetically to me, declaring: 'You've done marvellously, really. All things considered. Like, gold star for you.'

I flared with fury. 'It's *all* about money,' I said to Kenny, losing control of my volume. 'If you're skint and worried about getting into debt, it's a lot fucking scarier to start a degree or set up a company.'

Kenny shook his head. 'Again, only if you see the world a certain way. The debt will take care of itself once you're in a job.'

'Maybe, maybe not. I imagine it's easier to risk it when your family provides you with a massive financial safety net.'

'There it is. That's the attitude I'm talking about. Quitting before you've begun.'

Was this a fucking wind-up? 'It sounds to me,' I said to Kenny, bitterly, 'like you're admitting that you're no cleverer than the average state school kid.'

He shrugged, insouciant. 'That depends whether you think imagination is clever.'

There was a shift in the air pressure, like an intake of breath. Then, sounds from the hallway. The front door slamming, keys landing on a hard surface. Feet, thumping the floorboards. I sighed, thinking. Thank fuck for that.

When Bryn finally appeared, we gave little cheers and gentle admonishments: *Hey, man, what took you so long?* But he only gave us a half-hearted wave and dropped into one of the chairs at the table, his face like a locked door. I caught Sarah's eye, attempting to verify that the confusion I felt was shared, but she looked away. Eventually, Bryn gave us a smile. But it was a strange, unsettling smile, and when he thanked us all for preparing the meal, his voice rang like an instrument slightly out of tune. I had no idea what was going on, but something told me it wasn't the time to ask.

Kenny, emboldened by his earlier performance, felt differently. 'Hey man,' he said. 'Where'd you go?'

Bryn gazed at that mysterious extra place with its gleaming glassware and neatly folded napkin. The chair, its portentous emptiness. 'It's nothing.'

Sarah and Jamie busied themselves with the starter plates. Alexa locked eyes with me, and I responded with the tiniest possible shrug.

Unbelievably, Kenny ploughed on. 'If something's up, you can tell us—'

'What I'll tell you,' Bryn said, very softly, 'is to shut the fuck up about it.'

There was a pause. Taut, like the moment before a falling object hits the ground.

And then, Bryn gave a laugh like thunder, a heatwave breaking, flashed his eyes at Kenny. The others followed his lead, and Kenny smiled stupidly as if everything was fine. Although I laughed weakly along too, disappointment twisted like hunger pangs. I'd dreamed of being in this place, with these people, but my imagination had failed – this reality was nothing like my dreams at all.

We tightroped through the starter and the main like characters in a murder mystery, primed for a revolver in the bread basket, cyanide in the port. We drank resolutely to steady our nerves and, before long, the table was strewn with wine-spattered napkins and sauce-graffitied plates like something from a war zone (Sarah had already declared, quite seriously, that Bryn should throw the napkins away because getting red wine out of linen was honestly more trouble than it was worth). The only thing that remained pristine was the dessert, plated for later, a gleaming fruit tart that someone had carried conscientiously from Cambridge in a ribboned box.

Keen to keep the atmosphere cool, I pointed at the instruments huddled in the corner. 'Hey Bryn. You don't play piano, do you?'

He shook his head. 'My parents do. Obsessive about music, both of them.'

'Really?'

'Oh yeah. Not that they're any good. That Bach, on the stand? Frances can't do more than four bars, but she keeps it there because it looks good.'

I'd spotted it earlier. The Crab Canon. 'I learned that one,' I said. 'You'd like it, it's kind of maths-y. You basically play the same line of music forwards and backwards at the same time.'

Bryn shrugged. 'Maybe that's why Frances doesn't bother with it. I got my maths from my dad. Frances likes music with epic strings, stuff she can weep to. And they say my dad's the theatrical one.'

I imagined Frances draped across a chaise longue, consumptive. Actually, no: in a breastplate and horned helmet. 'I guess that's the thing with music,' I said. 'We can project our own stuff onto it. There's this thing with Shostakovich, where some people say his work was a coded message condemning Stalin's regime. Others say that's impossible, because anybody who condemned the regime was ...' I dragged a finger across my neck. 'You either hear it or you don't.'

Jamie half-stifled an ostentatious yawn, making more of a scene than if he'd just let the thing out.

Suddenly, Kenny sat up tall. 'Wait. Bryn. Your dad. Is this the house where he ...?'

A dark smile crept stealthily across Bryn's face. 'He has a workshop in the cellar. The locals said it was where he performed occult rituals, and that his ultimate goal was to bring people back from the dead.' He paused, thoughtful. 'He must have enjoyed that particular rumour, because it was one he never bothered to counter.'

Kenny literally spat out a laugh. 'Fuck,' he said, showing teeth darkened by wine. 'People are so stupid.'

Bryn's eyes narrowed almost imperceptibly.

'But *he* doesn't believe that stuff, does he?' Kenny went on. 'Like, he hasn't ended up fooling himself?'

Jamie and Sarah cast a subtle glance at one another. It seemed that, in the gloom, they leaned ever so slightly away from Kenny.

Bryn's voice was low, cold. 'My father is no actor.'

Kenny railed on. 'What does he say? He must talk to you about it?'

At this, Bryn seemed almost to flinch – his wine glass slipped from his hand, producing a sudden red bloom on the tablecloth like a silk handkerchief pulled from a magician's pocket. He swore, and Alexa dabbed quickly at the spill with napkins. Kenny only giggled stupidly at the small pandemonium. There was a hurry to right Bryn's glass and refill it, to replace the smiles that had slipped from our faces. Again, that empty, griping feeling in my gut.

Bryn nodded to himself. 'You're clearly interested in magic, Kenny. Must be why you've been hassling me so insistently for a bag of tricks.'

There was a pause that felt prickly. Jamie raised his eyebrow at Sarah, and she responded with a sly smile that I couldn't decipher. I looked from Bryn to Kenny and back again, neither understanding nor wanting to expose my ignorance by asking. Bag of tricks?

As if reading my mind, Alexa piped up. 'Didn't have you down as a budding magician, Kenny. Although you've definitely got a talent for making the party atmosphere disappear.'

Bryn cackled, grinned at her. 'That, and most of the *grand cru*,' he said.

'Yeah, he's mastered cups and balls too,' Alexa went on, returning Bryn's grin with a wink. 'As in, emptying his cup and talking balls.'

Laughter from all of us then – even Kenny, who couldn't take offence at Alexa's cheeky delivery. Finally, the room was righted again, order restored.

Still chuckling, Bryn reached into his pocket and retrieved a black bag, tied with a little drawstring. It was small, maybe only a couple of inches square – a coin trick, maybe? Fuck, was Bryn really going to share his trade secrets with this tosser? Kenny smiled, greedily, and held out his hand.

But Bryn stood, giving the bag a shake. 'Come on,' he called, disappearing through the kitchen door. At this, even Jamie and Sarah looked flummoxed. Even so, we all jumped up and hurried unquestioning after Bryn into the dark of the house.

Past the staircase with its gleaming banister, past the library with its cold fireplace. All the way to the back of the house, where the air became heavy and stale, through a door with an iron bolt and into a darkened room. As we piled inside, Bryn flicked a switch.

We were standing in what appeared to be some kind of storeroom. The bare bulb spilled light directly onto the floor, so although we could tell that the brick walls were the grubby white of a prison cell or an inner-city gym, the very corners were dark. From out of this darkness, large structures leaned like headstones: a box as big as a sarcophagus, decorated with lustreless stars; a wooden board painted with a red-and-white target, its surface pocked and punctured. Bits of furniture in faded carnival colours, the occasional swag of fringed velvet. Everything was veiled in cobwebs, as if it had long waited to be touched by something human. Shuffling into the space, we instinctively began to speak in whispers, as if someone might be listening. Compared to the rest of the house, this room felt hostile – a lair, occupied, something you're supposed to leave well alone. Without knowing why, I kept looking over my shoulder, to check that the door we'd come through was still open, the way out still clear.

The only sign of life was a path where the dust had been disturbed, leading from where we stood to a square in the middle of the floor. A trapdoor. Without speaking, Bryn followed the trail and knelt, lifting the trapdoor and revealing a set of wooden steps, descending. The movement produced a rancid breath of foul air.

We edged closer. There was something deeply sinister about those steps, floating down, about the intense darkness into which they sank. It was as if the gloom below was a presence of something rather than an absence of light, something that might stretch and flex and ease its way up towards us.

Bryn stood. With the drawstring hooked around his finger, he swung the little bag back and forth above the darkness below. With a turn of his wrist, Bryn let the bag fly. After a second, we heard it land with a soft *thunk*. 'All yours,' Bryn said.

Kenny rushed to the trapdoor and peered down. Then, with an anxious look at Bryn: 'Is that your dad's workshop?'

Bryn nodded, blithely. 'Where he does all his silly tricks.'

Kenny paused. Swallowed. 'Where's the light?'

'It's broken. Your eyes will adjust after a while.'

'Come on, man.'

'What?'

'Fuck, it's … it's creepy!'

The others cackled and mimicked Kenny's plaintive moan: *It's cree-pee*. God, seeing him there, his face creasing into concern, gave me the most exquisite champagne fizz of satisfaction.

Kenny approached the stairs into the cellar. Like a nervous skater testing the ice, he put one foot on the top step – then quickly drew it back. 'Jesus,' he said, 'did you hear that creak?'

We groaned: *Don't be dramatic, get on with it*. He tried again, settling himself firmly on the top step before moving to the next, his hands gripping the edges of the floor as he moved down inch by faltering inch. When he was up to his waist in the dark as if submerged in a pool, Bryn knocked him firmly on the head with a fist and we all laughed again. The smell from the cellar was really revolting, so earthy and putrid – I assumed the others were ignoring it out of politeness, so decided I should do the same.

Although there weren't many steps, it took Kenny a good minute to reach the bottom. We peered after him as he huffed and swore, noting the change in his footsteps as he arrived on the gravelly cellar floor. The hole he'd descended into was to us observers like a square frame, and soon Kenny moved out of it, beyond our view.

His voice drifted weakly up. 'I think I see it.'

We covered our mouths, smothering our giggles. Bryn's eyes had a bright glee. Kenny's voice came to us again, smaller this time. 'Bryn? What is ... Fuck ...'

And then, something peculiar. From the cellar came a strange scratching noise. But it wasn't the punctuated *scratch scratch scratch* you'd expect Kenny to make if he was scrabbling around in the dirt for his prize. It was a drawn-out, unbroken scratching, as if he were using two hands to keep the sound going. Weird. Was he was trying to turn the tables, to scare us for scaring him?

All the irritation I'd ever felt about Kenny seemed to blaze up, a burning, itching fury that I could hardly stand. The way he constantly took the piss out of me. The way he was always hanging around Bryn's neck, as if he held some kind of special status. He was as bad as Mona. Honestly, did any of us even *like* the guy?

Nerves aflame, I stepped forward, slammed the trapdoor and bolted it.

The thud was like the closing of a coffin. Beneath us, Kenny began to yell, and immediately came the sound of feet clattering on the wooden steps, hands slapping helplessly against the trapdoor.

Bryn looked at me, his eyes huge and mouth open. For a horrible moment I thought I'd crossed a line – but, giving me a look that said, *You read my mind*, Bryn burst into laughter. Taking his cue, the rest of us shrieked with delight, and I felt that swell of showman's pride.

Below, a cry, rising in pitch: 'Guys! Please …'

'We'll be back in a while,' Bryn called, stepping noisily away from the trapdoor as if we were leaving the room. 'Take it easy, man.'

People were doubled over, smothering their laughter. Kenny called again, but his voice sounded different somehow. In between his cries there was still that scratching. God, it must be really dark down there. After a minute or so, when the joke seemed to have landed, I returned to the trapdoor, unbolted it and tugged at the handle.

But the trapdoor wouldn't move.

More wailing from below, louder now. 'Please! Help me, please!'

'It's jammed,' I said, trying to keep the panic out of my voice. 'Kenny, are you holding on? Let go.'

How was Kenny making that scratching sound when he was banging on the door? I kept tugging and yanking, hard enough to make my back muscles scream, but I couldn't move the thing. Every second that passed seemed to stretch, endless, and gradually the laughter fell away as people realised: No, I was not kidding any more.

In the end, it was Bryn who managed to get the door open again. I expected Kenny to come up shouting and swearing, maybe even square up to me. But after scrambling out, he threw himself on the ground and lay, panting, like a shipwrecked sailor washed up on an unknown shore. We jostled around him, jovial again, loudening our voices to counter his odd quiet. But it was only when Bryn squatted beside him and patted his cheek that Kenny seemed to refocus his gaze, to stagger to his feet and force a laugh.

The light bulb above us must have swung softly, because when I glanced back down through the trapdoor the shadows seemed ever so slightly to shift. An illusion, the mind tricking itself. As we made to leave, I hung back, watching as Bryn lingered in the dark, staring down into the cellar. Strange – watching his rapt expression, I could have believed that something looked back.

Before I could say anything we were shambling out of the storeroom, shrieking with delight. Even Jamie giggled like a schoolboy. And when Bryn, beaming, took Alexa playfully by the hand, I forgot everything that had gone before.

The glow of this incident lasted the rest of the evening, which was even more enjoyable once Kenny had hurried early to bed. Then, after the rest of us said our messy goodnights, when I lay in bed and closed my charmed eyes, a thought repeated like a stuck record. I'd imagined that it would be the ultimate punishment to be down in that cellar, in the dark, alone. But I hadn't considered the possibility of being down there, *not* alone.

By the time we made it downstairs the next morning, the sun was high and bright over the chill gardens. We were jaded by the wine, but cheerful too, like an army unit that had survived a particularly treacherous mission. All cheerful except for Kenny, that is, who hadn't slept well and had a ghastly, shell-shocked look about him.

After a breakfast that was more like lunch, we strolled into the village, lingering in a quaint little bookshop and stopping at a café for coffee. Then we took a walk across some unchallenging fields. Leaving Alexa with Bryn (smiling to see him guiding her over unsteady ground or the occasional stile) and Kenny to trail alone, I walked beside Sarah and Jamie. For perhaps the first time, Sarah shared her own stories of calamitous school concerts, acting as if we had common ground despite the fact that her school orchestra toured in Barcelona while mine toured in Blackpool. Jamie didn't say much, but, whereas his previous aloofness had felt like hostility, it now seemed merely to signal disinterest.

When we returned to the house in late afternoon the daylight was already disappearing. I led everyone towards the kitchen, ready to make tea, but when I got there, something startled me, causing me to stop so suddenly that Kenny walked straight into my back.

There was someone in the room.

As I gaped, I felt a crazy certainty: *She's stepped out of the portrait.* Pale as a wraith. Tall and lean, her hair now roped loosely down her back. And those eyes. She was as commanding as I'd imagined. But in an unexpected way, like a holy woman or an empress.

However, the heavy wool coat and leather hand luggage suggested that Frances Cavendish had arrived not through sorcery but likely by taxi. I opened my mouth to say hello, but at her icy expression the words froze on my lips. Judging by the others, I wasn't the only one with no clue what the fuck was going on.

After an excruciating and confusing pause, Bryn stepped forward, beaming at Frances. 'Surprise!' he said.

Her voice was deep, silvery. It made me think of vaulted halls and bottomless sea caves. 'Yes, quite.'

Subtly, the rest of us exchanged mystified glances.

Bryn let his arms fall. Allowed himself a beat. 'Hello, Frances dear.'

'Care to explain?' she asked, her voice chill.

'But of course. Won't madam make herself comfortable first? Please.'

Bryn went to take his mother's coat, but she shrugged it off herself, revealing a fine woollen sweater, trousers that hung like silk. Then she sat, taking in the casual havoc of her dining table while Bryn introduced each of us. Frances already knew Jamie and Sarah thanks to their school connections – the two of them greeted her as if they were charm and courtesy personified – but she had to be reminded of Kenny's more businesslike family connection. Bryn acted as if everything was going to plan, whatever that was, while the rest of us stood, sheepish, a Greek chorus finding themselves in the wrong play.

'So,' Bryn said, 'I was messaging George, from the cricket club. And he said he'd seen Ivy coming to clean. So, I figured you must be staying the weekend, and … decided to surprise you.'

I blinked. What was he on about?

Frances practically snorted. 'Really.'

'Yes,' Bryn said. 'For your birthday.'

'My birthday isn't for weeks,' Frances replied.

'No, but you'll be in Geneva on the day, so we ought to celebrate now.'

Frances picked up one of the many wine bottles and inspected the label. 'And you enjoyed my birthday meal, did you?'

'Well, you're rather later than we expected, Mummy. But you're in time to cut the …' He gestured at the tart that had sat on the table since our arrival the previous night, its sliced fruits losing their shine.

'Ah,' said Frances. 'Your father's favourite.'

Something fell over Bryn's face, then, a cloud passing over the sun. But it was gone in a moment, and he chuckled to himself as he retrieved champagne from the fridge. 'You're so cynical, Mummy,' he said. 'It's not very festive.'

She set her face against his, belligerent. 'So. When would you like to do presents?'

There was a long pause. In it, Bryn removed the champagne foil and dropped it on the floor. 'Any time. In fact, why not now?' Then, turning to me: 'Just for you, Frances. A private performance of that wonderful Bach.'

He gestured towards the piano, and I realised with horror what he wanted me to do. I gawped at Frances – frowning gently now, as if genuinely intrigued – then back at Bryn.

'You want ... me ...?' I said quietly, my mouth suddenly very dry.

He gave me a big, straightforward smile.

Jamie sputtered behind me. I balled my fists, felt my fingers stiff and lumpen. How long had it been since I'd played that piece? A year? It was so short, probably only thirty seconds long. But it was so precise, each line so exposed. To fuck it up now would be mortifying.

Heat rose in my chest, my face. And yes, it was fear. But it was something else too, something like fury. A performance wasn't a casual offering. It was sacrificial: something that stripped you naked, that carved a piece from you. Yet here he was, handing me out, like corner-shop sweets from a paper bag. And for what? Some kind of joke. But what could I do, other than force a smile onto my face and trudge to my stage, a jester tumbling before a king?

I went slowly to the piano, vaguely aware of everyone taking seats at the dining table. There was maybe a ripple of pre-emptive applause. But all sounds fell away as I sat heavily on the piano stool. This isn't really happening, I told myself. It's a weird, nonsensical dream.

The thing about pieces like that: their intricate Baroque mechanism should tick over like clockwork, the notes falling neatly into place as if plucked by the revolving pins of a music box. There's no space to pause, to think. In fact, if your head gets in the way, you're fucked. So I tried to let my muscles do the remembering, allowing my fingers to travel the little notated paths they'd travelled so many times before. But, unsurprisingly, my lines were perfunctory and spiritless. Ordinary. I was glad when I came to the closing bars, when I could let the final notes ring in the silence.

My audience – not discerning – clapped politely, their confusion evident. Even on the spot, I was frustrated to deliver a performance so average. Frances shifted impatiently in her chair, searching for Bryn's eyes as if she wanted to speak with him very urgently.

Which is when I thought: If he wants a show for Frances, I can play along. 'Bryn,' I called. 'Shall we do the next piece now?'

A slight tilt of his head. The others shushed.

'You know the one,' I said. '"Is My Team Ploughing?"'

He laughed, sporting, gave me a rueful look that said: *Touché.* He had a good memory, would surely remember the words. And I knew the piano part by heart. Sure enough, unfazed by anything, Bryn stood and took his place beside me. He absolutely delighted in his guests' confusion – total, now – and, part of the joke, so did I.

When every guest had stilled, I put my fingers to the keyboard once more. Moving over the notes I seemed not to feel the keys themselves, as if my fingers belonged to someone else or as if each touch was the phantom sensation of a limb no longer there.

And then, those opening notes: that exquisite falling figure—

Extraordinary, how it came back to us. But the telepathy we'd developed was still there, a secret language sunk into my DNA. Yes, we had our misfirings, phrases where he pulled ahead of the tempo and I lagged behind. But it happened: that sorcery, when people go from playing notes to making music. That ebbing and flowing against one another, that push and pull between solo and accompaniment. The rhythm of the breath, the melodies rolling inexorably towards their resolution. Strange, that such an intensely physical act creates something so ethereal. That the sound, gone in a moment, leaves a mark that lasts a life.

Music is like pain. You forget what it was to experience it in the moment. You only know that there was no such thing as time, and your whole self was splintered into fragments, connected to everything that ever mattered and that ever would.

Even Frances – reluctantly but unmistakeably moved – clapped this time. From the others, the applause was ecstatic. When our audience had rightly enthused about Bryn's tone, his delivery, they poured their compliments on me. 'Those pianissimos,' Kenny murmured to Frances, wiggling his fingers. I smiled, thinking: Prick.

Sarah raved while Jamie looked reverently at my hands on the piano, their admiration clearly genuine. Alexa offered a quiet, sincere nod that said: *Nice one.* But the feeling their reactions gave me was nothing compared to what I felt when Bryn hugged me roughly, almost pulling me from the piano stool, forcing my face into the folds of his shirt.

Job done, he made to sit down again. But, God, I couldn't stand for this to end just yet. 'Wait,' I murmured, grabbing his elbow in a way that would have felt forward only days before. 'One last thing.' Then, turning: 'Lex, come up here. Er, Mrs Cavendish, please can we use your violin?'

Frances didn't protest, and the table understood. They started to cheer for Alexa, and the same terror that had dawned on me came over her. In fact, she might have refused had Bryn not stretched out his hands to receive her.

Tuning the violin, she glared at me as if betrayed. 'Don't worry,' I murmured, scribbling some notes on a sheet of paper. 'Just follow me.' Silence fell, and I savoured the collective bafflement, the knowledge that I, for once, was the one with the punchline.

Finally, I turned to the room. 'Okay,' I announced. 'You all know the words.'

Then I played our opening chord – preposterously dramatic, arpeggios dancing the length of the keyboard from bottom to top – and led everyone: 'Happy birthday to you …'

And then, that beautiful, bellowed tune, the perfection of untrained voices in happy unison. At the final lyric, some started to clap. But I didn't stop. I played the song through again, encouraging Alexa – smiling now – to lead us this time, to look Bryn in the eye as he improvised an imperfect but charming harmony around her melody line. The third time, even she became more daring, adding grace notes and flourishes above my stately chords, taking the tune up the octave with soaring strokes of the bow, an unmeetable challenge that made Bryn's resonant vocals turn to percussive laughter. I kept going. With every round the voices became louder and more experimental, the lyrics repeating like an invocation … Hands drummed at thighs, at the tabletop, feet pounded rhythmically at the floor, all of us whirling in a kind of willed madness until my climactic, crashing cadence brought us to a staggering, exhausted stop.

Cheers, then. They rushed to the piano, all except Frances, whose irritation had been replaced by something like resignation. Bryn thumped me on the back and then – equally thrilling – threw an arm around Alexa, kissed her firmly on the cheek.

Finally, Frances addressed Bryn wearily. 'I'd still like to speak to you, darling.'

Bryn looked unbothered. Sauntering out of the room, leaving his mother to follow, he called back: 'Help yourselves to drinks. It's a birthday party, remember.'

Kenny stared after them. Alexa smothered a smile. Jamie and Sarah looked at me plainly as if, for once, I might be the one who knew what was going on, and as soon as mother and son were gone we all burst into daft and uncontrollable laughter, the sound of it like a song I wanted never to forget.

After a while, almost dizzy from the praise, I went outside for some air. There, beneath the dark, starred blanket of sky, I was rocking on a garden swing when I heard behind me a scratch, a fizz. I turned to see Bryn, the lines of his face gilded by the glow of his lighter. Pulling on a cigarette, he took a seat beside me, his weight unbalancing the swing and lifting me upwards as if I were a child.

'The man of the moment,' he said, his voice warm against the cold air. 'I'm still in the shit with Frances – a long story, one for another time – but that was like a fucking spell. If she hadn't been so impressed, my bollocking would have been so much worse.'

I smiled, allowing our breaths to fall into a steady, satisfying rhythm. I knew not to ask any more about Frances, but dared a different question: 'So your dad didn't stop by too?'

Bryn tapped ash from his cigarette. Then, carefully: 'I thought perhaps he might. But his travels have taken him elsewhere.'

'Travels?'

'Since the TV magic got less popular, he's been away a lot. Exploring … esoteric stuff. Travelling the world, researching different belief systems.'

'And that's what the locals were gossiping about?'

He grinned. 'They think he's in league with the Devil or something. Some of the old churchgoing ladies would cross the street when they saw him. Saying Hail Marys as they went.'

I remembered the mums at the school gates, whispering behind their hands. 'Do the locals still act weird about you guys?'

His smile slipped then, and his face almost frightened me. So very sad. It was like seeing him with a shattered bone poking through his skin. 'Actually, no,' he said. 'Because my father isn't around much since he and my mother separated. It was a few years back. I've only seen him a handful of times since.'

A picture came to me of Louis Cavendish, descending into his cellar, further and further from his family, increasingly more concerned with the dead than the living. What did I feel, then? Sorrow, yes, bottomless and black. But maybe the slightest satisfaction too, that the darkness of loss was something we shared. 'Fuck. I'm sorry,' I said, daring to put a hand on his shoulder, imagining I could feel the pained throb of his heart. Then: 'It must be hard having people talk about him as if they knew him. I had the same thing with my dad.'

'How come?'

This was it. It felt like slicing open my own palm to seal a blood pact, and I wouldn't have hesitated to do it. 'So, you know my dad died? It was because he was an alcoholic.'

The look on his face was pure understanding. 'Fuck. I'm sorry too.'

'People talked about him. But not openly. All sotto voce, you know? If my mum mentioned him it would be in a whisper, like he was still there and might overhear.' I suddenly felt self-conscious. 'Sorry, that sounds weird.'

Bryn shook his head. 'Not at all. My father's alive, but when he's not around – I sometimes feel like he's here. I was practising a card trick the other day, and I swear I could hear his voice telling me how to do it better.'

That made me shiver. It seemed that, beyond the sprawling shrubbery, between the trees at the bottom of the garden, a shadow with the same stance as Bryn might be standing silently. Or maybe it was right behind us.

We looked at one another then, and I suddenly felt more exposed than I ever could at a piano stool, on a stage. But what a strange and pretty polyphony our vulnerabilities made. The moment became taut, almost painfully so: like the silence after an extraordinary performance, when the audience dare not clap and break the spell.

From behind us: the sliding of a patio door, the sound of Jamie's bellowed voice. Frances had gone out, was 'dining with a neighbour' and, fuck it, shall we just open the Pétrus?

I declared: After our dazzling performance, we musicians should be exempt from dinner duty. Incredibly, Jamie and Sarah thought this was fair enough, and they encouraged Bryn, Alexa and me to head to the roof terrace (Kenny had gone to bed early, citing a headache). We settled ourselves up there on the elegant garden furniture, blankets and booze protecting us from the freezing night.

'And then there were three,' Bryn announced. 'You know, Pythagoreans called the number three the noblest of all digits. Or something.'

'It's supposedly a magic number,' said Alexa, beside him. 'Father, Son, Holy Spirit.' She had a dreamy look, as if a song were playing in her head, and it suited her. The angles of her face were gentler, somehow, softened by the light of Bryn's company.

'Sex, drugs and rock and roll,' Bryn added.

'Three billy goats gruff.'

'Three blind mice.'

I stuck a hand in the air. 'The ghosts of Christmas past, present and yet to come.'

'It's a good job your girlfriend isn't here,' Bryn said. 'Four doesn't have the same ring.'

Fuck, I'd completely forgotten about Berenice. I hadn't even texted her since we'd left college. It was true, though: if she were here, she'd be telling us to take it easy on the booze, stop putting our feet on the furniture. In the event of any broken glasses or red wine stains, she'd be the first to grass us up to Frances. I resolved to text her later.

Bryn gave Alexa a top-up, allowing his fingers to brush against hers as he steadied her glass. She gave me a small, secret look. Something shy and hopeful, an unspoken acknowledgement of the crackle in the air. And in that moment I saw myself as a fulcrum between the two of them, the pivot chord linking different keys. Yes, there was something magic, something inevitable, about the three of us.

'Speaking of our trio,' I said, 'you two were brilliant. Riffing off one another.'

And then it was Bryn stealing a look at me, playful and wicked as if to say: *I see what you're doing, and I like it.* Everywhere, the hum of electricity – some glorious frequency, ringing. Trying to look casual, I made my way to the railing and looked down at the pool.

'Tell you something,' Bryn said, following me and laying a hand on my shoulder. 'When this terrace was built, I celebrated by jumping into the pool from here. I must have been even madder back then.'

I stared at the inky rectangle below. 'Jesus. What would you give someone to do that now?'

'Probably not three whole wishes from the lamp. But maybe one.'

The pool lights were off, and only the electric light leaking from the house illuminated the loungers that lay like gurneys in the gloom, the poolside paving that would shatter oncoming shins. There, in the middle, the black shape of the water. In the absence of light, it was impossible to see the bottom, and I wondered how cold it must be, how deep it might go.

I had a dull sense that, somewhere behind me, a door had opened and Jamie and Sarah had joined us, carrying clanking plates and cutlery. But, beneath the force of Bryn's hand, I was busy thinking how it would feel to go cutting through the air. I almost saw myself in slow motion: arms overhead, toes together, arcing gracefully to earth in a perfect mathematical curve—

Sarah's shriek startled me back into the moment. 'Whoa! What the fuck is he doing?'

I looked down at my hands. Having already kicked off my shoes, I was busily unbuckling my belt. I observed my own movements impassively, as if someone else was in control of my limbs, feeling nothing as my trousers rumpled at my feet.

'Jesus,' Alexa said to Bryn, 'he isn't ...'

Then, Jamie: 'He fucking is.'

And somehow, I was down to my underwear. It felt as unstoppable and unconscious as breathing or sleeping or falling in love. Bryn laughed, and the rational part of me felt a low shiver of relief: he was going to stop me. But he merely pointed again. 'That's the deep part,' he said. 'For Christ's sake, don't aim anywhere else.'

Grasping his arm to steady myself, I clambered onto the edge of the balcony, feeling like I was inhabiting someone else's body. Legs shaking, I focused on the frigid feel of the night air, the shush of the trees. Maybe this was what it felt like to be Bryn – to know that everyone's astonished eyes are fixed only on you.

And then I was plunging through the night, feeling the wind tearing across my skin, leaving my stomach high up on the balcony behind me—

—there was a cry that may or may not have come from me, before—

—the sudden slap of the water, something glancing my foot. But there was no time to register any pain, as I was too busy clawing myself up, sucking desperately at the air, feeling the cold clamping my ribcage like a torture device.

Unable to touch my toes to the bottom of the pool, I sank, panicked by the water closing above me. Finally managing to plant my feet, I pushed myself towards the lights of the house above, fractured through the distorting waves. Bursting through the surface again, I took a heaving, juddering gasp, splashing ungainly until I discovered the point where I could touch my toes to the floor and keep my head above water. Up on the balcony, figures jostled, whooping and shouting. I forgot the cold.

As I blinked and waved, not daring to call out in case my voice trembled, a blot appeared on my vision, hurtling closer. There wasn't time to turn my head before the waves exploded beside me, making the whole pool lurch. *Jesus.*

Bryn emerged like Poseidon, shaking out his hair and slapping at the water. 'You're fucking crazy,' he shouted, joyful.

Before I could reply, he lunged, grabbing me in a headlock. As my weight went backwards my feet came off the floor, and I felt myself dropping again like a stone beneath the water – there, an airless moment of thrashing limbs and white noise. Just as the panic began to rise, Bryn took me under the armpits and hauled me up through the surface, both of us spluttering and shouting, flailing wildly, our laughter eventually dissolving into even, exhausted breaths.

Water lapping our chests, we faced one another in the shivering dark. God, I felt so awake. Bryn's mouth fell slightly open, and I thought he might speak – but he only stared silently at me, his gleeful expression softening into something like seriousness. I became very aware of our exposed skin, waxen beneath the distant electric glow, of our breath, steaming in the chlorinated cold. The way the light rippled off him, he didn't look himself – his face, his eyes, unfamiliar.

He stepped towards me. Thinking I was in his way, I moved back – but he took another step, and another, making waves that wrapped around my trembling body like searching hands. When he was very close, close enough that he might whisper in my ear, I thought I felt the heat coming from him, like an aura, as if – even in this freezing pool – he couldn't ever be cold. Beneath the water, his hand moved so close to mine. There, alone with him in the frigid surge and swell, what I felt was abject terror.

Then, very slowly, Bryn sank below the water.

Seconds passed, and he didn't reappear. Rubbing my eyes, I scanned the surface. But I saw nothing moving in the black. 'Bryn?'

Something brushed my legs from behind, and I spun splashily around. 'Hey,' I said, my voice waterlogged and croaky. 'Stop messing about.'

Seconds slipped by. Still he didn't come up for air. Currents moved around me, and I jumped as something scratched softly at my calves. I rubbed at my arms, speckled now with gooseflesh. The water swirled around me in confusing patterns, and a shape shifted at the corner of my eye—

—no, wait, there was more than one shape, something that made me feel queasy, that made me think of that figure beyond the window or the shadows in the cellar—

And then: hands, wrapped tightly around my feet.

Then I was leaving the water, being raised onto Bryn's shoulders, while laughter and cheering fell like confetti from the terrace above us. My heart still thumped, but triumphantly now, and I waved and beamed, not minding the others pointing at my exposed body, enjoying the warmth of Bryn's hands as he gripped my shins. Once or twice, so as not to fall, I allowed myself to lay my hands on his wet curls. The realisation was exhilarating: nobody else was going to jump.

He stepped slowly through the water and deposited me on the edge of the pool, then I took his hand and helped him out. Panting, we collapsed onto the lawn.

Lowering his eyes, Bryn gave an exaggerated gasp. 'Oh shit,' he said. 'Look.'

As soon as I'd seen the line of scarlet running across my heel, it began to sting. On my damp skin, the blood spread quickly and dramatically. We stared for a moment in silence before bursting simultaneously into imbecilic laughter.

Then – I remember this vividly – he touched his fingers to my foot. Not to soothe or stem the bleeding. It was more like a gesture of curiosity, poking roadkill with a stick or prodding the flesh of a bad apple. When he took his hand away, the fingertips were red with blood. He looked as if he might smear it across his cheeks.

Holding out his fingers, he looked at me and whispered: 'An offering.'

Then he jumped up and bounded towards the house, leaving me shivering on the grass.

But then he was back, in one hand a roll of gauze, and in the other a ratty-looking blanket with trailing tassels. He threw the blanket around me and rubbed my hair, like my mum used to do after we'd been to the swimming baths, and I pushed him away and called him a dickhead. Then he took my foot in his lap as he looped the gauze around it once, twice, three times. And he leaned very close to my cheek.

'So,' he whispered. 'What's your wish?'

Still panting, I pretended to think. 'Genie. I wish for you to dunk Alexa in the pool.' Then, meaningfully, 'And I don't think she'll mind one bit.'

He laughed. Gave me a wink.

And then the others were there too, calling us insane, stupid, reckless, bloody legends. Alexa rushed over and knelt beside Bryn, her eyes racing over his body as if she couldn't believe him to be unscathed. God, she genuinely looked terrified. But her terror turned to delighted shock when Bryn lunged at her, scooped her up and sprinted to the pool, throwing the two of them into the water. I clapped when they resurfaced, Alexa still in Bryn's arms. And I almost punched the air when Bryn leaned in – a looming that made me think momentarily of old vampire films – for a long, cinematic kiss.

Stunned, Jamie and Sarah stopped their squealing, sought my eye as if to say: *What the fuck is going on here?* I gave them an insider's knowing smile.

And suddenly everyone was cheering, laughing, screaming towards the pool, all of us leaping now, the water exploding like pyrotechnics around us in our great subaqueous Bacchanalia. Limbs moved against one another in the churning waves, as if we were all part of the same spectacular sea creature; or as if we were tiny fish in the stomach of the same great whale. Tuneless sirens, we sang once more *happy birthday to you* – only now, on each round, the person named was the recipient of a hysterical dunking or splashy body slam. The giggling victim (happy birthday dear *Sarah*) would thrash uselessly away, before the rest of us closed in – lifting, howling, dropping, splashing. It was electric: the alternating touch of chill water and warm skin. The reassuring weight of bodies against mine, the weightlessness of my own frame supported in the water. The more I laughed, the more water I swallowed, and the more euphoric I felt. In this maniacal baptism, all the worries, the neuroses of which I'd seemed to be made, fell clean away and, finally, I was encompassed. I was in concert. Subsumed.

Much later, I lay clean awake in Bryn's bed. When my mind tired of replaying our glorious evening, it began to ponder what might be around me, hidden, in Bryn's room. Some cups with false bottoms? Another bag of tricks, whatever that was? I closed my eyes and told myself to be quiet. I was hardly going to go snooping around, was I?

Slipping from under the covers, I went first to his desk. A mayhem of papers covered in half-written paragraphs, columns of numbers stretching down, down. I peered at the pages in the gloom, telling myself that I wasn't snooping, merely noticing what had been left on display.

But of course, time being relative depending on

Askew on the page, a very expensive fountain pen, its cap not replaced.

this kind of time travel requiring an endless loop

Beside these papers, a calculator that looked a lot more complicated than the ones we used at school, a huge pair of headphones like a DJ might wear, scuffed. The latest iPod. Next to the desk, the wardrobe, its door open just a crack. Peering inside, I found no cursed portraits, no doors to other worlds. Only some photographs pinned to the wood, of school-uniformed youngsters looking fearless.

Then, across the room – someone staring at me.

I gasped, jumped backwards. But it was only a mirror on the far wall. Jesus Christ, I half scared myself to death. As I stood, trying to slow my breath, I remembered a Ghost Club story, one where you summoned a spirit by speaking its name into a mirror. Like the girl at Bryn's party, saying his name three times. It's not a very scary story, though. Why would I be afraid, when all I had to do to keep the spirit at bay was not speak of it at all?

Once my pulse had evened out, I slipped back across the room and lowered myself onto the bed, wincing at the squeal of springs. There, one last thing: his bedside cabinet. But that felt like crossing a line. It's one thing to gaze idly about a room, another to rummage through the closed-up places within it.

Then I thought: He'd look. If he were in my room, he'd have

been in and out of every cupboard, sampled my one expensive bottle of aftershave. He'd have put my slippers on, read my diary, and told me that privacy was a social construct or something.

I slid open the top drawer. There, a half-empty packet of Marlboro Lights, and a lime green lighter. A toiletry bag bearing the name of an expensive airline. The middle drawer, more interesting. Packs of cards, still in cellophane wrapping, apparently ordinary. Some grubby sponge balls, several black candles, two textbook-sized chalkboards, a piece of rope. Curious.

Now, just the bottom drawer. I paused, listened for the sound of approaching footsteps. Nothing. Not even any bumps or creaks as the house shifted in slumber, no whisper of leaves beyond the window. It was as if silence itself had crowded into the room to peer over my shoulder.

I pulled the handle, but it resisted. I frowned, searching for a lock that didn't exist. The drawer didn't seem jammed. It was more like – I know this sounds odd – someone was holding it closed from the inside. I tugged again, harder this time, and the drawer shot out of the cabinet completely, landing on the carpet with a thud and vomiting its contents onto the floor.

Shit, shit, shit. I hunched in the dark, poised for the voice that would call to ask: Is everything okay and, by the way, what the fuck are you doing in there?

Seconds crept by. No call came.

Releasing a long, shuddering breath, I gathered up the spilled bits and pieces. But the items made me pause. Each was strange. Unsettling, somehow.

There were sheets of paper, the colour of old newspaper, folded. I opened one of them, careful to touch only the very edges, to find that it was covered with pencil-drawn symbols, curling and archaic. Definitely not Greek or Cyrillic. I opened another sheet, and another, and found they were the same, just with a different pattern of symbols. There were also five or six photographs, as if from an old photo album – here, people sitting at a garden table, there a handful of boys wearing sports kit. But in every picture, all the heads had been cut off.

I dropped the mutilated photographs and turned to a small round tin, perhaps for boot or furniture polish, the label rubbed away. The lid came off with a sucking sound, revealing a number of teeth. Not little milk teeth, but long, yellowed molars, their hooked roots still attached. Maybe fifteen or twenty altogether, they were arranged around the perimeter of the tin so as to look like a horrible, yawning mouth, all strung together with strands of long, dark hair. Not wanting to touch it any longer, I closed the lid and put the tin away.

One other thing. A bundle of envelopes, held by an elastic band. Carefully removing the band, I saw that the envelopes all bore the same address – one in Italy – and their edges were slightly furred, as if they'd been handled many times. They were all addressed to the same person, one Louis Cavendish. What were they doing here? Had they been returned to sender? Why would Louis return Bryn's letters?

An image came to me then: me, knocking on my dad's door, and him not answering.

After putting the envelopes back as I found them, I rattled the drawer back onto its tracks. But, as I did so, I saw them sitting in the very base of the cabinet, beneath the bottom drawer itself: a little spread of black drawstring bags, just like the one Bryn had awarded Kenny. I ran my fingers over them, pressed and handled them. Some were empty. Others had a gentle weight, as if they were filled with flour or ash. Not a coin trick, then.

And then: a soft creak, beyond the door.

Moving quickly, delicately, like a man defusing a bomb, I pushed the drawer back into place. Then I threw myself back into bed. Silence, all around.

Rubbing my hair, I felt something catch in my fingers. A little piece of wool, from the blanket Bryn had wrapped me in. It made me think of a story – was it M. R. James? – where an occultist hexes a man by secretly slipping him a little piece of paper. Until he gets rid of the paper, the man is haunted, or hunted, by something. Lying there, I felt like someone had slipped me something too. But this was a blessing, not a curse. I was going through a good spell.

Perhaps that was when I finally got it, that feeling of being on the inside. Only later would I see that I had to fall – to bleed – to get there.

When I shambled downstairs the next morning, shirtless, there was nobody in the games room or the library. The kitchen was quiet. I was rummaging in the fridge when I was startled by the peal of polished vowels: 'Good morning.'

It was Frances, cold and statuesque as ever. 'Morning,' I replied, hugging my arms around my bare chest. Unsure whether it was better to offer a handshake or keep covering my nipples, I went somewhere in between: arms folded, I gave a small, cringing wave.

She waggled an espresso cup, and I nodded gratefully. Over the buzz of the coffee machine she explained that the others were up and packing the van. 'And is that a Lancashire accent?' she asked, handing me a cup of something that looked like tar. When I nodded, she added: 'Which school did you go to?'

'Oh, you won't know it,' I said, before wondering if that sounded rude. 'The only thing our school was famous for was some year elevens selling weed from the boys' toilets.'

She blinked. 'And what do your parents do?'

I knew this question was not really about what a person does – the actions they carry out daily – but who they are perceived to be. 'My mum works in a care home,' I said, wanting to explain that she'd been studying to be a solicitor before my dad cracked up, while feeling it shouldn't matter. 'And, er, my dad died. When I was ten.'

Frances didn't soften at that, like other people did. But she inclined her head as if something made sense. Then she asked an odd question: 'Have you found ways to keep him near?'

Had I? Memories, then: of me, inexplicably trying to persuade a curious classmate that I'd never had a dad in the first place, as if I were some kind of eighties' Jesus; stuffing Dad's things into the bin, including the shiny Zippo lighter that I'd always wanted. In the end, I replied feebly: 'I'm not sure.'

She sighed, looked out onto the gardens. Somewhere within the house, a clock chimed softly. 'You do realise,' she said eventually, 'that Bryn isn't here for my birthday?'

A shift in energy, here. It felt foolish to lie. 'Honestly, I don't know.'

Frances nodded, as if respecting my honesty. 'His father arrived in the UK on Friday. Bryn expected him here, but I imagine Louis' latest companion prefers a fine London hotel. Our cleaner was actually preparing the property for my own visit.'

There it was, the dove emerging from the magician's palms. If Bryn had hoped to see his father, it all made sense: his dark mood on Friday when he found the house empty. The dining table, the empty chair at its head, reserved for this ghost at our feast. All of us, destabilised by the force of a person who wasn't even there. Frances gave me a thin smile that said: *That's enough of that topic.*

'Actually,' I added, an attempt at cheer, 'my mum says that I got my love of music from my dad. I suppose that keeps him near. Did Bryn tell you we played for the fellows?'

She looked blank. It was hard to tell if she'd forgotten or never known. 'My,' she said, 'aren't you all very useful friends to have.' Then, fixing me with a cryptic look, she spoke in a voice of concern: 'One thing. Do remember that Bryn has a habit of … going over the top.'

It took me a moment. But I remembered what he'd confided that day, in the practice room that wasn't a practice room. 'Oh! You mustn't worry about him,' I said, glad to be the one reassuring her. 'He's on great form. The life and soul.'

Her eyes searched my face. Finally, as if unable to find what she was looking for, she collected her things and gave a polite smile. 'Your playing was beautiful,' she said. 'Bryn chose his guests very carefully.'

And she was gone. I stood, alone, feeling more than a little unbalanced.

Back in Bryn's room, I dressed and stuffed my things into my overnight bag. Then, confident that I was the only one upstairs, I slid the bottom drawer of the bedside cabinet open once more. There, the same objects that had looked so troubling in the night. Daylight poured onto them, illuminating fluff and curls of hair, and now everything seemed merely haphazard and confusing. Even childish.

This is where I did something odd. I took one of the pieces of paper, scratched with symbols, and slipped it into my pocket. When I jogged down the stairs for the last time, that paper seemed to throb at my leg like a walled-up heart.

Even then, I knew this little theft was ridiculous. Embarrassing. But the only way I can explain it is this: that I had a sense that those days – the greatest, that's what everyone said, that's how they felt – would not last. That I would need a token, a totem, to keep them near.

And so: the perfect end to the perfect weekend. Or it would have been, if not for the journey back. The juddering of Kenny's shitty driving, the stink of dust from the van's seats – all of it aggravated the gurgling in my stomach that had been getting worse all morning. We weren't even halfway back to Cambridge when I had to ask him to pull over so that I could puke into the grass on the embankment. When I was finally back at college and in my room, I staggered like a living waxwork between the bed and the sink, alternately vomiting, drinking water and dozing fitfully, the whiff of car air freshener still coming off my clothes.

I was ill for the rest of the evening and, weirdly, the whole of the next day. Which was an especial disaster, since this was the time I'd ambitiously earmarked to complete my two essays (the idea of begging for an extension would once have horrified me but, now, given my infirmity, it felt like the least of my problems). Tim came to see me, bringing rehydration salts and Lucozade, marvelling at the extent of my sickness and wondering if I might be better sticking to beer.

When I went to bed that second evening, I took the little paper I'd stolen from Bryn's room and tucked it under my pillow. I don't know why. But over those grim hours it only reminded me that he hadn't yet checked on me and, if anything, I got worse. During the night, in a fit of pique and fever, I tore it up and tossed it in the bin, and somehow I felt better when it was gone.

* * *

After our weekend at Bryn's, I thought more often about my dad. How, having perched me on his lap between his dancing hands, he'd pick out pop songs on the piano, how he'd sit in silence while I practised my exam pieces and clap noisily however they turned out. How he never once got annoyed when I, increasingly precocious, corrected his pronunciation of musical terms (Wagner, étude, Haydn).

How he drove me to my lessons, stopping at the shop on the way back: sweets for me, a scratch card or two for him. Also beer. Later, vodka.

Once, we were driving home – this must have been early on, when we were gauging my enthusiasm for this new hobby, when he was still gainfully employed, still married, still happy – when some classical piece came on the radio, one I didn't take the time to remember. And Dad told me: *Music is a time machine.*

This? he said. *It was playing in the hospital when I first held you. When I hear it, I can smell the washing powder on your little baby blanket.* He fell silent, smiled. I imagined them with us, in the car: my younger dad, me, in his arms. Is that why they call melodies haunting, I wondered? *I had long hair, back then*, he said, laughing. *Can you imagine?* At that time, I refused to believe that my dad had ever existed in any form other than the one he took now.

He didn't drive me so much after he'd lost his job. Not at all after he'd lost the job after that, the light from his eyes. Mum hid the car keys, not that he'd have remembered my lessons anyway. He was playing a different kind of music by then. He'd hammer tunelessly at the piano like a demon, slurring. Glasses would smash, cymbal crashes. I'd watch from the doorway, frozen – half of me wanting to throw my arms around him, the other half wanting to run as far away as possible. It's a peculiar agony, to feel so absolutely stuck.

But that's the maths, isn't it? When an object is acted on by two forces that are equal in strength but opposite in direction, those forces will cancel one another out – the result of which is that the object will stay completely still. I ended up paralysed, unable to move from the point where love and fear existed in perfect equilibrium.

Dad was only partly right about the time machine. Because it could only ever take us backwards. As an adult, I wondered endlessly about what had happened in his life to send him careening off course, but maybe I was looking for something that wasn't there. Maybe what haunted him was not some trauma from the past but the absence of a future.

When, a few days after our trip to Bryn's, I was back to full health, something odd happened. I was coming back from Bryn's room in Old Court, having presented him with a copy of Peter Warlock's biography as a thank you. And, as I jogged down S staircase, something gave me a start: a figure in a hooded coat, standing completely immobile, facing one of the ground-floor bedrooms.

It looked as if the figure was about to knock at the door, but its arms hung loose at its sides, a set of keys dangling from its fingers. There was something eerie about its absolute stillness – it was like an automaton whose seized mechanism might still spring into life. I didn't like to pass by. Then I realised who it was.

'Mona?'

She jumped, as if startled from sleep, and spun around. Her face shocked me. Not just because it was a bloodless white, but because she looked utterly terrified. 'Hey,' she said, her voice almost inaudible.

'I didn't mean to scare you. You okay?'

'Yeah. Fine.' She fumbled the key in the lock and gave me an awkward wave. I smiled vaguely and carried on out of the building and into the courtyard, supposing I must have interrupted some worries about coursework or something. Only later did I think: I never actually saw her go inside her room.

Was this the point I started to wonder? Or am I mis-remembering?

IV

'And how about work?' Tim asked above the drum roll of pub chatter.

This, I thought, is where people measure themselves against one another, trying to tip the balance of achievements in their favour: *You have a new job? Congrats, well I've just been given more team members to manage. Oh, you're a director now? That's great, well actually our company finds that titles can be anti-egalitarian. You've worked three weekends in a row? Yeah, I hear you, actually I haven't left the office in four years.*

Since Tim's day job involved saving the lives of children, there was no point trying to compete. 'Still working as a music teacher and occasional accompanist by day. Still running Voices from Before in the evenings. My CV may as well be carved on a stone tablet.'

'Got any operas coming up?'

'Tim, you've been to our concerts, you know we don't do opera.'

He frowned. 'What is it then?'

'Early twentieth-century songs. Don't you remember the stuff we did when you came to the town hall?'

'Oh yes,' he said, looking vacant. 'I remember now.' Only Tim could forget that kind of music, sprung in the brain as effortless as a seedling, the sort to be whistled beneath a fine arcadian sky. 'But you're happy?' he asked.

I paused. It might not have seemed much, to someone like Tim. But, after everything that had happened in college, I'd become grateful for the passing of one ordinary day into another, keeping my gaze lowered on the pavement of the present. Not all of us prized careers above everything else. Call me Mister Hallmark Cards, but finding love had shown me what really mattered. 'Yeah, I'm happy,' I replied, mindful of the catch in my voice, of the feelings stirred by Frances's letter. Then, tipping my almost-empty glass from side to side: 'Do you want another? Whisky or something?'

Tim literally recoiled. 'Nothing more for me unless it's a softie. Could you honestly manage a whisky now when you've got the auditions in the morning?'

'I wouldn't rule it out.'

'Christ, my head would be all over the place.'

Of course it would. At college, Tim had occasionally astonished himself by drinking a whole bottle of wine, whereas some of us in Bryn's group managed a whole bottle of port to ourselves before we left college for the night. I thought again back to that excessive time, before any of us were faced with the crashing mundanity of jobs and taxes, the screaming arrival of children, before hangovers became bad enough to make that final glass of wine Not Worth It. A time when our identity, our future, was still elastic.

I was going to suggest something gentler, wine maybe, but Tim spoke again, softer. 'Do you think it's a good idea? You, doing this?'

I laughed, grimly, rubbed my eyes. Said nothing.

'It's just,' he went on, 'I know that, with Bryn ... it was hard for you.'

Voices rose and fell around us in queasy crescendos. I tapped arrhythmically at the table. In a way it made me feel good, having Tim acknowledge the closeness between me and Bryn. But while he knew that things had gone wrong, he didn't know why. So I couldn't explain to him that it didn't matter whether this was a good idea or not (Christ, whether it was dangerous or not), because there was something that had haunted me for a long time and now I needed to face it – him – for myself.

He changed the subject. 'Okay, let's talk about happier things. Romance, maybe?'

I laughed, awkwardly. Even with Tim, who knew us both so well, I felt protective over my love story. Impossible not to be when its joys have always been countered by pain. I thought again of those hairbands, coiled into buds on the bedside table, the dreamy happiness they brought me. It made me want to get in the car and drive without stopping until I was home. 'You know,' I said, swallowing the last of my pint and nodding at the clock on the wall. 'I hadn't realised it was so late. We ought to call it a night.' As surprised as I was at the tricks played by time, Tim agreed.

Before we left, I needed to nip to the gents. I made my way to the end of the bar and down some narrow spiral steps, past posters announcing karaoke night and a new plant-based burger. At the bottom, on the right, was a door to the kitchen, from which came clanging and clanking and the whiff of deep-fat fryers. I turned left, through a fire door, beneath an arrow announcing the TOILETS.

The door swung shut behind me with a sucking sound, and I found myself staring down a long corridor. I looked with recognition at the curios adorning the walls, still here after all this time: the horse brasses and the silver pitcher, the tarnished trays and antique pistols. I also remembered the peculiar quiet. Strange, in these old buildings, how with a few steps you can feel so far away from the warmth and noise of the bar.

Inside, the toilets were just the same. Still cold, still cramped. Still stinking. In fact, the sulphurous smell coming from one of the cubicles suggested that a prolific visitor had recently left. Only my distaste was new, revealing that I was not so undiscerning as I had once been. Although the place was empty, I made for the urinal furthest from the door, and as I stood I fixed my gaze on the piss-chapped urinal cake below, choosing not to acknowledge the wall mirror, not wanting to show my changed face in its old glass.

There was a soft sound, like a scraping or a rustling. Mice? Jesus, the last thing I needed was a rodent running up my trouser leg while I was mid-flow. But even as I scanned the floor around my feet, I told myself: *That wouldn't happen, mice are nervous.* I was just tense, that was all. To calm myself, I tried to be grateful for Tim's inexplicable loyalty over the years. Would he have been this kind of friend to me if I'd told him the whole story? I forced myself to slow my breathing, each inhale and exhale loud and intrusive in the dank hush.

Without warning, a huge bang made me cry out. What the fuck? Fumbling with my fly, I looked over my shoulder. The door to one of the cubicles had clattered shut and was now bouncing, gently, to a stop. Still, I was the only one in the room. Scanning the space for an explanation, I noticed a little skylight at the ceiling, feet moving purposefully beyond it – the frosted glass was nudged open, a breeze creeping through a frame edged with grime and pigeon feathers. Fuck.

Breathe. At the sink I pumped at the empty soap dispenser, washed my hands with cold water. Then, drying my hands on my trousers, I felt something in my pocket. Something small and round. I slipped my hand inside to retrieve it.

A little rock.

The one from the car. The same soft grey, the colour of mist, the same smoothness beneath my fingertips. How the fuck had it got there? I pictured myself at the petrol station, dumping it in the bin, slamming the car door and speeding away. Yet here it was, returned to me.

I dropped the rock onto the ground as if it burned, watched it skitter on the damp floor. Feeling my knees turn to water, I staggered out of the gents and back into the corridor. The scratching continued, long and unbroken and much louder now, and the noise was joined by the static of blood in my ears, the dull thump of my heart. Everything felt fundamentally wrong, as if I were rereading a favourite book and finding the chapters out of order, the characters changed. There, as I looked up and down the corridor (so strange, on this busy night, that nobody else had followed me down here), I saw something that made my stomach pitch and roll. There on the wall, gleaming most brightly of all among the ugly antique brasses, a pair of scales, their arms reaching to the sides like the wings of a horrible angel.

There in the corridor, where there was no breeze, they began to tip.

I ran then, crashing through the fire door, back up the stairs, almost shouldering a waiter carrying a tray of ketchup-smeared plates. As I burst into the bar area, the thought rattled like a pinball in an arcade machine: *See. You wondered for a long time, but you finally have your answer, and the answer is that he's still here. He's still here, and he's been waiting for you.*

Why was it, my mind babbled, that he hadn't come for me in Manchester, in my poky flat? Or in the drab little church hall rehearsal space of Voices from Before? Perhaps my intuition was right, that he'd been making me wait – like Shostakovich, pacing, always expecting the knock at the door.

When I arrived shakily back at our table, Tim looked concerned. 'You okay mate?' he asked. 'You're white as a sheet.'

'Sorry,' I said, forcing a laugh. 'Just tripped on the stairs there. Made myself jump.'

Jump, ha. The word tasted sharp, electric.

Outside, Tim and I agreed that we'd meet tomorrow in the college bar ahead of the Cavendish dinner. Then he was strolling away, waving and beaming. Once he was gone, the night felt brittle and empty, a jar with a weakness in the glass.

As much as I hated to leave the rowdy solidity of the pub, it didn't feel right to loiter there, in our old stomping ground, alone. So I had no choice but to head back to the B&B. Although I could have walked, I called a cab, and while I waited for it to arrive I went back inside the pub and polished off a large single malt. The whole time, I thought back to something Bryn had told me: apparently, Newton merely saw the apple fall to earth. It never bounced off that curled hair, which, at Newton's death, was found to be suffused with the mercury from his alchemical pursuits. A myth. What would Tim think if I told him: That history of ours? It's never what you thought it was.

I thumped my empty glass on the bar, despairing. Of course Bryn was still here, and of course he was still playing with me. He wasn't going to leave me alone just because he was dead. Not when it was all my fault.

~

After our triumphant weekend away, college life took on a new gleam. I spent even more time with Bryn's wider group. And I had wild stories with which to entertain them – real, verifiable ones.

This company I kept made me feel different. More solid, some-how. I was coming to realise that study was only one part of the university experience.

It was an afternoon in March and I was in the post room, trying to craft an email to my supervisor that would satisfactorily explain the lateness of yet more of my coursework. So, I was not in the mood to speak to Mona, who, spotting me through the window, came creeping in. I gave her the merest nod, hoping she'd busy herself at the pigeonholes, but instead of taking the hint she took a seat beside me. The whole time I focused on the computer screen I felt her eyes searching for mine, a sensation that made me itch.

Unable to stand the tension, I eventually asked: 'You okay there, Mona?'

In my peripheral vision, she picked at the skin around her nails. 'I heard about your trip to Bryn's house.'

Ah. She was curious. And no doubt blisteringly jealous. 'Yeah. We had a blast.'

'People are saying you jumped off his roof.'

I nodded sagely, didn't clarify that it was actually the roof *terrace*. 'You know Bryn. Shit gets pretty crazy.'

'It sounds really very risky.'

'Well, if you're here to check that I made it …' I gestured at myself – all in one piece – and gave her a curt smile.

But as I did so, Mona's face shocked me. It had turned very pale, like when I'd found her outside her room. And very serious. Not her usual we're-here-to-learn seriousness. Something else. Very quietly, she asked: 'Did you really jump?'

'Of course I did,' I replied, huffily, 'there are plenty of people who saw it—'

'No, no,' she said, shaking her head. 'I mean … Did you *choose* to jump?'

I almost laughed. 'How else could it have happened?'

'It just doesn't sound at all like the kind of thing you'd do.'

That annoyed me. 'Then maybe you don't know me very well, Mona.'

At this, she looked stung. The truth hurts, I thought. Still, she went on. 'There'd be no shame in saying something. If he did something to you that – that wasn't right.'

She sat there with her home-cut fringe, her charity shop outfit. God, she would have bombed at the weekend away. She would have been a walking blunder, killing the chat, refusing the wine and going to bed early. True, I may not have had the most fashionable hair and clothes (is that why she spoke to me this way? Because we'd grown up in similar towns, been similarly tormented at similar schools?) but we were not the same. No doubt she'd come to the insulting conclusion that, since Bryn couldn't enjoy her company, he couldn't possibly enjoy mine.

'Look,' I said, 'I appreciate your concern – or whatever it is – but I think you've misread the situation. And I have things to do …'

At that, she lowered her head: *I see.* Then she stood, made for the door. At the last moment she turned.

Before she could speak, I called over my shoulder. 'Thanks though, Mona. You're a pal.'

The door fell closed. God, she honestly thought I meant it.

Bryn and Alexa eased very naturally into their role as college's Power Couple. They made sense: the two of them came from the same kind of family, the same kind of school. With their tall, dark leanness, they even looked alike. I, knowing them better than most, was delighted for them. I knew that Alexa was as mad as Bryn, as ready to sprint across courtyards pursued by porters, or to clamber over college walls in the dead of night. I knew that she, like him, hid her vulnerabilities beneath a superficial stand-offishness.

But I was delighted for another reason. Long before she'd become Bryn's girlfriend, Alexa had been my friend. I had the sense that her connection to Bryn strengthened my own bond to him, even when I wasn't around, a charm working quietly and constantly away. So, as I watched the two of them riding this wave of happiness – which I'd undoubtedly helped to generate – I felt it carry me along too.

In the weeks after our trip, we met more frequently as a three. For instance, when I walked Alexa back to the college bar after rehearsals, Bryn would now be there, waiting, and I'd eagerly offer to get a round in. At last, he was no longer a person disappearing out of every room I entered. He was there, ready to receive me.

At one time, I'd hoped to create a happy foursome: me, Bryn, Alexa, Berenice. But this seemed less and less necessary. The dynamics of the trio worked so well. And it was good for me and Berenice to have a bit of space now and again, especially since the topic of Bryn still made us irritable with one another. (In our latest argument, I'd declared it weird that she'd never mentioned Bryn's father being absent, she'd said that her cousin's life story wasn't hers to tell. This led to a painfully semantic argument about what constituted lying by omission.)

The one time the four of us fatefully attempted a double date was not long before the end of term. Bryn had messaged Berenice, saying they should meet for a stroll, and I'd suggested that we plus ones come along too. Which is how the four of us came to be wandering the

Botanic Gardens that mild, March afternoon, among the daffodils beginning to erupt from the soil, the budding cherry tree that would soon explode with its pink promises of spring. Only Berenice had a frosty look about her. She kept looking from Bryn to Alexa, from Alexa to me, as if the three of us were a thorny exam question she couldn't quite grasp.

We passed through a woody area, where shrubs reached twiggy arms to the sky and grasses nodded lacily like shrouded ghosts. Mimicking Bryn's hold on Alexa, I linked arms with Berenice, but it felt weird and we released one another almost immediately.

'Shame you couldn't come with us to Hillview,' Bryn said to his cousin.

Berenice gave him an ironic smile. 'It sounds like you managed fine.'

'Your other half certainly did. Made quite the impression on Frances.'

She said nothing. As we walked, Bryn unhooked himself from Alexa, edged a little closer to his cousin. 'Speaking of Frances. When you see her, how about suggesting that I head to Italy for the summer?'

Wait. Did Bryn want to visit his dad? And might Berenice be able to help? Glowing at the idea that she might win us some Brownie points, I unconsciously reached for her hand.

But she only shook her head, officious as a park ranger banning visitors from ball games. 'Bryn, we've talked about this. I stay out of your stuff.'

I pulled away from her, wondering whether Bryn would argue or turn sullen, but he only winked at his cousin as if to say: *It was worth a try.*

After that, the only sound was the rippling of the grass, the crunching of our feet on firm gravel. It wasn't an easy, Sunday kind of silence. It was tight and awkward. Part of it was my annoyance at Berenice, but I didn't want it to spoil the afternoon.

'Tell you what,' I said, artificially cheery, 'the other night, this really odd thing happened. I found Mona standing outside her room. But she was like a statue, just staring at the door, for ages and ages. Like, I dunno, she was scared to go inside.'

Alexa raised an eyebrow. 'Scared to go in her *room*?'

'Deadly pale. Keys in her hand.'

Bryn nodded, as if unsurprised. 'The room's haunted. I can feel the energies from my place upstairs.'

Alexa giggled, gave him a playful shove. 'Seriously, though. What's up with her?'

I made a peevish face. 'She's so weird, I swear—'

Berenice stopped walking. We paused too, startled by her stern expression. 'You know, most of us in this place are pretty weird,' she said, openly looking down her nose at me. 'And you weren't always so mean about Mona. When was the last time you had a proper conversation with her?'

'I *don't* speak to her,' I replied, a little petulantly, '*because* she's weird.' It was supposed to be a bit of entertaining gossip, not the beginning of another argument. Then, pointing at Bryn: 'Have you seen the way she hangs around him? It's creepy. She's completely infatuated.'

Berenice addressed Bryn. 'Has she ever said she's infatuated with you?'

I answered on his behalf. 'She doesn't have to, it's obvious.'

She kept her eyes on him. 'It's not obvious to me. And if her behaviour is so offensive, why do you allow her to follow you around like a dog?'

'Bee,' Bryn said, laughing now, 'I don't tell Mona what to do.'

She looked at the three of us, then, her expression cold. 'You encourage her. Then you make fun of her. And you think she's the weird one.'

I tutted, recklessly, drawing Berenice's attention. She gave me a look of such disillusionment that I recoiled. Then, in a tone of dripping scorn: 'How does he do it? Is it virgins' tears, offered on a full moon? Pentagrams drawn in his admirers' lipstick?'

I gaped. 'What are you on about?'

Alexa jumped in too, suddenly icy. 'Hey, wait a second—'

'Even more pathetic,' Berenice went on, her eyes on me, 'maybe you do it all by yourself.' Finally, to all three of us, as if delivering a verdict: 'Enjoy yourselves.'

In the split second before she made to leave, even I didn't know how I'd respond. But, from the look she cast me, she knew I'd stand, dumb, like a child admonished in front of the class. She knew Alexa would pause, half-heartedly, thinking to follow her, but that Bryn would catch her hand, would tell her that Berenice was like this sometimes, that it was best for us to leave her alone.

To me, Alexa whispered: 'Shouldn't you …?' But I shook my head. Best to leave her, I agreed. At least I had the decency to cringe when Bryn burst into loud, guilty laughter when Berenice was still well within earshot. In the end, though, Alexa and I laughed too. Then, exhausted by the theatrics, we threw ourselves onto a nearby bench.

'So. The Three Amigos ride again,' I said.

'More like the Three Stooges,' Alexa replied.

Bryn paused, drew a wonky triangle in the gravel with his toe. 'In engineering, the triangle is the most stable of all shapes,' he said. Then, arching an eyebrow at me: 'Must be how we managed not to collapse under that death stare from your girlfriend.'

I sighed as if to say, *Such a drama queen*, all the while thinking that the phrase couldn't have been less representative of who Berenice was. 'Your cousin!' I added, the disloyalty stinging as the spring breeze. Then, in a moment of improvisation, Bryn and I rounded on Alexa, declaring simultaneously: 'Your friend!'

Still feeling the force of Berenice's accusations, I asked: 'That stuff about Mona. Nobody's really being cruel, are they?'

'I actually think we're pretty fucking nice,' Alexa said. 'Most people would have just come out with it: Mona, you're boring. Go away.'

'I think Jamie did say that once, actually. But, seriously, would it be better to be honest? Like, to tell her to go away, but in a nice way?'

Alexa snorted. 'Go away *please?*'

I prodded Bryn. 'What do you think?'

He looked up at the trees, dark against a sky that was now the dull hue of bruised fruit. His eyes moved purposefully across it as if he were observing scenes that nobody else could see.

'I think,' he said, 'Mona has a philosophy: that there's only one thing worse than having your favourite people take the piss out of you. And that's having them not pay attention to you at all.'

I pulled a face. 'Mona? She's too smart for that.'

He sat up, slowly. His eyes fixed mine as powerfully as if he'd grabbed my face with his long, white fingers. 'You really can't understand?'

No string of words, no piece of music even, could have expressed as much as the silence we shared then. Because, in it, I saw Bryn's father, descending into a shadowy cellar, closing his door on the family who wanted him. My own father, staring into the blackness of a bottle. People we love, always just out of reach. And I needed no words to know that this was what Bryn was thinking too. It was almost spiritual, this soundless connection across worlds. Or was that spiritualist? It didn't matter. Saying nothing, I smiled soberly at him: *I understand.*

We didn't stay in the gardens much longer. The light was fading, and Alexa was getting cold. Back at college, I almost went to Berenice's room to talk it out, but I told myself that we needed time to cool down. In truth? I knew she'd tell me something uncomfortable, and I didn't want to hear it.

When we went home for Easter, the only thing that made me feel better about leaving my friends was that Berenice and I would get some space. When I stood at the train station waving her off, I made the gesture that meant *I'll call you*, and she looked back as if to say: *No rush.*

I don't remember the holidays. But I absolutely recall arriving back in Cambridge for Easter term, feeling that the city was more beautiful than I'd ever known it. The colleges, resplendent in the spring sunshine, the cool April sky generously donning the perfect hue to complement them. Yes, they were the same streets, the same corridors as before, but now they thrummed with life as if the air itself carried a kind of charge. Where my first Cambridge days had felt like a rehearsal, these had the electricity of a live performance, one in which I was not merely an extra but a main character. Perhaps for the first time, I was solid, substantial. I felt my feet firm on the university's esteemed ground.

Bryn, Alexa and I spent hours in the common room sprawled on the sofas together, watching daytime quiz shows and music videos. We visited Clowns café for huge bowls of cheesy penne pasta (Alexa's choice) and stopped at The Mill for pints of Old Rosie by the river (Bryn's favourite). Every day I'd wait for my friends to go up to the dining hall or into the bar, and these most routine things were so full of colour and music that my own body felt more vivid, more real. When we joked together, I laughed so hard that it hurt, my muscles moving in ways they never had before, as if I were breathing fully for the first time. At night, I replayed our conversations, reliving them in real life until they slipped into my dreams.

Yes, other people were there in those bright, mellow days, when spring yawned and stretched lazily across the city. But it seemed the three of us were the beating heart of that group. Now and again one of us would joke about it – the Three Musketeers – and my heart would lift like a flower smiling at the sun.

This was it, I told myself. This was what it felt like for university to 'open doors'. Not simply because of my studies (which, frankly, I'd been a little slack on the previous term) but because of the people I was with, who helped me to see the world differently than before.

It was an evening around this time when I found Mona standing in the staircase again.

I'd been up to Bryn's, to see if he wanted to go to the bar, but he wasn't in. So I was coming down the stairs alone, wondering at the unexpected rain lashing the leaded windows of Old Court, when I found Mona facing her door. Exactly like before, only now she was incredibly drunk. That in itself was odd. In our whole time at Cambridge I'd never seen Mona drink more than a glass of white at formal hall, never mind get completely shitfaced. Now, she tilted back and forth before the door, weight rolling from heels to toes and back again, making a soft whining noise that made me shiver.

I spoke softly, not wanting to alarm her. 'Mona?'

She looked listlessly around, her eyes watery and unfocused. Snot ran from her nose, and thick bands of saliva joined one chapped lip to the other. She whined again, a dreadful animal sound. I couldn't stand it. 'Are you okay?' I asked. 'I think you've had too much to drink.'

Her expression was filled with such despair that I almost felt sorry for her. She shook her head, and tears tipped onto her cheeks. Almost inaudible, she said: 'Make it stop.'

'What?'

'Please.'

'It's fine, you just need to sleep it off,' I said, touching her on the shoulder. 'Come on, let's get you inside.'

Her eyes locked onto me then, and she almost shouted: 'No. No, no, no.'

The word echoed around the staircase that stretched up and down, startling in the silence. 'Why not? Mona, what's the matter?' Beneath my hand, I felt her trembling. I realised with a chill that, yes, she really was afraid of her room. 'Give me your keys,' I said, reaching to take them. She jerked away from me then, but the keys slipped from her fingertips and onto the floor between our feet, and before she could react I snatched them up. Both frustrated and unsettled now, I found the right one and slotted it into the lock. Mona began to tug at her hair as I turned the door handle. The door swung open, as if eager for us to step inside.

I'd seen Mona's room, ages ago, so I knew roughly what to expect: mumsy duvet cover, unfathomably tidy desk, wall calendar showing po-faced cats of the kind her immune system couldn't handle. But, when I flicked on the light, there was something else. I wondered if there was something wrong with the bulb, whether it was giving a strange cast to the old corners. Maybe the walls, not quite perpendicular, were playing some Hitchcockian tricks of perspective. I'm not sure. All I know is that, standing on the threshold of that room, I had the stomach-dropping feeling of balancing on a cliff edge.

Trying not to show my unease, I beckoned to Mona. 'Come on. You need to go to bed.'

From her spot on the threshold, she shook her head. Then, slurring heavily: 'I know it's him.'

I frowned. 'What? Who?'

'Don't pretend you don't know.'

'I really have no idea what you're on about.'

'You know what he is, really. You do.'

Confused, I moved towards her, but she staggered back.

Then she whispered: 'You just think it won't happen to you.'

With that, she bolted.

I stood, stunned, listening to her uneven footsteps as she shambled down the stairs. Once she'd disappeared into Old Court and away, silence fell. It wasn't just heavy. It was padded, stifling. I looked around, unsure what to do.

I couldn't work out what it was that felt so abnormal. Everything was so banal: the worn armchair, the cheap coffee table, all commonplace if slightly garish in the harsh artificial light. It was a typical student room. But – there's no other way to describe it – there was a barbed, jittery feeling of danger. It was as if anything I touched might be electrified. I began to pace tentatively around the space, flinching at the charged stillness. An odour came from somewhere, and I stretched and dipped as I went, trying to find the source (was it the kind of dead fish smell you sometimes get with electrical problems? No, it was sharper, more like ammonia. It took me back to my first visit to Bryn's room, where the party odours were undercut with something feral). All the while, that horrible quiet. But not the kind of quiet you get when there's nobody around. More the kind of quiet you get in a game of hide and seek, when you lie under a bed wondering whether or not you've been discovered. Distinctly uncomfortable, I made for the door.

It took me a moment to see it. There, fixed to the glossed wood, was a large, silver bolt. Much shinier than the original lock and, judging by its amateurish positioning, fitted by Mona herself. This was disconcerting. Why would the sensible, rule-abiding Mona screw an extra lock into the door, knowing that the accommodation officer – who wouldn't even allow residents to pin posters on the walls – would flip their lid?

I looked back at the room again. Eyes attuned now to the strangeness, I saw other things. There, on the old, rickety window frame, a piece of string wrapped tightly around and around, as if the lock was not to be trusted. And, most disquieting of all: long smears on the glass, which, when I tried to rub them away, turned out to be on the outside. As though something had been pawing at the window, even though it was one floor up. I thought suddenly of Sajid's creature, crouching, and the curse that supposedly put it there. Not wanting to be in Mona's room a moment longer, I hurried out, my heart beating a faster tempo.

I eventually found Mona in the otherwise deserted library, curled into an exhausted sleep. Quietly, I placed her room keys beside her. Perhaps I imagined it, but she seemed to shift away from them.

I didn't tell Berenice about this incident with Mona, because by that time we'd broken up. It was very mundane. Having thought about it over the last few weeks, she suggested that we weren't a good fit, and I agreed wholeheartedly. She also said we could be friends, and I agreed to this too without meaning it.

The break-up didn't bother me in the slightest since I had Bryn and Alexa, my closest friends, now. And, in truth, it was this fact that precipitated my break-up. Berenice always complained about me spending time with Bryn, made comments about me preferring his parties to the chocolate-boxy Cambridge shit she wanted to do. Comments all, I felt sure, based in jealousy. Berenice hated that I felt more alive with her starry cousin than I ever did with her. And she hated the way people weighed her against him, since she was always found lacking. That bollocking she'd given us about Mona? She just wanted to make Bryn look bad, all while setting herself up as some moral authority. Berenice, patron saint of social rejects. Christ, she was so good, and I couldn't stand it.

It wasn't difficult to avoid Berenice, since Bryn and Alexa hardly went out of their way to spend time with her now. But if I did see her around college, I'd casually change direction. If I went to work in the library and found her there, I'd stroll by, eyes fixed on the bookshelves, before picking up a tome I didn't need and heading swiftly back out to the bar. I'm sure she would have been able to rewind the clock, to take us back to being college pals who could enjoy a drink and a chat together. I, on the other hand, preferred to act as though our relationship had never happened.

I thought about what Bryn had said about the number three, how it has come to represent balance and beauty. Interesting, though, that you can read it differently in music. If you sit at a piano and play an interval of three whole tones, the resulting sound is strange and dissonant. Together, the notes are uneasy, unsteady; they have a kind of pull, like they want to move somewhere else. The interval you're playing is called a tritone, and it has an exquisite kind of tension, one that the ear demands to be resolved. Composers gave it a nickname: *diabolus in musica*. The Devil in music.

One thing about this peculiar musical phenomenon is that it can lead you in very different directions. With its notes shifting stepwise, a tritone can relax, resolve into a satisfying harmony. Or, by different shifting steps, that same tritone can resolve into a completely different harmony, very far from the first. So this musical 'three' is a precarious place, a point from which a player might make unexpected turns.

But you don't necessarily hear those turns coming when the baton is beating. It's only in the analysis that we see the point where the key shifted from one harmonic territory to another, the moment we pivoted from major to minor.

A couple of weeks later, our college had a bop. Bops were twice-termly events in which participants, fancy-dressed as superheroes or pirates or whatever the theme demanded, would cram themselves into our tiny, antiquated bar, while undergrad DJs (posturing as if they were closing the party season in Ibiza) mixed tracks as well as a hand whisk might mix cement. Meanwhile, everyone bounced around like imbeciles, diligently performing the mandated dance moves to popular songs.

The theme of this bop was Good versus Evil, and I'd spent the afternoon making some angel wings out of cardboard and cotton wool balls. (Bryn had popped in at one point, ostensibly to use some of the bits I'd picked up at the craft shop for his Macbeth costume, and had ended up lying on my sofa with the student newspaper while I cut him a crown from one of my cardboard folders.) As the clock ticked towards seven, I donned my celestial costume and headed out.

The DJs were still setting up when I arrived. So I made my way into the common room to see who might be around. Some second years – Santa, fairy, Darth Vader – lolled around the pool table, idly nudging balls around the baize. Beyond them, a handful of faces turned towards the television, stupefied by the opening scenes of some action blockbuster, while along the back wall arcade machines buzzed and pinged and guzzled coins. I strolled aimlessly around until, somewhere around Big Money Trivia, a snippet of conversation caught my attention:

'Poor Kenny.'

'Yeah. It's bad.'

It was a NatSci girl whose name I didn't know, talking to Sajid, who I hadn't seen in ages. I paused, noting that neither wore costumes. From the TV came the sounds of an explosion, allowing me to hear only snatches of their exchange.

'He got really paranoid,' said the NatSci. 'It was starting to freak me out.'

'He kept talking about creatures, things touching him,' Sajid replied, slapping a flashing button. The machine produced a sad electronic trombone: *wah-wah-waaaaah.*

The NatSci dug around her pockets for change. 'Do you think he'll tell his parents what's going on?'

What *was* going on? While I'd seen Kenny around college, he hadn't really hung around with us since our trip to Bryn's. Also: creatures?

Halloween formal was ancient history, and I hadn't been cowed by Sajid since his star had fallen from Bryn's great sky. Seeing no reason why I shouldn't ask, I strolled up and positioned myself in Sajid's eyeline. 'Couldn't help overhearing,' I said, arranging my face in an expression of concern, 'but is Kenny okay?'

Sajid kept his eyes on the arcade machine. 'Sure, if by okay you mean totally fucking crazy.'

'What?'

Sajid and the NatSci conferred on the respective sizes of the world's mountain ranges. I stood, relieved and resentful that they at no point asked for my input. Eventually Sajid thumped a button and the machine emitted a loud jangling noise and several pound coins. Perhaps he hadn't heard me. Or perhaps he was jealous that I was still part of Bryn's group and he wasn't.

I don't know why it mattered. Maybe it was thinking about that cellar, my hand on the trapdoor. 'About Kenny,' I said, louder. 'Should I go and see him, maybe—'

Sajid finally looked at me. 'You can try, but you'll have to go to London,' he said, linking arms with the girl officiously. 'His parents collected him today.'

As they moved away, Sajid said one last thing, muffled by cinematic sounds of disaster. I can't be sure, but it sounded like: 'He didn't have the sense to get away.'

And then they were gone. Behind me, the quiz machine beeped. I sneaked a look at its silver bowl, just to see if Sajid had missed any coins, but there was nothing there.

The bar was finally beginning to fill up, partly thanks to the thumping bass of some 'ironically' chosen Westlife track, now blasting through an elderly sound system. I got myself a pint, then began to circle the place looking for my friends, nodding amiably as I went at nuns, Batman villains, Ghostbusters with cereal-box proton packs.

And then, a smiling face. 'Hey mate,' said Tim. He wore a shirt and jeans, the same as every day.

'Oh. Hey,' I replied. 'No costume?'

He shook his head. 'Just grabbing a coffee then getting out of here. I thought you said bops were for knobbers?' He inclined his head at a rugby blue who was dressed as a suicide bomber, armed with a belt of toilet roll cardboard tubes.

'Yeah, I know. I'm just … Trying to lighten up a little.'

'I thought you'd be at rehearsal tonight.'

I shrugged, adjusted my wings. 'I'm only missing this one.'

He looked suspicious. Over his shoulder, the door to the bar opened. In came Jamie, wearing a lab coat and a plastic Hannibal Lecter mouth guard, and Sarah, dressed in witch's garb with her skin painted entirely green.

And then, behind them, Bryn in his crown, Alexa as his sleepwalking queen with her hands stained with fake blood. Their faces, aglow in the lucent disco lights. God, individually they looked great, but, together, they looked incredible. I desperately wanted to wave, just not while I was standing with Tim.

'It's good to see you,' he said. 'Feels like it's been ages.'

I felt a teeny twang of guilt. Tim had been messaging me lately and I'd brushed him off every time. 'I know,' I said. Then, feeling like I had to ask: 'How's things?'

'Fine. Work has ramped up. I've been up late in the library all bloody week. You?'

'Got a bollocking from my tutor because I forgot to turn up to a supervision. Just lost track of the days.'

'That's not like you. Everything okay?'

'Yeah. It's only first year. Nothing important happens in first year.'

He frowned. 'That's not quite true, though, is it?' Then, his hectoring tone at odds with the joyful music: 'I don't mean to sound like a twat, but don't let your work slide. You're too talented. This funny little Cambridge chapter will be over before we know it, and we don't get a second go.'

God, I hated this tendency Tim had, to take everything so fucking seriously. I nodded vaguely, watching from the corner of my eye as Bryn and the others took their seats in the usual space, spreading territorially across the banquettes so as not to be accosted by those that Jamie referred to as 'shitmunchers'. The longer Tim talked, the more resentful I felt, the more panicky about claiming my own spot. I saw Sarah collecting wine from the bar, plus glasses (I'd have to go and get my own), saw them toasting one another, grinning—

'Hello?'

I started. Shook myself. Tim was staring at me as if I were a set of symptoms he was struggling to diagnose. 'Sorry, mate,' I said. 'Got stuff on my mind.'

He nodded. Then, giving me a look somewhere between recognition and resignation, he walked away. As I hurried towards my friends and claimed my seat, all I felt was relief.

The bar boomed with chart tracks, an inelegant mix of garage, pop and indie rock. As we shouted at one another over the thundering music, Bryn wondered aloud whether we should climb up onto the college roof. I was glad when Jamie pointed out that one of the porters was still patrolling outside, and perhaps our Scottish king was being a little impulsive.

Alexa looked indulgently at Bryn. 'Typical Gemini.'

'What else is typical Gemini?' Bryn asked, smiling. 'Dangerously sexy?'

'Indecisive.'

'Did you say incisive?'

She shook her head. 'Classic air sign.'

'You mean a breath of fresh air.'

'A fucking airhead.'

Bryn laughed heartily, kissed her hard on the neck. I looked at them both as if to say: *Sorry, what?*

'You don't know this?' Bryn said. 'She's pure woo-woo. Weirder than me.'

Alexa looked at me almost apologetically. 'At high school I was all henna tattoos and dream catchers. I used to do astrology for my friends whenever they crossed my palm with Marlboro Lights.'

'You don't believe in it, though?' I asked.

'No more than I believe in Christianity or Judaism or Sikhism or anything else. And, I suppose, no less.'

'How do you mean?'

'Well. What star sign are you?'

'Libra.'

'Of course you are. Imaginative. Bit of a daydreamer.'

'What?'

'You don't like being alone, you prefer to be part of a pair. And you can be insecure, a bit self-pitying if you're not careful.'

I pouted, not wanting to admit that, yes, that did sound a bit like me. Apart from the imaginative bit.

'But the thing is,' she continued, 'we're all a bit of everything. Everyone is curious about something. Everyone is stubborn about something. You can read a summary of pretty much any star sign and find enough of yourself in there to make it fit. Same with religious texts. You find what you need to find.'

I pondered this. 'So people pick the bits they want to believe. Which means it's all bollocks.'

Bryn took over. 'Yes and no. Take Tarot. It gives you this big, generalised life advice. Then you do the legwork of interpreting it, while giving Tarot the credit for whatever answers you come up with. Some people need their ideas to be legitimised by something bigger than themselves.'

Alexa nodded, *Exactly*, as if this were a topic they'd debated before, one on which they'd agreed a party line. I accepted their argument, still wondering how Alexa had never told me about her past as an incense-burning crystal botherer. Strange, to think of the secrets they must share when nobody else was around.

Before long, we went out into Old Court to get a break from the racket. The space was cool and quiet after the madness of the bar, no Snow Queens or Ninja Turtles out here. I took Bryn's crown reverently from his head and fixed his wayward ermine (cotton wool). As lighters scratched and cherries flared red in the dark, I remembered what I'd been meaning to ask. 'Hey,' I said to the group. 'I saw Sajid earlier. He said something about Kenny going back to London. Do you know what that's about?'

'No idea,' said Sarah, her lips leaving green stains on the filter of her cigarette. Then, gravely: 'But we will mourn him.'

Jamie closed his eyes briefly, opened them again. 'Okay. Mourned.'

I wasn't quite in the mood for piss-taking. 'Is anyone going to call him?'

Jamie looked at me as if I'd just farted.

After a long pause, Bryn turned to me with an odd smile. 'Maybe it's another curse,' he said. 'Perhaps poor Kenny was touched by something. When you locked him in the cellar.'

The joke hit me with a force I hadn't expected. 'Don't say that!' I said, squirming. The others laughed at my discomfort, and I laughed too and told them to piss off. It had come back to me so powerfully, that weird, falling feeling in my stomach that, yes, there was something off about that cellar—

And then, an atmospheric shift, the feeling that we were no longer alone. From our group, small gasps. I followed their eyes to see a figure, ghostly white, standing a little way down the path: Mona, shivering slightly in her pale summer pyjamas.

She said nothing, only stood. Something felt – how else to put it? – very wrong. Her face, sallow in the glow of the lamplight, had a wide-eyed, ghoulish look. Her breathing was shallow and strained, like a bird that had collided with a pane of glass. And instead of her usual library-induced pallor, her exposed arms and legs had a mottled redness. Almost as if she'd been running. Jamie sniggered openly, and Sarah looked away. Alexa seemed unsure what to do. I shrank into myself, pulling the neck of my T-shirt up to my nose, not knowing what exactly I was hiding from.

In the ticklish quiet, Bryn put a hand to his mouth, stifling a sheepish laugh. His eyes were wide. 'Oh shit.'

Mona didn't blink. 'What did I ever do to you?' she said.

When Bryn didn't reply, Mona raised her hand, and in her white-knuckled fingers was something soft and small. Her beloved stuffed cat. But now, parts of its fur were blackened, as if burned, and it was stuck all over with what appeared to be nails. It took me a moment to understand that the head had been removed, then reattached the wrong way around.

Muffled giggles from Jamie and Sarah – ignorant, knowing, I couldn't tell.

'Now,' Bryn said, ameliorating, 'my intentions were good. I know how you miss Tilly—'

Mona flinched. 'Lily.'

'—*Lily*, right, right. And I tried to do … a thing. But I got carried away. Anyway, it's like the film, right? With the pets? You shouldn't try to bring them back, because they end up all wrong and bad.'

He opened his hands as if to say *whoops*, and now Sarah laughed along with Jamie. I think Alexa did too. But these things dissolved into static when I noticed the backs of Mona's hands. Streaked with blood. From livid, red scratches that disappeared under her frilled pyjama sleeves. What the fuck? I fumbled instinctively for a tissue – but when nobody else moved to help, I let my hands sit heavy in my pockets, balled my fists to stop them from shaking. I felt a horrible tension, as if invisible forces were pulling me in two different directions, fixing me to the spot.

Mona held the little charred lump against her chest and glared at Bryn. There was something operatic about the scene: this small, dishevelled girl about to deliver a warning or a curse. I almost heard the low tremolo of strings, the timpani rumble that says: *Something awful is going to happen.*

But all she said, small and fierce, was: 'Just stop it, Bryn.' I almost admired the way Mona stood in the face of this onslaught.

'I'm sorry, okay!' he said, the glint in his eyes belying his apologetic tone. 'I'm sorry. Tell her. Tell her that I'm not a bad guy.'

A horrible moment, then, in which I realised he was talking to me. God, even in the dark the blood was bright on Mona's skin. I shook my head, beseeching: *Please ask someone else, this is the only time I want you to pick someone else.* But he kept his eyes, sparkling and wild, on me.

Finally, I turned to her, my voice barely a whisper. 'He's not a bad guy, Mona.'

The group assented, clapped. Sloppy and foolish. And then Mona was backing away like an exorcised spirit, stepping with solemn dignity back around the path to her staircase. When she was gone, Sarah nudged me. 'Fuck. Is she always like that?'

'What are you asking me for?'

'I dunno. I thought you knew her.'

I sputtered, horrified. 'What? Why would you—'

She shrugged. Presuming she was just pissed, I turned to Bryn. 'Mate. What just happened?'

He shook his head. 'Nothing.'

'Because in the park, we talked about Mona—'

But he turned away. He and Alexa exchanged a look, meaning moving silently between them. I felt as if I were looking at them through glass – as if, had I spoken, they might not have heard me. There was a story there somewhere, but they weren't telling it. Eventually, Alexa looked away.

Ready to move onto the next scene, Bryn clapped me on the arm, hard enough to make me wince. Then, hands clasped behind his back, he came closer until his face was just inches from mine. His breath was hot, and his skin smelled almost smoky, like the expensive whisky he always doled out at his parties. When he dipped his head, I realised what I was supposed to do. Obediently, I lifted the crown (which suddenly felt weirdly heavy) and placed it on his head. His smile showed the gaps between his small, neat canines, his tongue moving wetly behind them.

Duly coronated, he clasped the back of my neck and gave me a fond, firm shake.

'Come on,' he declared. 'Are we getting out of here or what?'

They began to move away, but I stared idiotically. 'Aren't we going back inside?'

'In there?' he replied, scornful. 'Course not, bops are shit. Queen's Ents, guys?'

And he was strolling away with Alexa, the others close behind.

I snatched a glance across the lawn at the lonely room belonging to Mona, our unquiet ghost. A movement in the doorway made me start – wait, was that her, watching? My skin prickled at the dark shape concealing itself in the shadows, and I almost called out to her. But no, I was being stupid. On second glance, there was nothing there.

Part of me thought I should knock on her door, see if she was okay (fuck, she was bleeding). But another part – my inner Libra, perhaps – refused to upset the balance between me and my friends. Even as I followed them out of college and onto our next adventure, I felt Bryn's hand on the back of my neck. Heavy. A sensation like the reassuring, controlling touch of a mesmerist.

TWO

I

There's that horrible sensation, when you're drifting off to sleep: you feel as if you're falling, and you jolt yourself awake. That night in the B&B, it must have happened five or six times. So, when I got up, I was feeling more than a little groggy. Hoping a walk would help, I made my way to the river, taking a route I never had as a student. Along the way, predictable Cambridge scenery emerged from unpredictable perspectives. Uncanny, as if seen in a mirror.

I paused by The Anchor to watch the morning light shivering on the surface of the river. There was very little sound but for the gentle clack of sandwich boards being set up by punting company reps, the murmur of tourists as they corralled family members for photos. I felt a million miles from the flat in Manchester, where the wails of the neighbours' baby would already be coming through the walls.

There, walking the Mathematical Bridge and its geometrically imperfect reflection, was a couple, hand in hand, silhouetted perfectly against the cold blue sky. It was the kind of idyllic scene you should photograph and upload to Instagram, but I'd never been a social media person. In fact, I'd thanked the universe many times that pivotal university moments – me, fancy-dressed as a

French maid, or passed out on the common-room carpet – happened before Facebook became ubiquitous, so were stored only in the memories of my fellow students. At least there they could be bleached and diminished by time. To be fair, I didn't mind posting work-related stuff online, but I kept my personal life analogue. Alexa was always the same. Hated having her picture taken, championed paper diaries.

Even if I'd been more 'online', I wouldn't have taken a picture. Things like bridges and balconies give me the creeps. I don't like to be reminded of the distance between a person and the ground, of how far it's possible to fall.

Seeing the couple, so easy and so comfortable, I wondered why my own route to love had been so arduous. Back at college, girls saw me as a Good Guy – the type who finishes last, the guy they talked to about other guys. That girl in Tim's group (God, I hated how Tim called her Casio, it was so annoying) would happily ruffle my hair in front of everyone, or link arms with me as we walked, because it was so clearly a platonic gesture.

Don't think I didn't notice: I only got lucky in love once I became The Bad Guy.

~

I was back north for the interminable summer holidays. I got a job in the local pub serving pints of mild to elderly gentlemen, who paid with mounds of coppers and asked wryly about my studies, baffled as to how my understanding of motets and madrigals would serve me in real life (they had a point). Now and again I met Gaz, Ben and Reedy, and while every meeting concluded with us saying how great it was to catch up, it felt like we were labouring to keep something alive when perhaps we should let it go.

In the end, I spent much of my free time at home. I'd help Mum in the garden, pulling weeds and deadheading roses under her careful direction, or I'd work with my stepdad on dubious home improvement projects, holding his ladder while he fiddled recklessly with old light fittings. It was nice, actually. Good to step outside my own head, to do things with my hands that produced a tangible, concrete result. To make simple progress on simple things. When our jobs were done, we'd order from our favourite takeaway and – while watching back-to-back episodes of our favourite reality TV shows – my mum and I would engage in our customary aggressive bartering: *No way, a barbecue spare rib is worth at least two prawn toasts.* Whenever I beat her to an answer on *Family Fortunes*, my mum would wink and call me a smartarse with conspicuous pride.

These were days before Zoom, before mobile phones did anything beyond calls, texts and games of Snake. And my rugged old Nokia was fairly quiet throughout the months that sighed by. Tim called once a week, and we talked about house parties and barbecues he'd been to with people from his course. At one point, having heard the information from Berenice, he mentioned that Bryn and Alexa were in Prague, and I felt a kind of panic. Although I'd been texting them, the thread connecting us felt worn and frail – as if it might snap, allowing them to soar away from me like kites on a current.

All of which is why I was so glad to get back to college for our second year. As I passed through the gates, my feet moved with the breezy confidence of one who knows where the nearest toilets are. And when I discovered everyone in our usual corner of the bar – Bryn at the centre, leaving the freshers in no doubt as to who owned the space – it felt like coming home. Together, we assessed each new undergrad: this girl, Footlights wannabe. And that guy?

Pure Christian Union. We spoke to a few, but mainly to offer unsolicited wisdom in patronising tones: Come on, nobody goes to Cindy's on a *Thursday*.

Michaelmas term unfolded predictably as Cambridge wrapped itself in autumn garb. I enjoyed seeing students in their box-fresh American Apparel, moving antithetically against those antiquated streets; also, observing their tweedy peers, in sensible cords and button-downs, tottering in and out of Tiki-themed clubs and neon-lit bars. Lecture timetables unfurled like college scarves, parties punctuated the weeks emphatically as fireworks. Shops sold pumpkins and jaw-breaking toffee apples. I felt as though I were listening to a piece of music that I'd heard before, enjoying it all the more now that I knew the tune and could hum along.

One evening in October, I found the common room crackling with a kind of static. The television, blasting out scenes from some musical talent show, was being ignored by those who clamoured around the huge noticeboard, their bodies obscuring the usual Students' Union announcements and poorly executed penis graffiti. I approached a third year medic whose name I couldn't remember. 'What's going on?' I asked.

'Check it out,' she replied. 'Bryn won the Conran Award.' She pointed at a double-page spread from the student paper, pinned wonkily but proudly on the wall. On it, a black and white photograph of Bryn, looking supremely comfortable in front of the camera.

'The what?'

'It's a university prize. For long form essay writing?'

This made no sense to me.

Bryn himself stood in the middle of the crowd, jostled and patted by admiring hands. Confused, I fought my way through the disciples until I found myself in front of him. 'So,' I said, with an uncertain smile, 'I hear congratulations are in order?'

He laughed, shook his head. 'It's no big deal.'

Jamie, standing beside him like a politician's personal spin doctor, chipped in. 'Sure. But five grand is a reasonable chunk of pocket money.'

Pocket money? I looked from Bryn to Jamie and back again. 'You won five grand?' I asked, a note of hysteria creeping into my voice. 'How?'

'I wrote an essay about John Dee. A Tudor mathematician. Also astronomer, astrologer, alchemist. Probably one of the most fascinating minds in history.'

'Right. As part of your course?'

'Nah, for this competition. I saw the application form online when I was on holiday and thought, fuck it. I never liked sunbathing anyway.'

I had the sensation of being slapped. My understanding had been that whenever Bryn wasn't grudgingly slogging through an assignment or hanging out with us, he was sitting on the sofa and scratching his balls. We didn't do extra-curricular stuff, did we? That was for the Monas of this world, no? I thought back to the hours I'd spent in my parents' local, talking to toothless old buffers about darts, and how he must have spent the time hunched over his books. He hadn't mentioned this to me, not once.

My brain reminded me that I ought to react, so I threw my arm around his shoulders and sputtered: 'I mean, wow. That's … awesome. So, what did you say about …?'

'John Dee? You don't really want to know.'

'Oh I absolutely do.'

He sighed, theatrically, *Go on then*. 'I wrote about his relationship with a guy called Edward Kelley. They did spiritual investigations together.'

I frowned. 'Spiritual investigations? Like séances?'

'Not quite. Kelley claimed he could see angels, and that they were going to tell him the secrets of a universal language, supposedly the language God used to create the world. The two of them spent years trying to find it.'

'That's weird.'

'It got weirder. Towards the end, Kelley told Dee that the angels had ordered them to swap wives.'

'Bloody hell. They didn't do it, though?'

'You don't ignore instructions from The Almighty.'

I wanted to ask smart questions, but my world was spinning slightly off its axis. 'So this Dee guy, supposedly so smart, gets taken in by this bollocks?'

'Yeah,' said Bryn, like a minister on his fifth breakfast interview of the morning. 'But my essay was about how you can't always set logical thought and magical thought in opposition. Often, people like him came up with brilliant ideas partly *because* of their belief in the weird and the supernatural, not in spite of it. Dee wouldn't have made his most important discoveries about navigation and astronomy if he didn't believe in things like astrology.'

The more he talked, the more panicked I became. This essay wasn't some half-arsed side project, dashed off on impulse. It was thoroughly researched, carefully thought through. How many more topics did Bryn just happen to be an expert in? How did he have so many opinions? 'Shit. Well. Congrats, man. Drink to celebrate?'

'Thanks,' he said, holding up a pint in progress. 'Jamie already got me one.'

I glanced at Jamie, who wrapped his arm around Bryn's shoulder. The two of them looked like brothers, impeccable in their Oxford shirts, jumpers knotted around their shoulders, signet rings glinting on their pinkies. Both beamed, not at me but at Sarah, who clicked away with a small, sleek, digital camera. When the photoshoot was over I clapped Bryn on the back, realised I'd done that already, and mumbled that I'd be back in a bit. As I moved away, others closed in around him. At the sight of each one, Bryn's face lit up anew, an arcade machine swallowing coins.

On the edge of the group was Alexa, observing Bryn as he received his public. Following her line of vision, I saw he was now talking to a pretty fresher with a heap of blonde hair. This fresher pretended to punch him on the jaw and, obliging, he made as if to fall backwards. Then, smiling, he leaned to whisper something in her ear, and the fresher held the straw from her drink between her straight, white teeth. She was conspicuously attractive, but in an obvious, unoriginal way. Like a pop singer or a soap star, respectably styled for a charity appearance.

'Lex,' I said, giving her a nudge. 'Fancy a drink?'

Although Alexa turned to face me, her gaze strained for a moment longer towards Bryn. Eventually she met my eye, produced a smile as if from a switch. 'Good idea.'

We found the bar in a state of lazy quiet, only a handful of students scattered around the timeworn banquettes. Alexa and I took a couple of stools at the bar and ordered the customary bottle of college red. 'You're not rowing tomorrow?' I asked.

'Fuck no,' she replied, 'I quit. From now on, I'm only awake at 5.30 a.m. when I'm on my way home from a night out.'

'Very sensible. I only managed the one term last year. I miss the river, though.'

'No, you *think* you miss it because that would be poetic.' She held her glass towards me. 'But it's not poetic, it's just cold. Have you spoken to Berenice recently?'

I shook my head, filling her glass, then mine. 'How is she?'

'No idea. Haven't seen her.'

I congratulated myself for still being part of the team, for passing a test that Berenice had failed.

'Speaking of which,' Alexa went on, 'did you hear about Mona?'

'What about her?'

'She dropped out. Had some kind of breakdown.'

'Shit, seriously?'

'*Mmm-hmm.* Dominic – you know, ginger NatSci, nice guy – told me. Said she'd been acting odd last term. He even spoke to her director of studies about it, to see if they'd get her some counselling or something, but he doesn't know if it happened. Apparently she came back last week because her parents pressured her, but she only stayed for one night and then put herself on the first train home. Told college she's done.'

I wondered whether I should have spoken to college about Mona myself. But what would I have said? I thought about her terror in the stairwell, the queasy feeling I'd had when I stepped over the threshold into her room. Those marks, on her hands. There in the comforting hubbub of the bar, I felt a strange impulse to glance into the darkened corners of the room, to check the shadowy space around my feet.

Alexa carried on. 'Classic Oxbridge. People go from being the smartest in sixth form to being average at uni, and it messes with their sense of self. I get that. But I have a coping strategy: I don't give a shit.'

We toasted Alexa's philosophy. But I knew she was wrong. Mona wasn't worried about being top of her classes. She *was* top of her classes. Why else had Bryn shared the same breathing space as her, if not to 'take inspiration' from her coursework when he'd left it too late to summon his own muse? Again I thought of her inexplicably nauseating room, the string around the window, the extra lock on the door. A peculiar image came to me of Mona, trembling under her bedcovers, and a second Mona, hovering outside the window, moon-eyed and raking her own skin with ragged fingernails. I shook my head, as if to fling the image away.

'The thing that amazes me most,' said Alexa, 'is that she hasn't emailed Bryn to say goodbye.'

'There's still time.' Then, desperately curious: 'Speaking of Bryn, great news on his prize.'

'Yeah. He's amazing. Hard work, though.'

I paused. She gave a thin laugh and waved a hand, *I'm kidding.* But after a beat she sighed, leaned a little heavier on the bar. 'He's just … Exhausting, sometimes. I was with him at their Highgate house when he was finishing that essay, and he was so stressed about it. I had to keep picking his notes out of the bin, giving him pep talks. And he'd get so cranky with me.'

'Come on,' I said. 'He's not that bad, surely?'

She looked strangely at me. 'Of course he is. His moods can be really … dark, sometimes.'

Yes, I remembered our weekend away. But was this different? The idea that there were sides to Bryn I didn't see – it felt like an ache.

'But that's the thing,' Alexa said, bright again. 'Big characters need a lot of attention. And we love them all the same.'

Yes. Some people were given leeway that others were not. Bryn would still have aced his Cambridge interview if he'd turned up wearing flip-flops and Bermuda shorts, but I wouldn't have made it through the first five minutes without my suit and tie, confirmation that, yes, even with my comical accent, I did know how to walk on two legs and eat with a knife and fork.

I don't know why I cared, but I asked anyway: 'Who was that blonde girl in the common room just now?'

Alexa gave me a guarded look. 'Which blonde girl?'

'The one talking to Bryn.'

Something like a sneer, then. 'Some first year English student. Dad's a property magnate, so she's quite the Cambridge celebrity I hear. Why, got your eye on her?'

'No! Just wondered.'

There had been something about Alexa's phrasing, as if this girl were on a different level. It was all relative, I supposed. Alexa rested a hand on the bar and I noticed, perhaps for the first time, how pale the skin, how fine the bones. Little wonder Bryn's hand always looked so powerful with Alexa's in it. In that moment, I wanted to cover Alexa's hand, protectively, with my own.

As we sat, silent, I thought about Bryn's prize. There, a tugging in my core, as if something not yet marked on any astronomical chart were pulling out of my gravitational field.

Later, I wondered: Could I have written an essay like Bryn's? Me, who'd spent my school days fetching up each textbook answer like a dog retrieving a stick? I'd always been good at presenting facts. But I'd failed to understand the need for original thought, for interpretation.

Perhaps I could have interpreted my beloved Warlock. I could have explored whether his drunkenness had any impact on his work. That, and his fascination with the occult. Supposedly, he believed boozing to be a route to mysticism – so, did it really help him to weave the past and present into new, unearthly chords? Did it help him as he stooped at his piano, choosing notes as if choosing words for a particularly potent spell?

As for Bryn, he hadn't deceived me, not really. Since he was one in a long line of university-goers, this kind of thing was built into his DNA. He read, wrote, thought without even realising it, and making a critical analysis of the world came as naturally and instinctively to him as flicking on the TV did to me. In this respect, Kenny was right: public school polish was about much more than money.

Thankfully I didn't need to acknowledge this rightness, since Kenny was long gone.

It was early evening in November, the dark sky cloaked by a billowing blanket of cloud, when I was woken from a nap by a hammering at my door. It was Bryn, wearing a beautiful but stained dinner jacket and a slightly manic grin. His hair was styled strangely, slicked close to his skull in a way I hadn't seen before and, for once, he was completely clean-shaven. 'You busy?' he asked, slightly out of breath.

'Not overly,' I replied, my voice still thick with sleep. Then, pointing at a case he carried in one hand: 'Is that a violin?'

'Do you want to do a gig?'

'A gig?'

'Those songs we played last year. Do you want to play them at an event?'

I felt suddenly, gloriously awake. 'Yeah, sure! When?'

'Tonight.'

'Wait … What?'

'There's a dinner at Trinity, for some society. There were musicians organised, but they fell through. We get free drinks. And it's just a couple of songs.'

'But we haven't rehearsed!'

'So? You could play those things backwards.' Then, with a shrug: 'And I'll manage.'

I held up my hands, palms out: *Let's all just settle down.* 'Bryn, why would Trinity want musicians from another college when they've got hundreds of their own?'

He leaned on the door frame. 'Do you want to do it or not?'

There was a hint of exasperation in his voice. In the silence that followed, I laughed, uncomfortably. I wanted to say: *This is ridiculous, we're completely unprepared.* But I knew what his response would be. What's the worst that could happen? In any case, perhaps any terror or embarrassment would all be worth it for us to be a duo again. Which is why I finally said: 'Alright.'

'That's the spirit! You should get changed.'

'Now?'

'Course, it starts at eight.'

'Jesus, Bryn.'

We armed ourselves with sheet music and ties and cufflinks, feeble props denoting professionalism, and made our way out of college and down Trumpington Street. With each step, Bryn swung the violin case aggressively, and I might have wondered why he carried it at all were I not too busy mentally rehearsing my piano accompaniment. By the time we reached Trinity, a fine rain was beginning to spot our unironed shirts. The moon hung orange in the restless sky, inauspicious.

Through the college gates, I had to skip, ungainly, to keep up with Bryn as he moved around the edge of the long, imperious courtyard. I chased him through a huge wooden door, set into one of the great stone walls, and up two, three floors of a tall, twisting staircase. I was still climbing when he reached the top, and I paused, slightly breathless, as he smoothed his jacket and approached a closed door.

'Is this it?' I called.

He said nothing, only pushed open the door – releasing the lucid sound of glasses being set carefully on trays – and beamed at whatever was on the other side. I stumbled up the stairs and followed him in.

It was some kind of reception room, the walls adorned with classical landscapes and decorative plates. Everywhere, dark furniture polished to a high gleam, velveted armchairs and ottomans that must have overheard more about politics and philosophy than I ever would. On one marble-topped table, champagne flutes ready to be received. When I sidled up to him, Bryn was speaking to one of the few people inside, a jolly man in an unusual gown. I caught the end of their exchange: 'We were starting to wonder if you were coming,' the man said.

'Sorry,' Bryn replied, not looking sorry. 'Last-minute run-through, you know, getting everything spot on.'

'Quite right. And here we have …'

The man turned to me. As I held out my hand to introduce myself, Bryn jumped in, staring at me in a way that was fierce and overpowering. 'Thomas,' he said. 'Tom. This is Tom.'

I looked at Bryn, then back at the man. Nodded, blankly.

'Well, Tom,' said the man, as people began to file in behind us, 'our guests are arriving. So, whenever you're ready.' At that, he gestured to the corner, where there was a lustrous black piano, its raised mahogany lid a glowering mirror. Thanking the man, Bryn placed a hand on my shoulder and guided me away, swiping a glass of champagne as we went.

'Okay,' I said, switching into concert mode. 'Remember what we did with the intro? The tempo will be quite fluid—'

He put the glass in my hand. 'Actually, I need you to do some solo stuff.'

'What?'

'Just in the background, while they're having drinks. Play anything you like, these people don't care.'

The room was filling with old duffers in suits and gowns. A few looked towards us, expectant. I had a low, sick feeling. 'But I thought … I haven't prepared—'

'Relax. You're not performing for *The Times* music critics. It's a room of fellows who aren't listening anyway.'

He pushed down on my shoulder and I plopped onto the piano stool. 'What happened to the other musicians?' I asked.

'I cancelled them.'

I almost dropped my glass. 'What? Why … why would you—'

He looked at me as if the answer were right in front of me. 'So that we could come instead.'

The logic was circular, a tune on repeat. I stared down at the row of keys as if they might bite. 'Bryn. What is going on?'

He shook his head, exasperated. 'What's the problem? Are you worried that they'll find out that you actually are a musician? That you can, in fact, just about be trusted not to fuck up some basic songs?'

I flinched. Arguing with him was like trying to hold a snake. When you felt you'd pinned him on a point, he whipped from your grasp, bit back. Still harder to deny was his expression where, beneath his mask of mischief, frustration lay coiled and shimmering. Even his sleek hair, so unlike his usual careless curls, threw me off – it gave me the feeling you get when you wave at a friend in the street before realising you're looking at a stranger.

The room was full now, and the man in the gown was looking at us rather pointedly. Sighing, I asked one last question: 'Who the fuck is Tom?'

Bryn shrugged, and suddenly the sparkle was back in his eyes. 'Whoever he is, he probably isn't drinking free champagne in the most private corner of Trinity.'

Completely lost, I downed my drink and began to play.

In our first secret rehearsal, Bryn's power had seemed some kind of divine right. Sublime. It had felt like grace.

But music is unusual among the arts. Paintings and sculpture stick around for centuries, but music lives in a moment. Once a piece is played, it'll never be played exactly the same way again. And the power that came from Bryn afterwards did not feel holy, not at all.

While I played some old exam pieces I knew by heart, Bryn strolled about, plucking canapés from platters, chatting to guests chosen by an unguessable system. At one point, I overheard him saying that he'd be playing after dinner, which made no sense whatsoever.

In between pieces, other guests came and spoke to me. I couldn't ask them what the event was all about, since that would have exposed me as someone who wasn't meant to be there – but a line about 'The story of our Saviour' on the invitations they carried made me wonder whether this was some kind of religious thing. In fact, I was worried that one priestly-looking bloke was going to make a bid for my soul, but after a monologue about some college collection of silver – used at the inauguration of the Archbishop of

Canterbury, or something, I wasn't even close to paying attention – I kind of wished he had.

Another guest who decided to say hello was a staff member who wore a grey bob and some of those colourful beads popular with women who want to appear quirky. 'So, Thomas,' she said, 'where did you go to school?'

Always the same question. I gave her the name of my sixth form, knowing she wouldn't have heard of it.

She hadn't. 'And where exactly is that?'

I named the town. She seemed not to have heard of that either, and only took a vol-au-vent from a passing waiter and deposited it on the piano. 'Were your parents always very supportive of your musical development?' she asked.

A memory came to me then, of something that happened when I was six or seven. Some kids from down the street had come back to mine, and as we barrelled into the front room we saw a shape stretched on the sofa, silent and still. It was my dad, on his back, skin the colour of raw pastry poking between his greasy vest and underpants. A cigarette, fallen from its ashtray, was slowly charring the coffee table and releasing a coil of foul smoke. It was only when the other kids started giggling that I noticed the muddy stain between his bony thighs, on the sofa, a stench like fertiliser mingling with the smell of what I now knew to be whisky. Then there was Mum, scurrying in with a washcloth, red-faced and garbling apologies that weren't hers to make. I never asked those kids around again.

'No,' I said, taking the woman's vol-au-vent and showily eating it.

She blinked. Searched for something to say. 'You know, there are some musical items in the collection of artefacts on display tonight—'

Christ, not this again. I explained that, regretfully, I must pause our chat and start my next piece. Looking relieved, the woman tottered off into the crowd.

After I'd played some simple Mozart, a bit of Brahms, a gong sounded. Drawn by its golden tone, the guests shuffled like a hypnotist's subjects through a side door and off to dinner. The man in the weird gown loitered at the back of the crowd, so that he could thank me for the music on his way out, and I nodded at him as if everything had gone beautifully to plan. Then I sat, waiting for the room to clear of everyone but me and Bryn, so I could ask him what the fuck had just happened.

But when the gowned man had gone and the door had fallen shut behind him, I found myself alone but for a waiter, who bustled silently about before disappearing himself. I waited, like a lost child standing stock still in a supermarket, thinking that Bryn would surely reappear soon. But as the minutes ticked by, my irritability shapeshifted into anxiety. I had the feeling, the feeling that drops like a stone, of being deserted.

Quitting my post at the piano, I headed out and checked the nearby toilets. They were empty. After that I called Bryn's mobile several times, but only his recorded voice answered me, flat and inhuman. I even went back and peered through the door that led to the dinner, in case for some reason he'd decided to eat, but he wasn't there.

I was about to go back down the spiral staircase when, looking down the corridor, I spotted a room at the very end to which the door was ajar. Mouth sickly with champagne, I stumbled towards it, almost tripping over my own feet, before pausing at the threshold and nudging the door open.

Electric light from the corridor bled into the room, creating a long strip of chintz across the floor, illuminating shapes within what appeared to be a large lounge. I could just about discern the limbs of chairs and small side tables, all skeletal angles, their colours muted in the gloom. To my right was a cold, gaping fireplace, either side of which were larger tables, swathed like altars, bearing towers of coffee cups and rows of dainty port glasses. To my left, where the darkness was heavier, was a gallery wall where huge frames hung, their contents nothing but still, black flags. Below them, another table, the size of a coffin. And, on it, detectable only because of the moonlight sighing through a small window, some kind of glass case – the kind for displaying museum artefacts, like Victorian medical implements or haunted dolls.

Then the darkness itself shifted, and I realised with a jolt: there was something in front of the case, something I'd been looking directly at and hadn't seen. A figure, slightly stooped. It seemed to be facing away from me, although I couldn't be sure. I stepped one foot into the room then immediately withdrew. The figure seemed to have moved, in the space of a blink, somehow, behind the table. For a second I thought I saw a streak of brightness where the face should be, like a row of small, neat teeth.

Another blink and the figure was back, in front of the cabinet, leaning towards it again. Impossible. My eyes, playing tricks.

I called: 'Bryn? Is that you?'

Although I'd spoken softly, my voice was stark and vulgar in the silence. The figure twisted. In the dark, I still couldn't see its face. A liquid feeling in my limbs – provoked by the memory of that shadow beyond the bathroom window, that shape slipping up an Old Court wall – made me clutch at the door frame. I wondered whether the guests in the dining room would be able to hear me from this distance, if for some reason I were to cry out. The figure moved a little, from beyond a fall of shadow, and I was finally able to make out his face. Fuck.

'Bryn, did you hear me?' I said, my voice barely more than a breath. 'What's going on?'

In the darkness, he put a finger to his lips. Clicked a nail on the glass cabinet: *tap tap tap*.

I looked around for a light switch. Unable to find one, I moved reluctantly into the gloom. 'I don't think we should be in here.'

He didn't reply. Instead, he turned to the doors of the case and touched them softly, as if he were stroking a girl's hair. Then, suddenly, he began to tug at the lock, making the glass rattle crazily in its frame.

Panicked, I held up my hands. 'Don't! You'll break it!'

But the doors of the case swung open. He paused, allowing the silence to settle. Then he reached inside the case and – very slowly and deliberately, as if it were the finale to one of his magic shows – retrieved something. From my position in the doorway I couldn't see it very well, but it appeared to be a small, silver cup. With a long sigh, Bryn cradled it in his hands.

'What's that?' I asked, hugging myself to try and stop my trembling.

He didn't reply.

I tried again. 'I'm pretty sure we're not meant to be touching it.'

When he spoke, his voice sounded different. 'Then don't touch it.'

'Please,' I said, looking over my shoulder, 'put it back and let's go. It's just a cup.'

He brought the thing to his lips, chuckling softly – it almost looked as if he were telling it a secret – and he looked off into the distance, a fierce light in his eyes. Was he drunk? From somewhere down the corridor a voice called something about dessert wine, and I held my breath until the sound had faded. I wasn't sure whether I was more afraid of being caught stealing college antiques or being alone in the dark with this person.

'It isn't *just a cup*,' he said.

My eyes hadn't quite adjusted to the darkness and, were it not for the unmistakable cadence of his speech, I might not have been sure I was talking to Bryn at all. My frustration and fear were indistinguishable now, blurred by the strangeness and the murk. 'Just leave it,' I said, trying to hold my voice steady. 'We need to go, now.'

'You know,' he said, turning suddenly as if only just remembering I was there, 'they only put this on display for very special occasions. Especially since my father's day.'

Realisation came like a storm, breaking. No, it wasn't just a cup. It was a chalice, one used at some of the most solemn Christian occasions since the early eighteen hundreds. One that went briefly missing, thirty years ago, courtesy of the infamous Cavendish Senior. Just the right size to slip out in an empty violin case. The most shocking thing about all this was not that Bryn was ready to lie, to steal (a relic, for fuck's sake, a priceless relic). Not even that he would make me his unthinking accomplice and put me in danger. The most shocking thing was that it was not a joke to him.

'That's why we're here?' I said, bitterly. 'Because you're hung up on some family story from a million years ago?'

He laughed, a mirthless sound in the dark, as if I'd surprised him. Still his face was distorted by shadows. After a while, he wagged a finger at me. 'Your hero,' he said. 'Warlock.'

'What about him?'

'Remember what he did, in the church?'

It took me a moment. But yes, I remembered how Warlock and his friends had broken into a church at night, how they'd joked about sacrificing a woman on the altar. How, at this, the church had been loudly and dramatically struck by lightning. Bryn must have read the biography after all. 'That was a story. Probably exaggerated.'

'All good stories are exaggerated. Shall we see if we can summon something ourselves?'

As I looked helplessly on, he grabbed one of the bottles of port, uncorked it, and poured a heavy slug into the silver cup. Remembering our first illicit rehearsal, I had the sensation of the world being flipped, seen through an old, foxed mirror. 'Stop it,' I said, the shake in my voice giving me away. 'This is stupid.'

'What? If you don't believe it, what have you got to be scared about?'

'I'm not scared, Bryn.'

He stepped towards me, slowly, looming out of the darkness like a moon appearing from behind a pall of cloud. In the silver glow that came through the window, his skin was luminous. As if he were made of cold stars. But as he came near he smelled darkly somatic, like iron and earth. 'Yes,' he said, 'you are.'

He came so close I thought he might take hold of me. His pupils were huge, a kind of cosmic blackness. Part of me wanted to step back, to escape the force of him. The other part wanted to fall at his feet and weep, clasp him around the legs and bury my face in his expensive trousers like a penitent. The more my terror grew, the more I wanted to clutch his hand, beg him to come, please come with me, let's get out of here.

But I only stood, dumb, while he offered me the port. When I refused, he drank it himself and thumped the chalice on a side table. Then he took the uppermost napkin from a neat linen pile. 'Let's see which devils we can summon tonight. Shall we?'

To my bemusement, he lifted the napkin and very slowly draped it over himself, covering his head completely – like a bride or a mourner, mute and veiled. I stared at my friend as if we were obediently following the steps of some dark liturgy.

Then he began to speak, so low I could hardly hear. A language I couldn't understand.

Fear danced over my skin like a breath. 'What are you saying?'

He kept going, the words spilling out of him, unfathomable.

'Bryn. Stop it.'

He had hunched his shoulders now, and the pale napkin hung low in front of him. You might have thought he had no head at all. Still, that horrid burbling.

'Seriously, Bryn, that's enough!'

Abruptly, he stopped. Silence enveloped us, like great wings. He took one corner of the napkin between a finger and thumb, began to inch it upwards, and I had a profound feeling of being in a nightmare. Something told me that, when the napkin was off, Bryn wouldn't be wearing his own face any more. Instead, something unknowably ancient would be looking back at me. Or maybe there'd be nothing – only a flat, awful darkness where his mesmerising eyes should be.

But no. When he removed the napkin, there he was, his hair escaping its austere style, his eyes indecipherable runes.

'Boo,' he said.

Suddenly, there was a rumble of thunder, and I staggered backwards, gasping – Jesus, what was happening? – but Bryn only covered his mouth with one hand, smothering his laughter at my horrified expression. The sound was only a trolley, clanking with plates and glasses, trundling down the corridor outside.

I settled myself. 'For fuck's sake, Bryn—'

And then: a bright rectangle of gold on the wall opposite. A door to an adjoining room had been yanked open, and in its frame stood a wide, bearlike man, straining from a liveried jacket. A porter. He looked immediately in the direction of the case, his expression a simple mixture of confusion and surprise.

'What do you think you're doing?'

Bryn looked at him, then back at me, his eyes wide and incandescent.

'Hey! You hear me?' The porter took a big stride into the room, into the shadows, fumbling unsuccessfully as I had for a light switch. 'I said, what do you think—'

Bryn raised an arm, and I thought I heard unintelligible words, spoken low and level. Then the scene became a set of static images, like a story told in stained glass. There was the porter lumbering forward. Then, something else, in the dark space around him, a darkness that stretched crooked and long – was it reaching for him? The final scene in this horrible tableau: the porter, suddenly almost horizontal, his burly frame seeming to hang unthinkably in the air. It was a moment when time seemed to stretch, to break. Only the sickening crack of the porter's head on a table as he fell made the world rush into motion again, a stopped clock shocked back into life.

And then Bryn ran, and I ran too, following faster than I thought I could go, the two of us streaming out of the room and down the staircase, across the courtyard and onto Trumpington Street, our jackets flapping behind us, my chest burning with the frigid air until we flew through the gates of our own college and into Old Court, into the dark.

Which part of a trick is the magic part?

Is it the moment things turn, when the card disappears under a cuff, when the coin drops unseen into the pocket? Or is the magic just as present later, much later, in the audience's retelling, in the words that recreate and refine the trick? *No, I'm telling you, he definitely wasn't hiding anything in his hand.*

I've been over this story many times now. Backwards, forwards, from every possible perspective. Whichever way, it's just as chilling.

The next day, I didn't go to lectures. I felt a cold panic about the porter's condition, kept imagining his head opened like a soft-boiled egg, so I wandered around college aiming to bump into Bryn in the hope he'd do or say something to put my mind at ease. But he didn't appear in the lunch queue outside hall, and he didn't show up in the library or the bar. Every minute of his absence, my fear intensified. Perhaps he'd already been visited by college officials. Or even, if the porter was badly hurt, the police. I imagined him in a cell. I imagined hearing news that the porter had died from his injuries. I imagined Bryn's face smeared across the front pages, the shock of the nation that this angelic-looking, well-spoken young man was in fact a simple thug. Or, in tabloid parlance: evil.

Eventually I found him in the common room playing pool with some of the first years. He barely looked up as I waved at him, just lifted his eyes as he leaned over the cue. 'Hey man,' I murmured, sidling up to him. 'Everything okay?'

'Yeah, good,' he replied, not bothering to mirror my surreptitious tone. 'You?'

'Fine, fine. Couldn't be arsed with lectures today, ha.'

He didn't reply. Elsewhere, people laughed unthinkingly at an episode of *Friends* they'd seen several times before.

I leaned close. 'You haven't heard anything?'

He sank a ball into the far corner pocket. 'About what?'

I made my voice even quieter. 'About … the porter.'

'Why would I?'

'I dunno. I'm just, you know. Worried.'

'What for?'

'He might be hurt.'

He moved down the table, sank another ball in another pocket. 'You might not realise it, being so busy with the bassoon, but there are worse injuries every week on the rugby pitch.'

'I just have this feeling—'

'And nobody even knows who we are. So how would they find us? The only thing that went wrong was you barging in and making a load of noise. We ran so fast I left the fucking cup.'

He turned back to the first years as if our conversation was over, said something that made them laugh furtively. Not caring how pathetic I looked, I followed him around the table. Because I still had a question about something else, something that was my real worry, even though the idea was still a half-formed thing, a creature swimming in a specimen jar in a sideshow's cabinet of horrors: 'Bryn. What did you do to him?'

He frowned. 'What?'

'The porter. You said something to him. And, somehow, he's flying through the air.'

Around us, the buzz of chatter, the whirr and clunk of the vending machine. Bryn placed the cue very gently on the table. Then he put a hand on my shoulder and turned us away from the first years, the subtle tightening of his fingers simultaneously soothing and threatening. Speaking so quietly that his lips hardly moved, he said: 'You really want to know?'

I nodded.

He stared, thoughtful, as if weighing me up. Then leaned even closer, so I felt each airy word landing on my cheek. The sensation made me shiver. 'When you learn magic,' he said, 'you start by manipulating objects. Coins, matches. Before long, you can manipulate other things. Like people.'

'You mean, psychological stuff? Like forcing people to choose a certain card?'

'Well, not just that.'

I stared, dumb. Did he mean …?

Then he barked a laugh and stepped backwards, numb space opening up between us. 'I'm kidding, you dickhead.'

'For Christ's sake—'

'All I did was tell him to fuck off—'

I shook my head, my face hot with frustration. 'Come on, he was a big guy. I hardly think being told to fuck off was enough to knock him off his feet.'

'—and he was so surprised that he came storming in and tripped over the violin case. More by luck than design, I must say, I'd chucked it by the door. Shit, Alexa's going to be pissed that I left it behind.' He frowned as if what he said should have been obvious to me. 'Guys like that, they're only tough because people think they're tough. But if you stand up to them, it puts them off kilter.' Then, to himself: 'I guess it is magic, really. Because it's about belief.'

I shook my head, mystified. 'It doesn't make sense,' I said, feeling surer of this than anything I'd felt in a long time. 'The way he fell. It was weird. Like, not natural. The way his head—'

He slammed a fist on the pool table, making the balls shudder and roll. I flinched. 'Just fucking forget it, alright?' he said, loudly, his tone dark and surprising. 'You're making something out of nothing. As usual.'

The first years looked at one another. I looked at my hands. Turning back to the table and picking up his cue, Bryn missed an easy shot and cursed under his breath. I wasn't even sure what he meant. But I wasn't about to make a thing of it in front of the others, one of whom, I couldn't help noticing, was that ever-present blonde girl. Silently, one of the freshers chalked a cue. Awkwardness hung, foul as cigarette smoke.

Somewhat penitential, I asked: 'Will you be in the bar tonight?'

'No, I've got plans.'

He didn't expand. For a few minutes, I made supportive comments about the game – the odd 'shot' – whenever the opportunity arose. But nobody replied, and so I stood in silence, unsure whether to stay or go.

Being in Bryn's bad books was horrible. Worse than being back in sixth form.

Strangely, my one comfort during this time was Alexa's comment about Bryn having 'dark' moods, the fact that he'd behaved oddly with her over the holidays. If he was having a tough time, maybe because he was more stressed about work than he let on, then his sharpness towards us wasn't personal. And if *we* were the people to whom he showed this vulnerable, irritable side of himself, it was flattering, really.

But this very active line of thinking was a distraction from something that swam below the surface of my consciousness: the question of what had actually happened to the porter. Bryn's explanation? It simply didn't fit with what I'd experienced, there in that funereal room. Sometimes, when I snapped awake from a dream in which I'd seen that man hanging in mid-air, I found myself unable to fathom the distance between what I'd seen and what couldn't possibly be true. And I held my knowledge of the incident like a new kind of talisman, a tiny power that I hoped might protect me. Against what, I wasn't sure.

I found myself in an unnerving equilibrium: feeling inexplicably and inexpressibly unsettled by Bryn while never wanting to leave his side.

II

When people find out I'm musical director of Voices from Before, they assume I must be a great singer. Sadly, not the case.

Singing is hard. You need to take a full breath, low in the belly, and then *allow* the sound into the world. You can't push or force it. You mustn't obstruct the sound with bad posture or tension in the jaw. Just let it emerge, honest and untainted and real. That's why singing is so exposing, like letting someone see you with no clothes on. No, it's like letting them see your insides. I was always too tight in the solar plexus and in the throat, gripping the air like I didn't know how to let it go. Perhaps that's why I always loved the piano: the keys are at arm's length.

But with Voices from Before, I don't sing. I direct. I study the words and music to understand what the composer is trying to say, and I help the singers to say it. For instance, why does this part of the music repeat itself? Why the shift to a new key, here? You're looking to reveal the essence of a piece. Which is why, with the prospective Cavendish scholars, I wasn't necessarily looking for outstanding technique – I was looking for someone who could give me the truth.

I went down the corridor, past anxious parents fizzing around, past one inordinately punctual vocalist hunched over his sheet music (a mistake, by the way, to go over and over your piece last minute – after a certain point, the repetition muddles everything). Past the library, into the auditorium, where the other judges were already parked at a table stocked with coffee and elaborate pastries. I introduced myself gladly to each one – ruddy Bach specialist, ancient choirmaster, sallow early music expert – and we did the usual small talk, complaining about the state of arts funding, smiling about shared connections. The smile fell from my face though when I saw that someone had brought their suit carrier, ready for later, and draped it across a chair like a body bag. Black tie still makes my blood run cold.

'There's a running order,' said the choirmaster, cheerfully handing me some sheets of paper stapled at one side. Before I could reply with a 'thank you', my breath stuck completely in my chest. On the front cover of this little booklet was a photograph of Bryn. The photograph from our matriculation day, the one used by several national newspapers when they announced his death.

It was a photograph I'd always hated. In it, Bryn's shirt was stiff and clean, so unlike the rumpled reality we'd loved. His gown, neatly arranged, a deep, unspoiled black. Even at the time, I'd thought: If Bryn had known that this picture would be the one all over the press, he would have lost his shit. Who chose it? They can't have known him at all.

This was the moment I was supposed to say: *I knew him, you know, he was my best friend.* Then, if I were really being honest: *That's why his family asked me to be here today. Not because of my unremarkable musical achievements, but because they knew how much I cared about him.* But it didn't feel real. That person, in the picture? A stranger. I put the booklet face down in my lap and closed my eyes.

Fighting the rising panic, I thought about the person who got me through these hideous times. I thought about her last text message, its gorgeous mundanity – *Have fun, see you soon xx* – its two kisses at the end, an upgrade from the days when there'd been none. Wishing I could call her that very minute instead of being stuck in that stupid auditorium, I mumbled her words like a prayer to a gentler god, knowing she was the reason it had all been worth it.

~

He was right. Neither porters nor police came for us. And when, a few days after our conversation in the common room, Bryn arrived at my door asking to borrow my phone charger as if no cross words had been exchanged, I was glad. I simply shelved my perplexing memories and thanked the universe that our orbits had aligned again.

For the rest of Michaelmas term, I drew closer than ever to him and the group. Whatever my commitments at the music faculty, I made sure to be back at college for lunch each day so that I could catch up with whoever was around. I skipped rehearsals and supervisions when their timings clashed with punting trips and room parties. My friends were the constellations by which I navigated those unpredictable days, and Bryn was, naturally, my North Star.

But the incident with the porter had made me very alert to any sense of distance between me and him. Whenever he joined a group of us in the bar, I noticed if he chose a seat far from mine, leaving me straining to hear his shining voice. And I developed an immediate and intense loathing of anyone who received more than an average amount of his attention – not so much the old guard like Jamie and Sarah, but new faces, from other years or other colleges. Like that cookie-cutter blonde girl with the blinding-white grin.

Sometimes, I wouldn't see him for a day (even two or three), and though this was nothing new I reacted differently now, with frustration and anxiety. Then he'd return, and the cycle would begin again. Him, moving brightly around our circle. Me, burning, wishing that mine was the shoulder on which he lay his pale hand, that mine was the ear into which he whispered soft and low.

It was around this time that I was surprised to receive a call from Tim, asking if I'd like to go to an exhibition at the Fitzwilliam about 'Music and Mathematics'. While I was puzzled by Tim's interest in the topic, I had nothing better to do, and I met him outside the museum just as the first snowflakes of December were beginning to fall.

Despite the exhibition content, we avoided any conversation about twelve-note scales and standing waves. Instead we talked blandly about how we'd hardly seen one another all term, how the last few weeks had been so busy.

In front of some art inspired by the Fibonacci sequence, Tim pulled up. Gave me a chastising look. 'Okay, I'm calling you out.'

I stared, oblivious.

'You just said "larst" instead of "lassed". Like a southerner.'

'No I didn't.'

'Yes you did! It's not the only thing either. When we spoke earlier, you suggested we meet at half parst two.'

I rolled my eyes as we moved silently past a cross section of a human ear.

Next up, fractals and the golden section. Beside enlarged musical scores, photographs of a shell, a fossil, a lightning bolt. Tim's forehead folded, and I had a horrible feeling he was going to ask me to explain what the hell we were looking at. But when he started to speak, he stopped himself, gave an awkward cough. 'You alright?' I said.

'Yeah, fine. I've just—' He paused. 'I've got something to ask, and it might be a bit weird.'

'Er, okay.'

He looked me in the eye, his expression sober. 'Would you mind if I went out with Berenice?'

I almost laughed. 'Berenice? Wow.'

'Is it too weird? Be honest.'

'No! I just didn't expect it, that's all.'

He spread his hands, as if the situation were as mystifying to him as the exhibition. 'I didn't either. But we went to the union this week, just as mates. And she said she liked me. We've been friends for so long, and I realised … I like her too.'

I blinked, slightly stunned.

He spoke carefully. 'Would you rather I … didn't …?'

'Oh, no. I mean, yes. I mean, go for it.' I waved a hand flamboyantly. 'You have my blessing.'

Tim beamed, and I realised that, bloody hell, he really liked her. 'She said she felt our friendship had changed,' he said, an excitement in his voice that was somehow excruciating. 'That's one of the things I like about her, how she's so matter-of-fact. There's no games.'

In other words, no mystery. No magic. 'Very true,' I said.

'She's just totally herself.'

'Yep, straight down the line.'

'No drama.'

'Less rock 'n' roll, more milk and two sugars.'

He looked a little thrown. 'I didn't mean it quite like that.'

'Sorry,' I said, knowing that was a bit much. 'Bad joke.'

Tim relaxed unquestioningly back into a smile. 'Thanks for being cool about it.'

I turned to the gallery of fractals and grinned fixedly at a weird broccoli.

The room had filled up and I was getting too hot. More and more, the little bits of explanatory text on the wall were obscured by someone's bobble-hatted head. Of course I didn't mind Tim dating Berenice. I was just surprised. Maybe I felt a little foolish, too, at being so surprised. Maybe this was the kind of thing every-one else had seen coming. Tim said something else about Berenice, how she too would really appreciate my coolness. Alright, I thought, no need to go on about it.

As we walked, the crowd bunched up around us. Tim stood on my toe without realising, and I looked away to hide my frustration. A tension began to hum in my head, almost a low whistling. There was that man, the one in the hat, blocking my view again.

But this time, the sight of him sent shock pulsing through my body. The folds of skin at the nape of his neck, the fair curls, the long, lopsided posture, I'd seen these before. I'd seen them, years ago, disappearing through our front door, heading in the direction of the pub.

Then the man turned, revealing a face round and smooth-shaven, not like my dad at all. False alarm.

'But it doesn't just happen,' I said after a pause, flustered and surprised by the waver in my voice, 'does it?'

'What?'

'Relationships don't just change,' I said, sighing, feeling argu-mentative without knowing why. 'People change them.'

Tim looked uneasy. 'I guess. But people change them based on how they feel. Which is something they can't necessarily control.'

'But you don't always have to follow your feelings. Sometimes, you might feel like ending a relationship, or a friendship, when the right thing to do would be to stay and … Stick it out, in case your feelings change again. See if things get better.'

He ignored the tourists nudging us forward and gave me a long, earnest look. Jesus, it reminded me of Berenice. 'I'm not sure I follow you,' he said, softly. 'Are we talking generally, or—'

'Yes, generally.'

'Because if you don't feel okay about me and—'

'Of course I'm okay about it. I'm just saying.'

An attendant asked me to move back from one of the exhibits. In my head, I told him to piss off, but I did as I was told.

'You know,' Tim said, his earnestness maddening now, 'Berenice would never break any confidences of yours.'

This was ridiculous. But for the bare and uncontroversial fact of my dad's death, I hadn't shared any material confidences with Berenice. I imagined her, po-faced, setting out these terms to Tim like the negotiator of some fucking peace treaty, taking everything too seriously as usual, taking this opportunity to present herself as a model of honour. 'Well I'm glad Berenice has outlined how this should work,' I said.

'I'm sorry, I thought it would be okay—'

'It is okay!'

'Because, to be honest, I wasn't sure you two were ever that serious—'

'Well, now I'm completely serious,' I said, my laugh glancing sharply off the walls, 'when I say that I don't bloody care. Have fun with Berenice. Go to naff restaurants full of middle-aged bastards, eat pretentious dinners with a *small* glass of wine—'

'Mate—'

'—then go home and sneer at all the ordinary folk playing drinking games in the bar, remind yourselves that you're *far too mature* to be having fun like the rest of us knobheads.'

In the pause that followed, Tim gave me a long, searching look. As if he were meeting a TV personality and finding them smaller than expected. 'What's this about?' he asked, gently. 'You're not yourself.'

I shrugged, petulant. 'Who am I, then?' Then, unwilling to interrogate my feelings any longer, especially not in the company of someone as emotionally astute as Tim, I pushed past people towards the exit.

If I hadn't walked away from Tim that day, perhaps I would have had someone to talk to when things went bad. Someone who could say: *Fucking hell, it makes no sense whatsoever, but you might be right about this, pal.* Perhaps, if I'd had somewhere else to go, I would have drifted away from Bryn's group, like an animal sensing an electrical storm.

It doesn't matter now. I can't change what happened, which is that I allowed Tim to think that I was angry about him and Berenice. It was better than having him know the truth: that I was only ever angry at him for reminding me who I was, for proving that relationships were mutable, and for not being Bryn.

As Tim predicted, Michaelmas and Lent terms flew by, and the Easter term of our second year began in an unexpectedly cold April. Spring hid beneath the blanket of grey sky and kept hitting snooze. Students slogged up and down overcast streets, while boat crews and rugby teams tramped to and from their crusades, damp and grim. College itself seemed to huddle against the glaring skies and sudden showers, its courtyards cold and quiet, its gardens yet to bloom. In the first few weeks, many students seemed to knuckle down, spying the dark shape of exams on the horizon. I still spent an awful lot of time in the common room, determined to be there when my friends emerged from their rooms, ready for the next bar visit or pub crawl.

May brought Bryn's birthday. I'd bought a bottle of cognac that, looking at the price, must have been bloody nice, and on the chilly Sunday morning that was his birthday, I delivered it to his room. After several knocks, he finally inched open the door and I burst into song. 'Happy birthday to you, happy … You okay?'

He looked tired. And distracted, as if he'd forgotten what day it was. When I presented the parcel he looked surprised, and only held it loosely at his side. 'Thanks. You shouldn't have.'

I shook my head, *It's nothing*, thinking about the fact that I'd be on tinned soup for the rest of the month. 'So,' I said, 'birthday drinks in the bar later?'

He shrugged. 'I dunno. Alexa's taking me out for dinner.'

'So, drinks after that?'

'Maybe.'

'What do you mean, maybe? It's a celebration!'

He rubbed his hair, which stood crazily in all directions. 'I know, I know. It's just – I'm not big on birthdays.'

Actually, that was true. The previous year, we hadn't done anything to celebrate.

It was only after I'd returned to the common room that the picture came to me: my bedroom, back home, hung with balloons; my smiling mum, singing tunelessly over a home-made cake; me, staring at the little collection of cards, feeling the absence of my dad's handwriting like a physical pang. Fuck, if Bryn missed his dad, birthdays must be a special kind of torture. I should have known.

Later that afternoon, not liking to leave him alone with his sadness, I decided to pay Bryn another visit. Maybe I could cheer him up with a pint at The Eagle, or a burger at The Maypole. Imagine if I could be the person to persuade him that, you know what, birthdays are okay really. And friends can be a different kind of family.

Crossing New Court, I had to shield my face from the rain – a relentless, driving downpour – which is why I didn't see him at first. He was standing beneath the archway into Old Court, talking to that girl, the one with the blonde hair. Together, they sheltered beneath Bryn's enormous coat, noses almost touching, the girl's hand resting territorially on Bryn's waist. Both of them wearing electric smiles. I hurried on, unseen, telling myself that it was likely nothing.

But the scene had given me a creeping feeling, a rash of goose-bumps. The girl's presence seemed to have perked Bryn up immeasurably. But the 'dark' moods Alexa had experienced didn't seem to dissipate so easily. Could it be that Bryn was happier around this girl than he was around Alexa?

The breakdown of their relationship would be terrible. Not just because Alexa would be devastated, but because the world was right and solid with my friends as a couple. A split would bring about an unnatural kind of scene change – like being in a haunted house and discovering that, while your back was turned, a chair has slid across the parquet.

* * *

That evening, I messaged Bryn to see how he was getting on, but it got to half past nine and I hadn't heard from him. Deciding that he and Alexa must still be at dinner, I headed to the college bar to see if anyone was around for a pint.

The night was unexpectedly close, a night for slinging your coat over your shoulder, for throwing your windows open and watching the curtains hang still. The sky was starless, and in the lamplight the college walls glowed rosy as cheeks, bright squares gazing from those rooms whose inhabitants were at home. I felt fresh and vital and very much awake. And, for reasons I can't articulate, I didn't make my way as planned into the clamorous bar. Instead, I went on past the stairs that led up to the dining hall, under the stone arch that led into Old Court.

The night there seemed denser. But on the second floor of the south wall was a slab of light: Bryn's room. The window was open, and from it sounds fell like blossoms, laughter and music and fragments of conversation. Moving urgently, as if I were late for a supervision, I jogged around the courtyard and up S staircase, past Mona's room (I mean, the room that had once been hers) and on up to Bryn's.

It was no wonder someone had thrown open the window, because the place was heaving. On Bryn's desk was a large jug of what seemed to be a fruit punch, surrounded by wine, beer, vodka and absinthe bottles, in various states of fullness. People lay on the sofa, the bed, the floor, leaned against the walls and windowsill. I shuffled through the bodies and, finding Bryn in the centre, tapped him on the shoulder.

He looked up, surprised, and a smile found its way onto his face. 'Hey. Lex, look who's here.' Alexa, appearing from behind him, peered at me. She wore a glamorous corset dress, as if careful to respect her role as magician's assistant, and a slash of red lipstick that emphasised her stark, asymmetric charm. The only thing she lacked was a smile, wearing instead an expression of weary drunkenness.

'I heard you from outside,' I replied. 'Good dinner?'

'Oh, yeah. Great. We've just got back. These guys surprised me and, somehow ...'

He waved at the chaos and I nodded, noticing that they'd made quick work of the drinks. Then he was apologising, saying that he needed to speak to someone, someone I didn't know, and he and Alexa were folding themselves into the crowd.

Was that Jamie and Sarah in the corner? Maybe. But I couldn't get close. And everywhere else, faces I didn't recognise. No Sajid. No traybake girl. I sidled towards Bryn's desk and looked at the spread. Next to the jelly, a bowl of crisps, mostly emptied, the last shards soggied with beer. A ravaged quarter of sponge cake, furrows where fingers had skied through the white icing. I found a clean paper cup, filled it with some warm wine and watched from the sidelines. Now and then I tried to strike up conversations with other visitors to that makeshift bar, but they tended to nod politely before disappearing into the throng. The only person who initiated contact was a girl who looked as if she was going to be sick, who asked if I'd seen a blue phone.

After some time spent shuffling, largely unnoticed, from one island of people to another, I managed to join the little crowd in which Bryn was talking to a tall, tattooed girl. 'Seriously,' I heard her say, 'don't let me text him later. That's the kind of thing Drunk Me will do.'

Bryn grinned. 'Give me your phone, I'll look after it for you.'

'Fuck off, you'll text him yourself! I swear, I need someone to upload my brain into a big fucking computer and delete our whole relationship.'

'Wasn't there a movie about that?' I chipped in. 'I don't think it worked out so well.'

'It'll be possible, soon,' said Bryn, still looking at the tattooed girl. 'To upload your brain to a computer.'

'What for?' I asked.

He finally addressed me directly. 'Make you live for ever.'

'That's … cool.'

'Or horrendous. Why would anyone want to live for ever?'

I had no answer to this beyond the fact that dying seemed incontrovertibly a bad thing.

'So would you be able to delete memories?' asked the girl.

'Maybe,' Bryn replied. 'Or optimise your brain. You might implant the ability to speak French or play the piano. Or something useful.'

'Okay,' I said. 'But … is it still me?'

Bryn gave a grudging smile. 'That's the thing. It depends what you mean by "you".'

'I've got a pretty clear idea of what I mean by "me".'

'Really? So what is it, then? Are you the physical stuff of your brain? Or, if you picked up that little network of synapses and fired it up in another place, another time, would that same physical mass produce a different person?'

'Why would it?'

'Because *you* are not just a physical mass. Your self, your identity, is constantly changing, based on your interactions with the world. Especially with other people, who are also constantly changing.'

I pondered this. 'In that case,' I said, 'you're saying you're a different person from one second to the next.'

'It's a legitimate philosophy,' said the tattooed girl. Then, as if presenting from a slideshow: 'Some people see their lives as a single narrative, played out by a single self. Others think their lives are made up of multiple selves – so, although they know that five-year-old me is somehow connected to the eighteen-year-old me, they're not the same person.'

I scoffed. 'Not the same person? Seriously?'

Bryn addressed the girl. 'You know the drunk person who called your ex last night? Was that you?'

'Christ,' she said. 'In so many ways, please no.'

I shook my head. 'This sounds like a philosophical trick that lets you dodge responsibility for any stupid shit you've done in the past.'

Bryn refilled his glass as if he hadn't heard.

'How can you *not* see life as a single story?' I went on. 'We're made of our pasts. Someone might be a CEO in a big, global company, with a Porsche in the drive and a million in the bank, but if they grew up on a council estate in Burnley there's probably a part of them that will always feel working class.' I hoped Bryn would think my comment incisive, but he rolled his eyes. 'What?' I asked.

'You're obsessed.'

'With what?'

'Class.'

'Well, maybe I can't afford not to be.'

Any triumph I might have felt at scoring a point was dimmed by the look that fell across his face. I had the feeling I'd committed a faux pas, like walking into a cocktail party in cargo shorts. The last thing I wanted was to upset him, today of all days. In the bustle of the party, ours became an awkward, silent bubble.

Perhaps he was irritated by this surprise, at these people who didn't know how he truly felt about birthdays. There he was, hoping to let the day slide unremarkably by, and look at the place. A melee of organised fun. Maybe he'd appreciate a break.

'Actually, Bryn,' I said, laying a hand on his arm and attempting to lead him away from the girls. 'Mind if I talk to you for a sec?'

Under the small pressure of my palm he remained completely still. 'Sure. Go on.'

They stared at me. I stuttered. 'Actually, I meant … can we go outside …?'

Finally, he acquiesced, arching an eyebrow at his tattooed friend as he strode out, leaving me to scuttle behind.

The corridor was cool, a spring breeze coming through the windows and carrying the party sounds up and down the staircase. Two massive blokes thundered towards us and, after a cheerful exchange of back-slapping, Bryn pointed them to his room. When they were inside, he faced me.

'Well?' he said.

Suddenly wishing I'd rehearsed this, I paused. Cleared my throat. Leaned in a little, as if someone might still overhear. 'So, I er … I just wanted to check. Is everything okay with you and Lex?'

He pulled away from me, kept his expression steady. 'Why do you say that?'

'Well, I … I saw you with that girl.'

'What girl?'

Someone else came trotting up the stairs. I waited until they'd passed. 'That first year, I don't know her name. Short. Big blonde hair.'

He made no attempt to keep his voice down. 'And what did you see?'

'Um, I saw you together. Earlier, when it was raining. And you just seemed quite … close.'

'You mean, we were standing close to one another?'

'Well, yeah, but …'

'So, in other words, you saw nothing?'

I held myself very still. This conversational path suddenly seemed booby-trapped. When I spoke, my voice sounded small in the deserted hallway. 'Bryn, if there's a problem with you and Lex, I want to help. If you're honest with her—'

'What? And tell her that I have friends, some of whom are female, and that I sometimes – shock, horror – talk to them?'

'No, but if you're interested in someone else—'

'I'm interested in lots of people.'

'You know what I mean.'

'No, I don't. Is there a limit on the number of friends I'm supposed to have?'

'Of course not. No.'

The muscles at his temples shifted as he clenched his jaw, and I felt caught off guard. As if I'd been petting a dog and it had suddenly bared its teeth.

A step, towards me. His eyes moved over my face, so purposefully that it almost felt as if he were tracing my brow, my cheekbones, with the knuckle of a balled fist. Eventually he whispered, warm and close like a rush of blood to my head: 'Are you jealous?'

My laugh sounded more like a sigh. 'What?'

The pause that followed felt like the moment a coin is flipped, and I held my breath to see how the situation would land. Heat seemed to come off him in waves, pulsing like a dark heart. Very slowly he put a hand to my chest, and I flinched as if the contact burned.

At this his door swung suddenly open, and the sounds of shrieking laughter and thumping music exploded into the hallway like glitter from a party cannon. From inside the room, guests called to

Bryn, lost without him, impatient for his vitalizing company. For the first time, I was happy for him to leave me.

But he didn't. He broke into an enormous smile, began to laugh, a full body cackle that almost sent him off balance. Then, as I gaped, he grabbed me firmly by the upper arms with those strong hands, pulled me close—

—and planted a loud, extravagant kiss on my cheek.

'You are one crazy bastard,' he cried, pushing me away, wiping a manic tear from his eye. 'Must be why you like magic so much. You're always looking, looking. It's also why you're so easy to fool.'

He knocked me on the side of the head, one, two, three times, not hard, but enough to make me shrink into myself. And then he was turning, striding towards the noise and chaos of the party. I stood, stunned and stupid, ready to creep dejectedly back to my room.

But, at the threshold, Bryn glanced over his shoulder. 'Well? Come on, then.'

The kiss seemed still to sit on my cheek. It tingled, like the feathery touch of a dandelion clock. Or a bite from the tiny teeth of a stinging nettle. Bryn disappeared back into his room and I – part relieved, part uneasy – followed as instructed.

The party smog was worse than ever, a cloud of body heat, alcohol fumes, cigarette smoke. A bottle in each hand, Bryn made his way through the crowd – which parted ahead of him like a great sea – topping up glasses as he went. Alexa lay on the bed looking more miserable than ever, her long tangled limbs and vacant expression making the scene look like a high-fashion photoshoot. I wanted to see if she was okay, but after my conversation with Bryn it would be foolish to have him see us speaking secretively. Did she too feel that something was seriously wrong? And if so, why hadn't she told me? Forlorn, I grabbed a plastic cup and filled it almost to the brim.

Having completed a circuit of the room, Bryn clapped his hands, gestured for someone to turn the music down. As if a curtain had been lifted, there was his performance face: luminous, all eyes and teeth. 'Okay,' he announced. 'Time for some magic.'

Sparks of excitement now, as people crowded in around him, murmurs of bubbling delight. Even the lights seemed to lower in expectation. Silence fell. Perhaps this would put the evening back on an even keel.

'Let me tell you a story,' Bryn said, 'about a man. A man named Pops.'

Everywhere, eyes shone with glee.

'Pops was a decent bloke. But he was always getting into scrapes. Because' – here he shaped his hand around an invisible cup, made a tipping motion – 'he was partial to a drink.'

The wine I'd just guzzled, desperately, suddenly tasted sour.

'One day, Pops was asked to guard a safe. Full of money.' Bryn took a coin from his pocket, held it up for us to see. Then he motioned to me, his finger curling, sinuous like an animal's tail: *Come here.* I looked hopefully around to see whether he might be directing his attention at someone else. But no, it was me he wanted.

While the crowd murmured expectantly, I stepped tentatively forward, through the sea of bodies until I was by his side. When all was still again Bryn dropped the coin into my palm. On one side of it, a face grinned. On the other, the same face growled. Realising I was supposed to inspect the coin for the benefit of the audience, I turned it over, checked it was solid. Satisfied, with the coin at least, I returned it to Bryn's palm.

'But while he was working, Pops' friend came along,' he continued, in a sing-song voice. 'The friend said, Pops, have a drink with me. And Pops said …'

Then, in a terrible northern accent: 'Ee, lad, bugger off and let me be.'

Everyone laughed, rowdily. Except for me. Had Bryn forgotten what I'd told him, about my dad? He can't have realised what he was saying.

'But the friend said, Go on. So Pops had a little drink. And another. And another.'

He gestured at our glasses. One by one, people began to down their drinks, messily, wine and beer tracking down their chins and onto their clothes.

'When he finally woke up, his friend was gone. And the money?'

He held the coin in front of my face, leaned towards it, and blew.

Suddenly I was blinded, coughing, people were shouting. My eyes burned and I rubbed at them, frantic, and whenever I opened my mouth it was filled with something dry, acrid. I gasped, grasped at nothing, feeling the crowd pull away like a retreating wave. In my sightless state, the cries of the room seemed even more dramatic. They fell quickly away into a taut, horrified silence.

When I could finally blink my eyes open, I caught sight of Bryn's dark mirror. There, something awful looked back: grotesque, goggling eyes, a wide, pink mouth. Monstrous. But it was my own face covered in a kind of thick, grey dust. Perhaps I was the only one who saw it, but I looked like a coal miner, emerging filthy from the mouth of a pit. Or something dead – ashen and mummified.

People held themselves away from me, pointing. The quiet was like that of a classroom when a teacher is about to dish out a bollocking, way more mortifying than laughter. As I brushed uselessly at my ruined T-shirt, Bryn did a little bow.

In those ignominious seconds, my instinct seemed to fail, and I had to decide how to react. Was I going to challenge him? In front of his friends, on his birthday? What if I'd read the situation all wrong, and it was a genuine mistake? The silence stretched out, waiting for my reaction.

After a beat, I burst out laughing. At that, everyone else did too.

Then I slapped Bryn on the shoulder, making sure to get some of the mess onto his expensive shirt. 'You absolute dickhead!'

He grinned, slapped me back. 'Try not to get it in your mouth, it might be a little bit toxic.'

'Shit, really?'

'Of course not, you knob.'

Strangers touched my skin, inspected the dusty tips of their fingers. Laughed, loudly, made me recount the moment the coin had seemingly exploded. That irritating blonde girl – yes, she was there – made me describe exactly what I'd seen of Bryn's hands as they moved in front of my face. But as soon as I could manage, I dashed out of the room and down the stairs, praying not to bump into anyone on the way.

The whole time, I tried to persuade myself: *Sure, nobody chooses to be the stooge, but the performance doesn't exist without him.* At least we'd been a double act again. The trouble was, deep down, I no longer felt like I was in on the joke.

On shaking legs, I stumbled back to my room. Inside, I retrieved a bottle of gin from my cupboard, drank two huge gulps, then threw myself into my armchair and waited for my heart to stop pounding. A strange, swirling feeling in my gut told me that we'd crossed a line somehow, stepped outside a salt circle. He wasn't feeling down, not about his dad or anything else. But he was angry, now that I'd said those things about him and Alexa. Furious, that I'd poked my nose into his business.

But this is what happens with friends, I told myself. You have difficult conversations and, in the end, they bring you closer. True, I never had conversations like that with Gaz or Ben or Reedy. Not even with Tim. But that's because, honestly, those friends didn't mean so much to me. I felt sure we'd speak later, Bryn would apologise for overreacting, he'd explain that I was right, actually, that things had in fact been going awry, but he and Alexa were fine now, thank goodness I intervened. Balance restored.

Still shaky, I made for my little washbasin and looked at myself in the mirror. Christ, what a state. I scrubbed hard at my face, eyes squeezed shut against the soap suds, streaking the little enamel washbasin with grey. It took a few goes to get rid of the dust, followed by a final rub around the sides of my nose, the underside of my chin. What the hell was this stuff, anyway?

As I stared at my reflection, something moved over my shoulder.

I gasped and spun, frantic.

It had seemed as if a shadow, long and thin, had slipped out of the darkness behind me and across the room. But my door was shut, locked. With my back to the sink now, I looked from bed to desk to piano, everywhere in between, searching crazily for the slightest movement. But there was nothing. No knot of limbs folded into the corner, nothing tucking itself behind my armchair. Cautiously, I lowered myself to my knees. Nothing under the coffee table, nothing under my bed. Maybe it really had been a shadow, caused by a light moving beyond my window? Fuck, I must be losing it.

I became aware of a sound, one I had to strain to hear. It was low and brittle and very insistent. A kind of hissing. Or a scratching. Careful not to make a noise, I took slow, cautious steps across the carpet, listening at corners and bits of furniture as I went. All the while, that strange dry scratch. It seemed louder near my piano. There couldn't be anything behind my piano, could there? Surely not inside it? Touching a hand to the instrument, lightly, as if taking its pulse, I leaned in. Held my breath.

There it was. The scratching was an unbroken loop, as if a circle were being carved into the piano's insides. Or was it more like the low, insistent crackle of a fire? No, not quite that. It reminded me of something, but I couldn't think what. Uncanny, like a sound that belonged somewhere else. I thought then of Kenny, floundering in Bryn's cellar, and I had the feeling of time rushing backwards – I was suddenly a child, and all I wanted was for a grown-up to come and put things right.

But nobody was coming. Hands trembling now, I eased open the piano lid, just a crack at first, little by little. As I peered into the belly of the instrument, searching between the bony hammers and strings, the scratching went on, uninterrupted, louder now. But there was something else, below that weird frictional sound. Something staccato. Something alive.

Was that *laughter*?

I cried out, and the piano lid slipped from my fingers, falling shut with a force that made the strings ring glassy and chill. Stumbling backwards, I grasped at my armchair as if the floor might fall away from under my feet. The whole room seemed to shiver with something like incredulity, or expectation, or dread. What was that?

Who was that?

I threw myself out of my room and staggered down the corridor. The door had slammed behind me before the piano's ghostly harmonics had stopped ringing.

I didn't know whether Mona would be checking her Cambridge email any more, or whether it was even live. So I got her Hotmail from one of her college friends, on the pretext that I had some CDs of hers that I needed to return.

It wasn't an easy email to write. Fixed on the digital page, the words could come back at me any time, so I had to tread carefully. That's why I didn't explicitly mention the night she'd refused to sleep in her room (what could I have said, anyway? What tangible, concrete things could I have said about the feeling I'd had, the dark and frightful feeling that I should get out of there as fast as I could, that the place was rotten and soiled and possibly dangerous?). I certainly didn't mention her horrifying appearance at the bop, or the thoughts that had emerged later like a dark continent on the horizon, crazy thoughts that explained the chalice, the tin of teeth and hair.

Instead, I said something vague. That I was aware she'd had a tricky time at college. That I was possibly experiencing something similar and wondered whether she could tell me more about what she'd been through. At the end, I added a kiss. Then I deleted it, deciding that Mona might think I was taking the piss.

What did I expect from her? What, honestly, were the chances of her telling me: You're right, I think Bryn might have put some sort of a hex on us, we must bring it up with the dean. Maybe I hoped that Mona – so clever and so capable – would have the evidence to prove or disprove my fledgling theory. Evidence, like my knowledge about the porter, that might somehow come in handy if I ever needed to protect myself.

Or maybe I just wanted to feel like I wasn't alone.

And, in fact, I wasn't alone. Because Alexa was having trouble with Bryn too. At formals, she'd glare at him as he conjured coins for yet another pretty dinner guest, her expression weary in the candlelight. In room parties, she'd squeeze herself between him and other girls just to stop his pickpocketing fingers lingering on pale necks relieved of scarves, on delicate wrists freed from bracelets and watches. I saw her shifting, softening at the edges: swapping her chipped nail varnish for neat manicures, flattening her natural waves with hair straighteners. Not that it helped.

Bryn and Alexa even went through a phase of arguing in public corners, but it didn't last long. Even if Bryn hadn't started out as the bigger, stronger character in every way, Alexa shrank a little with every exchange, afraid of pushing him too hard. I wondered, if Bryn was unhappy with Alexa, why didn't he just break up with her? Because he was not the type to relinquish things. He was the type to possess them. Why would he do the decent thing and release Alexa when he could have his cake and eat it (and get a second slice, on the house)?

Once, during a particularly raucous night when Bryn had been carrying girls up and down his staircase in the manner of a fireman, I saw Alexa in a doorway, her eyes rubbed red. Wrapped in someone else's limbs, Bryn saw it too. And I watched, horrified, as he turned from her with a look of pure disdain. I'd seen that look before. It reminded me of weird fragments: a curse delivered on a disrespectful party guest, a trembling figure descending into a cellar, a room with an extra lock on the door.

I thought of Alexa's warmth and wit, her dark, expressive eyes. Her imperfectly lovely smile. These were things that could make you feel ten feet tall, so it would be an extraordinary man to treat them so carelessly. But that's exactly what Bryn was. Extraordinary. Careless. I wondered when carelessness might tip into a more conscious kind of cruelty.

I also thought about my dad, about one of the times when he was boomeranging from home to dosshouse and back again, from being a man in recovery to being a man in freefall. He was back at home, eating properly, being decent to Mum. Then, one afternoon, when she was out, he told me he was going out to do a few jobs. Maybe the garden centre or the tip. And I knew, no ghost of a doubt, that he was going to come home drunk. There was nothing concrete to suggest this: there he was, looking nice and tidy in his polo shirt and clean jeans, his eyes still bright, the house keys that had only recently been returned to him swinging around one finger. But I had the same feeling I had now: that, while I couldn't say what, something was very, very wrong.

III

The first few auditions were pretty average. They included two sopranos singing the same Bach aria, both technically accurate but bland, and a kid singing Vaughan Williams as if he were rattling off the items on his shopping list. After an hour and a half, I was relieved to arrive at the gap in our schedule designated a 'comfort break'.

Sipping from my own reusable cup, so as to avoid the lukewarm coffee from the dispenser, I thought about the students still fretting outside the hall. Offering yourself up to another person, only for them to say, *Thanks, but no thanks.* It's hard. In any case, judges can be wrong. Had the first singer really played fast and loose with the phrasing, or was hers a more interesting reading of the music than I'd given her credit for? One of the hardest things about judging is staying open-minded – hearing a piece as if for the first time, rather than being disappointed when it's not how you think it should be.

Back in our seats, we called in the next applicant. Through the doors came a stooping boy, his rigid smile an unconvincing show of confidence. He raised his arm as if to wave, but then thought better of it, flapping weakly like a broken bird.

'Hello there,' said the choirmaster. 'Joseph, is it?'

'Yes,' Joseph replied, nodding hard.

'Good to meet you. You've come from Bolton?'

'Er, yeah.'

'Quite a journey.'

Joseph didn't know what to say to that. I thought of myself, arriving at Cambridge, not yet knowing all the things that were wrong with the way I spoke, the way I walked.

'And what will you be singing for us, Joseph?'

'"Is My Team Ploughing?", by George Butterworth.'

I couldn't have been more taken aback if Joseph had approached the judges, held my face in his hands and kissed me on the mouth. Blinking, I scanned the running order again, wondered how I'd never noticed. Was this really such a popular audition piece? To hear it now, here. Of all places.

A laugh bubbled through my lips, and faces turned to me, perplexed. Reddening, I pretended to cough, thumped myself on the chest. How strange. I wanted to announce: This was mine and Bryn's, you know. What we performed for the fellows, back when I still didn't realise who (what) he was. I might even have whispered it to my fellow judges, had they not already turned their eyes back to Joseph, who, along with our accompanist, was fussing with some rumpled sheet music. I rubbed my forehead and my fingers came away slightly damp.

Then a chord rang from the piano – infinitely gentle, as if it came from very far away – and that falling, melancholy melody was upon me.

Is my team ploughing,
That I was used to drive

I've seen a lot of singers in my life. I know how they transform themselves during a performance, how they can make you forget who they really are. But, as this boy sang, it was as if someone else inhabited his body. It wasn't just his facial expressions or the way he held himself. I mean he seemed to change, right in front of us. As his voice sounded, a whisper that somehow found its way across the hall, his frame somehow became more insubstantial until I could see the ghost: thin and wan, like mist over a river, asking after those who now work the horse and plough without him. It sounds ridiculous but, as he swayed in the spotlight, the light almost seemed to travel through his limbs. I told myself it was just the shock. I hadn't expected the song, and I certainly hadn't expected such a performance from poor, meek Joseph.

In the next stanza he was taller, broader, his voice rich and powerful. Here, the still-living friend, reassuring the ghost that, yes, the team is working and the horse's harness jingles still. The two characters, in one body. Joseph shone so brightly that the space around him seemed peculiarly dark now, and I found myself looking around to see if someone was dimming the house lights. Feeling my heart beginning to race against the pulse of the music, I gulped at the air. Something felt queasily wrong, almost as if the harmonies beneath the melody were darker, thicker. But no, our accompanist was note perfect.

Then the third stanza, the ghost returned again. As if the moments of my life had been reshuffled, I felt my fingers dancing over the keys, in that rehearsal room that wasn't a rehearsal room. Time was a repeated bass line, going around and around. My heart thumped so loudly that I thought the other judges must hear it, when I realised: there was a colour in the voice, a gravity that didn't come from this ordinary boy. A magic, playful but powerful. It wasn't possible. And yet, trembling, I knew it to be true: this was

Bryn's voice, sounding now. These were the exact turns and shapes he'd made with the music, the tugging at the tempo that we'd practised over and over, burned into our brains. It was beautiful and horrible all at once. I wanted to grab the judges, shake them and shout, Don't you hear him? But of course they didn't, they'd never heard that otherworldly baritone. I could do nothing but sit, fixed in my chair, while the whole room acted as if there was nothing wrong.

The ghost – Joseph, Bryn, I no longer knew – now turned to me, its gaze so livid and insistent that I couldn't blink. Its questioning was mock-mournful:

Is my friend hearty,
Now I am thin and pine,
And has he found to sleep in
A better bed than mine?

My lips moved helplessly along to the reply:

Yes, lad, I lie easy,
I lie as lads would choose;
I cheer a dead man's sweetheart,
Never ask me whose.

At the fringe of my awareness were the other judges, their faces angled away from me. I was suddenly deeply frightened that if they turned towards me their faces might not be their faces at all.

A dead man's sweetheart.

Over the years, there have been so many times when I've thought: He's come for me. In the crowded pub, a shape appearing in flashes between overheated bodies. On the bus home from a concert, a body in the corner with its back turned. I'd always been wrong. But here, in this haunted place, there was no mistaking those penetrating, familiar eyes and, as I looked into them, the room at the edges of my vision became undulating ribbons of blackness, a suggestion of endless space.

I made my silent retaliation: Did you ever think that maybe you didn't deserve her? Yes, you were witty and talented and charming and, truly, worshipped. But you were also selfish and cruel and thoughtless, and you got away with it because you lived according to your own rules. There was always someone ready to catch you if you fell.

No. I'm sorry. My phrasing was careless, I didn't mean—

Why was the piano still playing? This song should be finished by now. Beneath the ringing chords was something low and harsh and insistent, as if some of the strings were broken. As if something were chuckling.

I did the right thing, I went on, repeating the idea like a desperate mantra. *I know you wanted her, but that's not how the story was meant to end and you know it.* The ghost-man-child stared at me, unmoving, the darkness around him like a vacuum into which all air and light was sucked, and I thought: I'm going to lose it, right now, in front of everyone, I'm going to scream.

And then the room was still again, the auditorium lights soft. Silence.

Actually, not quite silence. There: a soft tapping.

Desperately trying to slow my breath, I realised that the other judges really were staring at me now. The cup I'd been raising to my lips when Joseph began to sing was hanging limply from my fingers, dripping onto the carpet, the liquid landing with a delicate *pat pat pat*. Crashing back into the present, I fumbled to right the cup, while Joseph hurried out to a chorus of 'thank yous'. The choirmaster asked me whether I needed to get some air, as I was looking rather pale, and I leapt up, grabbed my bag. Thank fuck I always had a bottle of brandy stashed in there, in case I ever needed to add something stronger to my coffee.

Outside, sweating beneath an overcast sky, I thought of the Three Musketeers. The ghosts of Christmas past, present and yet to come. The three wishes in *The Monkey's Paw* and their perfect, terrible fulfilment. In my head came the Latin, *omne trium perfectum* – every group of three is complete – and I cursed myself for ever imagining that the story could have gone on without him.

~

As May bled into June, Alexa and I kept up our walks back to college after rehearsals, and even the drizzliest strolls were high points in my week. Not simply because they were a reminder that I wasn't alone in worrying about Bryn. Alexa took me out of my disquiet, somehow, making me feel less like myself. Even when troubled, she retained her self-effacing grace, her quirky beauty, and I imagined that, when people saw us together, they saw these qualities reflected in me.

We'd crossed the bridge on Silver Street, the river slipping like a great eel below us, and Alexa had let our conversation fall into yet another extended pause. 'Are you okay?' I asked. 'You seem a bit quiet.'

She shook her head. 'It's no big deal.'

'So there *is* something?'

For a few seconds, the only sound was the rattle of our instrument cases (hers a replacement, after the incident at Trinity) and the wet thump of our tread. When it came, Alexa's voice was quiet, as if it didn't want to be heard. 'I had a difficult chat with Bryn.'

'Want to talk about it?'

She took time to find the words. 'He's been distant all term. I know he's stressed about work. But sometimes I call him and he doesn't answer or call back. I know you'll say this is pretty standard, which it is. But it shouldn't be. Not when he's been so ... up and down. He knows I worry about him. You know?'

Her faith in him made me shiver. After his birthday, I no longer believed this bollocks about dark moods, about Bryn being up and down. To me it sounded more like he was irritable with Alexa, making excuses to see less of her (behaviour I couldn't understand at all). Of course, there was the worrying question of what he might do if she challenged him. Would she spot something in her mirror too, something shifting silently between the bookcases in her bedroom? I sneaked a look at her freckles, like a sky of dark stars, at her eyes, which shone like faraway planets – at least, when she was happy – and felt very afraid for her.

'I told him that he shouldn't just disappear, not when ...' She paused. 'But he got angry and said I didn't understand. We couldn't agree on anything, and it was just ... It was horrible.'

'What's he up to tonight?'

'Out with some friends at King's.'

I nodded. 'So he's okay when he's out having drinks with his mates.'

She tried and failed to hold back a frown. 'I guess it's cheering him up.'

I suddenly felt terribly sorry for Alexa. Her devotion seemed such a prize – how many guys would kill to date a girl like her? Funny, clever, adorable? But Bryn held this prize carelessly, always wanting more, more. And the infuriating thing was, there would always *be* more for someone like him. I thought again of the porter's cracked head.

'Lex,' I said, thinking how fragile she looked as she hunched against the cold, 'are you happy?'

She slowed to a stop, gave me a curious look. 'This isn't about me.'

'Of course it is.'

'He needs my support.'

'And you need his.'

'Yeah, but right now—'

'Lex,' I said, firmly, 'Bryn is a great guy. But he's all about him. That need of his to be centre stage, it's why he's amazing and it's also why he's a nightmare. We let him have the spotlight because we enjoy the show. But he has responsibilities to you too.' Before she could say more, I held out my hands and presented my last words with a flourish, as if I were revealing the last step in a quadratic equation or pulling a pink-eyed rabbit from a top hat: 'Don't forget *you*.'

We stood in silence while the wind slipped between us. Alexa ducked further into the upturned collar of her coat, like an animal retreating into its burrow. Then, eyes on the pavement, she set off down the street. I wondered whether I'd sounded unsympathetic or disloyal, and I jogged to catch up with her, ready to backpedal. But when I touched her shoulder she nodded and, to my relief, gave a frail smile. 'I know, I know,' she said, sounding tired. 'Thank you.'

Don't forget you.

If he'd challenged me, I would have argued: I never said anything specific. I merely put an idea out there and invited Alexa to interpret it as she saw fit. My words were like Tarot cards or horoscopes: things that appear to bring foresight but really uncover the knowledge already inside us. Things with more power than we give them credit for.

On my next visit to the computer room, I got the email I'd been waiting for. It was a bit formal ('Dear … Regards …', that kind of thing). In very few words, Mona explained that she'd found that Cambridge wasn't for her. She hoped I'd have a better experience, wished me all the best for the future, and attached a link to a web page of local counsellors. She didn't ask any questions or encourage a reply. She didn't put a kiss at the end. It was as if she'd opened the door, with the security chain still attached, and was now closing it, politely but firmly.

There was something about the tone that I didn't buy. Something evasive in its brevity, even fearful. It was like a line written by a PR company, designed to discourage further questioning. Perhaps she was scared to tell me what she really thought, in case I told everyone she was crazy. Or maybe she was scared to talk about Bryn in case he found out.

Bathed in the blue light of the screen, I tapped out my reply. I gently offered that, far from the experience suggesting any mental weakness on Mona's part, it might be driven by darker forces (occult felt too strong at this stage). I told her that things had been strange lately, and there were lots of things that I wouldn't previously have believed that now seemed to make sense. Being as direct as I dared, I asked her: did she have cause to be frightened of anyone?

The next day my inbox contained a stern message, from an unfamiliar address that turned out to belong to Mona's father. He suggested that I not contact her again, and I felt I'd be unwise not to comply.

*   *   *

Over the following days, I tried to focus on work. Too ashamed to go creeping back to Tim and his friends, I stayed in my room, puzzling over essay questions that I would probably have understood better had I shown up to the lectures. But the rhythm I'd found so easily in those first-year study sessions was gone, my flow unpractised. In any case, I was distracted by a low, simmering anxiety – for some reason I kept checking that my window was properly locked, that my electrical sockets were clicked 'off', as if they might inexplicably spark and set my room alight.

One night I was working late, fretting over a four-part fugue that should have been submitted days beforehand, when there was a hammering at my door. The noise almost made me fall out of my chair. From beyond the room, a voice: 'It's me.'

Opening the door, I felt an inexplicable relief. 'Alexa, hey.'

She beamed, that charming, crooked smile. In one hand was a large, unopened bottle of vodka.

'Wow,' I said. 'Having a big night?'

She raised her other hand to display a similarly enormous quantity of rum. 'Didn't know which you'd prefer.'

'Wait, what?'

'Don't pretend you're working.'

She strode inside and dumped the bottles on my coffee table, shook out her hair. It was wavy, my favourite style of hers even then. 'I wanted to say thanks,' she said, taking tumblers from my shelf, giving them a subtle wipe. 'For what you said. About me and Bryn.'

'Oh. I mean, I didn't say much of anything.'

'You did, and it got me thinking. I spoke to him, about how he's been acting. I told him he was being unfair.' She lifted the rum, I shrugged an *Okay then* and she poured a preposterous amount into each tumbler, the bottle clinking unsteadily against the rims. We chinked, a muted cheers.

'So what did he say?'

'That I'm being unreasonable, that I don't get it.'

'Shit. Was he angry?'

She nodded. 'But I was too. I told him I wouldn't stand for it. And that was it.'

'What do you mean?'

'I mean, we ended it.'

She downed the rum and immediately refilled her glass.

I tried not to show how relieved I felt, how certain I was that Alexa was now safer than before. 'Fuck, Lex. Are you okay?'

'That's the thing,' she laughed, loudly. 'I feel fine.' Then, her hands fluttering like frightened birds: 'I've been released.'

I smiled, tentatively. 'So should I be offering congratulations instead of commiserations?'

'Ha, maybe. Either way, the least you can do is have a drink with me.'

In a spirit of solidarity, I downed my drink. She laughed, and it made me feel useful.

Alexa looked so different that night. Her whole body seemed to sing with a kind of fractious energy – it was as if, at any moment, she could make her excuses and dart out of the room. But she didn't. She stayed for hours, pouring ever larger drinks that didn't seem to dull her sparkling expressions, both of us preternaturally cheerful. Even though I'd come to think it for the best, I'd expected to feel sadness at the ending of Bryn and Alexa's relationship. But I felt glad. And I thought it spectacularly right when she leaned forward and lifted her hand to my cheek.

In a way, Bryn was the one who brought us together. The idea flashed through my head even as she touched her lips to mine.

* * *

Alexa stayed over that night. But we didn't do anything beyond kiss. Going from friends to lovers felt like meeting all over again, a strange backwards step, and we moved slowly to protect the friendship that mattered so much to both of us.

Once we'd gone to bed, I lay with my eyes open, my body curved behind Alexa as she slept. At one point I reached to touch her dark hair, but stopped myself, looking in wonderment at the movement of my own hand. Pulsing with satisfaction and pride, I had the feeling of being in someone else's body, in someone else's bed. How gorgeously strange, to be the kind of man who dated the kind of girl like Alexa.

But when sleep finally came, it was troubled and strange. I dreamed I was lying in my bed, on my back, staring into the near-total blackness. Except Alexa wasn't there. And there was a foul smell in the room, something burnt and filthy. I realised, slowly, that on the ceiling above me was a shape. It was big, at least the size of a person, flattened and completely still. However long and hard I looked, my eyes wouldn't adjust, and I had only a sense of arms or legs (or a tail, for all I knew). I lay there, too confused to be afraid, distracted by the soft sound of breathing: was that mine?

In the dream, I tried to move. But I realised with terror that my whole body was paralysed. I couldn't cry out either, not even as the shape began to descend, extremely slowly, towards me, hanging impossibly in the air like a spider on an invisible thread. As the thing came closer, it moved into a bank of starlight, and I saw small bright spots in what might be a head. Eyes, perhaps, or teeth. Too many to count.

My body jolted as if I'd been electrocuted.

Alexa rustled around in the duvet. 'What the hell?' she said, shifting irritably.

I rubbed my face, surprised by the dawn that was already creeping through the gap in my curtains, head woozing from the booze of the night before. In the smallness of the bed I tried not to touch Alexa with my clammy skin. The rustling of her feet beneath the covers sounded like someone sighing beyond the window. 'Sorry. I was dreaming.'

'You're a terrible sleeper.'

'I'm not usually.' I settled back into the pillow. Then shivered. 'What are you doing?'

She frowned. 'What?'

'That scratching. With your toes.'

'I'm not doing anything.'

'There. You're doing it now.'

'It's not me!'

'Can't you hear it? Scratching? On the sheets?'

We were quiet for a moment. Then she leapt up and sprinted across the room, brushing frantically at her legs. 'What is it?' she cried, not daring to look. 'Is there something there?'

Mouth mossy with rum, I stood and threw the bedsheets back. I tried to look controlled as I told her: Don't panic, Lex, it's just a mouse. Go outside and I'll take care of it. I wasn't trying to look like a hero. It was just easier than explaining that there was no mouse – and that, when I leaned in close, I could hear the unceasing scratching that had previously come from my piano, only now it was coming from deep inside my bed.

Yes. By this point, I *did* want Alexa and Bryn to break up. I saw how he'd tired of her charms, how their relationship was potentially becoming dangerous. And I'd finally realised how I felt, in her company. I just hadn't expected the aftermath of the split to involve me so directly.

The morning after she stayed over, I suggested to Alexa that we keep things between us a secret. Just for a bit. I said something about how it would be nicer to avoid people's inquisitorial stares and intrusive questions but, in truth, I had to work out how to reveal all this to Bryn gently. How to explain that it wasn't a betrayal, rather the result of powerful forces beyond mine or Alexa's control. Did I want to avoid his fury, or did I think I could maintain his favour too? There must be some mystic combination of words, arranged in just the right order, that could smooth things over.

When Alexa left my room – quickly, quietly, careful not to attract the attention of anyone who might realise that she was still wearing clothes from the night before – I told her that I'd be busy at the faculty for the rest of the day. And when she was gone, I turned my phone off and hid in the library, reading, dozing and listening to CDs on my Discman. Now and again, I ran through the logic in my head like a lawyer practising my closing arguments: that Alexa had already broken up with Bryn by the time I kissed her and, when you thought about it, she and I were a better fit anyhow. All three of us would be happier this way, in the end. The more I repeated these ideas, the more I believed he could even be pleased for us.

But when night came and I curled myself uncomfortably into the library sofa, I had a feeling that I was approaching something: a great corporeality, a land not yet drawn in any atlas. A dark place already visited by Sajid, Kenny. Mona (who I'd discovered drooling and fretful in this exact spot).

And as the sun set, I couldn't stop my mind from revisiting those indecipherable words, spoken softly by Bryn in the moments before the porter's body hit the floor.

* * *

The next day, I got an email from college apologising for the issues in my room, reassuring me that a thorough inspection would be carried out and offering alternative accommodation in the meantime. I was baffled by this until I discovered that Alexa, well-regarded by college staff, had bumped into the bursar in New Court and complained passionately about my pest situation. I was quite pleased with the plan at first. I mean, maybe college would discover that it *was* mice? But then I realised where I was being sent: to the room previously occupied by Mona, directly below Bryn.

I moved rooms that evening, when the sky was turning from a bright lavender to a heavy plum. Bearing a rucksack of essentials and a box of books and folders, I crossed New Court and passed underneath the archway into the fragile quiet of Old Court. With every step, my body tensed in anticipation of meeting Bryn who, shamefully, I still hadn't texted. But there was no sign of him. Once I'd shouldered open 'my' door, I dumped my things in the middle of the carpet and looked around.

Everywhere, blank. The room seemed surprisingly cold without Mona's floral duvet set, her slippers tucked under the bed, the neatly stacked notebooks and the calculator aligned just so beside them. It made me kind of sad. She'd been so proud to be accepted by Cambridge, had told us all how she'd dreamed of it for years. Now it was like she'd never been here at all.

Actually, that wasn't quite true. Because there, on the wall, were ghostly marks where Mona's extra lock had been removed. I thought of Bryn, one hand taking an apple from her hair, the other hovering inexplicably around her pocket. As I set pants, deodorant, drinks and glasses in their temporary homes, that story came to me again, the story of the man planting little written curses on his enemies. I listened for movement above my head. Was he up there? If so, was he listening too?

Before the kiss with Alexa, I was the guy who went along with everyone else: No, you choose where to meet, no, you pick the time, no, I'll fit in with you, you, you. I was the runner on a film set or the roadie on tour, there to help others shine, and people valued me for knowing my place. Which is why, when I thought of what I'd say to Bryn, I felt an overwhelming impulse to grovel: *I'm sorry that this hurts you, to be honest I don't even want to enjoy it.*

But I was a different person now, and part of me didn't want to apologise. Bryn hadn't been good to Lex. He treated her like he treated everything else, without care or grace. The idea that he might still want her, in spite of his flirtations and falsehoods, and that this might cause him to be angry with me – his level of entitlement had surely reached new and giddy heights.

While I awaited a pest update, I spent as little time as possible in my temporary room. I washed and changed there. And (having been evicted from the sofa by a concerned librarian) I slept there, or at least I lay fretting in the dark before a few hours' fitful dozing at dawn.

I suppose I could have asked to stay with Alexa. But, still feeling our fledgling relationship to be a bird that might flit at any moment, I didn't dare make such a big move. And I felt uncomfortable asking her to stay over with me – imagine us there, clasping one another like terrified animals while Bryn moved predatorily somewhere above us. So, outside of orchestra practice, we saw each other only in the college bar or in hall. There, I'd wait until those around us were distracted before adjusting a strand of Alexa's hair, before taking her pale hand briefly in mine.

A couple of evenings later, I had a concert at the faculty. So by the time I got back to college, the June sky was dark, only a dash of pink at its hem. Keeping my head down, as was my custom now, I dashed across Old Court as if I were trying out for track and field, my bassoon case clunking painfully at my thigh. But when I clattered through the double doors and into the corridor, something made me stutter to a stop.

The door to my room was slightly open.

Tiny, cold feet seemed to tiptoe down my spine. There were no bedders going in and out of rooms to make beds and empty bins, not at this time, and nobody else would have keys. In the soft, spring shadows, my terror seemed inappropriate. But the uncharacteristic warmth of the evening couldn't dissipate the underlying chill, the unsteady and unnatural feeling that I'd had when I'd found Mona standing in this same spot. With the tips of my fingers, I gave the door a push and watched it swing silently open.

Inside, the room was sombre, thanks to the tightly drawn curtains. A faint glow from the courtyard's lamps fought its way between them, falling over the desk and sharpening the edges of my books, my toilet bag, my displaced belongings. From my little radio came the low murmur of strings and piano (unmistakeable, the Andante from Shostakovich's Piano Concerto No. 2). And in my armchair was Bryn, hands folded across his chest, legs lazily crossed in his usual fashion. Much of his face was in shadow, as if the light itself didn't dare touch it without permission. His angles, his grace, his gravity – it was elemental. He was as splendid as fire, or the sea, and every bit as terrifying.

He leaned forward to show a full smile, the kind they call devastating.

'Hi mate,' he said.

'Hi,' I replied, my voice like a lackey, low and creeping. When I stepped reluctantly inside the room, the door fell shut behind me, the sound like a single, rueful 'tut'.

'So, we're neighbours now?' he asked, innocently.

'Just for a bit.'

'Well, I hope my music doesn't disturb you. Because if it does, I'm afraid I'm going to do fuck all about it.'

We stared at each other. Then he gave an explosive laugh.

'Only kidding,' he said. 'It'll be great. Keep your friends close, hey?'

I nodded, vaguely. 'How ... did you get in?'

'Thought we could have a welcome drink,' he said, holding up one of my glasses, filled with something red. 'I made a start, hope you don't mind.'

I moved towards the sofa – slowly, as if careful of quicksand – and lowered myself onto its elderly springs. I picked up a glass I'd abandoned on the floor, still shimmering with the dregs from my last serving, and poured myself a very large measure from the bottle Bryn had opened: an expensive port that I'd planned to share with my friends on a special occasion. I felt the distance between us, yawning like a great mouth. With teeth.

He raised his own glass, brightly, in a wordless toast. I copied him, but where his body was bright and buoyant, mine was sagged and heavy, a warped reflection in a funhouse mirror. 'So. How's things?' he asked, his tone aggressively pleasant.

'Oh, fine.'

'That's not what it sounds like.'

My insides tipped and rolled. 'How do you mean?'

He gestured around the room. 'Well, here you are. Out of your natural environment.'

I shrugged as casually as I could manage. 'There might be an infestation in my room. College is looking into it.'

'Yeah, I know,' he said, his expression congenial and bland. 'Alexa flagged it, right?'

Fuck. Did he know? About us?

But how would he know? Alexa wouldn't have said anything. Maybe it was one of the college staff. The porters and chaplains and bursars all loved him, gossiped with him as if he were one of them.

'You see,' he said, 'nothing gets past me.'

I could no longer appear nonchalant, not with my hands shaking, sweat tracking behind my ear. Fuck. He definitely knew. This was it, the conversation I'd been practising in my head all this time.

'Bryn,' I said, carefully, 'I've been meaning to talk to you.'

He gazed around the room as if he hadn't heard. 'It's weird, isn't it? What are the chances?'

'What?'

He shuddered emphatically, waggled his fingers like little thrashing legs. 'Eurgh. Creatures in your room. After what happened to Mona.'

I rubbed my arms, which had started to itch. Silence from the corridor and the courtyard. 'What? What happened to Mona?'

'And as for Alexa,' he went on, laughing, 'she's bad enough when she sees a spider. Never mind something bigger.'

(What did he mean, *something bigger*?)

'Bryn, please. About Alexa.'

He paused. Tilted his head: *Go on.*

'I can understand if you're pissed off,' I said, cringing at my own awkwardness. 'About what's happened. With me and her. And I get that. But – I really mean this – I don't want it to come between us.' I took a breath, realising I was very bad at this. 'I mean, as in, between me and you.'

He leaned back in the chair, his face like a lone candle at midnight mass, a brightness behind which everything else disappeared. The more he receded into darkness – and the more petrified I felt – the more I was drawn in, as if by grabbing him I could save myself from falling. But I sat, feeling the awful emptiness of my hands.

'I didn't realise you had such a flair for the dramatic,' he said, as if impressed. 'It's the kind of thing I'd do.'

'Bryn, please, the two of you are my favourite people in the world …'

He raised his eyebrows, gave me a look that seemed to mix amusement and pity.

'… and I wouldn't have done it if you guys were … still together,' I said, babbling. 'I swear. And I would obviously have preferred to speak to you first.'

'Obviously.'

'But, come on. I know you, Bryn, and you weren't happy—'

He leaned suddenly forward, and the wings of the armchair made him momentarily monstrous, a terrible angel, his face glowing as if he were lit from the inside. 'No,' he said, his smile gone now, his voice low and bitter. 'You don't know. Say what you like about who I am, but truly, you have no idea.'

He leapt up, then – Christ, he seemed so much taller than ever before – and in shock I stood too, moving crabwise so as to keep the coffee table between us. Butchered photographs, a tin of teeth. A man mid-air in a darkened room. Actually, I thought, maybe I know exactly who you are. I just didn't want to believe it. (Or perhaps I didn't want to believe how exquisite I found it, how very badly I wanted to see it, to prod around like a pathologist in a butchered body.)

Eyes locked on Bryn, I tripped, thumped my leg against the corner of the desk. Winced. As the pain spread through my flesh, so did my indignation. What fucking right did he have to be angry with me? What had I done that was so wrong?

'Listen, Bryn,' I said, finding a steadiness in my voice. 'Nobody was more excited than me when you and Alexa got together. I wanted you to be happy. But lately, you've been treating Alexa like – like shit. It doesn't take a fucking psychic to see that she's miserable.'

His astonished eyes followed me as I stumbled around in the shadows. My breath came in gasps, my leg throbbed like a broken heart.

I carried on, my tongue dry and stupid. 'You think the world is some … some fucking voodoo doll, for you to shape and bend however you like. And you know what?' I paused, realising that this was the worst part, that this was the darkest truth of all, 'I was fine with that. But then you went for Alexa, and she's my friend – I mean, more than that, now – and I won't have you do to her what you did to … to Mona.'

He tilted his head, openly sneered. 'Mona?'

The hastily applied bolt, the string securing the window lock. The marks on the glass. 'Had she worked it out, like I have?' I cried. 'Is that why you frightened her out of here?'

A laugh, sharp as a snare drum. 'Ah. She did take some of my little jokes quite badly. Even so, I hardly think it was me who sent her scurrying back home.'

A horrible clarity: the thing on the bathroom sill, on the Old Court walls, in Sajid's room. Down in the cellar. No, it wasn't necessarily Bryn who did the scaring. Why would he, when the job could be outsourced as easily as ironing shirts, shining shoes? In these matters, as in others, someone else – something else – did his dirty work. 'Not just Mona,' I added. 'You got rid of Sajid. Kenny.'

'What is this, a line-up of the wettest people in college? Face it,' he said, his voice pitying now. 'Some people simply aren't built to survive this place.'

I leaned against my little sink, felt my body sag. Imagined my name added to that ignominious list. What must it be like to be those people? To see Bryn moving around college like a great comet, only ever observing his dazzling presence from a bound and grounded world? What must it be like to know that there's another life you should be living, another person you could be if you could only follow in his wake? Please, I thought. I just want us to be okay.

But that's not what I said. He stepped towards me and – the self-preservation kicking in, overriding my wish to be closer to him – I held out a hand: *Stop*.

'Bryn,' I said, firmly. 'Leave me and Alexa alone. Or else I'll tell. That it was us, at Trinity, with the porter.' Then, softer. 'I wouldn't say this if she didn't mean so much to me.'

He looked at me for a long time, like a cat pondering a foundered bird. All the while, I stood, mute, somewhere between misery and fear.

Then he gave me a smile that would have curdled cream. 'My worry is,' he said, sauntering towards the door, 'that you're going to end up getting hurt.'

The words rang in my ears as the door slammed behind him. The emptiness felt like sickness, like hunger, and when I refilled my glass, my hands shook so hard that I spilled port over the carpet. The air felt stale and dead without him, and I wanted to call out, *Come back, please*. It was like having a knife pulled from my flesh – for all the agony and all the damage, I might have felt better if the blade had still been stuck there.

* * *

I often wonder about loyalty. Whether it can be a fixed thing, how it's earned as well as given. Whether it's ever offered without conditions. If the friend to whom you've been unfailingly loyal behaves in a way that you don't recognise, what then? Should you be loyal to the person you thought you knew or the person they've become? Can you ever do both at the same time? And what if, for better or worse, *you're* the one who has changed?

I said something else to Alexa, that night we walked home together, before she had the argument with Bryn that precipitated their break-up. I made her swear that she wouldn't tell anyone, especially not Bryn, what I was about to say. Then I told her what he'd revealed to me, in the practice room that wasn't a practice room, about his overdose. She knew already, of course. But then I told her how he didn't actually think he would die. How, later, he'd used his 'depression' as an excuse to get out of his exams. How that stuff was all, perhaps, an act.

She listened as I explained that I wasn't suggesting any particular course of action. I was only trying to help the two of them to understand one another better. I allowed her to imagine the rest: how disrespectful his actions, how false. Not the way you'd behave towards someone you loved.

Abracadabra, open sesame, presto.

Don't forget you.

Magic words, a language that can change the world. Or, at least, change how people see the world. Alexa had squeezed my hand and told me: 'You're a good friend.' I'd thought so too.

* * *

Hours after Bryn had left my room, when evening had turned decidedly to night, I was still on my sofa, thinking. Worrying (it came more and more, now, that sight of the porter hovering in the air like the subject of an exorcism). I hadn't wanted to upset him. It was the last thing I'd wanted to do.

A crash from the corridor made me jump to my feet. As I stood, listening, I heard it: a dry scrabbling, like something moving low to the ground. Trembling again, I stepped cautiously to the door and creaked it open, as if Bryn himself might be back, ready to deliver the hurt he'd spoken about. But it was Alexa, squatting on the stairs beside her dropped bag, her hands sweeping at a mess of spilled coins and keys. Around her, a hairbrush and a lip balm, a mobile phone in two pieces.

'Lex!' I said, bending to take her arm. 'Are you okay?'

She turned to me, her lovely hair arranged about her face as if she'd narrowly escaped a bomb blast. 'I'm fine.' Her voice came thick and pillowy. She was very, very drunk.

'You've hurt yourself.'

She squinted at the bloodied knee poking beneath her skirt. 'Oh. Yeah.'

'Come here, it needs cleaning.'

'Fuck. Am I a mess?'

Avoiding the lie, I pretended not to hear and instead helped to return her things to her bag, then led her inside and sat her on my bed while I grabbed a handful of tissues and dampened them at the sink. All the while, she was submissive as a child. I'd known she'd been out on a girls' night, so I wasn't expecting her, and I'd have been slightly embarrassed by her catching me drinking alone had she not been too pissed to notice. It was a miracle she'd remembered where my new room was. 'What happened?' I asked, kneeling, dabbing gently at the gravel-studded skin.

'I tripped.' She rubbed her face, spreading mascara further down her cheek.

'Oh, Lex. Did you have a good time before that?'

She flopped backwards onto the bed, legs dangling over the side, my bedsheets billowing around her. 'It was shit,' she said, foggily. 'All shit.' She fell silent, and I thought she was perhaps drifting off to sleep. But then she sat up, rigid, like a medium possessed, eyes flaring. 'Have you spoken to him?'

'Who?'

'Bryn.'

'Oh. I have, actually.'

'I knew it. It smells like him in here.'

I was momentarily thrown. 'What does Bryn smell like?'

'What did he say?'

I didn't want her to worry. 'He's angry,' I said. 'But with me, not you. He'll calm down,' I added, unconvinced. 'Do you want some water?'

She shook her head and sank back into the sheets, took her broken phone from her bag and, freshly disappointed by its fragmentary state, put it back again. This wasn't going to be like it had been with Berenice – me, preparing for our dates by pressing shirts and cleaning shoes, trying each and every time to be a more polished and more competent version of the person I suspected I was. Christ, I'd held Alexa's hair while she puked in a bin outside McDonald's, there was no point hiding ourselves from one another now.

Which is probably why I felt able to ask those questions, ones that were scratching at my brain like animals crowded in a cage. 'Lex. When you were with Bryn, did you ever think there was anything weird about him?'

'Obviously. He's completely weird.'

'I mean, weird in a way that you might be worried about.'

She shuffled up onto her elbows. Her voice was quiet. 'You already know that.'

'What?'

'How I worried about him. When he was feeling down.'

Ah, I thought. His 'troubled me' set piece, pretending to have dark moods while hiding something far darker. But that wasn't what I meant. 'No, not that …' I sighed and looked around the room. Still I saw his shape spreading on the chair, his fingers around the port bottle, around the glass. It was as if he marked the air itself, making a permanent impression on every scene. 'What I mean is, Lex – were you ever scared of him?'

She blinked, as if struggling to understand. Then cackled, sloppily. 'Scared of Bryn? I was scared of how much I liked him.' She checked herself. 'But you know that as well.'

It stung, but I'd asked for it. Maybe this wasn't the time to talk about him. Before I could change the subject, Alexa asked: 'Do you regret it?'

I scrambled up onto the bed and stroked her arm. It felt waxy and cold. 'Of course I don't. How could you think that?'

She looked agitated, her eyes overly bright, her breath shallow. I could have kissed her flushed cheeks, wrapped her in a comforting embrace, but it wasn't the right moment. 'I'm really sorry,' she said. 'It was selfish of me. I know how much you, like … worship him. And now …'

'Really,' I said, feeling sick at the thought, 'it's going to be fine.'

She turned onto her side, carefully, like someone very old. I took her hand, felt the pulse skipping allegretto in her wrist. Neither of us spoke for a minute, maybe more. As I sat, I thought about the first time I'd ever seen her, with Berenice, dressed as a zombie, when there hadn't been the faintest attraction between us. Funny.

'I don't feel so good,' she mumbled into the pillow.

'Do you need to throw up?'

'No. I need to close my eyes.'

'Well, why don't you do that.'

She nodded and pulled my duvet around her. I waited a moment before easing off my shoes, turning out the light and lying beside her. I didn't take off my jeans and T-shirt. I felt oddly vulnerable, unable to shake that impression of Bryn, his hands – his eyes – still there, in my chair, in the dark.

I thought about the things I'd entrusted to Bryn. Hopes, joys, worries, each little confidence a sign of my devotion. Perhaps these would protect me, like votives offered to a saint. Or perhaps they were the means by which I'd get burned.

One of my offerings: my deepest horrors. A group of us had gathered in the common room to watch a film about some kids getting lost in the woods, being chased for days by something awful. In the film, these kids come across a river and, if they follow it, they're bound to get out of the woods at some point. Right? But – and this was the bit that stayed with me, the bit I couldn't shake – after a day or two of walking, they find themselves back at the spot where they started. That's the part where you know the normal rules don't apply, and those kids aren't getting out at all.

When the common room lights were back on and we'd disguised our terror with blustering laughter, Bryn and I had talked about the things that scared us. We'd wondered: can visceral things like werewolves and aliens ever be more frightening than things like spirits and demons? Or are the intangible things always the worst? Never afraid of the difficult questions, Bryn asked me: 'What are you horrified by? Really?'

I thought for a while, knowing that 'snakes' or 'heights' was not what we were getting at. Then I told him about that day I'd asked those kids around to my house, when we were stopped in our tracks by the sight of my dad spread on the sofa, by the ripe stench of shit.

I even told Bryn the detail that I never, ever talked about, because it unsettled me deeply in a way that I didn't understand and couldn't explain: how, when we walked into the room that day, there had been something crouching on top of that dreadful quiet. A strange scratching sound, like a long, insistent mechanical breath. Staring at the scene, I'd wondered briefly whether it was the air itself, sick of my dad and rushing out of the room. But really it was the vinyl crackle of my dad's record player, the music finished but the record stuck and skipping, playing the sound of emptiness – a sound, an emptiness, from another age, scored imperfectly into a circular, material memory. Was it bringing the past to us, or taking us back into the past? As the record went around and around with that maddening scratch, I had the idea that time was not to be relied on, that it might run forward and backward all at once. And although, at that moment, I knew full well my dad was alive, I felt that on some level he was already dead.

Bryn didn't try to tell me that my dad probably wasn't all bad, that he was clearly troubled, blah blah blah. He just listened, respectfully. Then, when I asked the same question of him, he became unusually serious. And he replied: 'My greatest fear is that some of the things they say about my father are true.' Then he laughed, as if it were all a big joke.

But I knew better. I remembered Frances, at the weekend away. The empty place at the table. What did people say, about how little Louis Cavendish cared for his son? How hideous would it be for that son to believe it?

There was another question I never considered at the time: How do we know when to *stop* being afraid? Can we ever be sure that we've left the path that would lead us to disaster? Or will we always wonder whether we're lurching towards some horror, like those kids lost in the woods following the river, heading unknowingly back where they came from?

I'd trusted blindly in the path laid out for me. Doing well at school, going to a good university. This, I trusted, was my route to something you might call success, or approval. But the path is circuitous, deceptive. Sure, you might get into a good, even great, university. But when you're there, you may find you don't know which way is up or down. Like the Magic Circle, an in-crowd will pass intelligence amongst themselves, cards slipped invisibly from one palm to another. If you want to become part of this cadre, you will be tested. Depending on your performance – the right school, the wrong accent – you may gain admittance, or not. As with many of these things, the surest route is to be recommended by a friend.

You will knock and knock at the door. But even if someone opens it, they might not let you in.

A feeling of panic, a scrambling towards consciousness.

It was dark. Fuzzy from the wine, I didn't know where I was. Sensing a shape beside me, I nearly cried out – but it was just Alexa, her breathing heavy and slow.

There had been a sound. Feeling suddenly and violently awake, I shambled out of bed and moved to the window, pulling the curtain back a fraction. Old Court was lifeless. No nocturnal creatures tip-tapped around the lawn, no returning clubbers howled at the moon. My watch showed it wasn't yet four. As I let the curtain drop back into place, I heard it: a knocking at my door.

Each knock was light and unhurried, one, two, three. It was so out of place that, at first, I felt nothing at all. Slowly, my mind unfurled its logic: someone would only knock at this time if it was urgent. But if it was urgent they wouldn't knock like that, they'd hammer hard, to wake me up. This was such an ordinary sound. Which is exactly what made it so hideous.

I saw it clearly, now. I wondered what he'd do when I opened the door, whether he'd douse me with a bucket of iced water or punch me square in the face. But as I cowered there, feeling the hairs on my arms rising one by one, what I really feared (even though it was mad, too mad to contemplate) was that he'd speak arcane words, under his breath, words that would have me sprawled on the carpet or splayed against the wall. Or maybe he had other words, more potent still, for punishments I didn't yet know.

For two, maybe three whole minutes, I waited, appalled by the volume of my own breath. From beyond my room, silence. I stepped slowly towards the door and looked at the carpet, where light bled in from the perpetually lit corridor. Was there a darker patch, a suggestion of feet, planted a few inches away? Hard to say. I folded, putting my hands and knees carefully to the floor. Face against the carpet, one eye closed, I peered through the gap beneath the door.

Nothing there. I pushed myself to standing, waited for the rush of relief that didn't come, and turned to go back to bed.

There it was again, polite as before: *knock knock knock.*

I spun, heart thrumming like a moth in a jar, toes clutching at the carpet. Fuck. Who else could be doing this but him? My mind darted from one plan to another: I could wake Alexa to see if she heard it too. I could arm myself with the empty wine bottle and face him down. Or I could go back to bed, on the basis that the sound was probably only the college walls exhaling in the night, just the ancient pipes. I didn't believe this last thought, but I tried anyway.

Very gently I put my ear against the door, the gloss paint cold against my cheek. From the other side, quiet again. But it wasn't the quiet of empty space. It was the studied quiet of a hunter, held very still (a flash of memory: me, calling through the letter box of my dad's horrible new flat, knowing he was inside, wondering why he couldn't or wouldn't answer).

Then, from out of the quiet, a whispering, murmuring. Was that Bryn? Maybe, but it sounded like more than one voice. I pushed against the door, straining to hear.

And suddenly, from the other side, a thunderous banging, like something large throwing itself against the wood, but faster than that, much faster, as if there might be many things rather than just one, hammering so furiously that the whole door frame shook.

I staggered backwards, whining, clapping my hands uselessly over my ears. Please Bryn, I begged, silently, please don't.

Slam after slam, relentless. Praying for the ancient hinges to hold, I felt the air rasping in and out of my throat, heard a moaning that didn't sound like me. As I stumbled backwards, my feet collided with something and I fell, toppling the coffee table and everything on it.

Alexa threw on the bedside lamp, glared at me in the gloom. 'Jesus,' she said, in a voice like ground glass. 'What the fuck are you doing? You frightened me to death.'

I clambered to my feet, trembling. The air seemed to have shifted, become less dense.

'Didn't you hear it?' I said, breathing hard. 'That banging, at the door?'

'All I heard was you, crashing around like a fucking elephant.' Then, somewhat resentfully: 'Are you okay?'

I nodded. She threw off the bedcovers, leapt up and marched towards the door.

'Alexa, don't ...'

She flung it open.

Outside, nothing.

'There's nobody there,' she said, irritably, before returning to bed and turning towards the wall.

Slowly, unsteadily, I righted the coffee table and picked up the things that I'd knocked over. One of them: my book about Peter Warlock, a copy of which I'd given to Bryn. As I placed it carefully back on the table, I stared at the photograph on the front, taking in Warlock's Mephistophelian good looks, his mischievous eyes shining with occult knowledge. He stared back as if to say: *I did warn you*.

IV

I don't remember the last few auditionees or what I had to say about them. Nor do I remember leaving the faculty, arriving in the city centre car park. But I do remember that, as I walked through market square towards college, the sun was low and the summer shadows were long. Although there still stood the usual stalls with their candy-striped awnings, their unsold flowers and doughnuts and vegetables and crystals yet to be tidied away, the square was quiet enough for me to hear the sound of Joseph's voice momentarily pealing in my head. Even in the warmth, the hairs on my arms rose up like radio antennae straining to pick up the faraway tune. I hurried on past the little church whose name I never knew, past a row of Italian chain restaurants that hadn't been there in my day. Past The Eagle, that pub where those scientists discovered DNA.

The one thought that has always calmed me is Alexa. And I reached for her then: I pictured her making tea, curled into the sofa, brushing her long, dark hair. I imagined calling her right now and telling her everything, heard her calmly telling me to walk back to the car and get home immediately. In my head, I spoke her name like a psalm, a plea for protection. Because it wasn't friends or family or music that had sustained me across the dark years following Bryn's death. It was her, and the fact of our friendship blooming inexplicably into something more. People say that love makes them a better person. But Alexa choosing me? It had transformed me completely, made me unrecognisable to my meek and forgettable former self. Now, when I came home after a poorly attended concert and turned on the radio to hear one of my university peers conducting the London Symphony Orchestra, or when a pupil's parent spoke down to me because their estate agent salary afforded them better shoes than mine, I reminded myself: Alexa chose me. And everything I did – however terrible – I did for her. But I couldn't call her.

Jesus, had I tried to explain even a half of it, to anyone, the words would have stuck in my throat like tiny bones. Just change quickly and get straight to the bar, I told myself. Have dinner, leave early, then sleep in the car if needs be.

I was so lost in these thoughts that college came upon me abruptly, like a mugger. As imposing as the day I first encountered it, with its vast gates and impenetrable walls. I had the distinct feeling of being not wanted, but maybe that was normal. Maybe I'd never felt particularly welcome here.

While I stared, trying to stop my teeth from chattering, the slow shift from day to night spread gold across New Court. Soft light fell across the chapel in its reverent quiet, the immaculate lawn, just like that terrible moment all those years ago. The only difference was that time was mirrored – back then, night had been turning into day. In that glorious, terrible glow I recalled the stilled fairground rides, the courtyard littered with empty champagne bottles. And I heard again the porter's feet clattering on the path, his voice as he shouted at someone to *Call an ambulance, now*, his fierce composure useless as those beautiful limbs that lay splayed and broken on the unforgiving ground.

When I signed in at the porters' lodge, the porter – someone new, unfamiliar to me – gave me overly detailed directions to my room, and I didn't bother to say they weren't necessary. He also confirmed that I'd be the sole resident of my staircase, what with it being the holidays (a fact that wasn't as welcome as he assumed it would be), and looked at me strangely when I fumbled the keys he dropped into my hand.

The walls of Old Court leaned in close, and their windows peered guardedly down. Although I expected staff to come hurrying by, perhaps bearing fine wines or tableware for our dinner, nobody passed me as I made my way around the lawn. More than once I reached to adjust the record bag in which I carried my rumpled lecture notes and half-written essays, but that bag was long gone now.

Through the familiar double doors and into the hallway, the silence became more insistent and oppressive, so much like a presence in itself that it made me look over my shoulder. Straight ahead, the door to the room I'd booked as if I had no alternative. Mona's room. My room. Its immediate familiarity was a strange and partial kind, like something from a film or a photograph – something only ever seen through a lens, or else completely imagined. But my body remembered it better, and when I slipped the key into the lock I automatically jiggled it, just so, like I'd had to back then. The lock responded with a soft click, allowing me inside.

For a moment I was sure I was in the wrong place. In the spot where the desk had been there was now a sad, brown sofa. By the wall, where the wardrobe once sat, a thin-legged desk and its matching chair. The coffee table was gone, replaced by another that seemed equally unstable. Although there were no pictures, no books on the shelves, the space gave off a strong sense of belonging to someone else. I threw my case on the bed and shrugged off my jacket. Then I paced the ugly carpet, letting my fingertips slide over the bare walls.

I'm not sure why I did it. But I stepped towards the closed door and put my ear against the wood, like I had all those years ago. There was no sound but a near-inaudible white noise, which might have been the shush of wind outside or the rush of blood inside my own head. Then, very slowly, I bent into a crouch and lowered my cheek to the floor. Peered underneath the door. Nothing, of course. I couldn't help but notice the ache in my knees, the soft noise I inadvertently made as I leaned more weight into my hands.

Then, from above: a thud. Like someone landing two-footed on the floor. Instinctively I jumped to my feet, curved my hands above my head as if the ceiling might cave in. But after that, the only sound was my heart, thumping. What the fuck? The porter had explicitly said there was nobody else here. The distance to the lodge, to the common room and the bar, suddenly felt very great. It occurred to me that, while I'd started worrying about what might happen during the night, I might not even make it to dinner. Perhaps, in the next few moments, the lights would blink out and the door handle would turn and all would be darkness until Tim found me, gibbering and clawing at my own arms.

I unpacked my overnight bag. Dress shoes, new socks. The deodorant I only wore because Alexa said she liked the smell. Then I dressed, quickly. But not before jamming the chair under the door handle, the way people do in TV shows, and securing the

— 260 —

window lock with my tie. When I stared at my pale reflection in the mirror above the tiny sink, I wondered whether the room recognised me, or whether it was as surprised by the ageing, frightened face as I was myself.

Don't let him inside your head, I thought. Don't give him the power. He has enough of that already.

Tim didn't comment that I was late arriving in the college bar, that I'd left him alone to mingle with the other scholarship representatives. He merely pointed out the many things that delighted him: the jukebox, standing as brightly as before, the chalkboard still scrawled with special offers. Observing these things, I was momentarily my student self again. As if there was an essay deadline I was about to miss. Of course, Tim asked about the auditions (I almost spilled my pint when my mind resurrected the memory of Joseph's beautiful, horrible song) but he believed me when I said everything had been fine.

Because of my lateness, we had only a few minutes before it was time to head up the old staircase, to join my fellow judges gathered outside the dining hall. As we moved forward in a queue, I had the feeling of time being disordered: pages of music, scattered in the wind. Once more, I felt a room of eyes upon me. That terrible burning in my leg.

And the more I stepped forward, the more I seemed to be moving backwards, to that moment that was always waiting for me however hard I tried to outrun it.

~

May balls are possibly the most Cambridge thing about Cambridge. Huge, high-production events, they take place within the colleges during May Week: a period of partying which, despite the name, typically begins on the second Thursday in June, and which includes a day of heavy drinking known ominously as Suicide Sunday.

That year, our own college's ball had the cryptic theme of Dreamscapes – 'a night beyond your wildest imaginings' – and several of our group would be attending as part of a couple. Jamie would be paired up with Natalia, a horrible socialite who had, at our first meeting, made fun of my shoes for having rubber soles. Sarah would be bringing Jasper, a slow-witted bloke who had a rugby blue and was studying something called Land Economy.

And, of course, there was me and Alexa. Which was both a dream and a nightmare. How provoked might Bryn be by the sight of me and Alexa, the two of us slow dancing in our finery like forties' film stars?

I couldn't explain the whole situation. But I needed Alexa to understand that we mustn't bump into Bryn at the ball, the argument being: *We mustn't rub our happiness in his face, Lex.* This argument seemed best made over a nice dinner, and while my bank balance wouldn't stretch to a meal out – not with the ball and its myriad expenses on the horizon – I could cook for us, take the food to her room. So, keeping the details a surprise, I asked Alexa to block out the evening, then I called my mum and asked what the hell to do. Although Mum tried not to react to the news of my burgeoning romance, I heard her excitement as she talked me through some recipes that were not only seductive but manageable for a novice with access to one small hob and a kettle (bolognese, then).

Which is how, the afternoon before the ball, I came to be crying over a chopped onion, my fingertips papered with bits of garlic skin. All the while I dreamed of what it would be like to be at the ball with Alexa. Surely the comedians would be twice as funny, the food more delicious. Even better – with her hand in mine, I myself would be doubly charming. Alexa would be a witness to these experiences I never expected to have, able to say: yes, you were there, and it really happened.

I texted Alexa from the smoky kitchen, revealing what I was up to, and she responded with genuine shock at the effort I was making. Then, after what seemed a ridiculous amount of simmering, I headed out to pick up some wine. Outside college, I found myself peering in clothes shop windows, admiring eveningwear extras such as top hats and canes, wondering whether they'd make me look dandyish (or maybe more like a cruise ship conjurer?). Only that morning Alexa had collected her ball gown from the dressmaker's, and I imagined her inside an air-conditioned boutique, the walls lined with rails of silk and satin and lace; here, Disney damsel colours of powder-pink and duck-egg blue, there, alarming siren reds and arsenic greens. I imagined her surrounded by mirrors, rows of Alexas reflected infinitely into space.

I was inside the wine shop, working through the cheaper shelves, when my phone began to buzz. It was Alexa, and she sounded terrible.

'I'm really sorry,' she said, her voice scraping like chairs on a lecture hall floor. 'I can't catch up tonight. I feel awful.'

'What? What's wrong?'

'I don't know. I got a sore throat earlier, and it's been getting worse all afternoon. I had a nap to see if I'd feel better, but I'm really rough. I know you wanted us to have dinner—'

'Hold on, I'm coming over.'

'Really, don't bother—'

'Can I bring you anything? I've got cough and cold medicine, paracetamol—'

'Please don't worry, I'm just going to sleep it off.'

Hanging up, I ran back down Trumpington Street and towards college, scattering the pigeons. With every step, I tried to quell my rising disappointment and anxiety. When I made it to Alexa's I knocked gently at the door, as if the sound might cause her pain, and after a moment or two of shuffling and rustling she opened it, wearing her pyjamas and a weary expression. She didn't look sick – in fact, she looked lovely – but her eyes had a flatness I didn't recognise.

I gave her a sympathetic smile. 'Hey.'

She sighed, almost sheepish. 'You didn't have to come.'

'I wanted to check that you're okay.'

'I am. I just need to rest.' Then, after a pause, 'I'm really sorry. To cancel last minute.'

'Don't be sorry. Dinner will keep.'

She offered something between a smile and a frown. I hoped she'd invite me inside for a bit, as if my presence might be a tonic. But she seemed dazed. Behind her, a zipped-up garment bag, crisp and new, lay flat across her sofa. I nodded at it. 'Best that you get well for the ball. That thing isn't going to wear itself.'

She nodded, listless. I took a couple of cautious steps into the room, still hoping for that invitation to stay. In the silence, I looked over Alexa's shoulder at her desk, at her things in their comfortable chaos: a book of poetry, open like a bird crash-landed, next to a scattering of photocopies and a barely touched sandwich. Her Doc Martens, dumped in the middle of the floor.

And there, among the nail polish and the stray buttons, a post-card, writing side up. I say 'writing', but it was in fact a pattern of peculiar symbols. Loops and curls and crosses. They looked familiar, but I couldn't immediately say why.

Alexa gestured at her rumpled clothes. 'I'm not really fit for company …'

'Don't be silly,' I replied, eyes on the postcard. 'You look great.' I had the feeling of having forgotten something. As if I should pat my pockets: phone, keys, wallet.

Wait a second. These were the same scrawled symbols I'd first encountered in Bryn's room, on the paper that I'd stolen from his bedside drawer, during that weekend when I'd actually wanted him and Alexa to be together. Shaking my head, I tried to gather myself. Alexa, increasingly puzzled, continued to hold open the door. Fuck. I needed more time, to see, to think. 'So,' I said, stalling, 'you're just going to …'

'Go to bed.'

'Right, right. Good idea.'

Another glance. The corners of the postcard were neat and sharp, so it must have been either well looked-after or very recently received. There was no address or stamp, which meant it had been hand delivered, to Alexa's pigeonhole or to Alexa herself.

'You know,' I said, rambling now, 'call me any time. Like, even if it's the middle of the night. I don't mind.'

'I just need to rest up.'

I wished there was some way of me comparing this card with the paper I'd stolen, the one I'd carried back to Cambridge, the day I'd become ill.

There, that feeling of the floor falling away. The memory of that M. R. James story, tolling like a distant bell, of carefully written curses slipped from one man to another. The day I'd taken the paper from Bryn's room, I'd become violently sick. Now, Alexa had a paper bearing the same weird symbols, and she was sick too. Was there something slipped into Mona's pocket, something that had turned her mad? It wasn't possible. But hadn't I seen and heard enough now to know that, in fact, it was? Would I swear there was nothing poisonous about those papers, those charms, of his? Stupid, to think that he'd punished us enough. I knew all this, suddenly and surely, and there was nothing I could do to prove it.

If only Alexa would ask me to stay, I could take a closer look at the postcard. Maybe memorise some of those shapes, look them up. But she merely leaned against the door frame, her smile like a blown rose. *Think, think, think.* Every extra second I lingered, awkwardness accumulated, cloying as hospital flowers.

But then Alexa stooped to pick a tissue from the floor, and in that fraction of a second I pictured how Bryn would do it: he'd pretend to look at his watch and then, easy as you like, he'd put his hand on the postcard, slide it off the desk and into his pocket. Fuck it, he'd probably swipe the sandwich as well, just because he could. While Alexa's eyes were lowered, I mimicked those imagined movements: passed my hand over the postcard, pulled it towards me—

—felt it creasing as I stuffed it clumsily into my trouser pocket—

—saw Alexa clocking the movement, furrowing her brow—

'What are you doing?'

I stiffened. Blinked. 'Nothing.'

Her voice was flat. 'I saw you take it.'

'What?'

'Give it to me.'

She lunged at me, like a kid who can't believe that you won't let them play with that cigarette lighter, but I stepped backwards into the corridor and her grasping hand only grazed my chest. 'Lex—'

'Give it back!'

'Just hold on—'

'How dare you! You can't just take my things, my private things!'

As she glared at me, her face a sheet of fury, I felt surer than ever. Sajid, Kenny, Mona. Now Alexa. The people who displeased him were dealt with, sooner or later. 'Lex, please listen. I know this sounds crazy, but you shouldn't be near Bryn.'

Her eyes and mouth became huge. 'What?'

'When did he give this to you?'

'That's my business!'

I had to give her a reason, however feeble or beside-the-point it may be. 'Alexa,' I said, pleading, 'Bryn doesn't treat people well.'

'He's not the one going through my stuff like a fucking stalker!'

'Remember what he was like with other girls.'

She came at me again, but I put out a hand, fingers spread, ready to hold her back if I had to. When she finally stepped away, resigned, she let out a laugh that was bitter, ugly, new to me. 'You're fucking out of order, you know that?'

'Lex, I swear to God, I'm doing this to protect you. On my life, okay? I'll explain everything, if you'll let me, but I can't give this back to you, I have to do this …'

As we observed one another, I felt as if there might be someone, something, up the staircase, listening. A draught passed around my neck, as if a face leaned close to mine.

Then I took the postcard in both hands and ripped it in two. Ripped it again. I think Alexa shrieked, or maybe it was in my head. I kept pulling and tearing until the whole thing was unreadable, and when some of the pieces fell from my hands I didn't bother to pick them up.

The door slammed in my face. Somewhere, someone seemed to stifle a giggle. How long might it take for Alexa to go back to normal? Should I wait a while and knock again? No, I needed time to work out what to say. I trudged back down the stairs and through college, depositing different bits of the postcard in different bins along the way. It seemed safest, somehow.

When I got back to my own staircase in New Court, I headed up to the kitchen to grab some of the bolognese I'd prepared. There I discovered that, instead of turning the hob off, I'd actually just turned it very low. So, the sauce was now nothing more than a blackened residue, baked solid onto the pan, filling the kitchen with the stink of charcoal. I threw the pan into the sink and retreated to my room. All the while, an idea burned at the back of my brain. It wasn't just Alexa's sickness that had disturbed me. It was that she hadn't been herself.

When we act in a way that seems uncharacteristic, who is the new 'self' that feels so wrong? And where does the real self go? But the biggest question: How could I think he'd let us get away with it so easily?

The next day, lighting rigs and stage equipment sprang up in the courtyards, rides and inflatables and fast food vans. Everywhere was a kind of merry chaos, so unlike the imperious calm that usually characterised college. Crates of clanking bottles, instrument cases, elaborate flower displays – all made their way through the college gates in preparation for a night that, the marketing assured us, would live long in the memory.

I didn't see Alexa directly before the ball. It didn't seem wise. In any case, although a series of texts revealed that she'd calmed down after the postcard incident (her illness having disappeared remarkably quickly after my intervention, a fact that chilled me), I wasn't quite back in her good books. She'd decided to get ready with the girls, and I was going to find her once the celebrations were underway.

So, as the clock above the chapel chimed seven, I opened the champagne I'd bought for us to share and made a toast by myself. I thanked the universe for Alexa. And I made a quiet but fervent plea that we could avoid Bryn for the night. After tonight we'd be packing up and heading home for the holidays, where I'd have time to work out what to do.

Wishing for an extra pair of hands to help with my cufflinks (which I didn't particularly like and had only bought because he had some similar), I caught sight of myself in the mirror. They say a tux makes anyone look good, but I wasn't sure whether I looked better or just not like me. Maybe those things were the same. I added a pocket square, tied my bow tie. Then, knowing that all I needed now was Alexa on my arm, I drained my glass and stepped out into the evening.

New Court was so spectacularly beautiful that I momentarily forgot my fears. The walls were washed with turquoise light, creating the impression that we all stood within a Barbadian cove, or at least an enormous fish tank. Above us, acrobats whirled on invisible wires like fireworks exploding against the violet sky. Immediately to my left were two punts, beached on piles of glittering sand and painted seashells, lined with ice and filled with bottles of fizz. Most partygoers headed for the two attendants – mermaids, apparently, who were languidly presenting freshly filled flutes – while others yanked whole bottles from the ice and continued cheerfully on their way.

To my right was a row of stalls, decked in greenery and artificial flowers in the style of an enchanted forest. From the first came the smell of freshly fried doughnuts, all warm yeast and powdered sugar. From the next, onions, blackening sweetly, ready to be slathered on top of startlingly pink hot dogs. Crêpes, French fries, waffles and ice cream, the latter topped with dinky marshmallows and rainbow sprinkles and neon-red raspberry sauce. Childish pleasures from seaside days and circus nights, a subtle sign that we, even in our eveningwear, were still a long way from the adults we were destined to be.

I paused amidst the hubbub, texted Alexa to ask where and when we should meet. Pressing send, I spied Tim at one of the stalls, a hot dog in each hand, licking at some sauce dribbling down his wrist. The sight of him made me wince. Since our museum visit I'd been awkward around Tim, only ever agreeing to meet him when I was sure Berenice wasn't around (once literally running away when I saw the two of them emerging from the post room) and never once admitting the absurdity of my behaviour. While I wondered whether to scarper, Tim turned and spotted me. I felt like a school-kid caught in a sweet shop when they should be in double science.

But here he was, waving his steaming snacks in the air and smiling, striding towards me. Plain, dependable Tim, in his imperfectly fitted jacket and his clip-on bow tie, who was always there and who I didn't appreciate in the least for it.

'Everything's free, so I got two,' he announced simply, hands outstretched. 'Want one?'

'Yeah, go on,' I said, taking one. 'Thanks.'

He beamed, bright and unconditional as ever. 'So,' he said, 'I've done a recce. The main stage is in Old Court. Apparently the headliner is a Christina Aguilera impersonator.'

'The budget must have gone on the fizz.'

'Do you want to head to the bar? I think there's some comedy on.'

Actually, all I wanted was to find Alexa. But maybe the bar was a decent place to hide out, better than being in a wide open space where Bryn could appear from anywhere. I followed Tim's lead, stopping briefly at a gin stall to take a cocktail with my free hand.

Stepping inside, I scanned the crowded bar. Embroidered drapes swagged from the ceiling, punctuated by golden pantomime lanterns, and beyond the windows that usually looked out onto New Court, starry fabric hung, giving the impression that it was already night outside. Aladdin's cave, maybe, or Scheherazade's chambers? On a small stage a man and a woman improvised valiantly while audience members fidgeted and chattered. There was no sign of Bryn.

A familiar voice cut through the crowd. Was that Jamie? Yes it was, commandeering several tables with some boat club buddies. His black tie jacket was, confusingly, white, and I wondered whether the rules were deliberately designed to baffle or whether he was allowed to break them. Beside him was Natalia, stony-faced, weary at the world's constant failure in its duty to please her. As we passed, I leaned in to say hello – but there was a hardness in Jamie's eyes, as if he were pretending not to see me. Not surprising, really, that he'd sided with Bryn.

Tim and I squeezed through the crowd, careful not to blot ketchup against furry shrugs and dinner jackets, before settling ourselves at the back. I eased my phone from my pocket, to see if Alexa had replied, but put it away when I realised we'd picked the only spot that never got any signal.

The performers ploughed on over the ceaseless chatter. Tim ate his hot dog, I worked on my cocktail. Punchlines came periodically, and the audience reacted slightly behind the beat, distracted by friends appearing, disappearing. I very quickly felt restless. For all its glitter, the scene seemed flat. As my attention drifted, I found myself staring at the long, leaded windows that should have looked out onto the courtyard but now showed only an artificially created night. Our own selves shimmered in the glass, a sea of smiling expressions.

But there, standing right in the middle of the reflected audience, was Alexa. Only she looked different to the rest of us. Not smiling at all.

I turned from the window and scanned the actual room. But where Alexa should have been, there was only the chaos of the bar and its patrons.

Another look at the window. Yes, Alexa was there in that reflected scene, her face pale and forlorn. And looming behind her was another figure: one whose smile was unnaturally wide. Within this tableau, Alexa moved towards the door. The figure moved too. Fuck.

I leapt up and looked again around the space. But I couldn't see Alexa among that real-life mess of body parts, the wine-stained mouths. The crowd shrieked with laughter, a pointed, hysterical peal.

Once more I looked back at the window. Alexa was disappearing out of the bar, just a pale shoulder and a coil of dark hair now. The figure was following, its face a blur, like a pencil drawing smudged with the heel of a hand. But I knew it was him – the way you can conjure a whole person from a scrap of their handwriting or from the smell of their clothes.

Without a word to Tim I crashed into the crowd and fought my way out, ignoring exclamations about my rudeness. My one thought: that I had to reach Alexa before he did.

* * *

I ran around Old Court, scanning every silken silhouette and every band of black jackets. Here, a string quartet playing a stupid classical pastiche of some Britney Spears song while girls twirled the skirts of their evening gowns in a sloppy courtly dance. There, a collection of fairground games: a coconut shy, a hook-a-duck, a dunking chair on which a third year historian shivered nervily, bare skin prickling in the evening air. No sign of Alexa or Bryn. The garish colours of the soft toys, the novelty hats, the striped paper bags of sweets, were all sickening beneath the electric lights. Kicking uselessly at a balloon sculpture, I dashed back into New Court.

An arch of flowers bloomed extravagantly above the staircase that led to the dining hall. Deciding it was worth a try, I took the steps two at a time, moving beneath an undulating ceiling of green plastic vines. At the top of the stairs was the tail end of a queue, making its slow tread into the hall itself, and I fell in at the back, occasionally standing on tiptoes to peer above a sea of coiffed heads. If I didn't find them here, I told myself as I dialled Alexa's number, I'd go back to the bar and ask Tim for help.

I'd reached Alexa's answerphone more than once by the time the queue carried me through the large wooden door that opened into the hall. Inside, the lights were already low. Chairs, all occupied, were arranged in neat lines, divided by a central aisle. All faced the dais where the college tutors usually sat for dinner, which was now transformed into a stage. On this stage was a table. And pointing at the table, two cameras, each hooked up to a large projection screen. Presumably whatever happened onstage would be broadcast, to make sure that nobody missed a thing.

People pressed behind me, forcing me down the aisle, and a steward began ushering me towards the front, saying that the show, whatever it was, was about to start. I opened my mouth to object, but then, there on the right, a knot of black hair – it looked like Alexa, but I couldn't quite tell.

I allowed myself to be bundled towards the front row, the only place where a handful of chairs still waited, empty. In my seat, I half-stood, searching the scene for Alexa's bright eyes, but the crowd obscured the dark head I thought I'd seen.

I sat, stared at the stage.

Now that I was closer, I could see that the table on the stage bore a brown leather suitcase, and around it, little objects. Small rag dolls, made with a deliberate carelessness, with faces cut from colour photographs. Balls of hair, piled like after-dinner delicacies. All around the edge of the stage flamed squat black candles, neat and regular as tombstones.

Before my mind could arrange itself, a door behind the stage opened, causing everyone to clap and cheer. The screens flickered into life. And he appeared.

His face wasn't warped and strange, like when it had been reflected in the windows of the bar. It was open and beautiful as he took his place centre stage and made a deep, professional bow. When he held up his hands, his smile just the right amount of bashful, the applause subsided, leaving a quiet punctuated only by the odd ironic 'whoop'. Just like the first time I'd seen him, that day on the college steps, I was struck dumb by his effortless poise. Attention was a birthright. And didn't he deserve all of it?

'My name is Bryn Cavendish,' he announced, his voice firm and clear. 'And I have a question for you.'

A pause, for effect.

'What is magic?'

A begrudging silence from students who were used to having all the answers. Then, a voice from a few rows back: 'Magic is deception.'

Bryn gave a look, ready and wry. 'Deception,' he repeated, as if the word itself had an unusual taste. 'Alright. So, I tell you that the ball is here ...'

He raised his hands. We saw the small red ball in his left palm, the image doubled, magnified on the screens behind him. Then he closed both hands into fists.

'But I'm deceiving you,' he said, 'because it's really over here.'

There was the ball again, appearing behind the slowly spreading fingers of his right hand. A chuckle danced through the audience.

'But,' he continued, 'let's imagine I sell you a painting, telling you that it's a Van Gogh. And when you get home, you find it's a fake. That's deception too. But you're not going to give me a round of applause for it, are you? So, I ask you again: what is magic?'

Audience members sat tight-lipped this time, pupils reluctant to disappoint a favourite teacher. Eventually, someone else spoke up, a little cynical and a lot drunk: 'It's deception for people who *want* to be fooled.'

Bryn raised his eyebrows, gave a pout that said, *Interesting*. 'People who want to be fooled. You're saying that an audience member sets aside their logical mind in order to enjoy the performance? They see the levitating assistant and, becoming an active participant in the trick, they blindly accept the version of reality in front of their eyes?'

The speaker shrugged at this interpretation of his words, seeming not to know himself what he'd really meant.

'No,' Bryn said, shaking his head. 'I don't think so. When the assistant levitates, you try desperately to work out how it's happening, to find out where the wires are. The last thing you want is to suspend your disbelief. You're dying to know how it's done.' Here he raised his hands again and, even more slowly this time, had the red ball disappear from one hand and appear in the other. 'Any other suggestions?'

This time there was no word from the audience, who, like the ball, were in the palm of Bryn's hand.

'For me,' he said, conspiratorially, 'magic is a reminder that, for some of us,' – here, a glance around the rarefied room – 'anything is possible. Why should we accept an ordinary life when we can dream of more?'

The idea spun in the air, a planet waiting to be discovered. I turned and looked to the exit, wondered whether I should try to creep out. But at least I could keep an eye on him here. On stage, he couldn't do anyone any harm.

He took an oversized playing card from the suitcase. Turning to a girl a few seats along from me, he held the card in the air. 'Could you tell me what card this is?'

The girl arched an eyebrow at Bryn, trying to appear resistant to his charm. 'The six of clubs,' she said.

Bryn became still, held the card lightly at the corner for all the room to see. Then he gave it the faintest shake, turning it immediately into the queen of hearts, the screens showing the preposterousness and impossibility of this action. Gasps and applause rippled through the room. 'You see. Why should we accept things the way they are?'

Shaking her head, the girl failed to conceal a smile.

'Maybe that's why,' Bryn continued, 'some of the most pioneering thinkers in history have been drawn to magic. They explored religion, alchemy. The spirit world. Now, I need a volunteer.'

I saw it in my head before it happened in the room. Bryn, ignoring those who reached like congregants in supplication, meeting my gaze with an expression that could have been surprise, malevolence, or both. Pointing a slender finger. 'This chap, here. Let's have a round of applause, ladies and gentlemen.'

My voice came out small and pleading: 'Wait, no—'

'Up he comes. A warm welcome, please.'

Applause broke around me. I shook my head – *No, really* – but somehow my legs were taking me up the little steps onto the stage, through the fairy ring of candles, and I saw my own image appear on the huge projection screens. I looked terrible. Bryn's eyes followed me as I found my place beside him, and I suddenly felt feverish – as if I were standing next to an open fire.

'Thank you,' he said, letting his hand rest heavily on my shoulder. The touch was uncomfortably hot. 'Your name is …?'

I opened my mouth, but he put a finger to my lips.

'Actually, no. I'll tell them. Your name is John.'

I tried to pull away, but my feet stayed planted where they were. 'No, it isn't—'

'Yes. Tonight, you're John Dee. A man who studied right here at Cambridge, also known as Doctor Dee.' He turned to the audience, spoke as if from a pulpit. 'Born in the early sixteenth century, Dee was a remarkable man. Mathematician, philosopher, astronomer. Astrologer and alchemist, expert in cartography and cryptography. Explorers in the court of Queen Elizabeth I consulted him about finding the Northwest passage to China. The queen herself had him look to the stars to choose the most auspicious date for her coronation. You know what else John Dee did for decades of his extraordinary life?'

He'd told me the answer long ago, and, unable to extinguish my desire to please him, I almost raised my hand. But he was the one who said: 'He tried to speak to angels.'

I looked out at row upon row of captivated faces.

'This was pretty controversial,' Bryn explained, 'not because people didn't believe what John Dee said. They *did* believe he was talking to spirits. They just didn't believe those spirits could possibly be good spirits. They thought that, instead of talking to angels, Doctor Dee was talking to devils.'

Bryn moved slowly to the suitcase and reached inside. I reminded myself: at any time, I could just step off the stage, walk away.

'Whatever they were, Dee had a particular way of reaching them. In the way that fortune-tellers might use a crystal ball, he used something called a shewstone to see his spirits.'

From the suitcase he lifted a round mirror, framed, the size of a dinner plate. The one from his wall, its surface almost black, like looking into a well. He held it carefully, and I could see my reflection, warped and ugly.

'The problem was, Dee wasn't too good at using the shewstone himself, so he had an assistant named Edward Kelley look into it for him. So, Doctor, here's one shewstone for you. And another,' he said, pulling a second from the suitcase, 'for me. Tonight, I'll be your lovely assistant.'

The audience laughed. A prickling sensation rushed across my skin, as if long nails were being drawn lightly down my back.

'Spirits sometimes want to deliver a message from our dear departed,' Bryn said, casually, as if explaining how to enter the church raffle. 'Or to give us a warning of some kind. Sometimes they come for revenge. So let's see if any of them have a message for you, Doctor. Shall we?'

I breathed out, long and loud. Taking my unease for cynicism, the audience laughed again.

'Now, I need you all to stay very quiet,' Bryn said to the audience, serious now. 'Give the dead a chance to speak.'

The room fell into an obedient silence. Bryn stood, holding a mirror in each hand, searching for something in the unsettling black. He stayed this way for so long that it became almost awkward, as if something had gone wrong. But, at some point, the pressure in the room seemed to shift. The stillness became oppressive, panicked, like a person forced to hold their breath for too long. There was an odd sound, too – Bryn was muttering nonsense words quick and low, words that didn't sound like anything I'd heard before. They came faster and faster, sparking on his tongue, getting louder and stranger and more disorienting—

Then, a huge crack: Bryn had snapped the faces of the mirrors together, as if closing a book. He held them towards me, one on top of the other.

'Doctor,' he whispered, 'put your hands on here. Gently.'

I laid my hands on the uppermost frame.

'Can you feel it? Can you feel the spirits speaking to you?'

I shrugged, clueless, my mouth too dry to speak. The audience giggled again, but this time through tension alone. The whole room was braced, as if for a thunderclap. I didn't even move when I felt the heat in my hands, building, as if I were protecting a candle flame from the wind.

Without warning, Bryn shouted: 'Stop!'

I jerked my hands away.

'That's it,' he whispered. 'The spirits have spoken.'

In the silence, he slowly separated the frames. Those circular surfaces, which had both been black and empty, now bore writing, thick and chalk-white. The audience gasped, and heads moved, straining to see.

'Let's read the message,' Bryn said, holding the first frame aloft. 'The first one says: *She's just* ... and then, the second one ...'

The front few rows had already started to laugh.

'… *not that into you*. Oh. Love advice. Bad luck, John. The spirits can be a bit direct, but it's better to face the truth I suppose.'

Laughter rolled throughout the hall, and I tried to muster a magnanimous smile. But only for a second. Because, as the applause rose again, I saw something else on the stage, in the darkness, behind Bryn.

That shape. Long and dark and horribly thin. The same shape that had crouched beyond the bathroom window, that had clamped itself on the wall of Old Court. The one that had haunted me both dreaming and awake, never far from Bryn. Now it stepped softly, as if through a doorway, into the circle of candlelight, so that I could see its face in the cold, unforgiving glow.

He wore that same searching expression as in my dream, but, this time, he was the right age, the age when he died. I recognised his old polo shirt, faded from the wash, the paint-spattered shorts he wore whatever the season. He shifted his weight from one foot to another, unsteady. But not because he was drunk. I think he was frightened.

My words were lost in the relentless applause. 'Oh my God …'

I have the sense that Bryn lowered the mirrors, took a long, luxurious bow. But I can't say for sure, because I was staring straight ahead, stupefied, appalled. Trembling violently, I whispered: 'Dad?'

The clapping hands must have slowed, frowns must have appeared on the faces of those who were wondering what I was doing, who I was talking to, whether it was part of the act. I think I staggered.

'Can you see me?' I said, my voice barely a breath.

My dad's mouth hung open as he cast his gaze uncertainly around. His focus seemed off, as if he were seeing not the hall but another scene in another time. As if he were searching for something that wasn't there. I glanced, pleadingly, at the audience, before realising they had no idea what I was looking at. Again, that bitter smell of something singeing. Then, as if the movements were not his own, my dad came tentatively forward, hands raised, the twitching fingers groping and searching. His eyes flicked left to right, faster now, and I followed his frantic gaze – it was impossible, surely, that our eyes wouldn't meet, any second now. Slowly, as if trying not to break a spell, I reached out my hand.

But, as the tears in my eyes turned him back into a shadow, I pulled away, drew falteringly backwards. I didn't want him to see me, or touch me. I didn't want anyone else to see him. I didn't want them to know that he belonged to me.

Bryn's hand on my shoulder shocked me back into the moment. Standing there, his expression impassive, he didn't even have the decency to look triumphant. 'Get your fucking hands off me,' I shouted, shrugging him off as hard as I could. 'How are you doing it?'

'Mate—'

'I said, how are you doing it?'

'Jesus, just—'

'You're a fucking—'

'Your leg—'

Only then did I feel the heat, the flames from one of the candles lapping up my calf. There was that awful gasp from the audience, revealing that something has gone awry, that someone has made a scene. I twisted on the spot, pushing at Bryn and swiping at my smouldering trousers, my breath catching, voice leaking out in whimpers. Bryn grabbed at me once more, but then, somehow, I was off the stage and sprawled on the floor, patting madly at my calf, the smell of smoke in my nose, pain flashing up my leg. From my splayed position, I still saw two shadows on the stage, the sight enough to make my head reel.

But before I could say or do anything more, someone was helping me down the aisle, and in the background Bryn was joking that some people don't know how to behave around spirits, all while the applause rolled again, the room turned its back on me, and the tears fell freely down my cheeks and onto my rental suit jacket.

Outside the hall, members of the May ball team bustled around, headsets and serious faces on, as if they were stage managing an event at the United Nations and not a piss-up for a load of students. I slumped into a nearby chair and shooed the usher away, wiping at my face and telling him I was fine. Even then, some long-honed reflex hoped quietly that Bryn would come to check on me, and I had to tell myself not to be so stupid.

I stooped to inspect my leg, the skin unbroken but tight and red, and when I looked up again she was in front of me. She wore a blue satin gown, her dark hair in a tight chignon, unfamiliar but as beautiful as ever. 'Alexa,' I called, feeling immediately better. 'Don't worry. I'm fine.'

Kneeling, she peered at my scorched trouser leg. 'Jesus. Does it hurt?'

'Emphatically yes.'

She gave me a look of tenderness. 'Listen,' she said, 'that trick was mean. But don't take it personally. It was a joke. A stupid one, but still a joke.'

I pulled away from her, bewildered that she could still defend him. 'Lex—'

'That line, on the glass, he could have used it on any guy in the audience …'

Of course. She was talking about the mirror trick. And making excuses, like I had so many times. But excuses would be no help when he took his revenge on her too, when he finally burned her up like a moth in his irresistible flame. She needed to stay away from him. But I'd already made a poor case for that, and it had pushed her briefly away. So.

Sitting there, I wondered. Maybe there was nothing left but to tell her the truth.

But could I, really? Alexa would need to have a religious kind of conviction to accept, without proof, what I had discovered: that our world is subject to ancient, esoteric forces harnessed by only a few, according to rules that the ordinary among us will never understand. She'd have to consider that, on some level, she'd seen it in Bryn, but had chosen – like so many of us – *not* to see. And that, in walking away from him, she'd be walking away from something that was not just horrifying but utterly enchanting.

A sickly looking first year clattered out of the hall and swayed past us, determined as a mule, dragging his dinner jacket along the ground. When he'd passed, I decided that I had no other choice. 'Alexa,' I said, taking her hand, feeling as though it was someone else moving my limbs, choosing my words. 'Bryn doesn't do tricks.'

She furrowed her brow. 'What do you mean?'

'The magic he's doing. It's real.'

She paused, the curve of her lips drooping slightly. 'I don't get it.'

'It's not a joke.'

A beat, before Alexa's face folded into a genuine frown. 'Even Bryn doesn't pretend that's true.'

'I know, it's genius,' I said, laughing bitterly. 'He's pretending to be a magician, to hide the fact that he can actually do magic. It's the greatest piece of misdirection of all time.'

From the hall came another round of applause. Alexa nodded, slowly, and dropped my hand. 'When you fell, did you hit your head?'

'I know how it sounds, but I'm perfectly lucid.'

'Okay, calm down …'

'Alexa, I'm serious. That thing with the mirrors, and the writing, that wasn't the trick. There was something, someone, on the stage with us. Bryn, he conjured it—'

'What do you mean "someone"?'

I couldn't say his name. 'A spirit. An actual fucking spirit, or a ghost, or whatever you want to call it. Standing there, as clear as I can see you now.'

'This isn't funny.'

'I've told you, it's not a joke.'

'Stop it.'

'I fucking swear. On my mum's life. I don't know how he does it, but he … summoned something, to scare me. Because of what I did to him, because of me and you—'

Alexa's posture became rigid. 'Listen. It was really dark in there.'

'I was three feet away!' Then, trying not to think too hard about it: 'So close, I can tell you the colour of its eyes.'

She put a hand over her mouth. Looked more sad than scared.

'Alexa,' I said, grasping the folds of her skirt, 'this isn't just about tonight. Like, what about Sajid? Sajid broke the decanter that belonged to Bryn's family, and Bryn put a curse on him, then Sajid saw some creepy thing in his bedroom—'

'What?'

'And Mona? Bryn gets sick of her hanging around, and all of a sudden she's refusing to go in her room and putting great big fucking locks on the door, and before you know it she's left her whole course—'

She pushed my hands away. 'What's wrong with you? You know what happened to Mona!'

'Oh, that she had a "breakdown"?' I stood to do the scare quotes, and pain blazed up my shin. 'It would be so much easier to pretend everything is fine, that Bryn is a normal, cool guy. But the truth is, I think he's dangerous. I think he can make things happen, really fucking scary things, and yes I think it's because he has some kind of power I can't explain. I know how it sounds, Lex, I really do. And I'm only telling you this because I care about you and I don't want anything bad to happen to you.'

For a minute, more, we didn't look at one another. Eventually, she smoothed her skirt, spoke in a voice that was measured, cool. 'I don't know if you should come back inside.'

'You're going back in?'

She looked at me, for a long time, as if I were one of Bryn's tricks that she was trying to work out. Then, flatly, she told me that she had to get back to the show – one of her philosophy friends was in there, very pissed – and then she was disappearing, her skirts like a tide going out, back towards the danger that she couldn't or wouldn't see.

This, though I didn't know it yet, was my cue to raise the curtain on the final act of this horrible drama. To begin the falling action of our story that would not tie up loose ends or lead us to resolution, but would instead give the audience nightmares from which they would never completely awaken.

When I arrived at the St John's ambulance station, the medic was busy dealing with injuries from the bouncy castle (two sprained ankles, one slight concussion). So I limped slowly back to my room. With my trouser leg rolled up and a wet handkerchief taped around my calf, I sat in my armchair and stared through the window, watching helplessly as stage lights gave a noxious green cast to the immeasurable Cambridge sky.

I'd been there for some time when there was a movement in the air, a sound like a sigh as if the room itself felt sorry for me. By the time I turned, the door had already swung shut. He was there, close enough to conjure an apple from behind my ear or slip a curse into my pocket.

I blundered to my feet. Between us, only my coffee table, a small useless barrier. No place for niceties now, I murmured: 'What do you want?'

Although his tux looked tired, Bryn himself looked unnaturally fresh. His mouth turned up at just the one corner, almost rueful. 'I wanted to see you.'

Of course he wanted to see me. He hadn't finished the job.

He picked up a mug from my table, sniffed it. Replaced it, very gently. 'Look,' he said, his voice golden as a bell, 'I should apologise. I get carried away by the performance sometimes.' He paused, looking wistfully at the floor, as if remembering his own brilliance. 'Surely you understand that. Although maybe not, since you're always the accompanist.'

From beyond the window, howls of delight. I said nothing.

'Anyway,' he said, 'we've obviously had a little tension lately. And tonight,' he held up his hands, *Nothing concealed here*, 'I went too far.'

A pathetic, hopeful feeling rose up in me like cinematic violins.

'After all,' he said, lowering his volume, 'gentlemen ought to settle their problems behind closed doors.'

The violins became jagged, serial killer stabs. 'I don't see what's left to say,' I said, unable to stop the tremor in my voice. 'Things seem pretty settled to me.'

'Come on. It's hard work having enemies.'

I moved slowly around the table, trying to create a clear path to my door. This was it, wasn't it? I'd expected it to happen in a shadowed staircase or a deserted corridor, but in fact the ending would come amid the faraway flare of fireworks, the distant jangling of fairground tunes. 'Yeah,' I replied, shakily. 'Which is why you get rid of your enemies, right?'

A laugh. 'What?'

'Even Alexa. You made her sick.'

He clapped his hands together as he mirrored my movements around the table, the two of us circling like animals. He was enjoying this. 'She did say my laundry management left a little to be desired. But "sick" is a bit strong.'

'You've made your point, Bryn,' I said, feebly. 'I'm humiliated. Isn't that enough for you? You don't even care about me and Alexa anyway, so please. Just leave us alone.'

A fraction of a delay, followed by genuine surprise. 'Us? Oh my God.' He put his palms to his face, part appalled and part thrilled, as if watching a disaster unfold on the news. He turned in a little circle, performative, and the joyful physicality of him suddenly reminded me how insane it was that I could no longer reach out and clap him on his broad back, that he would no longer grip my shoulder and give me a firm, bantering shake. 'Fuck me,' he said, 'you still think it's going to work out. I swear it's kinder if I tell you: there's no happy ending, mate.'

Cold with fear now, I kept on creeping towards the door. Now, when I looked at him, he was backlit by the window, light streaming around his powerful frame. A small, defiant part of me asked: Why shouldn't there be a happy ending for us? Why shouldn't the good guys win? The other part of me replied that such things only happen in stories, idiot.

The silence that followed was so close that I felt I was drowning. As Bryn stood there, his eyes dark – and somehow flat now, like the eyes of a goat – I wondered what punishments might be running through his head. Smoke rising in my room, from a fire that nobody had started. A shape at my window, unhindered by locks. When I thought I couldn't bear it any longer, when I might cry out just to break the soundlessness (what might I shout? Let's stop this, start over at the beginning?) he spoke, slow and matter-of-fact:

'It's funny. Frances told me to be careful with you.'

There was a low thudding, somewhere in my head. 'What?'

He pretended to think. 'What was it she called you? *Such a poor, frightened boy.*'

I staggered to the door, the thudding intensifying all the time, sending me off kilter. Was it him, doing this to me? I grabbed at the door handle, tried to focus on its cold smoothness. I felt as if I might throw up.

'When the rest of us laughed at you,' he went on, his voice expressionless, without cadence, 'Frances said it wasn't funny. It was sad.'

It was relentless now, the *bang bang bang* in my brain, and despite having both feet on the floor I had a spiralling, vertiginous feeling – as if I were standing on a bridge, fighting not to throw myself off. This was coupled with a scorching kind of rage, the feeling of a naked flame coming closer and closer to my exposed skin, the reckless rage that makes dark words come from inside as if channelled by a medium. I staggered again, and all the while, that awful banging …

I snapped. Like a man speaking in tongues, I shouted uncontrollably about how I was going to speak to the chaplain, to the local press, how Mona and Sajid and Kenny would help me make sure he never hurt anyone ever again. I told him that Alexa regretted ever knowing him (a guess) and that I never wanted to see him again (a lie). Then, gripping the door handle, I paused to dream up one last dark benediction, a combination of words so precise and so cutting, intended not only to wound my opponent deeply but to win one last crumb of his grudging respect.

And at these, my final words, something clicked. Something cosmic: like a planetary alignment that shakes both the collective and individual consciousness, a shiver that runs from the stars right down to our cells; as if Mercury had at that exact moment occulted Mars or else slipped silently into retrograde. In the wake of this ecliptic shift, Bryn's face registered a mixture of emotions. Surprise. Hurt. Something like admiration.

And then I fled, out the door, right out of college, not knowing that this would be the last time I ran from him. The last time while he was still alive, anyway.

I often wonder whether this conversation could have gone a different way. Is there a version of this story where we utter the magic words: Look, let's stop this nonsense, let's start over? Or was it the case that, once I'd begun, there was no way off this darkening path?

Unable either to return to my room or rejoin the throng of the ball, I wandered the streets of Cambridge. I might have felt frightened or tearful, but I think I actually felt very little. Used up, like a drained battery or a blown-out bulb. The thing that pained me, besides my sore leg, was the realisation of my rootlessness – in this moment, I really did have nowhere to go.

But I couldn't walk for ever. So when, after several hours, I was sure the ball must be over, I returned to college. It was that odd, liminal time between the end of the ball and the beginning of the clear-up, and New Court was completely deserted. The sky bloomed pink, and the sun gave the scene a golden cast as if it were a dream. In another hour or so the Ball Committee would be back with a little army of tabard-wearers, all set to pick at the piles of discarded plastic glasses with long metal claws, ready to fold the silken banners down into neat, synthetic squares.

Even then, I didn't head to my room. I made for the staircase nearest the bar. Head bowed, I scurried up, checking over my shoulder with each surreptitious step. Unnecessary, in the end, since there wasn't a single person around. There was nobody to see me as I climbed the spiralling stairs, all the way to the top, before making my way down the corridor to the little window at the end. (Jamie's room was on the right, and it sounded like he was in there. Maybe others too. But I wasn't going to knock.)

I heaved open the window, wincing as it screeched in the frame. Ironically, it was only the memory of the pool party – my glorious jump – that persuaded me I really was capable of folding my body through the window and out onto the battlements, the way I'd seen Bryn and the others do so many times before. The muscles in my core screamed as I struggled to steady myself, every movement harder than I'd anticipated. Finally planting my feet, ignoring the cold that worked its hands around me, I pulled myself up onto the roof, careful of the ancient tiles, until I reached some kind of chimney stack to grasp onto. I rested against it with relief, trying not to think about how I'd get back down.

And you know what? It was breathtaking. The most beautiful view I'd ever seen. There wasn't a soul in New Court – only the unmoving amusements and unmanned stalls, sitting in the morning light like something from myth: the architecture of a deserted island or an abandoned ship. Beyond, slumbering colleges and dreaming quads, postcard-perfect beneath a pale pink sky. From somewhere below came the metallic rattle of a bicycle, the silver ring of a shop doorbell. Tears burned unexpectedly in my eyes. I did do it, I thought. I was here.

And then, as if it were inevitable: him. Clambering out onto the battlements below me, still in his black tie. My heart seemed to stop altogether – even if I'd had the energy, there was nowhere up here for me to run.

But he hadn't come for me. He didn't even know I was there. He stayed below, leaning brazenly out over the stonework, his jacket flapping around him like the flag of an anarchist or a pirate, his face turned defiantly to the sky. Crouching behind my chimney stack, I watched him with a sense of awe. As if I were seeing a rare bird, or a solar eclipse, or the lights of the aurora borealis bright among the blackness – a wonder you'd talk about for the rest of your days. A thing you can't hope to experience ever again.

Up there, it felt like there were just the two of us in the whole world. Only from my perspective, though, since he didn't see me. And that's why it was so magical. Supposing there to be no audience, he was simply himself. It was like the most exquisite piece of music you could ever hear. I allowed myself to sit for a while, taking him in, filled with the sad certainty that this would be the last time.

Some people say we're our true selves when we think nobody is watching. But how do we know our own identities without others' confirming gaze? If, like the tree falling in the proverbial wood, nobody is around to hear us, is our story a story at all? And when we're different things to different people, what then? My mum always said I was kind, considerate. Tim said I was a good bloke. I disagree. So whose version is true?

There's a type of spell called a 'glamour', which makes things more attractive than they really are. Perhaps most of us spend our lives looking in enchanted mirrors. How else would we get through our merciless, ordinary days?

Morning congealed into something solid, the sunlight glancing off discarded beer cans and broken glass. As I made my way back to my room, the chaos had already begun: the running of feet, the banging on doors, the first fretful voices. A plaintive wail, unseemly in that soft, decorous space. Rumour ran up and down the corridors like a hooligan.

It was Tim who knocked on my door, repeatedly enough that I couldn't ignore him. His face was ashen and harried, as he was hurrying Berenice to her parents' place. It was him who told me that Bryn was dead.

I already knew, of course. I'd seen Bryn's face – beatific, like an angel destined for earth – as he fell.

V

High Table, up on the dais, had been set for us judges and our guests, plus a couple of faces from the music faculty. In the main part of the hall, tables lay undressed. If I hadn't been so spooked, I might have laughed. The fact that such a relatively small number of us occupied the whole hall was evidence of the money the Cavendish family must be pouring into the scholarship and the strength of their relationship with the current master. I wondered whether Frances had insisted on this room, which seemed to me like a bad idea. The modest size of our party only emphasised the vast emptiness of the space, reminding us of those who weren't there.

Finding my seat at one end of the table, I looked along the bone white linen, the excessive silverware. All as it ever was. But at the centre, the one dissonance in this strange performance: Frances Cavendish, anachronistic in pearls and crimson silk. She *was* changed. That lustrous hair was shot with white, and the skin hung slack at her jaw. No surprise that the years without Bryn had been cruel.

Until this point, my nerves had been a background hum, an orchestra tuning up. But, as I stared at Frances, they began their slow crescendo. I realised: I was as frightened of seeing Bryn's mother as I was frightened of encountering Bryn himself. Because it suddenly seemed impossible that she didn't know. When I spoke to her – which I was yet to do, which I could hardly put off any longer – perhaps those eyes would reveal whether she knew why Bryn had gone over the battlements that beautiful, perfidious morning.

Tim waved a hand in front of my face, checking for a trance. I shook my head, laughing weakly, and tried to focus on the hubbub, on the familiar things that revealed themselves to be part of me – like the gong that pulled us to our feet, the corresponding Grace to whose words my lips moved as if I'd spoken them every day since graduation.

We sat, and waiting staff in bright white shirts and black waist-coats mirrored one another down either side of the table, bearing baskets of warm bread rolls. The first time I'd experienced this, I'd worried that it would be rude to take a roll with my hands and had instead tried unsuccessfully to prong a multigrain with my fork. Seeing Tim there, I felt dizzy. 'God,' I said, 'it's like we haven't changed at all.'

'Don't say that,' said Tim, pulling a face. 'That's the only thing more depressing than getting older. Anyway, since we first walked through those doors, a vast number of your cells have been completely regenerated. Which means you're practically a different person.'

'That's good, because my previous person had back acne and big ideas about Marxism.'

A hand appeared, silently filled Tim's water glass, retreated. 'It's funny,' he said, 'that on the one hand we know we're always chang-ing. And yet, at every stage of life we reckon we know it all. It's why I ended up getting a tattoo.'

I almost spat my wine. 'You *what?*'

'I was on my gap year,' he said, blithely, 'and I thought: I've lived in a foreign country, survived extreme food poisoning. I've nibbled the very edge of a magic mushroom. There's nothing more to learn about myself. So I got a tattoo of a Celtic symbol. You know, they were everywhere at the time. On my arse.'

I raised my eyebrows so far that I almost sprained them. 'Didn't Sporty Spice have one of those?'

'Shut up. Anyway, it was supposed to represent something, coming to maturity or some bollocks. But by the time we turned up for matriculation, I was sick of it.'

'Tim, how have I known you for so long and never known that?'

'It's not something I advertise.'

'It's a shame it didn't get replaced along with the rest of your cells.'

And then, a presence at my shoulder, causing me to flinch and drop my bread roll. It was Frances, making her way resolutely down the table towards the plummy chair of our judging panel. God, the thought of speaking to her made me feel sick. But it was better to do it now, I thought, while the mood was still festive, before the evening drew in. Better to show, by my dutiful presence and service, that I'd never wanted to hurt him, that all I wanted was for us to be friends. I took a breath. Then, as Frances passed, I reached for her slender wrist, grabbed clumsily in a way that made her startle.

Her eyes (fuck, his eyes) met mine, indifferent.

'I'm sorry,' I said, half standing, bumping the table and drawing looks from the other diners. 'But I just … I wanted to say hello, and how good it is to see you. And to thank you. For having me here. It's a privilege.'

Frances looked uncomfortable. 'That's quite alright,' she said, her manners impeccable. 'Tell me, are you a judge or a guest?'

Jesus, I must have underestimated the alterations in my own face. 'I ... I was friends with Bryn. I came to your house and played the piano, that's why you wrote—'

She gave me a bland smile, already turning subtly away. 'Ah, you must be another of the musicians from Bryn's year. The faculty was kind enough to share your details.'

'Oh. I—'

'Thank you so much for giving your time to this project, we must talk properly later. It's a pleasure to meet you.'

And then she was floating away like a ghost. Around me, murmurs. I sat again, wiped my reddening face with my napkin. Jesus Christ, her memory must be going. How fucking sad. Another tragic chapter in the fall of the house of Cavendish.

I might have been relieved that she bore no grudge, but in truth I felt no better. Because even if she didn't know what happened, I carried it with me always, inked invisibly but indelibly on my skin.

~

My memories of third year are shapeless. Towards the end of the previous year, I had – like several others, including Alexa and Tim – requested that my third year bedroom be in a student block around twenty minutes from college, and I spent a lot of time within its anodyne, rendered walls. I no longer visited those pubs in Cambridge where we'd met as the Three Amigos. And I avoided college, especially the bar where boisterous freshers had taken over the space that had once been ours. So diligent was I about this that, if I ever wanted a drink, I'd have a beer in my room.

Most of my time was spent at the music library. I was too far behind to expect much from my finals, but that was okay – all I wanted was for each day to be unremarkable. And to avoid the exquisite torture of hearing his name. This latter was made easier due to the fact that I never heard from Jamie or Sarah or any others in the group, not any more. Tim, however, either texted or stopped by my room every day.

Probably the only thing that stopped me going mad was Alexa. The mere thought of her affection allowed me to act as if I were bearing an ordinary grief. And, of course, an ordinary fear – because, even then, it didn't feel *over*. Some nights when I was alone, lying awake in bed, I'd glimpse movement beyond my window. Or I'd hear a slow, distinctive tread out in the corridor and I'd sit up, thinking: *He's back*. But the dream fog would lift, dissipated by the grumbling of a cistern or the creak of a bathroom door, the plebeian sounds of student rooms at night. In those moments, I'd grasp for Alexa's hairbands, those comforting little amulets resting on the bedside table, and I'd wonder which would be worse – Bryn being there or him being nowhere at all.

I also visited my mum and stepdad more often. One weekend, I went home to help clear out the spare room that was still packed with my old stuff, starting off with a load of crates that had been stored away since I was at junior school.

In the first crate was Snoopy, a little plastic dog I'd once carried obsessively around. Feeling his smooth, cold shape in my hand, I saw myself walking him across the chequered linoleum of our kitchen floor, dipping him in and out of a bubbled bath. Alongside him, pin badges from swimming club and Scouts, commemorative T-shirts from local orchestras I'd been a part of.

Mum tugged at a piece of parcel tape that held a cardboard box closed, and the box folded open to reveal a pile of photographs.

The photo on top had a seventies' look about it, like a promo shot from *Tales of the Unexpected*. 'Oh,' Mum said, her voice muted.

'What's that?'

She handed it to me. 'I thought we'd lost this. It's from when me and your dad got married.'

I'd never seen it before. In the middle of the frame, Mum looked towards the ground, lips pursed as if suppressing a laugh. My dad, one hand resting lightly on Mum's cheek, leaned close to her ear, his eyes sparkling in a way that I didn't remember. It felt like such a special, private moment that I felt awkward looking at it.

'God, look at those balloons,' Mum said, pointing to a mess of pink and white.

'Touch of class.'

'They looked very smart at the time. People said so.'

'That dress is interesting.'

'Careful,' she said, giving me a nudge. 'I've no idea who took this. We had a photographer take some pictures, but they were really formal – the standard stuff, bride and groom, parents, big group shot. They didn't really give you a sense of the day. Because our guests, they were so up for a party. You remember Fred?'

'Dad's uncle, from Blackpool?'

'That's him. He led a conga down the street. He was seventy at the time, nearly put his hip out. This photo, where we look so cheeky? That's what it was really like.'

For a moment, we sat. From downstairs came the sound of my stepdad cackhandedly washing up. 'Is it hard?' I asked. 'Looking at it?'

She shook her head. 'It's good to look at it.'

I rolled Snoopy from one hand to the other. 'I always thought … I dunno. I thought you hated him.'

Unsure whether her look was one of confusion or regret, I

wondered if I'd upset her. But she just stroked my back, like she used to when I was little. 'I did, sometimes. I hated him when he turned up at two in the morning, blood streaming out of his nose, shirt all ripped. Can you remember him, hammering on the front door?'

My stomach gave a gentle turn. 'I'm not sure.'

'You were maybe too young. It was after I'd changed the locks. He'd bang on the door with both fists, and I'd be thinking, Jesus, the neighbours. Then, when he'd sobered up, he'd be back, all apologetic, tapping at the glass like butter wouldn't melt.'

I gave Snoopy a firm squeeze.

'I hated him then,' she went on. 'And when he was gone I hated him for leaving me. But when he woke up in the mornings, he hated himself more than I ever could.'

I tried to focus on the ugly floral pattern of the carpet, on the wrinkled wallpaper, any banal thing that might help me not to cry. If my dad had been given the same chances and the same knocks I'd had, what would he have made of this life? How many paths might bring us to this exact point?

'You've got to remember,' she said, softly, 'the man in this picture, he wasn't the same man who used to drink a bottle of vodka before going to work. People used to say, kick him out, he's gone too far. But the hardest thing was knowing where the drunk ended and where my husband began. People don't get it. They think you have to either love someone or stop loving them. But you can feel everything at the same time.'

My throat felt tight. I cleared it, and Mum put an arm around my shoulder.

'Do you hate him, love?' she said.

I examined the idea, properly, perhaps for the first time. 'I don't know. Maybe I thought I was supposed to. But I don't actually remember him very well at all.'

After that trip home, I called Mum more often. She occasionally asked how I was feeling about Bryn, and she also talked about my dad. It was in those conversations that I came to understand how a person can feel bereft and freed at the same time.

That was also the year I wrote that essay about Warlock. I think, perhaps, I was trying to explain myself.

My essay explored the contradictions in Warlock's personality, whether you could read them in his music. I suggested that those who reach so close to the heavens that the sun itself feels like hell-fire – those devilish beer-swillers who live life like it's one long naked motorbike ride – are often as fragile as they are dangerous. You can see it in Warlock's letters, where his uncontrollable highs are often countered by soul-destroying lows. But, the thing is, it's hard to recognise this when you're travelling in your hero's wake, when he seems so limitless and alive. (You know, his name was actually Philip. Philip Heseltine. A boy whose father died when he was only two, never having known this Peter Warlock character. Perhaps it was hard to tell, even for Warlock, who he really was in the end.)

Nobody knows what tipped the scales for Warlock that Christmastime. Yes, he had money worries, but he'd always had those. He was irritated by the contemporary music scene, but that was nothing new either. Maybe it was something else. A little thing. Strange, that the final scenes of Warlock's short, bombastic life were so understated. Closing the windows, shutting the doors, and remembering, just before he turned on the gas, to put the cat out.

Yes, maybe it was a small thing that did it, a stone from a sling-shot, an arrow in a heel. This is how both gods and men are slain.

If so, did the person who launched it feel as shocked and horrified as I did when I faced Bryn for the last time, when I landed that final, fateful blow?

I also read up on John Dee, the subject of Bryn's prize-winning essay, and looked into the 'angelic' language he supposedly discovered. One particular word stuck with me: *telocvovim*. A combination of two angelic words: *teloch*, meaning death, and *vovin*, meaning dragon. Death dragon, a reference to Lucifer. However, the word can also be translated, they say, as a phrase that is somehow more prosaic and more poetic at the same time: he who has fallen.

Most of us only ever talked about Satan in jest: *Get thee behind me*, you'd say to the hand offering a packet of chocolate digestives. And, in the years after graduation, I'd learn that even the Satanic Temple had abandoned the idea of a red, horned beast toasting sinners on hell's hot coals, preferring to see Satan as a symbol of rebellion, a figure standing against tyrannical power. Of course, one story is that Lucifer was a heavenly being, unfathomably beautiful, cast down to Earth for trying to be greater than God. But, apparently, in some Bible translations, the name Lucifer refers to a King of Babylon. In other words, just a man.

My point is: Warlock wasn't the devil his contemporaries thought him to be. And maybe Satan himself wasn't either.

The truth is, on the night of that ill-omened May ball – after Bryn's terrifying magic show, when we faced off in my room – I'd thought *I* was the one heading for disaster. I'd shouted and raved, staggering on my scorched leg, and he'd looked on with faint amusement. Until that crossing of a threshold.

I spoke the words softly, knowing it would shame me to have anyone overhear. 'You're the one to be pitied, Bryn. Living in your dad's shadow. Sure, my dad doesn't bother with my birthdays either, but at least he's got the excuse of being fucking dead.'

His face wore the blankness of shock; the look of someone who has been struck hard but hasn't yet felt the sting.

I didn't stop. 'Your dad doesn't give a fuck about you. He upped and left. And the saddest part: however much you copy him, whoever you've become, whatever fucking powers you have? You can never bring him back. Do you understand? You can never bring him back.'

God. His face.

Those were the last words I ever said to my friend, shortly before he went up onto the roof and stepped out into the clean air.

I never knew I was capable of performing my own dark magic, of casting my own terrible spell. And I certainly never imagined that instead of raising myself to Bryn's level, I would bring him down to mine.

As the final term of our final year drew to a close, my peers readied themselves for the future. Jamie was going to work for some MP, and Sarah was heading to Canary Wharf to do something called management consultancy that nobody seemed to understand. Having become disillusioned with medicine, Berenice had secured an internship at a think tank. All of them, preparing for careers that revolved around opinions and concepts rather than messy, physical things like bricks and cars and bodies – jobs where money was counted not in greasy, palm-grubbied coins but in neat columns on a computer screen.

But the future was a concept I struggled to grasp. A blank page, an essay I'd forgotten to write. Thankfully, I took my direction from Alexa – she'd often talked about having old school friends near Manchester and, what with my family so close by, I was glad to look for flats and jobs there.

Packing my books and crockery into bags, setting aside my gown for graduation, I remembered how arriving at Cambridge had been like stepping into a new self: one that had seemed strange and uncomfortable at first, but that I'd grown to fill. Did it suit me, this self that was cleverer but more cruel? A self that was capable of destroying my most beloved friend?

VI

The main course was lamb two ways: thick slices of fillet, fleshy at the centre, with an earthy stew on the side. Feeling obliged, I spoke for a while to the woman on my left, while Tim told another guest about the food we'd been used to, back in the day: the watery fish pie, the gluey stir fry, served with rather less fanfare. All the while my nerves rang softly, like the echoes of a chord around a concert hall.

The wine refills kept coming, and I gladly accepted them. At one point I spilled a glass of water, and everyone did that thing of gasping overdramatically. Plates disappeared as smoothly and silently as they'd arrived. A gooey chocolate thing appeared, and I dripped a long brown blob of it onto my shirt. Tim, sipping his water, told me I was a mess.

From somewhere came the sound of a knife striking glass. As the voices around me fell silent, there was a plummeting in my stomach, and the knowledge hit me all over again. All these people, all this spectacle. It shouldn't be necessary. We shouldn't be here.

Frances was standing. She thanked us all for making this scholarship a reality and expressed her hope that it would run for many years to come. She joked about her love of music but lack of talent, and everyone laughed obligingly. Then she began to talk about

Bryn. About the time Bryn lisped his way through his first theatre role as the Artful Dodger, about his intense but brief passion for the trombone (which ended when he left his brand new instrument in the back of a taxi). About the singing lessons in which his teacher had described his voice as angelic. Looking at the candlelit faces, turned towards Frances like adoring shepherds at the crib, I thought: He was a better performer than any of you know.

The feelings exhumed by Frances's tales came in a sequence: total admiration, abject jealousy. Then fury, melting into hatred and fear. Guilt. Finally, back to admiration again. A repeating bass line that had begun to sound when he'd walked into this very hall, that Halloween night, decked in blood red.

But always, always, rolling inexorably towards guilt. All these years it had followed me down every overlit supermarket aisle, onto every overstuffed bus. It had hunched in the corner of every utilitarian music room I'd ever used, lay beneath the frame of every bed. The memory came to me of Bryn at our first rehearsal, crouching on the windowsill, eyes aflame, and I wished there was a door in the world that would open onto that unsurpassable, deathless moment. I'd close that door and lock it behind us.

His life was too short, Frances said, faltering into banality. But it was an extraordinary life. Now, through the scholarship, Bryn would help others to live extraordinary lives too.

Immeasurably weary, I rubbed my eyes. It was too gloomy, the lights were too low.

Turning, I caught sight of a figure in the doorway, past the long tables, standing completely still. The light from the staircase was behind it, leaving its features imperceptible. It seemed at first to have the casual, youthful stance of a student, but on second glance I thought: No, it's surely an adult. Yet the neck, the limbs, seemed out of proportion, the angles somehow wrong, and the thought was like a rush of cold, snapping me into wakefulness. Behind the figure, the corridor was unusually quiet. There were no waiters moving smartly to and fro, no distant clangs from the kitchen.

Frances talked on, saying that she still spoke to Bryn every day. When I looked back at the doorway, the figure was gone.

No, it wasn't. It was closer now, halfway down the main hall, standing between the long, empty tables. Without the light from the corridor behind it, it was even harder to see. But it was tall – or was it just thin? Its face, indecipherable.

Dinner guests leaned forward in their chairs, silently encouraging Frances Cavendish in her sentimental ramblings. I tried to catch Tim's eye, but even when I gave a meaningful cough, louder and more theatrical than I'd intended, he didn't react.

I looked back into the hall, but the figure was gone again. Now, there were only the tables, as empty and lifeless as before. My heart momentarily forgot its rhythm, my nerves sang again, discordant. Where the fuck had this thing gone? And how had it moved so quickly? This was a big hall, and to get halfway down it in the blink of an eye didn't make sense. No, it made one horrible kind of sense. I scanned the corners of the room, the doorways leading to those corridors we undergraduates had never been allowed to explore. Nobody there. I suddenly felt stiflingly hot.

Frances talked saccharin, greetings-card slush about how, when we love someone dearly, they are always with us. Sweat dampened the nape of my neck, so much so that the lightest breeze landed like cold fingers on my skin, and I felt compelled to look behind me. As I twisted, awkwardly, the legs of my chair complained against the floorboards. Some people tutted, but I ignored them. Only the old masters, for ever fixed in their frames, were behind me, looking over my shoulder. Come on, I told myself. Don't start seeing things that aren't there.

Discomposed now, I took hold of the tablecloth and very gently lifted it, as if the answers might be waiting for me on the floor. Under the table, Tim's shoes. A napkin, possibly mine, beside a fallen potato. I felt the person next to me shift in their seat, probably in irritation.

I let the tablecloth drop before draining the rest of my wine. Now, the person next to me seemed to be sniggering.

The lamb sat heavy in my stomach. The thought of it, pink mulch, made me queasy. There was an odour of something acrid, maybe a pan blackening on a hob or a dish left in the oven too long.

The laughter irritated me, like someone eating with their mouth open. I lifted a bottle of wine from the table, relieved to find it fairly heavy, but it almost slipped through my clammy fingers. Shit. Laughter again. I turned to my neighbour, ready to give them a look of disdain.

But it was Bryn beside me, his eyes huge and dark.

I leapt out of my chair with a shout, bumping the table and rattling everything on it. With a little collective shriek, people grasped for their wine glasses. Frances paused, but I barely noticed – I was scrambling out of my chair, voice strangled in my throat.

He was still there, staring up at me.

I might have cried out to the room: Don't you see him? Why can't anybody *see* him? But I could barely breathe, let alone make a sound.

I staggered from him, bumping my neighbour, not realising that the tablecloth was still gripped in my hand. There was another gasp, louder this time, as the candelabra teetered, spattering the table with wax. Tim jumped up to steady it then, rising slowly from his seat, reached out his hands, fingers spread. He looked like someone on a bridge, imploring: Don't do it.

Then I fled, leaping from the dais and stumbling down the long, judgemental room, casting chairs out of my way as I went. Nobody called after me as I burst through the double doors, knocking a trolley and sending a tray of coffee cups crashing to the floor. Even if they had, I wouldn't have listened. Because I was getting the fuck out of here, out of college and out of the city. Yes, I'd hoped that my presence here, my service to Bryn's family, would put something to rest. But he wasn't interested in my justifications or my explanations. All he wanted was to take me back to that awful moment, and I couldn't face it, I couldn't face—

Before I could finish the thought my feet tangled at the top of the staircase, and I fell, all the way to the bottom, each step a reprimand for every time I'd thought myself on his level.

~

The last night I'd been really drunk in Cambridge was the night before our graduation. I'd celebrated my underwhelming 2:2 by going to a club and drinking shots, all with revolting names like 'brain haemorrhage' and 'baby puke'. After a large kebab and a short stumble home, I dropped into a sweaty, fretful sleep at about three.

Then, I had the dream again.

There, in that uncanny kitchen, was that sound, *knock knock knock*. That door, about to whisper open.

And when I woke, whimpering, that certainty. It really was him. Coming back.

It made me think of a story I'd read about Peter Warlock, from his friend Augustus John. A favourite story of mine, once. In it, John describes how Warlock took his friends on a road trip to a Norfolk inn to hear some traditional folk songs. This night of music and beer was going well until, in the middle of an animated discussion, Warlock dropped to the ground, still and lifeless. Failing to revive him, all Warlock's horrified friends could do was respectfully cover his body and let it lie in the bar until morning, at which time they would make their sad arrangements. But when they returned the next day, they found Warlock sitting up, waiting, in better shape than the rest of the party. Extraordinary, to think your friend is gone for ever, to find yourself wrong.

The story rang differently now. I'd always known that Bryn wouldn't let others get in the way of what he wanted. I just hadn't realised something bigger: that he wouldn't be stopped by such a trivial thing as being dead.

VII

When I woke, laid out as if on a slab, I didn't know whether I'd been unconscious for five seconds or five hours. Above me, the sky, starless. Beneath my splayed palms, something chill and damp. When I lifted my head, my brain seemed to roll in my skull, and I had to close my eyes again.

After several deep breaths, I eased myself onto my elbows and looked around. I was in Old Court, lying in the middle of the lawn. My thoughts came slowly, hobbled, and it took a few seconds to remember leaving the dinner. Then, it tumbled upon me: the memory of Bryn, his impenetrable expression. Lumbering, gasping, to my feet, I wheeled on the spot, taking in every doorway, terrified of what might be hiding within. But my eyes confirmed I was alone. I rubbed my face with a dewy hand, puzzling how I'd got from the staircase to here, why nobody had come to help me. All I wanted was to speak to Alexa. Fuck. I felt suddenly, piercingly awake.

The glow of the street lamp did little to illuminate the court-yard, and not a single window shed light onto the square of dark grass. The silence felt heavy, like fog, as if it might subsume anything I tried to say. Shambling off the grass and onto the path, brushing uselessly at my rumpled trousers, I looked towards the room where I was staying. The one below Bryn's. I couldn't be there tonight, I knew that now for sure, I'd been stupid ever to think it possible. Imagine lying in the blackness, wondering when he'd come. I had to find Tim.

Perhaps he was still in hall. I wondered whether there was any way I could sneak back inside, into the comfort and safety of company, without looking like a madman. Unlikely. As I wondered what I'd say to the other guests, I spotted something on the path: something small and spectral white, a patch of brightness in the gloom. Feeling like a man condemned, I inched slowly closer until I could see what it was. When I realised, I almost threw up. It was that page, from the auditions, that sickening photo of Bryn. How? There was no reason for it to be here. I tried to look again, to confirm what I was seeing, but couldn't meet his faded, monochrome gaze. The humiliation of returning to hall was nothing compared to the terror of standing in that tomb-like quiet. I set off, half running, under the archway into New Court.

But when I found my trembling way to the staircase down which I'd plummeted, I found that the doors at the bottom were locked. The dinner must be over, the guests must have left. How could it be that nobody had noticed me, sprawled on the ground? Had not a single person passed through Old Court? I wondered whether there was another way back up to hall, whether I could sneak in and find a waiter to help me. But the thought of looking through the kitchens, creeping amongst the hanging pans, the freshly sharpened knives, made my stomach turn.

The bar would be closed now. Maybe Tim was in the common room. Even if he wasn't, I could grab a few hours' rest on one of the sofas, with the TV blaring reassuringly in the background. If I was lucky, a few international students might be hanging around too. Yes, they'd be a bit perturbed to see a ragged old bloke curled up and shivering in front of their telly, but we'd all just have to get along.

Hurrying to the common room, a pain in one leg making me lurch like the undead, I looked at the clock above chapel. It showed exactly two. I searched for shreds of comfort in the scene: the lawn, pristine as ever, silvered by the moonlight, the paving stones tessellating tidily around its edges. The library, with its precisely ordered shelves of logic and reason. The bedroom windows, some darkened by ivy, revealing nothing. Still, not a soul anywhere.

I thought again how quiet it was. No, it wasn't just quiet. There was a total absence of sound, as if the college were something sealed: a castle trapped in a snow globe or an insect fixed in amber. Increasing my pace, I bundled into the common room, desperate to hear the familiar sound of quarrelling around the quiz machine, the soft clicks and clunks from the pool table.

But there was nobody there.

With a steadying hand on the wall, I made for the banks of old sofas that faced the television. Vacant. The screen showed a man with huge sunglasses, gesturing at women in bikinis, no music to match his exaggerated moves. I grabbed the remote control and pressed the volume button, up, up. Then the mute button, on and off, on and off. Nothing. A thought, almost laughable, danced through my head: I'd gone deaf. Burst both eardrums as I bumped down the stairs. I didn't know whether that was medically possible, but I also knew that it hadn't happened, because I could hear perfectly well the shuffling of my scuffed shoes against the carpet.

In the silence, the jabbering of my mind was loud, voices clamouring over one another, tuneless. Where else to look? Christ, not the chapel, with its ancient corners and stone-eyed saints. Not the musty library, long shut. My nerves were drumskin-tight. Everywhere, an overwhelming sense of wrongness.

Hang on. The night porter would be on duty, making sure there were no students climbing the college walls or setting up their own personal traffic calming systems on the lawn. Sure that a word from someone else would break this unsettling charm, I blundered out of the common room and around the courtyard, the clapping of my feet a sarcastic applause.

At the lodge I knocked, waited. No answer. Finding the door unlocked, I slipped inside and approached the old, broad desk, with its signing-in book, its piles of letters. I dared to hope that the porter wasn't far away, as his jacket was slung over the back of his chair, his mug of coffee half-drunk. There was also a very faint smell of smoke, which would suggest that he'd had a cigarette break recently. Maybe he was out now, strolling around Old Court or checking the bike sheds. That would make sense, although it was strange that he hadn't found me splayed on the lawn.

As I waited for him to return, I distracted myself by studying the framed photographs on the walls. Rugby teams and drinking societies, fixed for ever in sepia. I supposed there'd be a photo of me, somewhere – perhaps a shot of the undersized college orchestra or the rowing squad I'd been an unhelpful part of. Not on a wall, but possibly in a filing cabinet somewhere, and however far I travelled from Cambridge, I would always be here, tethered to that moment.

The thought gave me no comfort, so I turned to examine the shelves, the staff pigeonholes labelled with names I didn't recognise. Sat down, stood up again. Nobody came. My breath became shallower, as if the air itself might be too thin, as if it wouldn't be enough to support my voice if I needed to speak, to shout. How much fucking longer?

I threw open the door of the lodge and almost fell back into New Court, my fingers worrying at the hem of my jacket. The smell of smoke was stronger now, even though there was no sign of the porter. As I paced the pavement outside the lodge, my eyes landed on the clock above the chapel. Its iron hands showed exactly two.

How strange, I thought, for such a clock to stop. Without knowing why, I made my way back into the lodge and searched the walls for a watch, a phone, anything that would confirm the time.

There, a clock behind the desk. The time, digitally displayed down to the minute: two.

At first, I had no reaction at all. Then a rush, like blood from a frightened face: I must have spent at least ten or fifteen minutes in the common room and the porters' lodge. It wasn't possible that the time was still two.

What came back to me then was the film I'd seen with Bryn, where the students get lost in the woods, where they follow the river but arrive back where they started. My body trembled as if I might shake myself apart, and I fought to suppress the idea, circling now, that perhaps it was possible that time would never move forward again. I turned unsteadily in small, pointless circles – what the fuck was that burning smell? – before deciding: I wouldn't wait for Tim, or for the porter, or for anyone else. I'd just go. I'd sleep on a bench, on a pavement, rather than stay here.

As I put my hand on the small door to the street, something dreadful ran through my head: an idea that, when I went outside, all of Trumpington Street would be silent too, shops and colleges closed up, pavements bereft of bodies. What if I walked for hours but heard no cars or footsteps or any other sounds of life, and what if nobody stirred when I pummelled doorbells and cast stones at bedroom windows? What if I kept going until it should be morning, but morning didn't come?

With no other paths before me, I pushed at the door, set within the ancient gates. Locked. Of course it would be, this time of night. I pushed again, then began to hammer, laughing senselessly, feeling the wood uneven beneath my palms, firm against my battered shoes. After a minute or so without progress, my knees folded and I dropped to the ground, and I listened to my breath, ragged, the sawing of a bow on strings.

But beneath this, out of the distant quiet, crept a sound. Something – how can I say – something that sounded *long* and angular, something that might have been music.

I leapt to my feet, eyes darting left and right. Then I looked up, directly up, at the blackness that seemed to be descending on me, falling, faster and faster, as if it were the essence of nothing, time was nothing, and I were nothing, nothing, nothing.

THREE

The Copper Kettle is a busy, touristy café looking onto King's Parade. When I arrived, head throbbing savagely, I was unsurprised to see it packed with Sunday brunchers. A gaggle of mummies dominated the room, too busy burping wrinkly babies to deal with the scrambled eggs cooling in front of them. Elsewhere, young people – applicants for next year, perhaps – sat, surly, with fussing parents. Tim was already at the corner spot we'd reserved, and I squeezed my way between the chattering diners to my seat. 'Morning,' I said, sitting heavily, my voice harsh as a fork on a plate.

Tim looked up only briefly from his menu. 'I ordered you a coffee,' he said, pointing to a full cup. 'Thought you might need it.'

I forced a laugh, but Tim didn't join in. Fair enough. Last night's events had done me little good with my esteemed colleagues, and evidently Tim was unimpressed too. No doubt that was Bryn's intention. Scant comfort that it could have been a lot worse.

A waitress, ridiculously young, came to take our order (full English, times two) and wrote it on her notepad in a slow and looping script. When she left, awkwardness hung between me and Tim like the stink of hot grease. Unable to avoid the obvious question, I asked: 'Did you put me to bed?'

He nodded. 'It looked like you were heading out of college, which didn't seem like a good idea.'

'Sorry. Thanks.' Unsure what to say, I lied: 'I don't remember.'

'You kept apologising.'

'Well, I really am sorry—'

'Not to me. To Bryn.'

I stopped, my coffee cup halfway to my mouth. My cheeks began to warm. 'Did I?'

'Yes, you did.'

One thing I'd hoped for from this weekend – aside from getting out of it unscathed, a result I might have interpreted as forgiveness, a result that had only ever been a dream – was that whatever confrontation was on the cards would happen between me and Bryn alone. That way, there'd be no need for explanations. But my punishment had been public. And I couldn't make Tim understand why I'd been gibbering apologies at the gate without explaining the relentless, rolling causality of the whole horrible story: the sinister punishments Bryn had meted out, my desire to protect Alexa, the kiss that put us in danger. The horrible words that were supposed to keep him away from me, just not like *that*.

Of course, I could allow Tim to think that I'd simply drunk myself senseless. While he'd be annoyed, I could live with it. But could I honestly take this burden back home again, not knowing whether it was truly over? Back to Manchester, where I'd once again do double-takes at faces on badly lit street corners, at certain silhouettes sweeping in and out of concert halls?

Taking a slow sip of my coffee, I wondered. Could Tim believe me? Rational, straightforward Tim, with his Cockapoo and his John Lewis gilet? Might he have seen something himself in that darkened hall, something that might illuminate the truth of this terrible story?

As the silence became uncomfortable, I thought of my dad: hunched humbly over an untouched breakfast, trying to outline the previous night's events in a way that would be acceptable not only to my mother but to himself. Who knew this type of narration was such a skill? Setting my cup carefully back in its saucer, I thought: Fuck it.

'Listen,' I said, 'I know this is going to sound really, *really* weird. But, when we were at college, things happened that … that I couldn't explain. God, I can't believe I'm saying this.'

The look on Tim's face was painful. Pure pity.

I ploughed on. 'Have you ever seen a ghost?'

'Have *you?*'

Sunlight poured through the windows. I took a deep breath. 'I saw Bryn.'

I blinked, waited. Maybe thirty seconds went by.

Eventually, Tim spoke. 'There was a lot of wine involved,' he said. 'And the whole event was about Bryn. It's not surprising that, in your state—'

I shook my head, aggravating the ache. 'No, not just last night. It's been happening since I arrived. And there were things, back when we were at college—'

Everything was coming out wrong, and I paused to figure out how to explain. Outside, tourists were removing jackets and cardigans, taking sunglasses out of bags. It made me feel even hotter.

Tim rubbed his face with both hands and sighed. 'Look,' he said, 'in a way, I'm glad this has come up.'

The waitress returned, thunked some condiments between us. Tim waited until she'd left before speaking again.

'The way you talk about Bryn?' he said, sharply. 'It isn't healthy.'

'Why not?'

'You present the past in a very ...' Here he placed the words extremely carefully. '... personal way.'

'What's that supposed to mean?'

'Well. You talk about Bryn as if he was a great friend.'

Silently, I spread my hands: *Obviously.*

'But, God,' he went on, 'be realistic. It was because of him that you stopped being friends with Mona.'

I laughed grimly. 'I was never that close to Mona.'

'Yes you were! What did we call her? Casio.'

'*You* called her that—'

'The two of you used to hang out at mine all the time. It was only when you realised that Bryn didn't like her that you dropped her like a hot potato.'

It's true that she became more annoying over time. But Tim was exaggerating.

'Also,' Tim said, 'Bryn didn't give a damn about you getting hurt. With Alexa.'

From somewhere came the spitting of a coffee machine, the spiky sound of crockery dropped into a sink. I looked for our waitress. 'I hope our food gets here soon, I'm starving.'

'I don't like to say this,' Tim said.

'Then don't,' I said, laughing in a way that sounded slightly delirious. 'Don't.'

'That thing with Alexa clearly meant something to you, I see that. Although I don't know why you gave a shit about her, because she wasn't very nice. Pretending to be everyone's friend when half the time she was only ever using them.'

I shook out my napkin, as if signalling surrender. 'Bryn and I, we hurt each other. I obviously feel bad about that.'

Tim adjusted his knife and fork, until the place setting was just so. 'But that's the thing. There's never been any reason for you to feel bad.' He spoke slowly and clearly, as if to a child. 'Alexa kissed you to make Bryn jealous. And he couldn't have cared less. He knew she'd come running the moment he clicked his fingers, which is exactly what happened practically the next day. You and her, it was one drunken kiss. Nobody took any notice, least of all Bryn.'

I grasped my coffee cup, to steady my hands. 'Alright, alright,' I said, 'thank you for the recap. You're not telling me anything I didn't already know.'

To my dismay, he went on: 'And I know you were … worried. About the way Bryn died. But I've told you before. It was a stupid accident.'

I looked into the darkness of my cup. Here was the thing that Tim didn't understand. 'No, Tim. I said some terrible things to him before he fell. About his father. The kind of thing that would make him feel—'

Tim made a *pffft* sound, shook his head. 'The only time Bryn cared about his dad was when he wanted money from him. They weren't close. At all.'

'They weren't close because Bryn's father had abandoned him.'

'I've told you what Berenice told me. Bryn even blackmailed his dad! He kept threatening to share his private letters, although I don't know who the hell would have cared about them by that point.'

'It's possible to have complex relationships with people you love,' I replied, too loudly.

Tim looked at me, weary. Folded his hands neatly together. 'Listen. Every time I see you, you talk about Bryn and Alexa like they were a big part of your life. I mean, I'm surprised you even call them friends. But I'm not surprised you see ghosts. Even I start to think I see Bryn, hearing that damned name over and over.'

I desperately wanted him to shut up, but he didn't.

'And I'm sad,' he went on. 'Because you spend so much energy on them, and they never did the same for you. They certainly don't now, not when they're both bloody dead.'

I gripped my coffee cup so tightly that I thought it might shatter.

The waitress arrived with two enormous plates, steaming beans precarious at the edges. She seemed about to ask something but, seeing our expressions, left without a word. One of the nearby babies began to wail.

'I'm not denying the things that happened,' I said. 'I've never denied them. What I'm trying to say is that, both before and after Bryn and Alexa … fell … there were things that …'

'Things that only you understand? Things that would connect you to them indefinitely? I don't want to hurt your feelings. But I think it's healthier for you to face the facts. If Bryn had lived, and he was looking back on our university days, I don't think he'd even remember your name.'

I sat back in my chair. I felt very old, somehow, as if all the years since college had suddenly collapsed on top of me. 'We should ask for some water.'

Tim kept his eyes on me. 'I'm sorry, honestly I am,' he said, very gently. 'When you were apologising to Bryn, I thought, maybe … Maybe you *need* to feel guilty. Because then, on some level, you'd be – how do I say this – part of his story. But the stuff with you and him, it was nothing. He wasn't some tragic hero, he was a stupid kid who died exactly the kind of reckless, accidental death we could have all predicted. Careless enough to take his girlfriend down with him too. And dwelling on it only keeps you stuck in the past. You need to … you know. Move on.'

For a minute, maybe two, neither of us moved or spoke. Tim's expression was hard to bear. I imagine it was the one he used when announcing to parents that their child has an inoperable tumour. Sympathetic but realistic. Grave.

In the end, Tim began to eat, and I sat quietly as my breakfast went cold. Outside, the sun blazed.

He'd climbed out of the window in Jamie's room, where they were having a post-ball afterparty. The others clapped and cheered once he was on the ledge. After a while Alexa stepped up too, something I didn't see at first from my position behind the chimney stack. They were dancing, people said, their hands clasped. Then, a simple misstep: Bryn pivot-turning into the air. By the time everyone had rushed to the ledge to check that this wasn't some spectacular trick, both Bryn and Alexa were on the ground. A porter, summoned by the screams, was sprinting pointlessly around the courtyard.

In dreams, I see them falling. I see Alexa on the ground, her eyes clouded, darkness spreading around her upturned face, a darkness that isn't simply her long black hair. But I never dream of Bryn that way. My brain won't countenance his extraordinary luminescence, extinguished.

On the nights when I wake from these dreams, gasping, I grab at my little bedside table and touch the talismans that live there always: the hairbands – fraying now, not as elastic as they used to be – that Alexa left in my room that night she stayed over, the ones I carried from one post-uni flatshare to another, all the way to Manchester. In the dark, I twist them around my fingers, tight enough to stop the blood flowing.

Not because they remind me of her. Because they remind me what it was like to be a certain kind of man, even for a short while. Yes, Alexa was a pretty girl. Yes, she made me laugh. But more than this, being with her made me into someone else. She made me feel like him.

Imagine if I'd been able to save just one of them. Who would I have reached for? There has never been any contest.

When Tim realised that I wasn't going to talk about it any more, he pulled a piece of paper from his pocket and gave it to me, pointing out the list of 'helpful' phone numbers he'd copied from some NHS website. I pretended to pay attention, simultaneously nodding at our waitress for the bill.

After that, Tim tried to lighten the mood by telling me about what some of the others were doing. Jamie, like his father, was very senior in the Civil Service and apparently quite secretive about it, while Sarah had two kids and ran a business that was something to do with sustainable homewares. Mona was back in Cambridge, a lecturer now, and Tim was still in touch with her. In fact, he and Berenice regularly had Mona and her wife over for dinner, and their children were firm friends. You wouldn't recognise her, he told me. I supposed not.

Tim talked about others too, including someone called Petra, an author whose books he'd enjoyed. It was only after he elaborated with a physical description that I realised who he was talking about. Traybake girl. Yes, Petra was her name.

Outside the Copper Kettle, Tim hugged me hard, declaring we should catch up again soon. I nodded, vaguely. He promised to call in a couple of days to see how I was doing, and I decided then that I probably wouldn't answer. As he set off walking, he looked briefly back, and his expression suggested that he knew it too. I ambled back to college, irritated by the sun's burning hand on the back of my neck.

When I got there, the college gates swarmed with tourists juggling cameras and ice creams. Eager to show that I was not one of them, I held my alumni ID ostentatiously out to the porter as I passed the big red sign that forbade visitors from going further. I made for the bar, thinking that, while I was here, I might take a quick look inside. Old times' sake, and all that. But on the door was a sign announcing that the space was closed for a function.

Through the glass panels I spied people milling around with little cups of Pimm's – tutors in rumpled jackets, young men in badly pressed shirts, young women in pashminas all dressed too old for their age. There were supposed to be more state school kids than ever before at Cambridge (do they know their way around better than I did?) but the bar scene looked exactly the same as in my day. There was a pile of hardbacks on a table. A book launch, maybe? A talk? Private.

I stood at the door, touching fingertips to the glass, wishing someone would let me in.

I chose Bach for the drive home, a playlist I'd made for myself. First up, the Crab Canon I played at Bryn's house all those years ago. The one whose lines of music can be played forwards and backwards simultaneously. It feels like those few bars of musical and mathematical genius, sharp as the facets of a laser-cut diamond, could circle on and on for ever, taking you always back to the same place whichever way you look at it.

Next, the cello suites. Beautiful but impersonal, music that reminded me only of strangers' weddings. I once heard the cellist Yo-Yo Ma on the radio, saying that every time he plays the suites he finds new truths to encounter. This idea appeals to me. It reminds us that the page of printed notes is not the music. The music is what happens when we interpret those notes and give them a life.

And what else can we do with the notes of our lives? In replaying even the most insignificant memory, simple as a nursery rhyme, there is an aesthetic choice, an interpretation. And yes, when I replay the music of my college days, there are all kinds of truths to discover.

So, my friendship with Bryn. If it were possible for you to play those notes *exactly* as they are on the page – say, as a computer would – they might describe a charismatic young man, fascinated with the occult, who loved to dazzle his friends with magic tricks. A lover of heights, figurative and literal, who scaled the walls of college and broke into people's rooms. Who, in his quest for sensation, would think nothing of spiking his friends' drinks, selling them drugs even when they couldn't handle it. A young man whose singularity did not stop him from being ordinarily cruel (I have occasionally pondered the blanketed wire box in Bryn's room, his fine for having something prohibited there – something, say, like animals – and the scratches on poor, allergic Mona's walls. Likewise, I can't deny that a hand dipping into a pocket may not necessarily be depositing a curse, but may instead be stealing a set of keys).

But the climbing, the drugs? These prosaic details could have applied to any number of posh, pretty Cambridge students over the years. And to be around Bryn was to *know*, on a level beyond black and white logic, that certain things about him could not be explained in words or numbers. It was a feeling that cannot be marked on a stave. It was to sense, almost physically, an invisible force, a law of the universe yet to be formalised in theorems. All of which is why, articulating our story, I allow myself to linger on certain parts: the shadows, the scratchings. My dad's sorrowful eyes.

In telling the stories of our lives – in replaying the music of our past – there is interpretation.

One thing that never changes in my replayings: this music is about love.

With friends, we say *I love him*, but not *I am in love with him*. And yet, can we not experience platonic love as total immersion? As if love were a great, dark pool within which we float, far from the edges, unable to touch toes to the floor, exhausted by the constant treading of water and in danger of being subsumed?

And it's true. I am in love. In love, I am.

Loving him, I existed.

Perhaps that's what he'd say, when I opened the pantry door.

Do you want to play those songs again?

Naturally, I'd collect my things and follow him into the dark.

One last thing: I found the answer to Bryn's question. An article in one of the Sunday papers explained how two specific parts of the brain 'light up' when we watch magic tricks. These parts are involved in high-level cognitive functions like working memory, planning, decision-making. Even ethics and morality. They help us resolve the cognitive conflicts of our day-to-day lives.

And I realised: magic is friction. It's that place where the possible and impossible meet, where belief and disbelief collide like a match against the striking strip. It's the exquisite tension, that solo-and-accompaniment push and pull of competing ideas, the connection between the things we see and the things that we know we can't possibly be seeing. Like Warlock's music: folky melodies set against modern harmonies. The man himself, demonic and demonised. Like Bryn, a blessing and a curse.

Maybe this explains why, when two very different people come together, the effect can be – there's no better word for it – magical.

I pulled into the communal driveway at about six, when the day's warmth had ebbed away. Once inside the flat I didn't stop to switch on the kettle or to take off my coat. I went straight to my bedroom, to the space under the eaves where, untouched since my last move, cardboard boxes and plastic crates huddled against one another like drunks. I dragged some into the centre of my room.

In the first were old programmes, including my first ever as musical director of Voices from Before. In the next, odds and ends: cricket gloves, watermarked paperbacks, a couple of old ties, and lots of loose change. Textbooks. The violin sonata that was my composition coursework. I'd forgotten I ever wrote such a thing.

The next box was the one. In it, photographs, some loose, others in their original shiny envelopes. A leather album, its cover dull and scratched. I turned the pages. Here, pictures from our gradu-ation ceremony. Snaps of Halfway Hall. An extremely civilised garden party, followed by an extremely uncivilised room party where someone is wrapped from neck to toe in clingfilm. Everywhere, phantoms of college days past: Alexa, in New Court, smoking a cigarette. Me in a punt, eyes half-closed, mid-blink. Mona, beside me, smiling.

There. The picture of Bryn in the pub. The whisky is on the table, like I'd told Tim, but Ruben the maths student isn't (he couldn't have been, I realised, as he only arrived in our second year). I was wrong about the underwear too. People are fancy-dressed as gods and monsters. In the background strolls Pan with his curved horns, an Athena with her plastic sword and shield.

There, sandwiched between a Lakshmi and an Anubis, is Bryn. But he isn't wearing a costume. In this divine company, he's come as himself.

Replaying:

There's something Tim hasn't considered. That Bryn falling from the building and taking Alexa with him would have been the most utterly diabolical act of revenge upon me. That's one interpretation, isn't it?

And what about this rock, in my pocket? I have no memory of putting it there.

Another thing I discovered was the sheet music of the Butterworth songs, marked up for Bryn ahead of our performance. I read the lyrics, as if I didn't already know them by heart:

Now, of my threescore years and ten,
Twenty will not come again,
And take from seventy springs a score,
It only leaves me fifty more.

I wished it was only twenty years gone.

That's the thing I always loved about this music. It describes so perfectly the tender, terrible feeling of past and present rubbing against one another. The feeling of longing for something that feels so clear and so close but just out of reach. Like when you enter a room and the person you're looking for is exiting at the other side – perhaps you catch the barest glimpse as the door closes softly behind them, and you feel that, if you were only to call out, you might still bring them back.

But now, as I stare through my drizzled windowpane at the smudging headlights, the peaks of brick and concrete, I'm not listening to the Butterworth. I'm listening to 'Ha'nacker Mill', my favourite of Warlock's works. A choral piece, about a ruined wind-mill. A song of time, decay. The lyrics describe the mill's great clapper silent, the briar grown wild around it. The collapse of the mill means something more, not the end of a building but of an era, now that the mill is gone and there are no more ploughmen, no more pipes or dancers.

But, terrible as this moment of loss may be, I press a button to begin the song again for the tenth, twentieth time, I don't know. Because I too am for ever on that hill, memories whipping about me like leaves ripped from ancient trees, the sky like a face I almost recognise, never getting any closer to the summit however hard I climb, the rain beating me back—

—beating on my window as I look at that bone shard of the past. It's not healthy, they say, to dwell. But, even if I wanted to leave it behind, I couldn't. You know why?

Because he always comes back.

I pour another drink, begin the song again.

The feeling in this music, it isn't nostalgia. Because nostalgia is a simple longing for the past. Even *saudade*, that word I learned from Warlock – grief for something lost – doesn't reflect what I hear in these transcendent sounds. But there is a word from Wales, born of the exquisite, wild landscapes Warlock adored. *Hiraeth*. A whisper of a word, a word to seal a hex. There's no direct English equivalent, but people describe it as the feeling of longing to be where your spirit lives. It can describe anything you yearn for. A person, a place, an era. Even places you've never been and times you never experienced.

Hiraeth. This is the magic word I reach for now, as I yearn for so many things. For those days when the story was still to be written, our mistakes not yet fixed on the page. For the kind of love that sank heavy in your bones like a break that will never completely heal. For heights we might have reached. For doors, not yet closed. For everything that might have been.

ACKNOWLEDGEMENTS

My first thanks must go to my agent, the incomparable Rosie Pierce, for taking a chance on this book – who knows where I'd be had you not worked your magic. Big thanks also to Tanja Goossens, Mark Williams and to everyone else at Curtis Brown who has helped to get this story out into the world.

In the UK, I'm so very grateful to Katie Bowden and Lola Downes – whose understanding of my characters has bordered on the uncanny – and to Eve Hutchings, Charlotte Webb, Penny Isaac and Helena Caldon, along with everyone at 4th Estate. Thanks too, to Ola Galewicz for the beautiful cover design.

In the US, I'm forever indebted to Dan Milaschewski, Franck Germain, Laura Schreiber, Stefanie Chin, Barbara Berger, Christina Stambaugh, Patrick Sullivan for the stunning cover design, Lisa Forde, Kevin Iwano, Sandy Noman, and the whole team at Union Square. I couldn't have hoped for better champions.

Thanks to Rob at The Fiction Desk who, years ago, published my short stories and gave me hope.

Some books were extremely helpful in the writing of this novel. In particular, *Experiencing the Impossible: The Science of Magic* by Gustav Kuhn is a fabulously entertaining look at what happens in our brains when we experience magic, while *The Queen's Conjuror:*

The Life and Magic of Dr Dee by Benjamin Woolley is a fascinating account of the mathematician and astronomer (and occultist) John Dee. *Frederick Delius and Peter Warlock: A Friendship Revealed* by Barry Smith is a collection of correspondence that revealed much about the inner life of the enigmatic Peter Warlock.

Thanks to The Octagon and all my other college friends for the inspo, and to the staff who patiently ushered me through my degree at Corpus Christi College, Cambridge.

To Tarik O'Regan, for introducing me to Peter Warlock in the first place, and to Joanna Wyld, for helping me with the many musical details (any errors are absolutely mine): thank you.

To the Faber Academy, Shelley Weiner, and to our class of 2020: you are the most outstanding writing buddies. A special shout out to Rebecca Keane, who read the whole story very early on and gave the kindest and wisest counsel. Thanks also to my other amazing writer friends, Zara Hayes, Michael Mann, Nick Asbury and Tim Rich. Your encouragement and advice have been invaluable. You are all ace.

Finally, love and thanks to my whole family. To the Baxters, to the Farrells, to the van der Borghs. To my wonderful mum and dad, Alan and Iris, who spent half of the 1990s driving me to music lessons and have given me more than I could ever describe or repay. To Pongo, who has given me mainly hassle but is perfect anyway.

And to Leo. This book would not exist without you. You supported me page by excruciating page, and you dreamed the dream when I really couldn't manage it myself. If every writer had the same amount of support, there'd be far more stories in the world. I love you. YNWA.